Melanie Clegg is a blue haired ..... historian, gin taster, lapsed got| ...... versailles obsessive, proud Ripperologist, Georgette Heyer fanatic and Victorian Prostitute re-enactor who lives in deepest darkest Bristol with her family but would rather be in either Whitechapel or Paris. *From Whitechapel* is her fifth novel.

She blogs as Madame Guillotine at

www.madameguillotine.org.uk

Also by Melanie Clegg

The Secret Diary of a Princess
Blood Sisters
Before the Storm
Minette

FROM WHITECHAPEL

Melanie Clegg

Burning Eye

This edition published by Burning Eye Books 2014

www.burningeye.co.uk

@burningeye

Burning Eye Books
15 West Hill, Portishead, BS20 6LG

ISBN 978 1 90913 643 4

For my fellow GIN FIENDS with much love.

WHITECHAPEL, NOVEMBER 1888

Tom Bowyer whistled tunelessly to himself as he strolled down Dorset Street, pausing every now and again to flip a coin to a passing street urchin or tip his hat to one of the grubby women already hanging about like flies around carrion outside the Britannia pub, gripping glasses of gin and with their shawls pulled tight about their shoulders to keep out the chill.

'Morning ladies!' he called cheerfully with a suave grin, garnering himself a response that ranged from catcalls to outright abuse.

He was a familiar figure about Spitalfields, Tom Bowyer, and not an altogether popular one although in the personal private fantasy that he had created for himself, he was loved by all and hailed with joy wherever he went. Poor Tom. In the real world he was rent-man and hired bully boy for Mr McCarthy, who owned most of the flop houses and rented rooms in the area and did his rounds every morning, feared and despised in equal measure by the residents of Dorset Street who had long since come to hate the heavy tread of his large feet outside, the knock of his chubby knuckles as he went from house to house gathering up Mr McCarthy's pennies and his mean little eyes peering around corners and sizing up belongings to see if there was anything more that could be squeezed out of his employer's already beleaguered tenants.

'Good morning, old Steve,' he said to the crippled old soldier who always sat by the entrance of Miller's Court. 'A fine day today.'

Old Steve grimaced at him from beneath his hat. 'She's not

there,' he said.

Tom sighed. 'I'll be the judge of that,' he said briskly before throwing a penny into the other man's lap and sauntering off down the dark, stinking little alley that led to the yard. It was a chilly, overcast morning and he shivered a little as he walked through the gloom, pulling his overcoat closer and wishing that he'd thought to put a scarf on before leaving the house.

The alley was short though and he soon found himself standing opposite the door to number thirteen. 'Rent,' he said, hammering against the rickety old wood. 'Open up now, Miss Kelly.'

There was no response. 'Bleeding tarts,' he muttered, hammering again with his fist, louder and harder this time. 'Come now, Miss Kelly. You're several weeks late and Mr McCarthy is fast starting to lose patience.' Not that he had much to begin with and Tom could never quite understand why it was that he let Miss Kelly fall so far behind when usually she'd have been out on her ear within a week of falling into arrears. 'Open up now.'

He gave the door one last thump with his hand then went round to the window. He couldn't hear any sound of movement from within the hovel, but she was a cunning one, Miss Kelly and not above hiding beneath the table or even the bed when he called around and caught her inside.

'The sooner she's kicked out, the better,' he said to himself as he pressed his big face up close to the window and looked inside, half expecting to see his quarry whisking herself away underneath the bed. 'More trouble than she's…' He broke off and gave instead a squeak of mingled panic and alarm before recoiling away from the window, almost falling over backwards in his haste to get away from the thing that lay inside, splayed and terrible on the narrow blood soaked bed; the ripped apart and ruined thing with exposed horribly grinning teeth, wide staring terrified eyes and long red hair that fell in a tangled blood matted mess across the side of the slashed and ruined sheets and towards the floor…

8

Chapter One
Emma, Calais, August 1887

I knew at the time that I should never have looked out of that window. In fact, I could kick myself now when I think about it. It was Marie's idea of course, just like everything else, good, bad and downright awful, that happened to us both that long hot filthy summer at Madame Lisette's and, knowing that, I really should have known how things would be as soon as my friend, for that's what I thought she was back then, pulled the grimy red velvet curtain aside and gave a theatrical gasp of shocked surprise, the one that made the other girls, the silly cows, say that she really ought to be on the stage instead of making a living on her back.

'Come and see this, Em.' She leaned heavily against the dirty glass, her gin scented breath steaming up the cracked and mould covered pane so that she had to scrub at it squeakily with her black lace mittened hand to be able to see again. 'What's that thing down there?' She demanded in a dramatic whisper, screwing up her freckled face as she peered into the gloom. 'Can you see what it is?'

She impatiently beckoned me over and I rolled my eyes but still rather thankfully put aside the red woollen stockings that I was clumsily darning and went to the window, expecting to see nothing more remarkable than some cats having a fight or a drunk fast asleep and snoring noisily on the doorstep while a dark little puddle of urine spread silently around his feet. Life was boring as hell at Madame Lisette's, when we weren't on our backs anyway, and even then, it could be a chore pretending to look interested when all the while we were thinking about what to have for dinner or totalling up how much money we'd made that day and wondering if it would stretch to a new pair of gloves and maybe some stockings too.

'Look there.' Marie pointed, squashing her finger flat against the window and I heaved a great sigh and looked into the yard, preparing myself to be thoroughly underwhelmed. It took a few seconds for my eyes to adjust to the darkness but I instantly wished it had been something as ordinary as fighting cats or a passed out drunk when I finally made out the two figures, a man wearing a cloth cap and a woman with fair straggling hair, struggling frantically on the slippery, rain slicked cobbles of the yard.

'They've got a bit of a cheek doing that down there,' Marie observed with an angry sniff, turning her head to the side as she tried to make out what was happening down below. 'Taking bread out of our mouths, she is.'

'Maybe it's one of our girls,' I said uneasily, thinking that there was something wrong, that the woman's feet drumming and kicking against the cobbles and her muffled squawks of alarm had little to do with the feigned passion that Marie and I both knew so well and, in fact, specialised in. 'Do you think we should go down and see if she needs help?' I said doubtfully, wondering why the woman had agreed to lie down on the wet cobbles when it would have been dryer and easier by far to do the business standing up in a nearby alleyway.

'Not a chance,' Marie scoffed. 'And get an earful for scaring off her client? Business isn't exactly booming right now, is it?'

'I'm glad of the rest,' I said with a sigh, tossing back my hair, which I had spent the best part of the day painstakingly bleaching with ammonia and rinsed with dye to make it even more brassily yellow and which still clung in damp annoying tendrils to my neck. 'The hot weather does something terrible to men, doesn't it?' There'd been a heat wave a few weeks back and we'd spent most of our days exhaustedly entertaining one gentleman after another in the sweltering little rooms, painted pink and stinking cloyingly of musk and roses, at the back of the house. It was a blessed relief when the weather finally broke and the rain came thick and fast, thudding against the rattling window panes and drumming noisily on the roof tiles above our heads, clearing the air and driving all the men away.

'Look there.' Marie grabbed at my arm in genuine alarm,

sinking her fingers into my flesh so that I yelped with pain. 'He's got a knife.' We both stared in horror as the blade flashed once and then again in the dim light cast by the sliver of moon high above and the woman's feet became ominously still.

'What should we do?' I whispered, licking my lips and clearing my throat which had suddenly gone completely dry. I looked at Marie and with a certain grim satisfaction saw that for once she was struck dumb and pale with fright, which made her freckles stand out like brown lace on her face. 'Should we go down there and see him off?'

Marie stared at me, working her mouth angrily as she tried to find the right words. 'Are you completely off your head?' she said at last, gripping my arm even tighter and enunciating each word coldly and carefully from between gritted, chattering teeth. 'He's. Got. A. Knife.'

I shook her off and even as Marie flung out a hand to stop me, I'd forced up the window and shouted 'Murder!' as loudly as I could down into the yard. The man paused and I caught my breath, my heart lurching in terror as he looked back up over his shoulder at our window before carefully pulling down the woman's disordered skirts which had been lifted to just above her hips and wiping his hands on them. 'Murder!' I shouted again, more shakily this time but louder as he calmly got to his feet and walked briskly away, tucking his bloody knife into an inside pocket as he went.

'If we go out now, we can still catch him,' I said, rushing to the door, pausing only to throw a tatty silk shawl over my corset and white chemise. I planned to run down to the porters downstairs, four taciturn and burly local men, who were employed to act as both doormen and protectors of the poor geese working upstairs but before I could leave the room, Marie had planted herself in front of the door and was staring at me with her mouth hanging wide open. 'What did you do that for?' she demanded shrilly, sounding more Irish than ever despite all her pains to hide her real accent. 'The silly cow was already done for so why did you have to go and let him know that we had seen him?' She was trembling with fury. 'You could have sent one of the men out to him. They'd have known what to do.'

I stared back at her. 'I couldn't just stand there and do nothing,'

11

I said, flustered. 'That poor woman...'

'Never mind that poor woman,' Marie snapped, interrupting me. 'What about us? I bet he clocked a right old view of the pair of us standing there at the window like a pair of lemons. What's to stop him coming back for us one day?'

'Why would he?' I asked, but my mouth was suddenly so dry that my voice came out as a pathetic squeak of panic. 'I could hardly see anything of him so I doubt he could see either of us clearly.'

'You willing to stay here and take that chance are you?' Marie shouted at me, her hands on her hips and cheeks flushed with anger. 'You happy to stay here in this stinking hovel and wait for him to come for us with his knife?' She stormed across the room and dragged her battered brown trunk out from beneath her bed then started flinging clothes into it. I noticed one of my own new dresses get dumped inside but decided to hold my tongue and quietly retrieve it later on. 'You can do as you please but I'm not hanging about this bloody place, waiting to be murdered!'

'Oh for God's sake.' I pulled the door open and gathered my thin nightdress around me before hurrying down the rickety stairs to the porters' tiny parlour below, which was thick with smoke and the stink of rum as the men played cards on the beer stained table in the middle of the room. 'There's been a murder,' I gasped as still holding their cards, they stared up at me uncomprehendingly. 'Une femme mort!' I tried again, remembering that their grasp of the English language was somewhat imperfect. 'Maintenant, dans le yard. Elle est murdered.' I drew my finger across my throat. That they understood and immediately they pushed back their chairs, which fell onto the grubby tiled floor with a clatter then rushed past me down the corridor to the yard door.

'What's this bloody racket about?' I gave a guilty start as Madame Lisette herself appeared at the top of the stairs, a flamboyantly patterned Chinese silk dressing gown wrapped around her generous figure and her brassy blonde hair hanging in tangled ringlets around her face. Without the deceiving layers of rouge, kohl, powder and paint that she applied with a heavy but practiced hand every morning, she was grey faced and piggy eyed with exhaustion. 'Emma,' she said with resignation when she saw

me standing trembling with fright in the hal
known you'd be involved somehow.' She hurried
and I took a step back as her heavy musky scen
resoundingly defeated the pungent fumes fr
abandoned cigars which lay carelessly on the t
piles of cards and grimy coins. I wistfully thought
a few of the coins into my corset but then reminded myself that
the porters were as sharp as tacks and had broken dozens of
fingers and noses for far less.

'There's been a murder in the yard out back, Madame,' I said,
stepping aside and pointing to show where the men had gone.
The door was still open and the cold air was creeping towards us,
making me wish that I'd put on a coat before dashing downstairs
'The porters have gone out to see.'

Madame Lisette stared at me. 'A murder?' she snapped, the
refined almost caressing accent that she so carefully cultivated
vanishing at once to be replaced by broad Bristol tones. 'In our
yard?' A board creaked on the stairs and we both looked up to see
Marie standing at the top, her eyes round with fright and a pair of
bright green stockings hanging from her hands. 'Oh, here she is,'
Madame said, rolling her brown eyes. 'I suppose you know all
about it, don't you. Always poking your bleeding nose in where it
isn't wanted. I knew it was a mistake to take you two sluts on.'
She didn't wait for a reply but sailed on down the corridor and
out through the door.

'Still leaving are you?' I whispered to Marie as she came down
the stairs.

'Course I am, but I heard Lisette ranting on at you and thought
I'd see what was happening first.' We were creeping quietly down
the corridor now and could hear voices in the yard as Madame
hissed instructions at the porters in fluent French. Oh, don't be
fooled. Despite the name, Madame Lisette was about as French as
Queen Victoria but she'd done well for herself when she landed
up in Calais and decided to set up a knocking shop there, catering
mainly for passing English gentlemen but also any locals who
fancied an occasional bit of English meat and had plenty of spare
money to pay for it.

Once a year, Madame took the trip back across the Channel to
London and discreetly scoured the brothels of the West End for

.d girls who fancied a new silk dress and a free trip to
. That's how she found Marie and me. We were both
working at an extremely elegant establishment on Jermyn Street
when Madame Lisette stepped out of the shadows one day and
put her glossy calling cards into our unwilling hands as we
walked down to Hyde Park in our best silk frocks and bonnets to
gawp at the fashionable ladies in their swanky carriages and be
seen by all the gentlemen.

'Haven't I been saying that I want a change of scenery?' Marie
said, her Irish accent lilting and her eyes round and misty as she
fingered the flimsy card and daydreamed of the Eiffel Tower and
handsome French men with glossy black moustaches. 'I've always
wanted to go to Paris.'

I snorted. 'She didn't say Paris,' I pointed out as she gave me
an annoyed look. 'She said Calais.' I looked doubtfully down at
the embossed card in my hand, which had 'Madame Lisette's
Establishment of Young Ladies' scrawled across the middle in
curly black writing and a cluster of lurid purple pansies printed
on the corner. 'I'm not sure about this, Marie,' I said doubtfully.
'My Mam always said that if something seems to good to be true
then it probably is.'

'Well, you can do as you please,' my friend said with a laugh
and a little dance that showed off her pretty ankles and attracted
admiring looks from a group of passing gentlemen. 'I'm off to
France!'

I remembered all of this as we crept silently down the corridor
to the yard, where Lisette was bending over the body that still lay
spreadeagled on the cobbles. 'She'll have to be disposed of,' she
was saying in brisk English to someone who was standing just out
of sight. 'We can't have word of this getting out. Business is
already bad enough without my girls getting ripped apart like
bags of grain on our own doorstep.'

Marie and I looked at each other in horror - so it was one of
our lot after all. I craned my neck, trying to see who the dead
woman was but could only see one out-flung pale hand and her
booted feet, which lay at odd angles to each other.

'What about the gendarmes?' someone said and I recognised
the calm Welsh voice of Lisette's right hand woman, Mrs Bell.
'They ought to be called, Lisette.'

'I won't allow it,' Lisette replied angrily. 'I'm not having the police crawling all over this place. They've been looking for an excuse to close us down for years - I'm not about to hand it to them on a plate.' She looked down thoughtfully at the dead woman, gently toeing her with her boot. 'No, we'll have to deal with this ourselves before they get wind of what happened here.'

'The person who did this should be brought to justice,' Mrs Bell persisted but I could tell by her resigned tone that she knew there was no way of changing Lisette's mind once she'd decided on a course of action. 'If you do nothing then you leave him free to kill again.'

'We'll deal with him in our own way,' Lisette snapped before beckoning the porters forward and speaking in incomprehensible French to them again, sometimes pointing to the corpse at her feet and other times out across the town.

'Lisette, no...' Mrs Bell interjected, sounding shocked. 'She should have a proper burial.'

Madame snorted and gave the corpse another fastidious nudge with her foot. 'And so she will have. Sailors have been burying their men at sea for centuries and see nothing wrong with it. I've told the men to say a prayer over her before they throw her in, that's no less than any vicar would do for her.'

'But what of her family?' Mrs Bell stepped forward from the gloom and I could see that her pale kindly face was drawn close with worry. She knelt down beside the dead woman and gently lifted her head, which lolled at a precarious angle as she'd had her throat cut clean through. 'Her family deserve to know what became of her,' she whispered to Madame.

'If her family gave a damn about what happened to her, she wouldn't have ended up here,' Lisette replied coldly before turning and walking away, pulling her silk robe close around her shoulders. 'I've given my orders and expect them to be obeyed.' She noticed Marie and I skulking in the shadows then and gave a small nasty smile that revealed teeth browned by decades of tea drinking and tobacco. 'I suppose that I ought to say that you should both let this be a lesson to you about what happens when you tarts don't know what side your bread is buttered on, but what would be the point?' she said before sweeping past us back into the house, leaving in her wake a sense of unease and a strong aroma of expensive French perfume.

As soon as she had gone, Mrs Bell stood up and wiped the damp and dirt from her dark grey cotton skirts. 'I wish that I dared to disobey her damned orders,' she said wryly as Marie and I crept slowly out of our hiding place, 'but I'd find my stuff thrown out of a window and myself speedily following it within minutes of the gendarmes arriving at this house.'

'Who is it?' I whispered as the porters bent over the body and prepared to lift it into a large sack that had been brought from the dilapidated stable at the back of the yard. 'She said it was one of her girls.'

Mrs Bell gave a sad nod. 'It's Bea,' she said. 'I thought she was in bed but she must have gone out to earn a few more bob.' She swallowed hard. 'Whoever it was slit her throat and then cut her open. She hasn't just been murdered; she's been slaughtered.'

I was close enough to see the body now and instinctively recoiled as I looked down at Bea's pale face, which had a dark smear of blood on the chin. Her hazel eyes were wide open and her rouged mouth hung slack in an expression of startled dismay. 'We saw it happen,' I whispered as I took in Bea's torn and bloodstained pale blue dress and her damp blonde hair, which had come out of its usually carefully coiled and pinned bun and trailed across the dirty cobbles.

Mrs Bell gave me a sharp look. 'Are you quite sure, Emma?' She glanced up to where she knew our window was. 'It was very dark. Perhaps you were imagining things?'

I shook my head, ignoring the warning pinch that Marie gave my arm. 'No, I definitely saw something. I saw his knife and everything.' With much huffing and puffing the porters lifted up the body, doing their best to support poor Bea's wildly lolling head and deposited it as carefully as they could into the sack.

'Did you see his face?' Mrs Bell asked softly. 'Think carefully, girl.'

Marie pinched my arm again and after a pause, I gave my head a regretful shake. 'It was too dark,' I lied, crossing my fingers behind my back as I had used to do as a little girl.

Mrs Bell looked at me searchingly for a long moment then gave a satisfied nod. 'Very well.'

We all turned to watch as the sack was placed carefully on to the floor of Madame Lisette's rather shabby black carriage, which had plainly seen better days before she'd snapped it up at an auction house. One of the porters, who looked most displeased about having to drive out in the middle of the night, climbed heavily up onto the perch and gathered the reins in his gloved hands. He then briefly touched his cap to Mrs Bell before driving briskly out of the yard, taking Bea with him and leaving the other porters to throw icy cold buckets of water and thick handfuls of straw onto the bloody cobbles, grumbling to each in French as they did so. It seemed that Madame Lisette had thought of everything in her determination that this crime should go undetected.

'Come on, let's go,' Marie whispered to me, shivering as she pulled her thin red shawl closer about her shoulders. 'I want to be as far away as possible from this place by tomorrow.'

I nodded and followed her back into the house, with one last curious look over my shoulder at Mrs Bell who continued to stand quietly in the middle of the yard, while the porters went about their grim business around her.

'Poor old Bea, eh?' Marie said as we clomped back up the stairs to our room. 'Still, she was almost at the end of the road anyway.'

I gawped at her. 'Leave it out, she was only thirty one. That's hardly ancient, is it?' I was just trying to be kind though and didn't quite mean it. I'd turned seventeen my first week in Calais and thirty one seemed unimaginably old to me. Old enough to be a grandmother in the part of the world that I came from. Old enough to be dead already.

Marie flounced a little. 'It is in our line of work, sweetheart,' she said with a pout. 'If she was a horse, she'd have been packed off to the knackers yard soon enough. Shame she couldn't find something better for herself before it happened.'

'She never got the chance,' I said quietly, feeling suddenly terribly sad.

Marie shrugged. 'I wonder what's going to happen to her stuff now that she's gone?' she said thoughtfully, looking across at Bea's closed door, which lay across the landing from our own. 'She had some lovely things, didn't she?'

'Madame will have first pickings no doubt,' I replied listlessly, following Marie's gaze. 'We should probably wait until...' I spoke in vain, of course, as the other girl had already turned the door handle and stolen quietly into the dark room beyond.

'Are you coming in, then?' she called out and I heard her crash heavily against a piece of furniture and swear with pain and annoyance.

'I'll fetch a lamp then, shall I?' I said rather resentfully before going into our room, picking up a small gas lamp that stood on a rickety blue painted chest of drawers next to the door and then returning to Bea's cologne scented bedroom, where I put it down on the small table beside her carefully made bed, which was covered with a pretty patchwork counterpane that I suspected she'd brought from home, folding it carefully so that it fit into her trunk. I touched it gently and felt sad all over again.

'I reckon we're the first to come in here,' Marie said with much satisfaction, pulling open a drawer and rifling through poor dead Bea's stockings and lace edged petticoats. 'I told you that she had some nice things, didn't I?' she said with glee as she pulled out some pink ribbed stockings and a petticoat with a blue ribbon laced through the edging which she threw onto the bed. 'Mind you, she always did look like she thought she was a cut above the rest of us poor tarts.'

'I'm not sure we should be doing this,' I said, looking around but not touching anything. It made me feel miserable to be standing there in a dead woman's room, seeing her things lying there just had she had left them and knowing that she would never be coming back.

Marie had moved on to the wardrobe beside the window and threw it open to reveal half a dozen light coloured dresses hanging together with little lavender and rose scented sachets tied to each one by a pale pink ribbon. 'What does Bea care?' she said over her shoulder as she pulled a pale lemon yellow dress out, held it up against her then threw it onto the pile on the bed. 'She's probably at the bottom of the Channel by now.' She pulled out a pink dress with a pretty rose bud pattern and added it to the pile. 'I always liked that one and didn't think it did anything for her. It'll look much better on me.'

I sighed and opened a drawer, not really intending to take anything but at the same time curious to see Bea's things for reasons that I couldn't really explain other than that she had been murdered and that, in a way, gave her belongings a certain tawdry glamour and allure. Inside the drawer there was a small blue watered silk box and underneath that, a sealed envelope, stamped and waiting to be sent. I looked warily across at Marie, who was busily trying on bonnets and pouting at herself in front of a tarnished mirror then picked up the envelope, which was addressed to a Miss Alice Redmayne at 18 Grosvenor Road, Highbury, London. I slid it into my corset then opened the box, which held a pretty amber pendant, engraved on the back with 'To my lovely Beatrice from her Alice.' I looked across at Marie again, who had now moved with great relish on to Bea's shoes, which stood in neat rows at the bottom of the wardrobe, then hid the box in my fist.

'I hope you've got enough money for the crossing back to England?' Marie said, buttoning up a pair of shiny red leather boots and turning her slender ankle from side to side, the better to admire the effect. 'Only, I don't have enough money saved up for both of us.'

'I haven't said that I'm coming with you,' I huffed, quietly closing the drawer. 'I might stay here for a while.'

Marie stared at me. 'Are you simple?' she demanded. 'That madman could come back at any time. Didn't you hear what Mrs Bell said about what he did to poor Bea?' She pulled off the boot, picked up its fellow and added them to the ever increasing pile. 'He gutted her. Now I don't know about you, but I'm not staying here to see if he comes after me with that knife of his.' She picked up another pair of shoes, pale blue this time, and threw them on to the bed. 'Don't forget that he clocked a look at you as well.'

'Where should we go?' I said with a heavy sigh, resigning myself to the inevitable.

Marie grinned then. 'I know just the place.'

Chapter Two
Cora, London, August 1888

I rubbed my eyes then clambered out of bed, careful as always not to wake my elder sister, Cat who slept on, her face buried deep in her pillow and the blankets pulled up high around her shoulders. I tiptoed carefully to the window and pulled the threadbare yellow cotton curtain aside to look down into the backyard, where a few cats were already prowling, on the hunt for scraps and perhaps a scratch behind the ear if they were lucky.

The station was usually quiet at this hour, most of the policemen were either out on the beat or inside getting briefed and ready for the day ahead. I knew that Pa had already gone down as I'd lain awake in bed earlier on, listening to him pulling on his boots then cursing softly as he hunted for his helmet which my little brothers had hidden in their room while he was asleep.

Today was different though and as I quietly pulled on my clothes, I could hear shouts coming from the station below, the slamming of doors and the sound of the policemen's heavy boots stamping on the wooden stairs. Something had clearly happened and as I fastened up my dress, I wondered if Pa, always so keen to help out and be useful, was in the thick of it as usual.

I padded on stockinged feet to the main room of our quarters, a plain whitewashed chamber that smelled faintly of sweaty feet, stewed cabbage, boiled beef from last night's dinner and carbolic soap, where my sister and I did most of the cooking, ate our meals, worked at the sewing we took in from a fancy dressmaker in Mayfair and oversaw the boys' reading and where Pa slept on the small truckle bed in the corner, preferring to let we girls have the relative privacy of the big main bedroom while the boys shared a bed in the other bedroom. The small window, which had been painted a cheerful bright blue by Cat, overlooked the street and I stood on tiptoe to look down on Commercial Street, which already bustled with activity with several hawkers and street girls selling their wares, the traders heading to Spitalfields Market to start the days trading, a few worse for wear soldiers shambling back to their barracks and an incessant trail of wagons and carriages trundling down the middle of the dusty thoroughfare chased by gangs of ragged little street boys.

As I watched, the great doors of the police station opened and about half a dozen officers ran out, some of them clearly caught unawares for they clumsily did up their navy blue tunics and straightened their helmets as they hurried down the street towards Christ Church. I looked to see if Pa was one of them but didn't spy his thick thatch of red hair, so easily picked out in any crowd, and so relaxed, relieved that he wasn't going to be in the midst of whatever trouble was occurring.

'What's happened?' It was Cat, drowsy and yawning her head off in the doorway, her pale pink pinafore apron held up by just one button while the other strap trailed down to her knees. She wasn't exactly a morning person. 'I heard shouting down below.'

I shrugged. 'Dunno. Some of the men have just run down the street.' I saw my sister open her mouth to ask the obvious question and cut her off. 'Not Pa though. He must still be downstairs.'

We'd lived in the station for three years, ever since Ma died giving birth to baby Alfred. We'd had our own place back then, a pretty little house on Brick Lane but then Ma died and Pa brought us all to live above the station, thinking it would make it easier for him to carry on working and still keep an eye on us all. My sister should have been long gone by now, flown off to her own life and family but instead she stayed to help care for the boys and Pa until they were able to take care of themselves and did her sewing work in the evenings to help make ends meet.

'What do you think has happened?' Cat said, turning away to make porridge for the boys, first measuring rough oats from a chipped blue ceramic jar into a pan then adding milk. 'Another riot maybe? Or do you think there's been a murder?' She sounded hopeful. Whenever Cat had some spare money, she liked to spend it on editions of the Illustrated Police News, a grubby rag that specialised in gruesome, and according to Pa, wildly exaggerated illustrated reports of all the latest murders and executions while my secret vice was collecting play bills and posters from the local theatres and music halls then daydreaming over them when I thought no one was looking.

I turned back to the window and peered over the dingy roof tops and smoking chimneys to where Christ Church soared in the distance, its huge white tower looming over the surrounding houses, forbidding and angular as a pagan temple. 'I hope not,' I said with a shudder. I never could abide the sight of my own blood, let alone anyone else's.

Cat scoffed. 'Oh you, some policeman's daughter you are,' she said, stirring the porridge until it began to bubble then solidify. 'Faint at the sight of your own shadow, you would.'

I felt myself go hot and red with embarrassment. 'I would not,' I protested, knowing that actually my sister was right but I would rather have died a thousand times over than admit it.

Cat laughed then, not unkindly. 'Yes, you would. Gawd knows what would happen if you was to see an actual killing.' She spooned the porridge into four brown earthenware bowls and sprinkled a little of our precious store of sugar on each one. 'To keep the little blighters sweet,' she said with a wink to me just as our four little brothers charged noisily into the room, auburn hair tousled and eyes grimy with sleep. It was drawing to the close of the school holidays and they were looking forward to a long sunny day of lazily kicking about the streets with their friends and perhaps earning a few illicit pennies fetching and carrying in the market.

Alfred, the youngest, put his arms up to me and I smiled with real love as I picked him up and pressed my lips to his sticky cheek, which was still warm from his bed. 'Sleep well, sweetheart?' I whispered and he nodded before struggling to be let down again. Unlike the other boys he was still too young for school or to be allowed out to play on the street and so stayed at home with Cat and me to look after him while we worked on our sewing and did the housework.

'Why don't you go and see what's happening?' Cat said, jerking her head to the door as she spooned out a helping of porridge for herself then put the rest aside for me. 'Maybe Pa will know.'

I hesitated for a moment then nodded, pulled on my boots and scampered out of the room before the ever mercurial Cat changed her mind and decided to go instead of me. Although I made the trip downstairs several times a day to use the privies in the yard or go out on to Commercial Street, I was a bag of nerves this time when instead of crossing the yard, I opened the door into the station itself then went down a brown painted corridor that smelt strongly of male sweat, leather boots and pipe smoke to the main lobby, a large shabby room with a scratched and battered wooden desk along the back wall which was usually manned by a couple of sergeants. Just beyond this I could see the cells, which as usual housed a motley collection of vagrants, petty criminals and drunken prostitutes. Sometimes they would keep me awake at night with their shrieks, tuneless singing and demands to be set free but this morning they were all quietly slumped on the floor, all of the stuffing knocked out of them by a night in the cells and clearly longing to be elsewhere.

'What are you doing down here, Cora?' a voice said close to my ear and I whirled around in panic only to smile with relief when I saw who it was.

'Ned,' I said, putting my hand to my breast as if touch alone could calm my leaping heart. Ned was a new recruit, a local boy who had gone to school with my sister Cat and, I suspected, was more than a bit sweet on her. 'I just came down to see what was happening.' I looked around for Pa and saw that the usually stern policemen behind the desk were unusually animated as they chatted with a tall young man with shining dark brown hair that I'd never seen before. I reluctantly dragged my eyes away from him and smiled at Ned. 'Cat thinks there's been a murder.'

'There's been a woman knifed in George Yard,' Ned whispered with relish, leaning so close that his lips almost grazed my cheek and he jumped back in embarrassment. 'Nasty business by all accounts. Stabbed over and over again.'

I was wide eyed now. I knew George Yard, which despite the misleading name was actually a narrow street and not a yard at all, well as I often used it to get from Brick Lane to Whitechapel High Street, where it came out as an archway between a pawnbrokers and the distinctly down at heel White Hart pub with its grimy bow window. It was a dingy ill lit alleyway, lined with cheap lodging houses and stinking of urine, rubbish, horse manure and the foul smoke generated by the tall chimney of the Whitechapel Board of Works' rubbish incinerator on the corner of Wentworth Street. Most would take pains to avoid it at night but it was safe enough during the day, mainly thanks to the presence of a large ragged school for poor children at the Whitechapel High Street end. 'Is she dead?' I asked.

Ned looked at me in amazement. 'Course she's dead,' he said as if to a simpleton. 'She's been stabbed all over.'

I felt a bit sick but managed to swallow it down. 'Is she still there?' I whispered.

Ned shook his head. 'Nah, they've taken her to the workhouse mortuary on Old Montague Street,' he said. 'Just waiting for someone to identify the body now.' He peered closely at me. 'You alright, Cora? You've gone awful pale. Your Pa is around here somewhere if you need looking after.'

I closed my eyes and shook my head. 'No thanks, Ned.' I felt irked though; this was the second time that morning someone had suggested that I needed looking after in some way, that I was too squeamish and pathetic to cope with anything gruesome.

'Your sister always says that you are as weak as water,' Ned said with a nervous laugh, obviously terrified that I was about to faint and cause a fuss that he would get the blame for. 'I shouldn't have said anything about the stabbing. I'm sorry.'

That did it. My eyes snapped open and I forced myself to smile. 'It's alright, Ned,' I said as jauntily as I could even though I was seething inside. 'I haven't had my breakfast yet, that's all. I'll be right as rain in a minute.'

He smiled at me uncertainly, obviously unconvinced. 'Well, that's good. I have to be off now.' He looked suddenly shy and a crimson flush spread up from his collar to the tips of his ears. 'Be sure to say hello to Cat for me, won't you?'

'Oh, I will,' I said grimly, my mind working swiftly as I formulated a plan that would show them all that I wasn't the hopeless little milksop that they all thought I was. Weak as water? I'd show them. 'Wait, Ned, who is that at the counter?' I whispered, jerking my head towards the newcomer who was still chatting away with the policemen as if they were all old friends. He was nice looking with dark grey eyes, a firm clean shaven chin, full lips and waving hair that even I knew was quite a bit longer than was fashionable and which fell just short of his slate grey coat collar. There was something open and friendly about his expression that made me want to look at him for a long time but even so I hastily dropped my gaze, feeling my cheeks go red with embarrassment, when he turned and looked at me for a moment over his shoulder.

Ned pulled a face. 'That's Henry Mercier, he's studying to become a lawyer and comes in to help people with legal matters if they can't afford to hire anyone proper.' His expression was scornful. 'Although what good it does, I'm sure I don't know.'

'That's kind of him,' I said faintly, watching as Mr Mercier followed a policeman to the cells then squatted down on his haunches to talk quietly to one of the miserable looking women slumped on the floor. As I watched, the woman started to cry and he took her grimy hands in his own to console her, talking soothingly all the while.

'I don't know why he wastes his time with them. If they're in here then they're past all help, aren't they?' Ned said with a snort of disgust before nodding briskly to me and strolling off to the briefing rooms that lay in a warren behind the lobby.

I waited a few seconds to make sure that he wasn't coming back then slipped out through the front door of the station and ran as fast as I could down Commercial Street, pulling my shawl close about my shoulders as I went. I'd show them that I was tougher than they thought. They'd rue the day they called me weak as water because I was going to do something that not one of them would ever dare to do.

I carried on running until I could go no further then leaned against the grimy railings of Christ Church to catch my breath, doing my best to ignore the curious stares of the homeless people who spent their miserable days sleeping and drinking themselves into a state of forgetful oblivion among the mossy stones in Itchy Park, the local nickname for the former graveyard. I then dusted myself down before carrying on more slowly to the turning on to Wentworth Street. The day before had been a bank holiday and there was a distinctly louche atmosphere in the air with litter everywhere on the sun warmed pavements, everyone nursing hangovers and tattered bunting hanging from the dusty windows of the pubs that stood on almost every corner and everyone nursing hangovers.

Pa had had the day off and, being brave and also somewhat foolhardy, took us all off on the train from Liverpool Street to Southend for a day at the seaside, using money he'd been saving for months to pay for it. He grew up next to the sea in Norfolk and it made me feel sad to see him standing on the pier at Southend gazing wistfully out into the great expanse of blue where sea and sky met and merged together. 'Are you alright there, Pa?' I asked eventually, slipping my hand, which was sticky with melted ice cream, into his. He looked down at me with a start of surprise as if he'd forgotten that I was there then gave me a sad smile. 'I'm alright, sweetheart,' he said with a deep sigh. He sighed all the time since Ma died. 'I was just watching the gulls and wondering what adventures and strange foreign lands the breeze will take them to.' Poor Pa. I squeezed his hand and turned to watch the gulls with him, admiring the way they soared and dipped without a care on the wind and envying them their freedom.

Caught up in my memories of the day before, I remembered too late that my route would take me straight past George Yard where several of my father's colleagues were even now hanging about the street entrance and doing their best to keep curious locals from seeing anything, pushing them back none too gently with their hands and truncheons when the large crowd that had gathered threatened to surge past them to the murder scene. 'Not that there's anything worth seeing,' an elderly woman huffed with annoyance as I pulled my shawl up over my head and tried to sneak past the entrance to the alley. 'It all happened indoors in George Yard Buildings. There's not a spot of blood to be seen on the street.' She clicked her tongue against her teeth. 'I wish I'd known that before I wasted my time trundling all the way down here to have a look.'

Once I had skirted around the crowd and avoided all of the policemen, it didn't take me long to reach the entrance to the workhouse mortuary, a low shabby, red brick building, no better than a shed, reached via a pair of black painted gates on narrow, winding Eagle Place. Next door was the Davenant Foundation School and I thought how odd it was that the mortuary, encased as it always was in a heavy pall of death and decay, should be directly next to the schoolyard where, if it hadn't been for the holidays, the sound of children playing and laughing would have drifted over to me as I hesitated then pushed open the gate, which led on to a tiny yard.

There should have been a policeman on duty to let people in but to my great relief he was nowhere to be seen and had probably nipped off for a cigarette and a cup of strong tea with his mates down at George Yard. I hoped that he wouldn't get into trouble should I be caught inside but even that fleeting feeling of guilt wasn't enough to make me waver from my purpose as I crossed the cobbled yard. There were two more doors in front of me, one straight ahead leading to the bin shed and the other on the left which led directly into the mortuary itself. 'Oh cripes,' I whispered to myself before putting my hand to the black painted handle and turning it, not even thinking of what I was going to say should anyone else already be inside.

The door opened and luckily the large room beyond, which reeked of antiseptic, soap and the harsh metallic tang of old blood, was empty. Thanking my lucky stars, I swiftly made my way to the post mortem room, a small white tiled chamber entirely dominated by the examination table in the centre, upon which lay a body entirely covered by a grubby white sheet with 'WHITECHAPEL WORKHOUSE' stamped in faded red ink on the bottom left corner. The body beneath looked large enough to be a man's but I could see a woman's scuffed and much mended boots and a few straggling brown cotton petticoats peeping out from beneath the sheet.

I carefully closed the door behind me then took a deep breath and stepped up to the table. For a few horrible seconds, it seemed to me as if the cloth covering the dead woman's mouth was being sucked in and released as if she still breathed and I instinctively gasped aloud with fright. The moment soon passed though and before I could give myself a chance to change my mind and run away, I closed my eyes, put my hand to the cloth and gave it a sharp tug.

I had seen death just once before when Ma died and I helped Cat and Aunt May wash and lay out the body, carefully plaiting her fair hair and tying it with a pretty blue ribbon then pulling the blankets up to under her chin so that she looked as if she were only sleeping and could still wake up at any minute. This was entirely different.

Whereas Ma had been pale and serene, the slight smile on her pale lips giving no clue of the terrible pain she had endured for days on end before she'd finally given up and quietly bled to death in Pa's arms, this woman was mottled and bruised, her mouth hanging slackly open to reveal rotten teeth and a swollen tongue while the dark blood splattered over her face and neck was clear evidence of the violence of her end. She stank too, of blood, stale beer, sweat and a horrible pervasive damp, the dank scent of loneliness and desperation that I had smelt before on the vagrants and sad street women that Pa locked up in the station cells.

Horrified and sickened, I gave a little cry and dropped the sheet back over that terrible, twisted face before taking a step back. Weak as water I may well be but my sister was wrong in one respect - I hadn't fainted and this was something far worse than my own shadow.

Swallowing down my revulsion, I looked around the room and spotted a pile of what looked like rubbish lying on a slate counter next to the sink but which on closer inspection was clearly the dead woman's few paltry belongings - a crushed black bonnet, two shillings, an old glove missing most of its buttons, some pills in a wrap of old newspaper, a small tin of tea and a bulky blood stained envelope.

I stared at them for a moment, thinking how pathetic it was that this was all the poor woman had on her when she died and glad that at least Ma had left behind a sweet little baby for everyone to remember her by and not a pile of old trash. I gingerly picked up the envelope, holding it between thumb and forefinger so that I wouldn't touch any of the blood and read the name written on it aloud. 'Miss Alice Redmayne, Highbury.' I looked around at the dead woman, my gaze resting thoughtfully on the battered old boots and ripped and tattered petticoats. She didn't look like an Alice and she certainly didn't look like she'd come from Highbury, which even I knew was a serious cut above even the nicest parts of Spitalfields.

It occurred to me then that it was all very well saying that I'd seen the dead woman but no one was actually going to believe it unless I produced solid evidence of the fact. I looked down at the envelope in my hand and then, before I really knew what I was doing, I shoved it deep inside my pocket.

'What are you doing in here, girl?' I didn't hear the door open behind me and gave a guilty start before turning around with what I sincerely hoped was a look of perfect innocence as I faced an angry short man with a neatly clipped brown beard and small grey eyes that coldly scrutinised me from behind a pair of round glasses that I recognised at once as Dr Killeen, one of the police doctors. His gaze darted away just for a moment to the corpse on the table, doubtless checking that it was as it should be, before returning to my face with a look of enquiry.

'I was just looking for my Pa,' I said in a shaky voice, relieved that I had remembered to tuck the sheet back over the woman's face before I went to look at her things. 'He's a sergeant with H Division. They said he might be in here.' I glanced at the covered shape on the table and swallowed hard, willing myself not to faint as I remembered those rotten teeth, the blood, the stink of her. 'I didn't know that I wasn't allowed.'

The doctor made an irritated sound. 'Of course you knew,' he said curtly, shrugging out of his tweed jacket and briskly beginning to turn up his sleeves. 'I've often thought that the women and girls,' at this he looked me over dismissively, 'of this God forsaken district have the most disgustingly morbid curiosity that I have ever encountered.' He went to the sink and began to angrily soap his hands and arms up to the elbow. 'Do you not see enough death already without feeling compelled to actively seek it out for your own vulgar amusement?'

I felt my cheeks go red with shame. I could have told him that I'd only ever seen my Ma dead before but quickly decided that I didn't want to share anything so personal, so raw with this man so instead I sadly shook my head. 'I'm sorry, sir,' I mumbled, bobbing an awkward and unnecessary curtsey under his cold gaze. 'I should go and find my Pa now.'

The doctor rolled his eyes then selected a sharp looking scalpel from a small metal tray on a table next to the sink. 'See that you do.'

I ran from the mortuary, almost colliding on the doorstep with another girl, not much older than myself and dressed in a flounced and much mended faded pink cotton dress with a little

29

too much rouge smeared on her round cheeks. She almost didn't see me coming as she was chatting away to the young police constable who had returned to his duties in the yard while I was inside. 'Oops, careful now.' The girl stepped quickly to one side and grinned at me before something about my appearance, probably my red cheeks and the tears in my eyes, made her smile drain away and her eyes narrow. 'Have you been to see the body?' she whispered, putting out a hand and placing it on my arm.

I nodded, glad of a sympathetic ear after the roasting I had just got from the doctor. 'It was horrible,' I murmured queasily. 'There was blood and her face…' The policeman made a little clucking noise and awkwardly patted my shoulder.

The girls nodded as if she completely understood. 'Do they know who she is yet?' she said, still whispering even though the policeman could hear every word. 'Just that word on the street is that it's an old friend of mine and she had something off me a few days ago that I'd like to have returned.'

'I don't know who she is,' I said, noting that the way the girl said 'friend' didn't actually sound very friendly at all. 'I've never seen her before. Maybe you should go and have a look at her things? There's not much but it's all in there with the body.'

'Maybe I'll have a look then,' the girl said more cheerfully, fluffing out her flaxen curls which looked far too yellow to be entirely natural. 'I always told the silly old cow that she'd come to a bad end and now look at her.' She looked up at the young policeman and gave him a sharp nudge with her thin elbow. 'Shall we go and have a look then, bobby?' She grinned, displaying surprisingly nice teeth and gave me a jaunty little wave over her shoulder as they disappeared together into the mortuary.

Chapter Three

Back in the room I shared with my sister, I carefully pulled the envelope out of my pocket and tipped the contents out into the palm of my hand. Whatever it was I expected to find among the seedy belongings of the murdered woman it wasn't a delicate amber pendant with a sweet little message engraved on the back. I looked in the envelope again to see if there was a letter to go with it but there was nothing at all, just the necklace and a few grains of dirt.

'Where did you get to this morning?' Cat was lounging in the doorway watching me. 'I thought you were only going down to the station to ask Pa what all the fuss was about. You were gone so long that he came up to take his break and told me all about the nasty business himself.'

I shrugged, quickly hiding the necklace and envelope in the folds of my dress. 'I had to go out.'

Cat gave me a look and stepped into the room. 'Where to?' she said, her hazel eyes gleaming with curiosity. 'Have you found yourself a lad?'

I felt my cheeks redden. 'Course not,' I muttered, mortified, and trying not to think about Mr Mercier's broad shoulders and the gentle way he'd comforted the woman in the cells. Pa and his colleagues were never rough with the women, usually sad prostitutes the worse for drink and occasionally opium, who entered their care but not many of them would have taken one's hand like that or spoken to her so gently.

'I don't know why you're going so red,' Cat said with a laugh. 'You're almost seventeen now. It's about time you found some nice lad to cheer you up.'

'So where's yours then?' I said without thinking before straight away putting my hands up to my mouth in shock, wishing that I could drag the words back into it again where they could remain unsaid and unheard.

Cat's face darkened and for a horrible moment, I thought she was going to slap me. It wouldn't have been the first time and she'd dispensed summary justice for far less sisterly treachery in the past. 'You know why I don't have a lad,' Cat said at last with resignation. 'I can't leave you and the boys and Pa to fend for yourselves. I have to stay here, to take Ma's place, until no one needs me any more.'

I sighed then shoved the envelope into my pocket and got up to give my sister a hug. 'There's always me,' I whispered, resting my head against Cat's sturdy shoulder and enjoying her special Cat smell of fresh linen, boiled pease pudding and coal dust. 'I can take care of Pa and the boys if you want to go.' I smiled. 'I know that Ned downstairs is sweet on you and would be glad to hear that you're thinking of getting wed.'

Cat made an irritated sound and pushed me away but her cheeks were flushed with pleasure. 'Get away with you,' she muttered, failing to hide a grin. 'I can't be thinking of that right now.'

'Then nor can I,' I said with a smile before lowering my voice. This was the moment I had been waiting for. 'Do you really want to know where I was this morning, Cat?'

My sister shrugged. 'It's no skin off my nose,' she grunted, busying herself straightening pillows and folding up our matching cotton nightdresses, which she had made herself and trimmed with a few stray scraps of left over lace and ribbon from one of her jobs, a wedding dress for a young lady in Islington.

I wasn't fooled by this display of indifference and rushed on anyway. 'I went to see the body,' I announced proudly. 'The woman who got stabbed in George's Yard. I went to see.'

My sister whirled around to stare at me, crushing a nightdress to her thin bosom. 'You never did,' she breathed, her face completely astonished before she firmly shook her head, looking almost annoyed. 'No, I don't believe it. You're telling fibs again.'

I grinned, not at all offended for I had been anticipating this very reaction. 'I really did,' I said before plunging my hand in my pocket and bringing out the envelope but not the necklace, which some instinct warned me to keep out of sight. 'I took this,' I said, handing it to my sister. The blood stains didn't bother me so much now, in fact I regarded them as medals of honour, proof that I wasn't the same squeamish silly Cora who had gone out that morning.

Cat gaped down at the envelope. 'Alice Redmayne. Is that her name?' she asked, transferring her astonished stare to me.

I shook my head, laughing now even though I knew I shouldn't. 'You should have seen her, Cat,' I said, hiding my disgust beneath a charade of light hearted mockery and knowing all the while that I just sounded crass and nasty. 'Oh, she looked a fright with big fat cheeks and her mouth hanging open and nasty old boots that were coming away at the soles. If she came from Highbury then I'm the ruddy Queen.'

Cat was still clutching the envelope and I was pleased to see there was a new respect in her eyes as she looked at me. 'I don't believe it,' she breathed, clearly not knowing whether to be appalled or full of admiration. In fact I could tell that she still didn't know if she quite believed me. 'Who would have thought you of all people would go and do such a thing?'

I preened myself a little. 'Not you, that's for sure,' I said, making a grab for the envelope and putting it back safely in my pocket.

Cat shook her head, as if coming around from a terrible dream. 'You'll need to give that back,' she said with a frown. 'It's evidence.'

'Oh, they won't miss it,' I replied, cheerfully patting my pocket. 'It's just some old tat the old trull had in her pockets. It doesn't mean anything.'

'Even so...' Cat said dubiously. 'You never know. What would Pa say if he knew what you'd done?' She started to laugh. 'Lord, can you imagine his face? Poor Pa.'

'He wouldn't mind,' I said, joining in my sister's laughter. 'He's always telling us that he used to get up to far worse when he was a boy.'

Cat purses her lips then. 'Worse than stealing something off a murdered woman?' she said with a raised eyebrow before putting the folded nightdress under our pillows and going back to the door. 'I'd better get back to the boys before they notice I've gone and tear the place apart. Mind you put that envelope back where you found it, Cora.' She gave me one last severe look then left the room.

As soon as she has gone, I took the envelope and pendant out of my pocket and looked at them thoughtfully. Of course I knew that I really ought to take them straight back to the mortuary and somehow slip them in among the dead woman's things again but something stopped me. Maybe it was the message on the back of the locket, or maybe it was idle curiosity about what sort of girl Alice Redmayne was or perhaps it was just a simple and entirely wholehearted desire never to have to go back to the mortuary again but I knew that on this occasion and for perhaps the first time in my life I was going to disobey my sister and do as I pleased.

My decision made, I popped my head around the door to let Cat know I was going out again, an announcement that was greeted with an uninterested shrug as my sister was busy wiping crumbs from Alfred's hand while he struggled to get back to his battered tin soldiers, hand me downs from our brothers, which were lined up in neat rows on the scrubbed wooden kitchen table. The other boys were nowhere to be seen, which ought to have struck me as ominous but I was too preoccupied to care as, relieved to have escaped another interrogation, I skipped down the stairs with a happy heart and went out on to Commercial Street again.

The sun was properly up now even if a few dark clouds in the distance promised rain later on and as usual I enjoyed the sensation of being part of the crowd, lost in the everyday hustle and bustle of the East End. News of the murder in George Yard had spread far and wide by now and everyone I passed was talking about it, relishing the gruesome details of the dead woman's injuries and shaking their heads sadly over the steady downward decline of the area that such a thing should happen on their own doorstep. Shamelessly listening in, I discovered that the woman had a name now as well: Martha Tabram and by all accounts she was no better than she ought to have been, rather worse in fact - a mean drunk and a bully. I thought of the corpse's fat jowls and slack mouth and shivered despite the sunshine.

I didn't have much money left after our day out in Southend the day before but there was enough to pay for my fare up to

Highbury and back on the cheap horse tram from nearby Moorgate Street so I headed straight there, strolling happily along shop lined Brushfield Street then crossing busy Bishopsgate, picking up a warm meat pie gleaming with a shiny egg glaze, from a stall by the police station, before hurrying through the grimy back streets around Liverpool Street station, munching on my pie and wiping my gravy wet fingers on my blue cotton skirt, until I came out on Moorgate, the heart of the City and home to several financial institutions whose gentlemen strolled in groups along the street, several abreast and dressed in sombre grey and black suits, their brows furrowed with concentration as they talked to each other in soft educated voices that sounded like they came from a different world to the harsh East End accents that I was used to.

There was a red painted horse drawn tram just about to leave so I skirted quickly around a group of raucous City men and jumped on board, giving a sigh of relief as I took the last remaining seat next to a sullen faced old lady in shiny black satin, who fastidiously moved her skirts away from me and with a huff of annoyance averted her face to stare out of the dust encrusted little window.

I didn't care in the slightest about being so obviously snubbed and settled myself comfortably into my seat, fully prepared to enjoy my adventure and looking about me with keen interest at my fellow passengers, who ranged from a sad faced young woman in fashionable clothes with a baby on her lap to a couple of grim looking City men hidden behind their huge newspapers to a white whiskered elderly gentleman in a bright pink waistcoat embroidered with oak leaves and lilies who was completely immersed in the book he held on his lap.

The tram seats were arranged in a row on either side of the straw strewn aisle so that the window was behind me and I had to either peer between the newspapers of the two City men sitting opposite or crane my neck at a painful angle to be able to see anything as we rattled slowly and laboriously through the jam packed city streets, jerkily stopping every now and again to let on new passengers or let people off. The old lady got off by Old Street and was instantly replaced by a young boy who noisily munched on an apple as he thumbed through a grubby copy of the latest Illustrated Police News that he pulled out of his back pocket. I peeped over his shoulder to see if Martha Tabram was in it yet but of course it was far too soon.

The tram creaked on up New North Road then slowly crossed Essex Road, where we almost collided with several irate pedestrians and cart loaded full of crates containing noisily protesting chickens and geese, then went on to Canonbury Road where the cramped dark houses of the East End gradually began to give way to elegant pale stone terraces of tall town houses and pretty white painted detached villas with short drives separating them from the main road. Even the people here looked different, the women were pale and willowy in their fashionable flower coloured dresses while the men sauntered slowly beside them, clean and well fed with shining pomaded hair and whiskers and even shinier boots.

I suddenly felt very self conscious about my faded blue cotton dress, red wool shawl and scuffed boots even if they were clean and in relatively good repair. Pa might not have much money but he liked us all to look decent, just as he placed what my brothers thought was undue importance on boring book learning at school, constantly telling them that it was the best and only way out of the slums of the East End. He willingly paid a penny a day each to send the three elder boys to school and would do the same for Alfred as well when his time came, money that they bitterly resented but knew better than to complain about.

We reached Canonbury Square, which comprised four neat rows of white painted houses around a pretty little patch of greenery, where children played in a well mannered fashion under the eyes of their sombrely dressed governesses, and which was one of the last stops on the route. Pushing aside my last minute misgivings, I followed the other alighting passengers off, pausing to hand my fare to the cheerfully grinning conductor and then giving one of the matching chestnut horses that pulled the tram a friendly pat on the nose.

Following my instinct I went north up Compton Road then asked directions of a passing chimney sweep, who pointed me in the direction of Grosvenor Road, the wrinkles around his eyes and his teeth showing stark white against the soot stains that covered his face. 'You looking for work, miss?' he asked with a friendly nod, looking me over. 'Only I know of a house on Highbury New Park that's looking for a decent girl to work as a maid. It's a nice big house with a good lady in charge. I could put a word in for you, if you like?'

I smiled and shook my head. 'I'm not looking for work,' I said, wishing that I had enough money left to give him a penny, 'but thank you kindly.'

I carried on, walking briskly up Highbury Grove then turning on to New Park as the sweep had directed. The houses here were huge and I stared about myself in amazement as I went, taking in the swagged curtains that I could see hanging at the massive windows, the shiny carriages waiting in front of glossily painted front doors and the pretty, neatly ordered flowers that filled the flower beds lining the driveways. Everything here was clean and neat and my heart ached with something that felt a little like homesickness as I considered how different it all was to the familiar ramshackle mess and dirt of Whitechapel.

After walking for what felt like hours, I found myself standing in front of number eighteen and if I already felt intimidated by the quiet elegance of the street, I felt doubly so now as I looked up at an imposing detached white painted mansion arranged on three floors with several polished marble steps leading up to the red front door, which was flanked by a pair of tall triple arched windows that looked to me as if they really belonged on a church.

'Blimey,' I whispered, staring at the the ivy covered pillared portico that sheltered the front door and the pink and purple flowering rhododendron bushes that stood to either side of the steps, shedding their heavy blooms all over the gravel drive. I put my hand in my pocket and uncertainly fingered the now sealed envelope inside. Had I got it all wrong? The vague idea but very pleasing idea I had been fostering all the way from Whitechapel of Miss Alice Redmayne as an ordinary girl just like myself evaporated like a phantom to be replaced by something altogether less friendly.

As I watched, the red door swung open and I quickly ducked out of sight as a plump lady with greying brown hair and small dark eyes that sank like currants in the soft dough of her face swept out followed by a stern faced butler in an immaculate black suit. 'Pray do tell Miss Alice that I am sorry to have missed her,' she said irritably, opening a yellow silk parasol and holding it at an elegant angle above her head. 'Perhaps another time?'

'Perhaps,' the butler said with a polite sneer before firmly closing the door upon her.

I waited until the lady had sauntered rather crossly down the road before taking a cautious step up to the front door. My original plan had been to knock and then ask to see Miss Alice in person but now that I had seen the house and the butler's scornful treatment of the last visitor, I could feel all my last scanty vestiges of confidence leak away and instead hastily decided that it might be better to simply knock, shove the envelope through the door and then make a run for it before they had me arrested for trespass or worse.

However, no matter how grand the house and the mysterious Miss Alice clearly were, it still felt only fair to offer some sort of explanation for the envelope's sudden arrival and after a moment spent mulling this over, I felt in my other pocket and pulled out a small blunt end of pencil with which I clumsily wrote 'From Whitechapel' in my best hand on the envelope, pressing down hard so that the letters would be legible. Surely that would be more than enough information for someone who lived in a house like this?

'Here goes,' I said to myself, feeling almost dizzy with fright as I lifted my hand to the door knocker which was shaped like a giant lion's head. The sound as I dropped it against its metal mount was terrifyingly loud and in a panic I scrunched the envelope through the flap before almost tripping down the steps in my desperate haste to get away. I heard the door open behind me as I plunged on to the street and a young female voice called out for me to wait but I did not dare turn back and instead gathered up my skirts above my knees and ran as fast as my legs would carry me towards Canonbury Square and safety.

CHAPTER FOUR
ALICE, AUGUST 1888

I had to cover my mouth with my hand to stop myself laughing as I hid behind the morning room door and listened to Swift, my father's butler and, since childhood, one of my closest conspirators, summarily dismiss Mrs Snaith from the premises with his customary disdainful aplomb. It wasn't that Mrs Snaith was a bad woman really, she was just intensely dull, incredibly persistent and overly fond of trying to push her opinions on others and I am afraid that, short of patience as I am at even the best of times, I was in no mood to deal with her right now, not with two dozen guests due for dinner that evening and goodness only knew what else I had to deal with.

Swift coughed discreetly from the hall once the unwelcome visitor had departed and I peeped out from behind the door. 'Thank you so much,' I said with a smile, stepping into the hall with a show of reluctance as if Mrs Snaith might still be lurking there, perhaps hiding behind one of the marble statues of ancient martyrs arranged against the walls. 'She really is quite dreadful isn't she? Last time we let her in, she stayed for almost two hours, talking all the time about a séance she went to in Bloomsbury and trying to persuade me to go to one with her.' I gave a sigh of amused impatience. 'Everyone knows that it isn't polite to stay for more than fifteen minutes on an afternoon call. I would have thought that someone like Mrs Snaith, who is so fond of talking about the decline of modern manners in the young, would know that.'

'She brought leaflets with her this time,' Swift said, gesturing with clear disapproval towards a pile of pamphlets that had been left littering the round table in the centre of the hall. 'Shall I dispose of them?'

I suppressed a shudder as I looked at the pamphlet that lay on top: a lurid illustrated tract about the physical benefits of making contact with the Spirit World. 'I think that is an excellent notion, Swift,' I said briskly. 'The incinerator is by far the best place for them.'

I was just turning back to the morning room when there was a knock on the door, followed shortly afterwards by a crumpled envelope falling with a soft thud on to the floor. 'What on earth..?' I instinctively put out a hand to stop the butler and swiftly picked the envelope up myself, frowning a little when I saw the rusty dark stains around the edges and then giving a small cry of surprise when my eye fell on the address and, with a pang of shocked delight, I recognised the hand with which it had been written.

'Miss Alice?' Swift took a cautious step towards me, his elderly face creased with concern. 'Are you quite well? Should I ring for tea?'

I shook my head impatiently. 'Never mind that,' I said before running past him and wrenching the door open. Having spent the entire day indoors, lazing about in the morning room with a pile of poetry books, I was blinded for a second by the bright sunlight so that everything was a soft blur as I ran down the steps and out on to the street. In the distance I could just about make out a young girl in a blue dress and red shawl running down Grosvenor Road as if the hounds of hell themselves were snapping at her boots. Her long auburn hair had unravelled from a careless bun beneath her bonnet and was tumbling about her shoulders as she ran. 'Wait! Come back!' I cried, waving my arm but the girl didn't stop, didn't even turn around. I sheltered my eyes against the sun and peered down the street, looking for a likeness or something, anything, familiar about the fleeing girl but hardly daring to think that I might see anything that I recognised. The hair was all wrong for a start but then dyes these days were really quite remarkable so who knew?

It occurred to me of course to pick up my heavy apricot silk skirt and give chase but the thought of my father's dismay should wind of such an exploit ever reach him was enough to make me stay put and just stand and watch in hopeless despair as the girl turned the corner and vanished from view. 'Damnation,' I said with heartfelt annoyance, before looking down at the envelope I had crushed in my hand. 'From Whitechapel,' I whispered, only now noticing the pencilled writing so hastily inserted after the address.

'Should I call for a police constable, Miss Alice?' Swift asked with some alarm as I slowly made my way back up the steps to the house, weighting the envelope thoughtfully in my hand as I went. 'I expect there is still time to apprehend the young person should we act now.'

I hesitated for a second, tempted by the prospect of putting the entire matter into more capable hands than my own, then regretfully shook my head. 'No,' I said. 'Let her go. She must have been frightened, poor thing, to run like that for no good reason and sending the police after her won't help matters.'

'As you wish, Miss Alice,' Swift bowed and went off, taking the offending leaflets with him and clearly thoroughly enjoying the prospect of consigning them to the flames of the kitchen oven downstairs. I almost wished that I could go with him but instead I waited for a moment, listening to his retreating footsteps then lifted my skirts above my ankles and ran full pelt up the stairs to my bedroom on the first floor, a large and very pretty room with floral wallpaper that matched the curtains at the windows and around the bed and which overlooked the well maintained garden at the back of the house. I was relieved to see that the room was empty and closed the door firmly behind me before settling on the comfortable blue silk upholstered sofa in front of the open window. The sun was still up although it was now beginning its slow descent and sounds of children whooping and shouting in the neighbouring gardens floated up to me along with the usual barking dogs, calls of anxious nursery maids and the regular rumbling and whistling of trains slowing down on the tracks at the end of the garden as they pulled into nearby Canonbury Station.

I looked for a long time at the front of the envelope, tracing my finger lightly over the well known and much loved writing that I had seen so often before. 'Oh, Beatrice,' I whispered, tears gathering in my eyes before I finally and rather tentatively put my hand inside and pulled the necklace out. I recognised it at once and in fact my mind immediately fluttered back to the day that I picked it out in the jeweller's shop window, drawn in by the cat's eye like gleam of the orange amber and ignoring my Mama's gentle protestations that a pretty sapphire would be far more suitable for my sister's fair colouring.

'No, that one,' I said stubbornly, pointing to the pendant until finally my soft hearted Mama sighed, shrugged and gave in just as she always did. 'Beatrice will like that one best.'

I was right of course and Beatrice was delighted when she opened my present on her birthday, immediately demanding that I fasten the pendant around her slender neck then turning and giving me a big kiss on the cheek. 'Sweet Alice,' she whispered, folding me in her arms and surrounding me with her own warm, fresh scent of violets and roses. 'You are the light of my life. My own little angel.'

That was six years ago now, when I was just eleven and Beatrice had just turned twenty six, perhaps a little too old to be still at home and unmarried especially as she was so pretty but she didn't seem to mind about that. She vanished shortly afterwards, just a few weeks after her birthday. I had gone sleepily into her room across the hall just as I always did every morning only to find the bed cold and empty and all of Beatrice's pretty sugared almond coloured dresses missing from the great wooden wardrobes that lined the wall. I never saw her again, had not even heard from her until this moment when 'Whitechapel' had delivered the precious amber necklace back to me once more.

I'd heard of Whitechapel, of course I had. Who hadn't? It ought to have astonished me, I supposed, that it was from such a hotbed of criminality that I heard the first news of my sister that I had had in six years but really it surprised me not one bit as for all my self admitted ignorance of the world, I had always thought that the dingy, crowded streets of the East End, a melting pot of the lawless, immigrants and the dispossessed, sounded like just the sort of place where people went if they wanted to vanish out of society's sight.

I played with the chain, which gleamed dully and would need cleaning before I could wear it, twisting it around my fingers then looping it thoughtfully about my wrist so that the pendant drooped against my forearm, its yellow cat's eye winking sleepily in the dying sunlight that floated in through my huge windows.

Had Beatrice run away to Whitechapel all those years before? Or perhaps she had been abducted away from her family? I had read about such things in the awful gothic novels that my friend Lucasta secretly lent me but had some doubts that such things actually happened in real life to real people like my own sister.

I got up and went to the little bureau next to my bed, which I kept locked with a small key that I hid beneath a loose floorboard. Once inside I rifled through a few yellowing letters and elderly lace and ribbon trimmed birthday cards until I found what I was looking for - an old photograph of two girls, Beatrice and myself, sitting stiffly side by side in front of the usual decorated backdrop, this one painted to look like a country garden with hollyhocks, roses and a few urns.

I was about eight years old at the time and stared out of the photograph with a decidedly mutinous glint in my wide eyes. I had been carefully dressed for the occasion in a pretty pink frock with a huge floppy pale blue velvet bow at my waist, while my strawberry blonde hair had been brushed until it shone then arranged over my shoulders. 'Don't move a muscle or your hair will kink,' Mama had whispered, patting my tensely folded hands reassuringly before backing slowly carefully away, out of the camera's view.

Beside me, Beatrice shook with nerves and as a result her image was a little blurred so that there was a soft, translucent effect, almost as if she was not really there, like one of the ghosts in those dreadful spiritual photographs that Mrs Snaith was so fond of. She had been there though and even now I could remember the firm feel of my sister's arm around my waist as we posed unsmilingly for the photographer. When I was little, I had always wanted to smile for photographs but by the time I was eight I knew better and had learned to stare at the camera almost ferociously, as if resenting its intrusion.

There was a brisk knock on the door and I hastily shoved the photograph, envelope and necklace into the drawer and slammed it shut before locking it and dropping the key back in its hiding place beneath the floorboard. 'Miss?' It was Minnie, my maid, come to dress me for that evening's dinner party. 'Can I come in?'

I sighed and threw myself back down on the sofa as if I had just woken up from a nap. 'Come in, Minnie,' I called, resigning myself to the inevitable although it seemed obscene really to be thinking about dinner when the sun was still up.

The maid bustled into the room, carrying a pile of clean white towels. 'Sorry if I woke you, Miss,' she said as she carried her load through to the bathroom then began to run a bath, liberally sprinkling the water with rose bath salts as the house's elderly water pipes groaned and rattled with exertion. 'Have you had any thoughts about what you want to wear this evening?' she said, popping her head around the door. It'd been a long day and her white linen mob cap was decidedly askew on top of her mousy curls, which no amount of brushing or coaxing could ever calm down.

I shook my head. 'I expect that Papa wants me to look impressive so perhaps the new yellow silk?' I got up and stretched then went to the window. Another train was pulling in to Canonbury and I watched a little wistfully as its trail of grey steam floated above the trees at the bottom of the garden, wondering as always about the people on board and where they had come from.

'Minnie, have you ever been to Whitechapel?' I asked almost dreamily, forcing myself to turn away from the window.

The maid almost dropped the dress she was carrying in astonishment. 'Course I haven't, Miss!' she said with a reproachful look as if she hailed from the most opulent mansion in Mayfair rather than a tenement in Hackney. 'It's a right old rough house down there and no mistake.' She lowered her voice. 'Why there was a woman murdered there just this morning. Stabbed almost forty times, I heard.' She sniffed and arranged the dress on the bed. 'Although she was apparently no better than she ought to have been so what do you expect.'

'I've never fully understood what that phrase means.' I mused as the maid undressed me, first deftly unfastening my dress then releasing me from my blue watered silk corset. It looked gorgeous but the fine French lace trimming itched so terribly that I was always thrilled beyond measure when I was allowed to remove it.

'What phrase would that be, Miss?' Minnie said, going off to turn the bath taps off and carefully test the water with her elbow. 'Needs a bit more cold,' she pronounced with authority.

'No better than she ought to have been,' I said, following her into the small bathroom, now filled with a warm fug of rose scented steam, which my father had fitted up with all the most modern conveniences, including a sink and matching lavatory embellished with garishly pink and red carnations and roses that swirled ominously around the base like octopus tentacles. 'I don't quite understand why not being any better than one ought to be should be a matter of such censure. We are what we are, after all,' I continued, ignoring my maid's rather ominous silence. 'Unless of course we are all living to different standards in which case what the poor woman in Whitechapel ought to have been is less than you and I, which hardly seems fair does it?'

Minnie stared at me with undisguised reproach then gave a tiny shrug. 'I'm sure that I don't know what you mean, Miss,' she said stiffly, turning off the cold tap and helping me remove my linen chemise then step gingerly into the water. 'Do you need me to wash you, Miss?' she asked, her unusually formal manner making it clear that she was somewhat affronted.

I smiled and waved her away as usual. 'No, I can take care of myself,' I said, reaching for the lily scented soap that rested on a china dish on the side of the bath and thinking that I didn't know quite what I meant either.

By the time I had climbed out of my now rapidly cooling bath and wrapped a large towel around myself, the sun was beginning to set and Minnie had busied herself closing the heavy taffeta curtains and turning on the gas lamps on the tables, giving the room a warm, cosy glow. She came forward to help me dry myself then handed me a fresh chemise.

'Why are you so interested in Whitechapel anyway?' she asked at last while lacing me back into my corset. 'Begging your pardon, Miss, but I didn't think it was the sort of place that a young lady like yourself would ever hear mentioned.'

I smiled. 'I hear all sorts of things that would surprise you, Minnie,' I said lightly, holding in my breath then releasing it with a gasp as the maid gave the corset laces one last ruthless tug. 'I was just curious.'

'My Ma always says that curiosity killed the cat,' Minnie said, turning away to fetch my dress, a pretty primrose silk trimmed with pearls and French lace.

'I'm not a cat,' I reminded her with a grin, stepping into the skirt. I was very fond of Minnie's Ma's apparently endless store of proverbs and sayings. 'And besides your Ma also says that cats have nine lives so even if curiosity kills me once, I'll still live on eight more times to fight another day.'

'That's not the point,' Minnie huffed, helping me into my silk bodice then fastening it at the back. 'The point is that it never pays to be curious.'

'Gracious, Minnie, have you never been curious about anything?' I asked as the maid straightened the elaborate folds and ruches of my bustle to her satisfaction before hiding the fastenings of the skirt beneath a large bow.

'Of course not. It's not my way, Miss,' Minnie said stoutly, giving the dress a nod of approval before opening my lacquered wood jewellery box which stood on the lace and ribbon bedecked dressing table. 'Pearl choker as usual, Miss?'

I sighed and rolled my eyes, knowing that there really wasn't any hope of jollying Minnie along when she was in this intractable mood. 'Yes, the pearls, Minnie,' I said, sitting down in front of the dressing table mirror and leaning back a little so that the maid could fasten the six stringed choker of perfectly matched pearls, an inheritance from my mother, around my neck.

'Well, don't you look a picture,' Minnie said then, picking up a brush and beginning to ply it through my hair as I watched her in the mirror. 'Your Papa will be so pleased.'

I smiled. 'He has been looking forward to this evening for quite some time,' I said, idly playing with some cut crystal bottles of scent on the table in front of me. My father, the artist Sir Edwin Redmayne had finally completed his most ambitious piece to date, a painting of Mary, Queen of Scots at her execution which was destined to hang at Balmoral but which he had been graciously allowed to show off at a private unveiling that evening before it was despatched to Her Majesty. I myself had posed as the tragic Queen of Scotland, with my hair hanging loose to my waist in a way that was definitely most inconvenient for a beheading and holding an awkward pose, half kneeling, half fainting for hours as my father sketched and barked orders at me from behind his easel. 'It must be a relief to him to have it finished at last,' Minnie observed, sticking her tongue out of the corner of her mouth as she wrestled with my hair. 'It feels like he's been working on that painting for years.'

I laughed and dabbed some carnation scent behind my ears and then, daringly, at the base of my throat. 'He has been working on it for years,' I said with a grin. 'I swear that I was still in short skirts when he began.'

'Surely not, Miss,' said Minnie, who had no great understanding of hyperbole. 'There now, don't you look nice,' she pronounced, putting the final pearl pin into place and stepping back with an air of satisfaction.

I stared at myself for a moment, thinking as always that I looked far too pale but then gave a smile of pleasure because that was expected of me and I knew Minnie would be disappointed if I didn't plus I wanted to make some amends for being such hard work that evening. 'Thank you, Minnie,' I said, pulling on my long white silk gloves and picking up my favourite ostrich feather fan, which had diamonds set into the resin handle. 'Have a good evening, won't you?'

'Oh I will,' Minnie said fervently, dropping a curtsey. 'I like to see everyone coming and going.'

I smiled and left the room then made my way quickly downstairs to the hall, where I guessed my father would be impatiently waiting for me. The staircase was lined with his paintings, but not the best ones for they were elsewhere, in stately homes, galleries and even palaces all over the world, as people frequently liked to remind me. He kept some smaller works back though, mainly rough studies, some landscapes painted when on holiday and family portraits of myself and Mama. The paintings of Beatrice had gradually disappeared over the years, whisked away either to the attics or to auction rooms, I had never dared ask which.

As I had predicted, my father, looking tall and dignified in black with his grey hair brushed back from his broad forehead, was waiting for me by the hall table, his brow furrowed with a frown which cleared as soon as I appeared. 'Alice, my dear!' He held out his arm to lead me into the drawing room, where we could enjoy some quiet time together before their guests arrived.

'You look delightful.'

The maids were busy putting the final touches to the house, giving a final polish to the statues in the hall, straightening the silver and porcelain dishes on the dining table and tweaking the enormous (and rather vulgar, I privately thought) flower arrangements that had been delivered earlier in the evening by the most expensive florist in London and now decorated the hall and dining room. My father adored lilies so there were masses of those along with roses and huge white peonies, their scent filling the air with an almost funereal cloying sweetness that made me feel strangely despondent.

'Is the painting ready for its grand debut, Papa?' I asked as my father peered impatiently outside from between the drawn brocade curtains which I remembered with a pang had been chosen because they exactly matched the faded blue of my mother's eyes. The painting in question was propped against its easel in front of one of the walls of the drawing room and was almost completely concealed by a large crimson velvet cloth that I had never seen before.

He turned and smiled at me. 'Yes, all ready and waiting,' he said with great satisfaction. 'Swift found an old velvet bedspread in the attic which makes an admirable curtain for the unveiling.' He pulled a face, as always irritated and resentful that his precious time should be taken up with such tiresome matters as cloths and unveiling when he would rather be devoting himself entirely to his art. 'I was rather worried that I would have to send you out to buy something for the occasion but it turned out not to be necessary.'

I laughed. 'What a relief,' I said, eyeing the cloth, which was clearly threadbare in a few places. 'Although are you sure that an old bedspread has sufficient gravitas for the occasion?'

My father gave me a sidelong look from his small grey eyes. 'You are poking fun at me again, Alice,' he said mildly.

I smiled, showing my dimples, which I knew he could never resist. 'I am afraid that I am, Papa,' I said, reaching up to kiss his cheek, which as always smelt of his favourite Italian lemon cologne. 'Anyway, I do believe that I can hear our first guests arriving so we should probably ready ourselves for the onslaught.'

Chapter Five

Impatient as always, my father insisted upon giving a speech and unveiling his painting before dinner instead of waiting until afterwards as had been the original plan. I stood proudly at his side holding a glass of champagne as he gave the velvet covering a tug that brought it to the ground and everyone politely applauded. 'It really is a most wonderful painting,' my aunt Minerva, a statuesque and rather terrifying lady in stately black bombazine that was almost hidden beneath huge amounts of of the glittering jet and diamond jewellery made so popular by the Queen, whispered to me as several guests surged forward to congratulate my father and the lady harpist stationed by the window with her tall, finely carved instrument began to play a melancholy Celtic air. 'Dear Edwin has managed to capture the poor Scottish Queen's dignity and despair so eloquently.'

'I am so glad,' I said with a wry smile. 'I spent a long time trying to hit the perfect expression while all the time Papa shouted at me to look this way, turn my chin down a little and pout a bit less. Never having been executed, I'm afraid that it was quite difficult for me to hit upon the correct attitude.'

Aunt Minerva gave a snort of laughter that made the jet tassels on her black silk bodice sway from side to side alarmingly. 'You got there in the end though.'

'We always do,' I replied dryly before changing the subject, suddenly struck by inspiration. 'Aunt, do you do any of your voluntary work in the Whitechapel district?' Like many obscenely wealthy childless widows, Aunt Minerva was fond of philanthropic ventures and being of a rather managing and bossy disposition liked to take a hands on approach to her good works which led to her terrorising soup kitchens, reform schools and women's refuges all over the metropolitan area with a particular emphasis on the indigent East End.

My aunt gave me a long quizzical look then shook her head. 'Not at present but I know of what is apparently a very excellent women's refuge there, on Lamb Street. Why?'

I considered telling her the truth but then decided the resultant fuss would be too hideous and so instead gave a small shrug. 'Well, you are always talking about how I need a purpose in life…' It was true, Aunt Minerva had very decided views on the apathetic indolence of modern young ladies and was keen that we, and in particular me, should improve ourselves with good works.

'But why Whitechapel in particular?' Aunt Minerva persevered with a frown between her plucked and pencilled eyebrows. 'It is hardly the sort of environment that I thought would have piqued your interest, my dear.'

I sighed. This was going to be harder than I had anticipated. 'It's just that my maid said that there had been murder there this morning and I thought, well, I thought that it sounded like the sort of place that needs as much help as it can get.' I put on my most wide eyed and innocent expression but my aunt, who had known me all my life, was not to be so easily fooled.

'You are up to something, Alice Redmayne,' she said a little crossly before throwing up her plump hands in an attitude of dismay. 'Alright, I shall see what I can do but I make no promises, my dear! And I need hardly remind you that your father will no doubt be rather less than pleased by this notion of yours.'

I grinned and kissed my aunt's cheek. 'Thank you, dearest aunt,' I whispered.

'Never mind all that flummery,' Aunt Minerva said, patting my shoulder awkwardly. 'Besides, I see that we are about to be interrupted by one of your suitors.'

I turned abruptly to see Patrick, Lord Woollam, a friend and occasional patron of my father's rapidly approaching us through the crowd standing around the painting. 'Oh bother,' I said before fixing my most pleasant smile, the one I had spent hours practising in front of my bedroom mirror, to my face.

'He won't be fooled by that,' my aunt whispered, digging me in the side with her chubby elbow. 'You can do better, Alice.'

I sighed and widened the smile until I was showing all of my teeth. 'Better?' I muttered.

Aunt Minerva gave a crackling laugh. 'Much better. You look positively wolfish,' she said before giving Patrick an arch nod of greeting and sailing off to greet some friends.

'You can stop pretending now,' Patrick whispered to me as he drew nearer and I gave him a look of surprised relief before letting my face relax. 'Although I'll admit that I would like you to greet my appearance with unaffected pleasure, I don't think a cheshire cat grin is quite your style, my dear.' He was a handsome young man a few years older than me who had come into his title while at school at Eton and had all the easy charming arrogance of one who was well aware of his place in the world and did not care who knew it.

I laughed then with all the unaffected delight that he could ever wish for. 'And there I was thinking that I was favouring you with my very best smile,' I said. 'Clearly I need to try harder in future!'

'Please don't,' he said with a pained expression that was entirely belied by the laughter in his bright blue eyes. 'I don't think I could bear it.'

We smiled at each other, genuinely this time, before I shook my head a little and turned my face away. 'Has your father been extolling my virtues again?' Patrick gently whispered.

I looked at him then. 'Just a little,' I admitted with a tiny shrug, accepting another glass of champagne from a passing footman. I had known Patrick since we were both horrible little children and it had been the fondest wish of both our fathers, who were the best of friends and distant cousins besides, that we should one day be married. A wish that in the absence of the young baronet's father, my own Papa continued to champion with an often mortifying vigour.

Patrick grimaced. 'I do wish that he wouldn't,' he said, sipping champagne and looking about the room where, I noted with amusement, a few of the ladies present were trying their best to catch his eye. 'Anyone would think that I was quite incapable of wooing someone without their father's assistance. It wouldn't do my fearsome reputation any good at all should word get out that your father was having to egg you on to accept me.'

'How improper you are,' I teased, thinking that two glasses of champagne in such swift succession was surely a mistake. 'Surely you know by now that you shouldn't be talking of such things to me?'

He gave me a suddenly serious look that made my heart stop for a minute. 'But I absolutely should be talking to you about such things, Miss Redmayne,' he said simply before shrugging his slender shoulders. 'Although perhaps such a conversation would be better suited to another time.'

I gave a watery smile. 'Perhaps.' I looked over his shoulder and caught the eye of my friend Lucasta Brennan who was standing a little apart with a bored expression on her pretty face as she pretended not to listen to her parents have yet another whispered argument. They'd arrived late, just after the unveiling of the painting, then proceeded to make a terrible and rather pointed fuss about the logistical difficulties of getting from Belgravia to Highbury at night, as if their house on Eaton Square was the apex of all known civilisation, while Highbury, a perfectly respectable area nowadays, was some murky backwater frequented by thieves and villains.

Patrick followed my gaze and grinned, immediately understanding my dilemma. 'I should do the noble thing and let you go to her rescue,' he said with a bow. 'Your father has asked me to take you in to dinner. I do hope that is acceptable?' he added in an undertone.

I looked up at him and smiled. 'Of course it is,' I murmured. 'More than acceptable.'

He bowed again and left me, his place being quickly taken by Lucasta who kissed me soundly on both cheeks before putting her arm through mine. 'A walk, I think,' she declared before leading me through the double doors that led to the enormous blue and gold dining room, which was laid ready for dinner. My father loved to entertain in grand style and the long table was carefully set with thirty places each with its own little blue glass vase holding a single budding white rose.

We did not pause to admire the table though but instead carried on out through the tall French windows which led to a stone terrace overlooking the garden. Lucasta closed the windows behind us then dropped my arm and pulled a small blue enamel cigarette box from the depths of the spangled pink silk reticule that hung from her plump wrist and perfectly matched her ruffled and slightly too fussy pink taffeta and gauze gown.

'Arguing again?' I asked with much sympathy. Lord and Lady Brennan's arguments had achieved legendary status in polite London society, conducted as they usually were in public and with often dramatic consequences for all concerned. No one would ever forget, for example, the time Lord Brennan, enraged beyond all reason by something his wife had hissed at him, had rushed out of a crowded ballroom and straight into the path of an omnibus. It was only the quick thinking of a group of passing young gentlemen that had saved him from certain death or at least severe injury and the whole incident had been the talk of London for months afterwards.

Lucasta gave a shrug then lit her cigarette with a match that she casually struck on the stone balustrade. 'Aren't they always?' she muttered, inhaling deeply and closing her eyes.

I watched my friend curiously. It often seemed to me that everyone was so busy gossiping about the argumentative Brennan couple that they always managed to forget that they had a daughter who was being damaged by the endless drama of her domestic life. 'It must be hellish for you,' I said, reaching out to take Lucasta's hand.

Lucasta gave another shrug. 'I'm used to it,' she said, opening her eyes and giving me a lopsided and rather rueful smile. 'The funny thing is that they aren't quite so bad when they are at home. They can actually be quite affectionate with each other in fact.'

'How peculiar,' I said, remembering the way that my own well mannered parents had been so quietly considerate around each other. They'd been a trifle undemonstrative perhaps but I'd never, not even for one instant, had cause to think that they didn't love each other. 'So it's all just an act then?'

Lucasta laughed. 'Who knows?' She inhaled on her cigarette again. 'The funny thing is that I have this feeling that should anything happen to one of them, the other would be absolutely devastated. You should have seen Isabella after Richard ran out in front of that dratted omnibus.' She examined her cigarette thoughtfully. As usual she referred to her parents by their christian names and I realised that I'd never heard her use anything else for them. 'She was quite bereft. Even Dr Gull, and we all know what he has had to deal with from Her Majesty, had to admit that he'd never before beheld such a prolonged attack of hysterics.'

'I will never understand adults,' I said gravely, just as I had often done when we were children together, hanging about at the edges of some awful children's ball in Bloomsbury or whispering to each other during the art and dancing lessons we had shared. I couldn't remember a time when Lucasta hadn't been a part of my life.

Lucasta grinned then. 'We're the adults now,' she reminded me with a shake of her head. 'Worse luck.' She took one final drag on her cigarette then put it out on the side of a stone urn before slipping a tiny enamel box full of violet pastilles out of her apparently bottomless reticule. 'Anyway, did I really see you making sheep eyes at Patrick just now?' she asked, popping a pastille into her mouth.

'Lamb eyes more like,' I muttered. 'I am being sent to slaughter, Lucasta.'

'Heavens, you are starting to sound like Isabella,' Lucasta said with a sidelong look of amusement at me. 'Not long now before you're hissing insults at Patrick over dinner and accusing him in a not so discreet whisper of giving all your friends the glad eye.'

I sighed and leaned on the balustrade, peering through the darkness into the garden. Another train was making the slow approach to Canonbury Station, the chimney emitting a long mournful whistle that was answered by a chorus of barking dogs and wailing babies from the neighbouring houses. 'I can't imagine being in a marriage like that,' I said, shivering a little.

'I don't suppose my parents could imagine it either,' Lucasta said sadly. 'I don't think anyone does. When was the last time you heard of a new bride weeping with dread and trepidation as she went up the aisle? Well, outside bad French novels anyway.' She leaned against the balustrade beside me and inhaled deeply before coughing and choking into a lace edged handkerchief plucked from her bosom. 'London air,' she said with a laugh. 'There's nothing quite like it.' She hunted again through her reticule and this time brought out a small battered silver tin, which she deftly opened before tipping a small white lozenge out onto her palm.

'Mama's cocaine tablets?' I asked, raising an eyebrow.

She shrugged and popped it into her mouth. 'How else do you

think I'm going to get through this evening?'

I sighed then changed the subject. 'I do like Patrick, you know,' I said hesitantly. 'It's just…'

Lucasta pulled a face. 'I know. He's terribly handsome though, isn't he? All those blond whiskers and those lovely melting blue eyes.' She nudged me. 'You could do a lot worse.'

I laughed. 'Usually, when people say that they really mean that you can't do any better.'

Lucasta grinned at me. 'Well, there is that too…'

I swiped at her with my ostrich feather fan. 'Remind me again why I am friends with you?' I asked, still laughing.

Lucasta lunged forward and kissed my cheek. 'That would be all down to my devilish charm and wicked sense of humour,' she said impishly. 'As well as the sad but true fact that no one else will put up with you. Or me either for that matter.' We heard Swift hit the great gong in the hall that announced that dinner was about to be served. 'Shall we?' she said with a bow, offering her arm.

'I think we should,' I agreed, putting my hand on Lucasta's arm. 'Remember that you have to deliver me to Patrick though. He's been given strict instructions from Papa.'

'Lucky you. I've been lumbered with someone old enough to have squired my great grandmother when she was a girl.' Lucasta sniggered and I noted that the cocaine was already taking effect as she had a decided flush about her cheeks and a brightness in her eyes that I didn't quite like. 'By the way, what's this I've heard about you going to Whitechapel?' she asked suddenly as she pulled the French windows open and stepped into the dining room. The maids had been busy while we were out on the terrace and all the candles in the silver candelabras in the centre of the table had been lit, casting a soft amber glow over the room and making the precious blue and gold Chinese wallpaper shimmer.

My heart stopped. 'What about it?' I asked a little breathlessly.

Lucasta turned to look at me in surprise. 'Oh nothing much. I just thought that I heard your Aunt Minerva haranguing your poor Papa about letting you do some work in a refuge there.' She hurried me past the dining table. 'Oh, do get a move on, Alice or we'll miss the procession into dinner. I'll never hear the end of it if I make you late for poor old Patrick.'

CHAPTER SIX

A few weeks later, I was sitting in my aunt's coach and making the journey from Highbury to Whitechapel, clutching my blue silk reticule nervously on my lap as we trotted down Grosvenor Road then turned to go across the stone bridge that passed over the railway line. A train had just gone through and the air was still heavy with dense black smoke, which made Aunt Minerva, who was sitting opposite, click her tongue against her teeth with irritation and angrily yank the window blind down.

'I really don't know how you can bear it,' she huffed to me, as I watched her with some amusement. 'It's so incredibly vulgar to live next to a railway line. Why on earth can't your father move to Chelsea or even Bloomsbury like all the other artists I know? Heavens, he ought to be able to afford a house in Mayfair by now!'

I sighed, only too familiar with this well worn refrain as I'd been listening to variations on the same theme ever since childhood. 'He likes Highbury,' I said with a shrug. 'And he loves the railway line. He likes to hear the trains go past while he's working in his studio - he says that it keeps him sane and makes him feel modern and connected to the world even when he is painting scenes from history.'

Aunt Minerva sniffed and twitched her grey cashmere shawl into place about her shoulders. 'That's all very well for him but what about you, my dear?' She put the blind up again and peered out disconsolately at our surroundings as the carriage bowled down St Paul's Road, a wide thoroughfare lined with pleasant terraced houses and prosperous and well looked after little shops. There had been torrential rain the previous night, one of those sudden summer storms that seemed to come out of nowhere, turning the sky black seemingly in seconds. This morning had dawned bright and clear however and so the streets were full of people: young couples strolling arm in arm and gazing soulfully at each other and parents out with their children, who laughed as they skipped and jumped along the sun warmed pavement where only a few puddles remained as testament to yesterday's deluge. Everyone was smiling and cheerful and clearly looking forward to the day to come but Aunt Minerva remained entirely unmoved. 'This was a village until not so long ago and it's still practically rustic out here. Don't you feel cut off from your friends?'

I shook my head, a tiny smile touching my lips as I remembered Lucasta's parents squabbling about the distance between Belgravia and Highbury on the night of my father's unveiling. 'Not at all,' I said with absolute sincerity. 'I like to be with Papa and have no great desire to be anywhere else.'

My aunt fixed me with a penetrating look from her huge blue eyes, the only and rather disconcerting resemblance she bore to my softly spoken and rather fragile looking mother, who had been her younger sister. 'Well, that won't always be the case, I am sure. We shall have to put our heads together and find you a house in town once you are married,' she paused to give a knowing little smile, 'unless, of course, your husband already has a decent property of his own.' Needless to say, as well as Honywood Hall, his estate in Essex, Patrick also owned an enormous and very elegantly furnished town house on Cavendish Square, a castle in Scotland and several thousand acres in Derbyshire.

My fingers tightened on the gold cord handle of my reticule and I turned my head to look out of the window, not trusting myself to answer straight away even if my aunt's meaning had been all too clear. We were rattling down Kingsland Road now, a long and dusty thoroughfare which would take us directly from Highbury to Whitechapel and never having been there before I craned my head to look at the red brick houses and shops that lined the road, thinking how pleasant it all looked if a bit scuffed and battered around the edges. A description that suited the poor but respectable people of the area just as well as the buildings.

This all changed though when we turned on to Shoreditch High Street, where the tall terraced houses and shops were much shabbier and the dirt and straw strewn road became narrow and congested with a mass of vehicles, horses and people, all shouting, gesturing and shoving past each other while stray dogs dashed barking between the horses' legs and small grubby faced children, their lopsided grins revealing blackened teeth, shoved their hands into carriage windows and begged for pennies.

I was just hunting in my reticule for some money to give them when we came to a sudden and rather abrupt halt that almost threw me forward off my seat and on to the floor. 'Have we crashed?' I asked, righting myself on the seat and straightening my hat. 'Perhaps I should have a look outside and see?'

'You will do no such thing, Alice,' my aunt insisted in her most commanding tones as she adjusted her own bonnet and peered crossly out of the window to where a crowd of young boys was staring at us and pulling faces, crossing their eyes, pushing back their noses with their fingers and lolling out their tongues. She majestically turned away. 'It would be most unseemly. Pray remain where you are and let the driver take care of it.'

Ignoring her, I reached up and pulled the window down before poking my head out to see what was holding us up. 'Two van drivers up ahead have had a bit of a collision and come to blows over which one is to blame, Miss,' my aunt's driver, Gideon, cheerfully shouted over his shoulder from up on his perch. 'We'll be moving again soon enough when they've either cooled their boots or knocked each other out.'

I grinned, spotting the two drivers, a pair of middle aged men with decided paunches and greying whiskers on their ruddy cheeks, up ahead. They'd both thrown their dilapidated coats and waistcoats on to the filth and dust of the road and were squaring up to each other in their shirt sleeves, while several other men, most of whom were clearly drunk, roared at them to stop and tried to forcibly restrained them as they threw half hearted punches and hoarsely shouted challenges to 'come on then, if you think you've got the sauce' and 'let's have a taste of your fists, boy' at each other.

'I'd quite like to put sixpence on the one with ginger hair,' Gideon confided in me, laughing. 'He's got a wicked punch on him. Just wait and see, if his friends will only let him go for a minute.'

Most of the crowd of men, women and children that had gathered in the middle of the road to watch the fight was laughing at the two men but there were a few shaken fists too, mainly from drivers and passengers who were being held up by the impromptu and rather undignified spectacle, and there were some yelled insults as well, using language that made me go a bit pink and put my head back in the carriage before resolutely closing the window with a snap.

Aunt Minerva was pointedly holding her lavender oil scented handkerchief up to her nose but her eyes, as I took my seat again, were amused. 'You'll have to get used to such robust language if you're planning on coming here again,' she said, her voice muffled by the handkerchief. 'We're very far away from Highbury now, my dear. We're very far away from everything in fact.'

I shrugged. 'I don't mind about that,' I said, feeling decidedly mutinous and wanting to shock her a little. 'Although Papa wouldn't approve at all.' With a shudder, our carriage started moving again, gradually picking up speed as it turned on to Commercial Street. In the distance, if I angled my neck sufficiently, I could make out the tall angular spire of Hawksmoor's Christ Church, looming white and faintly sinister over the smoking chimneys and grimy roofs of Whitechapel. For some reason the sight of it made me feel oddly uneasy, maybe because its austere beauty looked so out of place in such squalid surroundings - it ought really to have been presiding over Westminster or Kensington rather than one of the most down at heel corners of the capital.

'Your father will come around eventually,' Aunt Minerva said kindly. 'Edwin has always had the most peculiar ideas about charity, believing that it's far better and more dignified to throw money at a problem than roll one's sleeves up and lend a hand. I entirely blame his parents for this as they were a shockingly tight fisted pair whereas he isn't at all hard hearted really and nor are you.' She gave me an approving nod. 'I am sure that he will see sense in time.'

I gave a faint smile. 'He worries too much,' I said with a shrug. 'Which I suppose is entirely understandable in the circumstances.' This was as near as I had ever come to mentioning Beatrice, the ever present spectre in the room, to anyone.

My aunt looked momentarily confused then gave a sad little nod. 'It was all very unfortunate,' she said, which was the closest she had ever come to mentioning Beatrice to me as well. 'At some point though one really must let go of one's fears and try to live a little. It's no good living in the past.'

For a brief moment, I considered telling her all about the necklace and the real reason why I had decided to come to Whitechapel but then realised just in time that Aunt Minerva would almost certainly insist on taking the whole matter over and looking for Beatrice herself, pushing me quite out of the picture which was something I really didn't want to have happen. I had taken this quest on and was determined to see it through to its end, whatever that might be.

'Were you going to say something, my dear?' Aunt Minerva was looking at me with a concerned frown between her eyebrows.

I closed my mouth with a snap and shook my head. 'No, aunt,' I murmured before looking again out of the window.

Our carriage rumbled past a large pub, the Commercial Tavern, which Minnie would have admiringly called a proper gin palace with green tinted windows beautifully embellished with an intricate design of vines and juniper leaves and richly carved and gold painted curlicues above the doors and window frames. As we drew level, the great double doors swung suddenly open and a man dressed only in his shirt and trousers was ungraciously thrown out on to the dusty street, his checked cap following him a few seconds later. 'I ain't done nothing!' he bawled at the now closed doors before rounding furiously on a gaggle of women standing beneath one of the windows, glasses of ale in hand and a couple of them jiggling crying toddlers on their hips. 'What you looking at, you bloody tarts?' he yelled at them as they laughed at him before staggering away down the street, straightening his cap and shoving his shirt with an absurd and upright dignity into his trousers as he went.

'It isn't considered respectable for women to drink inside a public house,' Aunt Minerva said in response to my enquiring look, 'so they stand outside instead although how on earth drinking spirits in plain sight in the street can be considered more respectable is anyone's guess.'

'I think people down here have very different notions about what respectability means,' I said, my smile hiding my sudden feeling of intense trepidation. It had all seemed so simple but now that I had actually seen Whitechapel for myself, I could tell that I was almost completely out of my depth. 'It's almost as if we have entered a different country not simply a different area of our own city,' I whispered, my eyes taking in the poorly dressed women standing with their babies outside the pubs, the filthy barefoot children that ran in screeching gangs behind the carts that rumbled down the road to Spitalfields Market and the surly grimy men sitting on the pavements, pipes clamped between decaying teeth and caps pulled down low on their brows. The overall atmosphere was one of decaying hopelessness, of bleak despair. Was this really where Beatrice, my lovely shining haired Bea, had ended up? 'I can't believe that people are living like this only a few short miles away from us.'

'Quite so,' Aunt Minerva said with a definite and most annoying air of 'I warned you how it would be and you wouldn't listen'.

The road narrowed even more as we rumbled down Commercial Street and I began to feel oddly oppressed as I looked up at the endless rows of narrow, smoke darkened houses that pressed in on either side, which as Aunt Minerva now explained to me had once made comfortable and perfectly respectable dwellings for the Huguenot weavers that had made this district their home two centuries earlier but which were now either lodging houses where beds could be rented on a nightly basis or divided up into mean dwellings for the poor of the area, many little more than a single miserable room for an entire family.

'This is the police station,' Aunt Minerva said, pointing with her gloved hand to a tall wedge shaped building that stood on a corner. 'God knows they need it. I've heard that some of the streets around Christ Church are so violent and riddled with criminality that the policeman are required to enter them in pairs lest they be attacked and woe betide anyone who enters them alone.'

I looked up at Whitechapel police station, smiling when I noticed that someone had put some small terracotta pots of red geraniums out on a window ledge. As I looked, the window, which had been painted a bright cheerful blue inside was pushed up and a pretty girl with long plaited red hair popped her head out before producing a small battered tin cup which she used to water the flowers, giggling a little as some of the water spilled over the ledge and splashed a woman walking underneath.

For some reason this sight cheered me up enormously, giving me a timely warning that even though things looked grim on the surface, scratch it and there was still happiness, simple joy and even love underneath. I was therefore in relatively high spirits again when our carriage turned on to Lamb Street and pulled up outside a tall red brick house, blackened by years of exposure to smoke and grime like all the others we had passed, with a chipped and peeling green door.

'Here we are,' Aunt Minerva said bracingly, pulling her shawl about her and preparing to get out of the carriage. 'The Whitechapel Women's Mission. It doesn't look like much from the outside, does it? I'm sure things are very different once we get inside though.'

A crowd of small children, barefoot and dressed in the ragged remnants of what had once been clothes, had gathered to stare at the coach and one of the larger ones, a boy of about ten with straw coloured hair that stuck out untidily beneath his cap and a dirty red handkerchief knotted around his neck, tentatively reached up to pat one of the horses on the nose, talking soothingly to it the whole time. 'I love horses,' he said to me, his nasal accent one that I recognised immediately as Cockney. 'This one is ever so nice, Miss.'

I smiled at him, instinctively feeling in my reticule for a coin until Aunt Minerva reached across and put her hand warningly on my wrist. 'If you start giving out money, you will never stop,' she whispered. 'You must find other ways to help these children.'

'They look half starved though,' I protested, hardly able to bear looking at their blackened, swollen and bleeding little feet or their eyes, which were drained and flat with hunger and exhaustion. 'Surely a shilling to buy some bread won't hurt?'

'If you give them shilling then someone bigger will come along and take it from them, probably badly hurting them in the process,' Aunt Minerva said, her hand still on my wrist. 'Your shilling won't go far in Highbury but here in Whitechapel it will buy enough gin to make someone forget their sore feet and the ache of hunger in their stomach for several hours.'

For a moment, I considered ignoring her and emptying my

entire reticule on to the pavement so that they could take their pick, but then gave a sigh and removed my hand. 'I will have to think of something better then,' I said coldly.

My aunt shook her head. 'Don't take your anger out on me, my dear,' she said softly. 'Reserve it for those who truly deserve it - the employers who won't pay a living wage, the men who drink their money away and leave their families starving and in need and the landlords who extort every penny from the poor just so that they can keep a roof over their heads.' She fixed me with a look. 'I could go on forever but I fear you will find it all out for yourself soon enough. These are dark streets, Alice. Are you really sure that you are ready for this?'

My hand was already on the handle of the carriage door but at that I removed it and turned to look at my aunt, who continued: 'You can always change your mind, you know. No one will think any less of you and I am sure that I can find some other worthy cause that requires your help. I know of a refuge in Westminster that is quite genteel and would be perfectly suitable should you wish to busy yourself with something less challenging. I know that your father would be relieved if you were to go there instead.'

I hesitated, sorely tempted to give in and go home, but then I remembered the necklace and blood stained envelope locked up in the drawer beside my bed and resolutely straightened my shoulders. No matter what my own feelings were about the place, Whitechapel was the last link that I had with Beatrice and so in Whitechapel I would remain. I shook my head. 'That is very kind of you, aunt, but I am afraid that I am quite determined.' I forced myself to smile, feigning a confidence that I did not altogether feel. 'Besides, I am expected here and should hate to let anyone down.'

My aunt gave a brisk nod, that may well have been one of approval although I could not be sure. 'Very well then,' she said before tapping the ceiling of the carriage with the silver head of her ebony walking stick, alerting Gideon, who was happily chatting with the horse loving boy, that we wished to get out and that he should help us down. 'They won't thank you, you know,' she said rather cryptically as we waited for the door to be opened for us.

I gave a slight smile. 'Perhaps I don't want to be thanked,' I said before getting out of the carriage.

We were admitted into the entrance hall of the mission house by a very short maidservant with a snub nose, anxious expression and mousy brown hair straggling from beneath her none too clean linen cap. 'Missus will see you in the parlour,' she said breathlessly before bobbing up and down several times in what was intended to be an approximation of a curtsey. 'Will you be wanting tea?'

'Tea would be wonderful,' Aunt Minerva said with a kind smile, looking about her appreciatively and sniffing the air, which smelt strongly of beef stew, lavender soap and clean laundry. The hall had been painted a pale sage green and there were still touches of elegance, remnants of its past life as a once very handsome family home, in the carved wooden bannisters of the staircase and plaster work on the high ceiling. 'You'll have to show us where the parlour is though as we've never been here before.'

The maid went crimson with mortification. 'Course you haven't, ma'am,' she said, looking as though she was about to burst into tears. 'I'll take you there directly.'

I followed the girl and my aunt from the hall into a small cosy room overlooking the street. Like the hall this room had been painted pale green with matching curtains at the window and a bright but somewhat tatty Turkish rug on the floor. Although the maid had described it as a parlour, it felt more like a study with several crammed to overflowing bookcases lining the walls and a large cherry wood desk pushed up close to the window.

'If you'd like to wait here, I'll just go fetch the missus,' the maid said, bobbing another curtsey before rushing from the room, slamming the door behind her.

'How extraordinary,' Aunt Minerva said to me, raising an eyebrow. 'If they try to foist one of their inmates on you as a maid, I think it might be wise to gracefully decline.'

I smiled and sat down on a shabby green velvet sofa by the fireplace. It was a fine day still and the window had been left slightly open, letting the noise and smells, not all of them pleasant, from the neighbouring Spitalfields Market waft inside. As Aunt Minerva restlessly paced the room, lifting up ornaments to examine their bottoms, flicking through the books left out on the desk and peering at the old engravings that had been framed and hung on the green walls, I closed my eyes and let the sound of the market wash over me, enjoying the yells of the traders, constant rumble of carts and carriages and barking and growls of the dogs that hung about the stalls hoping for scraps.

'Goodness, what a racket,' Aunt Minerva said, closing a book with a slam and throwing herself down in a crimson leather upholstered armchair on the other side of the fire. 'I don't know how anyone can bear such a noise.'

'Is it worse than our trains at Highbury?' I said, opening my eyes.

Aunt Minerva gave a snort of laughter. 'Far worse,' she said. 'I'll concede you that.'

The door opened then and we both hastily got to our feet as two ladies, one tall and slender with cool blue eyes and blonde hair arranged in a neat chignon and the other short and heavy with dark intelligent eyes and untidily arranged jet black hair that seemed intent on escaping its pins and falling about her shoulders, entered the room, closely followed by the little maid who was struggling beneath the weight of a wooden tray laden with tea things which she noisily dumped on the desk before rushing from the room again. 'You must be Lady Coudland,' the tall one said in a clipped Scottish accent that belied her graceful appearance as she advanced to take Aunt Minerva's hand. 'What a pleasure to meet you at long last. I've heard so much about you.'

'Likewise,' my aunt said graciously before drawing me forward. 'This is my niece, Alice Redmayne.'

'I am very pleased to meet you, Miss Redmayne. I am such a great admirer of your father's work,' she said with a nod. 'I am Mrs Lightfoot and this,' she gestured towards the other woman, who stepped forward and took my hand in a firm grip, 'is Miss Lawler.' She smiled then, revealing a lot of big white teeth. 'We share the running of this establishment between us.'

'And what sort of establishment is it?' Aunt Minerva asked then as Mrs Lightfoot imperiously gestured for us to sit down again and busied herself with the tray of tea things, carefully lining the flower patterned yellow china cups and saucers up in front of her then pouring tea into each one.

There was a slight pause, broken only by the chink of the cups

65

against each other and the ticking of the fine wooden clock that stood in pride of place on the carved mantelpiece. 'Initially this was to be a refuge for the married women of the district,' Miss Lawler said at last just as as Mrs Lightfoot was opening her mouth to reply. She had thrown herself down next to me on the sofa but now she leaned forward earnestly as she spoke. 'However we now open our doors to any woman who needs our assistance, whatever her circumstances.' This last was said with a challenging look at Mrs Lightfoot, who tightened her lips together but said nothing. Miss Lawler smiled then as if she had scored a point and took a biscuit from a plate on the tray. 'My colleague doesn't altogether approve of some of the cases I have agreed to take on,' she said as an aside to me.

'You mean prostitutes, I suppose,' I said, liking Miss Lawler already.

'Really, Alice...' Aunt Minerva protested faintly. 'At least try to maintain an illusion of maidenly ignorance.'

'It was you who brought me here, aunt,' I reminded her with a wink as Mrs Lightfoot, quivering with disapproval handed me a cup of tea.

'It isn't that I disapprove of the prostitutes,' she said, pulling forward another chair and sitting beside Aunt Minerva. Her posture was marvellous, very straight and erect and I instinctively found myself sitting more upright in response, whereas Miss Lawler just seemed to burrow herself even deeper into the sofa beside me. 'It is just that I would prefer to concentrate on preventative measures to ensure that women don't feel compelled to fall into a life of wickedness to support themselves.'

'Nonsense,' Miss Lawler said briskly, taking another biscuit and then as an afterthought offering the plate to me. 'You can't cherry pick in an area like this - either you help everyone or you help no one. Personally, I would rather throw the doors wide open and assist each and every woman who comes to us.'

Mrs Lightfoot threw up her hands. 'We would be overwhelmed if you did such a thing,' she said, sounding actually worried that Miss Lawler, whom I was beginning to see was something of a loose cannon, might actually do just that.

Miss Lawler shrugged and carelessly brushed the crumbs off her dark brown cotton skirts on to the rug. 'Not necessarily,' she said gruffly. 'Most of the women here would rather throw themselves in the Thames than accept our help, which is why it is so crucial that we offer assistance to anyone who will take it.'

Mrs Lightfoot pursed her lips a little at that. 'You are wrong, Catherine,' she said curtly before turning to me with a very false smile pinned to her lips. 'Besides, I am sure that Miss Redmayne has no great wish to hear any of this.'

'I am sure that Miss Redmayne doesn't mind in the slightest,' I said, placidly sipping my tea as the smile on Mrs Lightfoot's face wavered then vanished altogether. 'If I am going to be helping here then I am, of course, very keen to know all about the place and how it is run.'

Miss Lawler grinned at me then shot a triumphant look at her colleague who had gone a little pink and was making a great show of finishing her tea as Aunt Minerva looked on with amusement. 'Well, seeing as that's settled,' she said, clapping her hands to her knees and getting up from the sofa. 'I think it's time for a bit of a tour.'

CHAPTER SEVEN

Miss Lawler led us back out into the hall and then down some rickety wooden stairs to the whitewashed kitchens below, where several young women dressed in aprons were gathered around the long scrubbed wood table earnestly listening and watching as a much older woman with grizzled red hair gave them a lesson in kneading bread. 'This is Mrs Russell,' she whispered to me. 'She is actually Lady Earp's cook but her ladyship kindly loans her to us twice a week to give cookery lessons to some of our girls.'

'How wonderful,' I replied, admiring the dexterity with which Mrs Russell was resolutely pounding the bread dough against the counter. 'Although that must play havoc with her dinner party schedule.'

Miss Lawler sniggered. 'She assures me not,' she said before addressing one of the women around the table, a short slight girl with huge blue eyes and hair so fair that it was almost white. 'How are you finding it, Meg?' she asked kindly.

Meg went a little pink. 'Oh, I'm enjoying it so much, Miss,' she said in a rush, hardly leaving a gap between each word so that it came out all garbled together. 'Mrs Russell makes it look so easy though and I am sure my bread won't turn out half so nice.'

'I am sure that it will,' Miss Lawler reassured her before turning to me. 'Like all the young women here, Meg is training to take up work as a kitchen maid. Mrs Russell teaches them the basics but the rest they will learn on the job.'

'As I did myself when I was a girl,' Mrs Russell said, pausing her kneading and grinning at me. 'It's hard work but satisfying.'

'Like anything worth doing,' Aunt Minerva agreed, looking about her with approval. 'You have everything set up most excellently,' she said to Mrs Lightfoot, who was examining the delicious smelling contents of a huge pot that bubbled on the black kitchen range.

Mrs Lightfoot gave what I thought must be the first genuine smile that I had yet seen on her face. 'We are very proud of our efforts here,' she said, replacing the lid on the pot. 'Our girls have been placed in some of the very best households across the city with excellent results.'

'Of course not all are able to be trained for employment,' Miss Lawler said sadly as we left the kitchen and went back up the stairs to the hall. 'Many of the women who come to us are already married or too mature to be trained for domestic service. Instead we work with them as best we can to build their confidence and set them on a proper path.'

'It doesn't always work of course,' Mrs Lightfoot interposed with a sniff as she led us up the stairs to the next floor. 'Some of the women who come here don't actually want to be helped at all.'

Miss Lawler smiled and shrugged. 'We always do our best,' she said, 'but to some working on the streets and the camaraderie that brings with others like them is preferable to travelling away and beginning afresh.' She pushed open a door on the landing and gestured that I should step inside. 'Was it Shakespeare who said that misery loves company?'

I smiled and shook my head. 'It was Christopher Marlowe,' I said. 'In Doctor Faustus.'

Miss Lawler laughed as she followed me through the doorway. 'I always get them confused. I'm afraid that I am not very well read.' I knew she was lying though, there was no mistaking the bright intelligence and curiosity in her dark eyes and I also suspected that the vast majority of the books that littered the parlour downstairs belonged to her as well.

We were standing in a large bright room with tall curtainless windows that looked down over Lamb Street. Several desks had been arranged in rows down the centre of the room and at each one was sitting a young woman with a book open in front of her, diligently copying letters and words into a chapbook. 'This used to be the drawing room when this was a private house,' Mrs Lightfoot said. 'It is now our school room, for want of a better name. Here we encourage our girls to learn their letters and to read.' As she spoke, a pink cheeked young woman in a blue cotton dress stood up from behind a desk at the top of the room. 'That is Mrs Jacks, she is in charge of the lessons here and does a most excellent job.'

I smiled at Mrs Jacks and paused for a moment to look over the hunched shoulder of the woman nearest to me, who was diligently copying out a poem by Keats in a very fair hand. 'Are you enjoying your lessons?' I asked her when she looked up.

She shrugged and smiled. 'This poetry ain't exactly to my taste being all flowery and such but it'll all be worth it in the end, I'm sure.'

'Rosie here has already been offered a position as a clerk in a shipping yard office,' Miss Lawler said proudly. 'Mainly thanks to one of our benefactors who owns the business. He has been very generous when it comes to offering our women work.'

'Well done, Rosie,' I said as she blushed and dipped her head back down to her book.

Mrs Lightfoot ushered us from the room, closing the door softly behind her. 'We are very fortunate to have several extremely generous patrons who assist us with the running of this venture,' she said, leading us across the landing to the next room. 'Of course, Miss Lawler and I have also had a hand in funding it.'

Miss Lawler grinned. 'I inherited a very handsome fortune from my grandfather when he passed away,' she said, entirely unabashed. 'I could have squandered it all trying to catch myself a nice equally rich husband but decided instead to put it to some good use.' She opened the door and stood aside so that I could enter. 'Funnily enough, after a few years working here and hearing the stories some of the women tell about their husbands, I no longer have any taste for marriage.'

I stepped into a smaller chamber, painted a soft pale blue and with pretty flowered chintz blinds at the windows. Inside there was just a rather ropey looking blue velvet sofa and a desk with two chairs placed either side, in one of which sat a thin middle aged woman with neatly arranged dark hair and a green wool shawl wrapped around her shoulders, while the other was occupied by a handsome young man with slightly too long dark hair and eyes the colour of a stormy sky who was showing her something in a book.

Mrs Lightfoot gave a discreet cough and they both looked up

then and smiled, a little wanly in the case of the woman but enough to show me that she had once been very pretty before life had taken a downward plunge and added a hard edge to her gaze and sharpness to her features. 'This is Mr Mercier,' Mrs Lightfoot said and I discerned a new almost flirtatious note entering her voice. 'He is training to be a lawyer and comes in every other day to assist the women with their legal issues.'

I must have looked confused because Miss Lawler jumped in then to explain further. 'Many of the women and girls who enter our care do so because of family break up or circumstances that leave them unable to provide for themselves. It is surely no surprise to you, Miss Redmayne, to learn that the law is no friend to our sex and in fact is often our avowed enemy?'

I shook my head. 'I am afraid that I am ignorant of such things.' I caught Mr Mercier's eye and he gave a sort of smirk and looked away. 'I do not doubt that it is so, however,' I added silkily, glaring at him. 'How fortunate you are to have Mr Mercier on hand to assist you.'

Miss Lawler smiled then. 'We are very fortunate indeed. He has been a most invaluable help to our ladies and has helped several of them gain proper independence from husbands and other menfolk that have mistreated them. We would be very sorry to lose him.' She put her hand on the shoulder of the seated woman and gave it a reassuring squeeze.

Mr Mercier smiled at her. 'You know that you have my services for as long as they are required,' he said before turning his gaze on to me. 'I grew up in Spitalfields and my family have lived here for several generations, Miss Redmayne and although I am not blind to the areas faults and distinct disadvantages, I love it still and would give my life to be of service to the people here.'

'What a very noble sentiment, Mr Mercier,' I said woodenly before turning my attention to the woman sitting in front of him. 'And what help are you giving here?'

He gave a small smile. 'I am helping Annie here make a case for seeing her children again,' he said in a soft voice, surely knowing that each word filled me with a terrible shame and made me regret my arch high handedness. 'Her husband turned her out of doors six months ago and kept the children from her. He won't let her see them, claiming that Annie is a drunk and no fit mother.

I am going to change that.'

'I see,' I said, feeling very small indeed and smiling again at Annie as she lowered her eyes in mute misery to her lap. 'Then I wish you luck and earnestly hope for a happy outcome.'

'Mr Mercier is a very fine young man,' Aunt Minerva said as we climbed the stairs to the next level of the house, having poked around a few more rooms where women were having lessons in various aspects of housekeeping or sitting reading quietly to their children. 'You are fortunate indeed to have his services.'

Miss Lawler nodded in agreement. 'Oh yes, very fortunate indeed. His father is a lawyer as well and was of immense help to us when we were setting up this venture. We couldn't have done it without him.' She smiled at me. 'In fact, this house used to belong to him but he agreed to sell it to me at a very low price so that I could use it for a refuge.'

'I expect that it would have been turned into yet another doss house if you had not bought it,' Aunt Minerva observed, ducking her head as we entered a long and very bright white painted room lit from above by several windows set into the ceiling. Here there were several beds lined along the wall, some of them with cribs next to them. There were women sitting on most of the beds, many of them nursing infants at their breasts while they kept an eye on the small children who played and ran in the centre of the room.

Miss Lawler grinned as a small girl in a pink cotton dress ran up and embraced her around the knees. 'This was once used as a workroom by the weavers who originally built this house.' She lifted the girl up into her arms then pointed up at the windows above. 'The windows were put there to create enough light to work at their looms by.' She kissed the child's cheek and put her back on her feet. 'Nowadays we use it as a dormitory for the women with children who come to us in need of refuge. There are other, smaller, bedrooms for single women but we find that the ones with children prefer to be together where they can support each other.'

I went to a window and looked down at the garden that lay at the back of the house, it was well tended and filled with flowers, probably looked after by the women, a few of whom I could see sitting on a blanket spread on the grass, enjoying the sunshine with their children.

'The garden is my own particular project,' Mrs Lightfoot said, coming to stand beside me. 'I've always found gardening so soothing and rather hoped that some of the ladies here would share my enthusiasm.'

'And do they?' I asked.

She smiled a little ruefully. 'Not all of them, no, but I like to think that it has had a beneficial effect on some. There's nothing quite like connecting with God's earth to make one feel at peace with the world, don't you agree, Miss Redmayne?'

Aunt Minerva laughed. 'I don't think my dear niece has ever taken the slightest interest in gardening,' she said with a fond look at me.

I felt my cheeks go warm under Mrs Lightfoot's disappointed gaze. 'It's true, I'm afraid,' I said. 'We've always had a gardener and I was never encouraged to take much interest in the gardens beyond occasionally picking flowers for the drawing room and,' my voice faltered, 'my mother's bedroom.'

Mrs Lightfoot put her hand on mine for just a moment. 'I too lost my mother when I was very young,' she said, her great blue eyes sympathetic. 'It is a blow that one never quite recovers from.'

The awkward silence that followed was eventually broken by Miss Lawler suggesting in an undertone that perhaps we should go downstairs and leave the women in peace. I dutifully followed them all down the staircase to the hall, the wooden steps creaking beneath my feet and my head spinning with all that I had seen and heard. Of one thing I was certain though - I was more resolute than ever that I should find Beatrice and I believed that the Whitechapel Women's Mission was the best place to do so. Surely someone here would know her whereabouts?

'Well this is all more than satisfactory,' Aunt Minerva said when we reached the hall again. There was now a distinct aroma of boiled cabbage and meat pudding in the air and to my shame my stomach gave a small growl of hunger. 'I am sure that my niece will be in good hands with you.'

'We would be delighted to have her here,' Mrs Lightfoot said, flashing us that big fake toothy smile. 'I think that she will be of great assistance to us all.'

There was the sound of soft footsteps coming down the stairs

73

behind us and I turned to see Mr Mercier standing on the bottom step, regarding us all with a rather amused expression on his handsome face. 'Is Miss Redmayne to be a permanent fixture then?' he asked with every appearance of delight even though his eyes as they looked me over were cold.

I raised my chin, determined not to be cowed by his obvious disapproval of me. 'I certainly am,' I said with a smile. I'd show him not to dismiss me as just another rich girl slumming in Whitechapel for fun and some vague sense of validation. No, even though I had my own personal reasons for being there, I was still determined to make myself useful and do my best to assist the people of the area, starting with those unfortunate children who lurked outside. 'I shall be back tomorrow.'

Miss Lawler laughed. 'I'm glad that you are so keen,' she said with a smile. 'However, you may want to wear something a little less elegant when you return. This can be dirty work and I'd hate for your pretty dresses to be spoiled.'

There was no trace of malice in her voice but even so I felt my cheeks go red with embarrassment as I looked down at the new dark blue flower patterned dress trimmed with soft brown velvet bows that, after much deliberation with Minnie, I had decided upon that morning. 'I'm sure that I can find something suitable,' I said, hardly daring to meet Mr Mercier's eyes which I knew rested on me with a not altogether friendly amusement. As was traditional, I regularly made presents of my old clothes to Minnie so that she could either keep them for herself or sell them on and make herself a bit of extra money. However, I kept a few old day gowns back to wear when I was helping Papa in his studio and they would have to do. I didn't suppose anyone at the Mission would mind a few paint and charcoal smudges.

Aunt Minerva clapped her hands together. 'Then that's all settled then,' she said briskly with a nod to me. 'I think we can dispense with any further chaperonage from me so I will bid you both goodbye now.' She opened her purple watered silk reticule and felt inside for a slip of paper, a cheque in fact, which she then discreetly slipped into Mrs Lightfoot's hand and which vanished into that's lady's pocket as quickly as it had appeared.

'You are very kind, Lady Coudland,' she said, smiling. 'We shall be so pleased to welcome Miss Redmayne back again.'

'I am sure that you will,' my aunt replied with an ironic glint in her eye and I wondered just how much her cheque had been made out for. 'Anyway, we must be off. Thank you both for such an instructive introduction to your work.' She beckoned me to follow her from the hall. 'Come along, Alice.'

I smiled at both ladies and pointedly ignored Mr Mercier before hurrying out through the door and onto the front step. 'I bet that's the last we'll see of that particular fancy young lady,' I heard Mr Mercier say with a laugh as the battered green door closed behind us.

Ugh. I seethed with annoyance all the way back to Highbury, slumped gracelessly as an adolescent boy in my seat and taking no interest at all in the houses and shops that we passed on our way home. At first Aunt Minerva tried to make some conversation with me but eventually she too fell into silence and turned her head to stare majestically out of the window, a frown settled between her thinly plucked eyebrows.

When we reached my house, she didn't accompany me inside only leaned across from her seat to kiss my cheek then took my hands in hers. 'It is up to you to show that young man that he is wrong about you,' she said in a low voice. 'Don't go in there tomorrow all petulant and full of girlish indignation. Be a woman and show him what you are made of.'

I grinned at her. 'I don't know what you mean,' I said as Gideon opened the carriage door for me.

'Pish,' said my aunt fondly, waving me away. 'Take care, Alice. I still don't know what you are up to but at least I can be sure that you will be in good hands.'

I hurried up to my room where Minnie was waiting for me, her gaze expectant and a little anxious. 'Well, how was it, Miss?' she asked. She'd been exceedingly relieved that morning when I told her that she wasn't required to accompany me and was clearly keen to ingratiate herself now.

I carelessly threw my reticule on to the bed and sat down heavily so that she could remove my dusty boots. 'Exhausting,' I said. 'I think I will enjoy it though.' I leaned back on my hands and stared around me, contrasting my pretty bedroom with the simple rooms the women at the Mission inhabited. Although Mrs Lightfoot lived in her own house in Chelsea and travelled in each day to help, Miss Lawler lived on the premises and had briefly shown us her room at the top of the house with its plain iron bedstead, sprigged white and blue wallpaper and simple rag rugs spread on the wooden floorboards.

'It must have been a shock to see how people live in Whitechapel,' Minnie said, getting up from the floor with my boots in her hands. 'My Ma says it's ever so rough down there.' She put the boots outside the door then went off to the bathroom to run a bath for me.

I sighed. 'It is very rough,' I said, standing up so that she could help me out of my dress. 'It feels so strange and wrong that there is so much want and harshness only a few short miles away.'

Minnie gave a small shrug. 'That's London for you, Miss,' she said smartly, folding up the dress and putting it on the bed before starting to unlace my corset. 'You look right peaky though. Shall I ring for some tea?'

I opened my mouth to agree but then closed it again almost immediately. No, a day like this required something far stronger and my eye instinctively fell on the bureau next to the pink marble fireplace. Minnie followed my gaze and gave a smile of understanding. 'I'll fetch it,' she said.

'It' was a bottle of finest French brandy, a birthday present from Lucasta, which lay hidden beneath a pile of snowy white cotton and lace nightgowns, along with a cut crystal glass pilfered from among my father's collection in his study downstairs. 'I'll have it with my bath,' I said as Minnie, frowning a little lest she spill a single precious burnt amber drop, carefully poured me out a measure.

'Very good, Miss,' she said, handing the glass to me before dashing to the bathroom to finish pouring my bath.

A few moments later, I lay back with a sigh in rose and lily scented water and took a much needed swig from my glass of brandy, savouring the rich burn of the liquid against my tongue and then the pleasant and very relaxing warmth that spread through my limbs as it hit my stomach. I gave a sigh, closed my eyes and slipped further beneath the steamy water.

'Would you like me to wash you, Miss?' Minnie whispered, obviously unwilling to disturb me.

I shook my head then opened my eyes, took another reviving

sip of brandy then picked up a fresh bar of rose scented Marseilles soap that rested in a little marble dish on the side of the bath. I thought again of the unfortunate women at the Whitechapel Women's Mission and felt a smart of shame that I should be surrounded by so many luxuries when they had barely anything to call their own. I lifted the soap to my nostrils and inhaled its almost spicy sweetness, thinking how sad it was that even a simple luxury like this was unheard of in Whitechapel. 'I can do something about that though,' I said aloud, suddenly struck by inspiration. 'After all, what's the use of money if you can't do anything good with it every now and again?'

Minnie stuck her head around the door. 'Did you say something, Miss?' she asked with a concerned look.

'No, nothing,' I said, gleefully waving her away and grinning happily to myself as I imagined Mr Mercier's expression when I turned up the next day with boxes full of several dozen bars of the very finest rose scented French soap for the ladies of the Mission.

CHAPTER EIGHT
EMMA, 1888

I woke up sore headed and feeling like shit. That's what a night in the Brick Lane Night Shelter did for you. I wasn't about to complain though - it was hard work getting a place on their wards and however uncomfortable, noisy and cold it might be, you knew you were a damn sight better off than the poor wretches who had nowhere else to go and had to spend the night walking the streets and sleeping in doorways or barns.

I wearily sat up in my bed, which was more of a wooden box really. The beds at the night shelter looked like open coffins, all lined up in rows either side of the room with a pillow at the head, a thin sheet covering the straw filled mattress and a very itchy blanket with STOLEN printed all over it to pull over yourself. I didn't know why they bothered with the whole 'STOLEN' business, there wasn't a soul in Whitechapel, except the babes in arms obviously, who hadn't nicked something one time or another and we all knew it wasn't our business to tattle on anyone who did.

'Sleep well, Em?' the woman in the coffin next to me said with a grin, scratching at her thin ribs beneath her dull grey dress that might once have been green, it was hard to tell any more. She pulled a barely serviceable old comb out from a pocket and started to run it through her dirty blonde hair. She wasn't much older than me, maybe nineteen at the most but looked nearer thirty, all thin and battered about the edges, much like we all did I suppose. 'I reckon we'd have got a better night's sleep on the streets.'

I laughed. 'I dunno about that, Liz,' I said, checking that my few belongings were still where I had left them, tucked underneath my pillow. 'Didn't you hear the rain last night? It sounded like the world was about to end. I pity any poor soul who got caught out in that.' I rubbed at my eyes, which were grimy with exhaustion then tenderly felt the bruise high on my cheek. I didn't need to look in a mirror to know that it was a proper shiner.

Liz winked at me. 'Got on the wrong side of some swell, did you?' she said with much sympathy.

I shook my head, pulling my hair over the bruise to hide it a little. 'I don't work on my back no more,' I said. 'Or at least, I try not to. I had a falling out with a door, that's all.' I was lying and she knew it. The fact of the matter is that a girl has to earn a living somehow and I'd taken to picking pockets to get money for my keep. This had gone fairly well until I was detected in the act by a very angry looking gentlemen on Middlesex Street, who had taken all my earnings and smacked me about the face for my trouble. Which was why I was spending the night in the shelter rather than in my usual fourpenny lodging house on Thrawl Street.

'I wish someone would paint over that,' Liz said, pointing with her chin to the end wall where ARE YOU READY TO DIE was painted in big red letters. 'It gives me the horrors lying here in my bloody coffin and seeing that written up there like, I dunno, the word of God or something.'

I glanced at the words and gave a disdainful shrug. 'Bollocks to it,' I said. 'Don't let it scare you, Liz. It's just something the God botherers have thought up to try and set us all on the straight and narrow.' I stuck my tongue out at it. 'Sod them. I'm not read to die and nor are you, neither.'

More of the women in the room were starting to wake up now, sitting up with coughs and sighs of discomfort and rubbing their sore heads and limbs. There wasn't much room to move in the coffin beds so you either had to get comfortable on your side and stay put or lie flat on your back like a corpse until morning. Some of the women started crying again when they woke and saw that they were still there while others just sat in a silent daze, starting into nothing almost as if they didn't know where they were at all. Someone started to tunelessly sing The Boy I Love Is Up in the Gallery, a popular music hall song, but she was quickly shushed and shouted into silence.

'Did you hear the rain last night?' a girl close to me said to another. 'Scared the life out of me, it did. I've never been so frightened.'

Liz grinned and leaned close to me. 'Someone's had a sheltered life,' she whispered, jerking her head towards the other girl. 'She'll soon learn.'

I laughed mirthlessly. We were scared all the time on the streets of Whitechapel, from the second we woke up glad to have survived another night to the moment we fell asleep again, relieved to have made it through another hungry, miserable day, we were frightened. It was the only sensible way to be, the only way to survive. 'A piddling thunder storm's nothing compared to some of the sights I've seen,' I said in a low voice, thinking about that night in Calais a year before when everything had changed. I shook myself and gave a shrug. 'I hope Poll found somewhere to stay,' I said to Liz, thinking about one of my friends from the lodging house on Thrawl Street, who hadn't had enough money to pay for her bed either but hadn't managed to get a place in a shelter. The last time I saw her, she was prancing about outside the Frying Pan pub on Brick Lane, so drunk that she could barely stand upright and telling anyone who'd stop to listen that she was sure to earn plenty of money now that she had a nice new black bonnet to entice the men down alleyways with her.

'Typical bloody Poll,' I said now with a fond smile, shaking my head as I remembered her excitement. 'No money to pay for somewhere to kip for the night but still manages to find the pennies for a fancy new hat.'

'At least she'd have been able to keep her hair dry,' Liz said with a wink and we both laughed. 'No, seriously, she'll be alright. Poll's not that bad looking really so I'm sure she'll have earned her fourpence to pay for a bed for the night, with some to spare.'

I wasn't so sure though, remembering the rain in Calais and how it had chased all the men away. What sort of man was desperate enough to brave last night's tempest in search for a bit of skirt? I shrugged. 'Ah well, good luck to her,' I said. 'I'm sure I'll see her later on, nursing a sore head and swearing never to touch a drop of drink ever again.'

Liz grinned. 'We've all been there,' she said, stretching her arms up above her head and yawning. 'Bleeding hell, I'm knackered.'

A nun, one of the Sisters of Mercy who ran the night shelter, appeared and rang a bell at the end of the room as a signal that we should all heave our miserable cramped carcasses out of our coffins, arrange ourselves as decently as possible and file into the eating hall for breakfast. 'What do you fancy this morning, Em?' Liz said, putting on a swanky voice and giving herself some airs as we hid our things beneath our clothes and brushed ourselves down. 'I was thinking maybe some kedgeree followed by kidneys on toast, all washed down with a pint of brandy. How about you?'

I grinned. 'I'll just have the brandy if it's all the same to you, milady,' I said, sniffing the air appreciatively as if it smelt of a delicious breakfast rather than last night's accumulation of stale breath, rotten flatulence and sweaty underarms. 'Mm, I do declare that I can discern a waft of gruel.'

Liz laughed and clutched her hands to her breast as if in raptures of delight. 'Ooh, gruel,' she said in a high wavering voice, mincing like a lady down the aisle between the coffins as the other women laughed at her. 'Delicious. One's butler swears by it.'

We were still laughing when we sat down on the scarred and dirty wooden table in the dining hall where, as usual, we were served with a slop of thin gruel, a slice of hard dark bread and a chipped enamel mug of lukewarm and very stewed tea. I'd heard rumours that they served hot chocolate on some mornings but had never actually seen any evidence of this. After that it was off to the yard for a hold your nose and hope for the best visit to the cold, stinking privies, a quick wash in the troughs of water and then out on to the street again.

'See you here later then?' Liz said to me as I pulled my shawl close about my shoulders and stood uncertainly on the pavement, wondering where to go first.

I grinned. 'I bloody hope not,' I said before waving and heading to Dorset Street. It was a lovely morning and even though it was early, the streets already heaved and hummed with life and activity as shop keepers opened their shutters for the day ahead and housewives strolled down the road together with their baskets to buy the day's supply of bread and milk, assiduously avoiding eye contact with the more floridly dressed and still obviously intoxicated men and women who were clearly making the walk of shame back home from wherever they'd landed up the night before.

'Alright, Em,' one woman hailed me and I smiled back, raising my hand in greeting. 'Didn't see you out last night.'

'I went to the shelter, Cathy,' I said with a shrug. Unlike the village where I grew up, there was no shame here in saying that you spent the night in the homeless shelter. We'd all been there.

Cathy pulled a face. Her coarse reddish hair was coming down from its bun and her make up was smeared all over her face and around her eyes. She also stank of gin and had a trail of livid love bites all down her neck and one on her breast. Whatever she'd been up to the night before, she'd clearly had fun. 'Ooh, bad luck, old cock,' she said. 'You missed a right old night down the Frying Pan. There was some nice looking soldiers there. You could have taken your pick of them if you'd had a fancy to it.'

I shook my head. 'Did you see Poll at all?' I asked, still worried about my friend. 'She didn't have enough for the lodging house either and I hate to think of her out in the rain all night.'

Cathy considered this for a moment then shook her head. 'Nah, not after about midnight when she upped and left to get some more pennies for her drink. I offered to buy her a jar of beer but she was in one of her proud moods and wouldn't let me, you know how she gets.'

'I know,' I sighed. Oh Poll. 'Ah well, see you later on then.' We smiled at each other and continued on our separate ways, me down Church Street and Cathy staggering on to her lodging house on Fashion Street, trailing her blue shawl on the road behind her and waving merrily to the shopkeepers, most of whom she owed money to.

It took just a few moments to walk down once elegant Church Street, which ran alongside the massive white edifice of Christ Church then cross the road by the Ten Bells pub, weaving quickly in and around the traffic, covered wagons taking goods to Spitalfields market and a few horse drawn omnibuses mostly, that moved in a continual noisy, dirty stream up Commercial Street. I then whisked down Dorset Street, sauntering past the huge three storey Britannia pub on the corner, which everyone locally called the Ringers on account of its fearsome landlady, Mrs Ringer.

However, Mrs Ringer's terrifying reputation was nothing compared to that enjoyed by the street, known as 'the worst street

82

in London', upon which her pub resided. It wasn't actually that bad, not during the day anyway and not for a local like me who was on nodding terms with most of the tarts and bully boys who sat out on the doorsteps of their lodging houses, enjoying a companionable cup of tea in the rare sunshine as their barefoot, grubby faced children played in the middle of the road. At night, it was a different matter though when the pubs along the street were full to heaving and vicious fights between both men and women spilled out on the vomit, blood and excrement splattered pavement and the tarts didn't even bother taking men up alleyways but just did them then and there in the street, not caring who was looking.

I walked about half way down the street then turned down Miller's Court, a dingy little alleyway next to McCarthy's grocer's shop, which was just wide enough for one person to pass down. 'Alright, Stephen,' I said to the mad old soldier who usually sat on the corner of the alley. 'How's things?'

He grimaced up at me and pushed his dirty cap back on his greasy grey hair. 'Could be better, Miss,' he said gloomily. 'You watch yourself now. Dark times are coming. Oh yes, they're a coming alright.'

I laughed at this and carried on down the alleyway, coming out into a small overlooked courtyard with a water pump and some nasty looking privies at the far end and knocked on the first door on the right. 'Marie,' I whispered when there was no reply straight away, 'are you in there?'

I heard the sound of something breaking, the whisper of skirts against wood and then someone swearing before the door is opened a crack. 'Who is it?' An eye appeared in the crack and then the sliver of a face. 'Em, is that you?'

'Course it's me. Who'd you think it was? The bleeding Queen?' I said, wondering what mess Marie had got herself involved in this time. 'Now are you going to let me in or not?'

She gave a sigh of relief and half heartedly opened the door to let me in. 'I wasn't expecting you,' she said gruffly by why of an apology and greeting as I looked around the room. It was small, damp and shabby with plain white washed panelled walls and only a few pieces of rickety old furniture, namely a wooden bed, a chair and two knackered and very dirty tables that wobbled on the unvarnished wooden floor when she brushed past them. Instead of curtains she'd made do by hanging her clothes over string at the two cracked and mould covered windows and as far as I could make out the only decoration in the whole sad little room was a faded old print of a miserable faced woman staring out to sea which hung over the tatty plaster fireplace, which was black with decades old smoke and grease. 'It's a bit different to Madame Lisette's place, isn't it?' Marie said with a shrug as I looked around. 'I'd offer you some tea only I've run out.' She bent down to pick up the pieces of the already handleless mug that she'd knocked over before answering the door.

'It's alright, I've just had tea at the shelter,' I said, sitting on the only chair as Marie, after some hesitation, shoved the pieces of broken cup into the fireplace then perched on the edge of the bed which had not been made and was covered with a tangle of not very clean sheets and blankets. 'I only came to see how you are doing.'

Marie gave a small smile. 'Och you know,' she said, patting her auburn hair which hung loose down her back and not meeting my eyes. Her Irish accent, never particularly strong unless she was angry or drunk, had faded even more and was now melded with a slight Cockney twang. 'Same as usual. You know how it is.'

I looked around the room, looking for some evidence of male occupancy but didn't see anything, not so much as a pair of socks or a twist of tobacco, that would declare that a man lived there too. 'You still with that bloke?' I asked.

She went a bit pink about the ears. 'You mean Joe?' she said vaguely. 'Yeah, I'm still with him. He's out looking for work right now but he'll be back later on.'

'I thought he was working as a porter in the market,' I said, trying to recall Joe to mind. I'd only met him once in passing when he came to the Ten Bells to chivvy Marie into going home with him and he seemed nice enough - tall with a thatch of dark hair and kindly pale blue eyes set into a slightly too long face. He wasn't Marie's type at all but if he made her happy what business was it of mine?

Marie gave a sigh. 'He got laid off,' she said, suddenly angry. 'They said he was stealing but he never took nothing. It was all made up, so it was. The buggers believed it though and sacked him, the stupid sod.'

I looked around the mean little room again, noticing the absence of food and the meagre pile of coals heaped in the fireplace. 'How are you doing for money?' I asked gently. 'I can't give you anything but if there's any way that I can help then you only have to ask, you know that don't you.'

Marie smiled then and pushed her hair out of her face. 'I know, Em and I'm truly grateful for it.' She gave a sigh then dipped her head and fished under the bed to produce a half empty bottle of gin. 'There's no glasses as I've already hocked them both,' she said with a rueful grin, handing me the bottle. 'We'll have to take it in turns.'

I unscrewed the top and took a small swig of throat burningly rough gin then wiped my mouth on my sleeve before passing the bottle back to Marie. 'So how is it then?'

She grimaced and took a long slug from the bottle. 'It's been better,' she said, wiping her mouth on the back of her hand before taking another even deeper swig. 'We're completely flat broke and several weeks behind with our rent.' She shrugged and handed the bottle to me. 'It's a total bloody mess.'

I took a sip of gin and handed it straight back. 'You need it more than me,' I said with a smile. 'Are you getting evicted then? Does your landlord know?'

She pulled a face. 'Oh, old McCarthy knows all right,' she said. 'The thing is…' She took another shot of gin and coughed as it went down the wrong way. 'The thing is that he's said we can stay and make up the arrears if I go back on the tralala again.'

I stared at her. 'I thought you said that Joe made you give all that up,' I said. She'd been furious at the time, seeing it as interfering but in the end had become reconciled, had even started seeing it as a bit romantic that he should want to have her all to himself.

She put the bottle, now almost empty, down on the table between us. 'He did,' she said softly, picking at the label until it peeled off in clumps on to the table.

'Are you giving sauce to McCarthy as well?' I asked bluntly.

She laughed then and shook her head. 'Gawd no. You should see him.' She peeled off some more of the label and wouldn't quite meet my eye. 'Sure, I wouldn't touch him with someone else's.'

I sighed. I could always tell when she was lying. 'Are you sure?'

Her face crumpled. 'Oh alright, I might have sucked him off a couple of times but nothing more than that and it's worth it to keep us off the streets, isn't it?' She leaned forward then and clutched at my hands, her fingers cold and dry as bone. 'You mustn't tell Joe,' she whispered urgently. 'He'd kill me if he ever found out why it is that we're allowed to stay. The stupid bugger thinks McCarthy lets us keep the room out of the kindness of his heart and it'd kill him if he ever found out the truth that...'

'That it's down to your kindnesses to him,' I finished her sentence, shaking my head. 'Marie, this isn't right. You should just move out. Tell him to stick his bloody rent where the sun don't shine and do a runner.' I clutched at her hands. 'You've done it before, why don't you do it again?'

She pulled her hands away. 'Because this is Dorset Street,' she said flatly. 'If we do a runner from McCarthy he'll send some of his bully boys after us and they'd mess us both up so badly that neither of us'll ever work again. I couldn't do that to Joe, not after he's tried so hard to look after me.' She stood up and went to the window, peering out between the petticoats and shirts that had been haphazardly hung up there in the absence of curtains. 'There's no point letting him evict us either as we'd never find anything as good as this for this cheap.'

'It's not really cheap though is it?' I said quietly but she shook her head and refused to listen to me.

'And what about you?' she said, changing the subject as she put the top back on her bottle and hid it underneath the bed again. 'Did you say you stayed in the shelter last night?'

I nodded. 'It wasn't that bad,' I lied. 'The nuns are kind enough and at least they don't expect us to work for scraps of food unlike some places. I'll be glad not to go back though.'

Marie sighed. 'I don't know why you waste your time thieving to make ends meet when you'd make three times as much on the game.' Clearly it was now her turn to lecture me about my shortcomings. 'It's different for you,' she went on angrily, when I opened my mouth to remind her that she wasn't all that happy to earn a living on her back either. 'You don't have a bloke to stay nice and clean for. You can do whatever you like.' She sounded a

86

little wistful and more than a bit drunk. 'And look at the state of that bruise. You never got hit like that when you was a tart.'

'No, because no one ever hurts tarts, do they?' I said with a meaningful look that made her glance quickly away as the shared and never to be spoken of memory of Calais reared its head again between us.

'You could always go home,' she said quietly. 'It's got to be better than this.'

'I can't ever go home,' I said, feeling miserable and wishing that I'd had more of her gin to take the edge off it. 'My Ma and Pa would die of shame if they knew what I'd been up to since I left.'

'As if they don't already know,' Marie scoffed. 'Oh come on, Em, all you need to do is turn up again and give a pretty little speech about how sorry you are and they'd welcome you back with open arms.'

I shook my head and stood up to leave. 'I doubt it,' I said, straightening my shawl. 'I reckon they were glad to see the back of me.'

Marie shrugged and stood up as well. 'Promise you won't tell Joe if you see him?' she asked as I put my hand on the door latch. 'Honestly, he'd kill me if he ever found out what's been going on.'

'Course I won't tell,' I said reassuringly, opening the door. 'Nothing to tell, is there?'

She came to the door as I started to walk down the alley back to Dorset Street. 'You take care of yourself, won't you, Em?' she said softly.

I looked back at her and smiled. 'You too, Marie.'

Chapter Nine

I hadn't gone far down Dorset Street when I was hailed by another familiar voice and turned to see Annie, a lairy old tart that I'd known ever since I first came to Whitechapel, hurrying down the street towards me, almost pushing people over in her haste.

'Alright, Annie?' I said without enthusiasm as she got nearer. 'What's up?' I started to feel nervous when I saw the intent look on her podgy face. Annie was a nasty drunk and I'd seen her lash out, mostly at other women and usually over nothing, more times than I could count. I stopped and waited for her to huff up to me, wondering what, if anything, I had done to offend her this time. 'Anything wrong?'

'There's been another murder,' she said abruptly, panting a little. 'Over on Buck's Row.' Marie's once upon a time description of Annie's face being like a bulldog chewing a wasp wasn't far wrong, I thought, as she stood before me, jowls trembling with annoyance and exertion and small, mean eyes swivelling suspiciously from side to side.

I pulled a face. 'It wasn't all that long ago that Martha got stiffed as well,' I said, wondering why she'd made such an effort to deliver this bulletin to me.

Annie frowned, which made her look absolutely murderous. 'You mean that woman in George Yard?' she said dismissively, folding her arms over her bosom. 'I didn't know her but sounds like the nasty piece of work had it coming.'

I shrugged. 'Yeah, well...' I didn't disagree with her, after all the last time I saw Martha she'd nicked the envelope with the pendant I was meaning to hock for doss and food money out of my pocket, the bloody cow, but even so it still felt wrong to speak ill of someone who'd died so horribly. 'The thing is, Annie, what's this got to do with me?'

'Coppers want to talk to you about it,' she said, rolling her eyes as if I was the stupid one for not being able to magically read her mind and work it out for myself. 'They think it was one of your friends from Thrawl Street and want you all in to identify her.'

My blood ran cold. 'Which friend?' I asked faintly. I thought of Poll dancing around on the pavement outside the Frying Pan and felt queasy with dread. Why couldn't she just come to the shelter with me when I asked her to?

'Polly? Is that her name?' Annie said with a pretence at forgetfulness. 'The short one with a scar on her forehead. Looks and acts younger than she is and got a very high opinion of herself even though we all know she's on the run from the coppers for thieving.'

I sighed, feeling all cold and empty inside. Oh Poll. 'I'd best get back there then.' I turned to go back up towards Commercial Street, my heart heavy. 'Thanks, Annie.'

She sniffed and shrugged, exuding a dank aroma of stale beer, cigarette smoke and bad living from her stained and torn black dress. 'Cheerio then.'

I walked slowly back up Dorset Street then turned right down Commercial Street, which was busier now with carts and omnibuses standing still in places as they waited for the traffic to ease up. Spitalfields Market, a huge building opposite Christ Church was in full swing and I heard the shouts of the market traders as I walked away, passing a group of blind musicians standing on the corner of White's Row, playing their violins and nodding thanks when they heard the clink of pennies in the enamel cup placed at their feet.

As was usual for this time in the morning, Commercial Street was crammed full of people, mostly tired looking housewives carrying baskets of shopping; out of work men who sat aimlessly in the doorways of the tall old weaver's houses and dozens of noisy street children who darted underfoot and had their hands permanently outstretched for money. The whores were all sleeping the gin off in their pokey lodging houses in the rookeries and wouldn't be out again until much later on.

I crossed the road further down, darting between a couple of carters who were close to having a full on brawl about their right of way on to Whitechapel High Street then carried on to Thrawl Street, a miserable thoroughfare lined with smoke blackened dilapidated houses, most of which were in use as cheap lodging houses where anyone with fourpence could pay for a bed for the night and the use of a dingy little kitchen. The atmosphere, never exactly jolly at even the best of times, was unusually sombre as I headed straight for number eighteen, probably because the police, who were intensely distrusted and disliked in this corner of Whitechapel, had come knocking earlier on, an event that would almost certainly have driven virtually every resident of the street indoors so that the only sounds to be heard were the insistent hungry wail of a baby from an upstairs room and the barking of some dogs chained up in the overgrown backyards.

A young woman with sloppily pinned up mousy brown hair and a filthy pale blue apron fastened over her red dress sidled out of the house next door as I paused for a moment on the doorstep of number eighteen, also known as Wilmott's thanks to the cracked and peeling wooden sign that hung above the door. 'You heard then?' she asked without preamble, her accent one that I could never quite place other than to recognise it as Northern in origin. 'The coppers have been.'

I sighed. 'I heard,' I said, imagining the scene. 'Did they speak to everyone, Mary?'

She shook her head. 'We all went indoors when we seen them coming.' She shrugged and smoothed down her apron with grimy hands. 'Mister thought they might knock and ask us questions but they only wanted to speak to the people lodging here.'

I nodded. 'Poor old Poll,' I said, feeling miserable again as I said her name. 'If it is her.'

Mary pulled her mouth down at the corners in an expression of regret and sorrow. 'It's right sad,' she said. 'Poll was a nice woman. A bit dim, right enough, but there was not an ounce of harm in her, not really.'

'I know,' I said, putting my hand on the door handle and bracing myself for whatever lay inside. 'I hope to God it's not her after all.'

Mary shrugged. 'Well, if it's not her then it's some other poor cow, isn't it?' She gave me a nod and went back into her house, leaving me with nothing else to do but turn the handle and step into Wilmott's lodging house.

It was usually a hive of noisy activity with both men and woman hanging about in the corridors and kitchen at all hours of the day and night, keeping themselves warm and dry and enjoying a bit of company but today I was greeted with a heavy silence, all the usual residents having clearly scarpered onto the streets after the police's visit. 'Anyone home?' I called, grinning to myself a little at the strangeness of calling such an inhospitable place with its damp, dirty walls and filthy loose floorboards 'home'.

I walked down the corridor to the kitchen, which lay at the back of the house and was a dark cavernous room with smoke and grease stained walls and ceiling, ominous splashes of long past dinners and tallow candle wax all over the floor and tables and a row of knackered old chairs arranged here and there around the fire. A couple of chipped plates, still with a few crumbs of bread and scrapings of cheese and some mugs half full of now cold tea had been left out on the tables, telling me that the kitchen had been vacated in something of a rush earlier on and that no one had yet dared to return.

'Em?' I heard a familiar voice whisper from the stairs that I had just passed in the hall. 'Is that you?'

'Course it's me, Emily,' I called back. 'Bobbies been have they?'

A small dark haired girl with huge blue eyes crept timidly into the kitchen, smiling with relief when she saw me standing alone by the dead fire. 'Been and gone again,' she said, her voice trembling as she picked up some of the cups and plates and took them over to the sink. 'Most people scarpered but I stayed to talk to them.'

I sat down heavily on a chair by the fire and mournfully surveyed the kitchen as Emily half heartedly scraped some crumbs of food into an overflowing tin bin on the floor and tipped tea down the sink. 'Where did you get to last night?' she asked eventually, turning back to me. 'Bloody hell, I was right worried about you.'

I sighed and stretched my feet out in front of me, noticing as I did so that the upper part of one of my boots was coming away from the sole again and would need to be mended. 'I went to the shelter on Brick Lane,' I said. 'Some geezer caught me stealing his

91

handkerchief and took all my earnings to teach me a lesson so I had no money to pay for my doss.'

'Gave you a smack too by the looks of things,' Emily said with a slight smile, sitting down next to me. She smelt like she'd spent the night beside a bonfire and I noticed that she had some dark smudges of black ash on her pale green dress and on her face. She pulled my hair away so she could get a proper look at the bruise on my cheek. 'My Mam would have put a bit of beef on that to make it come down a bit,' she said with a tut.

'If we had a bit of beef, it'd be in our stomachs not wasted on bruises,' I said, more sourly than I intended. 'What happened with the coppers anyway?'

Emily's face fell. 'They wanted to ask about Poll and if any of us saw her last night,' she said in a low voice. 'Then they took some of us down to the workhouse mortuary to have a look at her.' She gave a shudder. 'It were horrible, Em. She looked all pale and her eyes were open a little bit so it was like she was looking at us and even though they'd tried to hide it, you could see the cuts on her neck…'

I felt sick and looked away from her as she gestured with her hands to show where Poll had been cut. 'Did you see her last night?' I asked eventually.

She nodded enthusiastically. 'At about half two in the morning, going by the church bells. There was a huge fire down at the docks so a group of us went to have a look, you know, as you do.' That would explain the stink of smoke and dark smuts on her face then. 'I bumped into Poll outside the grocer on the corner of Osborn Street and Whitechapel High Street on the way back. She was completely off her head with gin, could hardly walk in fact.' She smiled at the memory, as I did too, remembering Poll and how funny she could be when she was helpless with drink. 'Anyway, we had a bit of a natter about this and that and I tried to get her to come back here with me but she was having none of it. I said I could get her in for the night if we promised to pay double tomorrow but she said she weren't taking no charity not even from me and wanted to earn her own doss money.' She laughed a little sadly. 'She had this stupid bloody new hat, you see. Said no man could resist her in it. Silly bitch.'

I sighed at the mention of Poll's bonnet. 'She'd have been

better off hawking it and getting her money that way,' I said unhappily.

'Too late now though, isn't it,' said Emily, her mouth downturned.

I stood up, suddenly desperate to get out of that stinking kitchen, to breathe proper outside air even if it was thick with smoke and dirt from the factories and stables that jostled for space with the houses in this part of Whitechapel. 'You sure that it's definitely her?' I asked.

Emily nodded, her wan little face miserable. 'I seen her with my own eyes,' she said. 'It couldn't have been anyone else.' She lowered her voice to a whisper. 'I heard two of the coppers outside talking about what was done to her. They said that her throat was cut so deep that her head almost came off and that she was all cut open so that her guts was hanging out but that no one even noticed until they'd got her off the street and into the mortuary.' She frowned, considering this. 'How did they not notice something like that? I know the coppers round here are as thick as mince and mostly on the take too but they've got eyes ain't they?'

I shrugged, looking away from her as she mimed cuts to the front of her torso. 'Maybe it was dark?' I suggested, wanting more than ever to be away as the long suppressed memory of that awful night in Calais and Bea's fair hair spread out over the bloody cobbles came back to me.

She thought about this for a moment. 'Maybe,' she concluded eventually. 'They said to me that it was very early when she was found, just an hour or so after I seen her on Osborn Street at half two. She was just lying there on Buck's Row with her skirts up and throat cut for all the world to see.' She paused to roughly wipe away a tear with the back of her hand. 'Poll never meant anyone no harm. Soft as shite she was. What sort of man does something like that?'

I shook my head. 'I dunno, Emily. I dunno.'

It didn't take me long to reach Buck's Row as I followed in the footsteps that Poll had taken the previous night, turning right out of Thrawl Street onto Brick Lane with the Frying Pan on the corner, where she had got royally and, I thought, fatally drunk then walking down to where Brick Lane merged into Osborn Street. Emily had bumped into her by the grocer's shop on the

93

corner of Whitechapel High Street and I paused there for a moment, leaning my hand against the wall just as she had described Poll doing and feeling horribly, immeasurably sad in a way that I had not felt for Martha or any of the other women who had vanished off the streets in my time there.

I turned left down Whitechapel Road, a wide busy road that had a more prosperous feel than nearby Commercial Street but was similarly rammed solid with carriages, carts and omnibuses while the pavements overflowed with all manner of people from Orthodox Jewish men rushing along with their skullcaps and black curls hanging about their ears to Chinese sailors smoking tobacco in long white plaster pipes to smiling red cheeked housewives popping in and out of the shops while gossiping with their friends. It was decidedly down at heel compared with, say, the likes of Regent Street but definitely lacked the ominous and ever present threat of imminent violence that hung in the air like a black pall over Commercial Street and the dark festering warren of streets and courts that ran off it.

About half way down, it widened even more and became even smarter, bordered on both sides by several flashy pubs, proper gin palaces with shiny coloured glass in the windows and the gleam of mirrors everywhere inside and shops, all covered from floor to roof with gaudy advertising billboards for everything from tooth powder to rat poison to pipe tobacco. Across the road I saw the East London Theatre, which was usually too pricey for the likes of me but where you could see all the latest music hall acts perform as well as the usual plays and such. A bit further along there was also the London Hospital, a vast pale stone building set a little back from the road and surrounded by a small park where it was whispered that they sneaked out in the dead of night to bury the chopped up remains of human carcasses that had been experimented upon. Maybe that accounted for some of the suspicion and dread with which the hospital was regarded in Whitechapel, to most of us it was where you went to die and none of us would have gone there willingly. Certainly I wouldn't set foot in the place unless I was in the direst need of treatment and in full expectation of death anyway.

I gave it one last wary look over my shoulder as I turned off Whitechapel Road on to Thomas Street and then took the first right on to Buck's Row, a narrow cheerless road with looming dark brick warehouses running down one side and a tall ominous looking school building, a length of brick wall and a row of squat little two storey cottages on the other. There was no need to ask anyone where Poll's body had been found as there was still a crowd gathered around a spot on the narrow pavement in front of a pair of tall wooden gates next to the cottages and directly across the way from a solitary street lamp. She really had been left out in the street for all to see.

I slipped closer, gently elbowing my way through the crowd until I was near the front and could see what they were looking at. If anyone had come here expecting gore, then they were no doubt sorely disappointed when they realised that all there was to see was a damp, slightly pink and obviously recently scrubbed patch of pavement and a handful of nervous looking young policemen struggling to maintain calm as they were harangued by the crowd for not keeping better order of the streets.

This then was where Poll had died. I looked at the cottages right next to the gates, home no doubt to respectable workmen and their families and wondered what they had heard in the depths of the night. Heard and ignored. A struggle perhaps? Maybe a scream? I then looked back over my shoulder at the huge hulking building behind us, a deeply unlovely three storey warehouse with ESSEX WHARF painted in huge white letters on the side. Was this the last thing that Poll saw as the killer struck at her with his knife? Or was it the distant clock of the London Hospital, just visible between the roofs of the houses that lay between Buck's Row and Whitechapel Road.

The ground shuddered beneath our feet as a train passed underneath us, creaking and rumbling along a railway line that was hidden from view by the brick wall next to the gates and its fellow on the opposite side of the road. I felt a bit foolish now as I'd assumed the wall was concealing the board school playground when in fact it was hiding the sheer drop down from the bridge that we were unknowingly standing on.

'The playground is up on the school roof,' I heard someone mutter behind me to their friend who had made the assumption as me and I looked up again at the board school, a four storey red brick monolith with, I now saw, tall metal railings lining the roof to prevent the children falling over the edge. 'They could have had one on the ground if it wasn't for the bleeding trains.'

The crowd started to melt away then, finally satisfied that there really wasn't anything much to see and that they wouldn't feel any closer to what had happened or have any better understanding of it by being there. I lingered for a moment longer though, straining my ears to hear the distant racket of Whitechapel Road in one direction and the rumble of trains from the other and gazing up at the warehouses that presided menacingly over the squalid little road. Even by Whitechapel standards, this was a miserable place to die.

I turned to leave, feeling in desperate need of a drink and somewhat regretting the odd impulse that had brought me there to look at the spot where my friend had died, feeling that even though I had known her, I was still no better than the random strangers who had turned up there for no better reason than to gawp in slack mouthed curiosity at where some poor woman had met her end.

And it was at that moment, as I stomped past the board school feeling deeply ashamed, trying my best to ignore the growl of hunger deep in my belly and wishing that I was somewhere, anywhere, else, that I saw her, a pale and familiar face amongst the crowd, staring fixedly and with wide eyed horror at the pink stain on the pavement. I couldn't place her at first, but then it all came back to me: that dreary day when I'd gone to the mortuary to try and steal my stuff back from a dead woman. She'd been there before me, the girl with red hair and sad eyes.

Chapter Ten

She looked up at me and I saw an expression of confusion followed by dawning recognition that must have mirrored my own, spread across her pretty face. There was a moment of indecision, during which I half expected her to turn tail and do a runner but instead she surprised me by smiling and shyly raising her hand in greeting. I hesitated for just a moment before shrugging my shoulders, fixing a smile to my own face and strolling over to her.

'Nasty business, isn't it?' I said by way of a greeting and she gave a slight nod, her eyes nervously fixed again on the wet stain on the pavement where Poll had bled her life out.

'Did you know her?' she asked in a thin, small voice, pulling her red wool shawl closer around her shoulders as a shadow fell across the sun overhead and a light breeze rose in the sky, scattering some rubbish that lay in thick clumps around the edge of the pavement. 'The dead woman. You knew the other one as well, didn't you?'

I nodded. 'We all know each other in our bit of Whitechapel,' I said. 'Poll, the woman who died here, shared a room with me, which I suppose made us friends of sorts.'

The girl gave a half smile and turned away from the pavement. 'I suppose you all have to look out for one another,' she said quietly. 'I have my sister for that but you have to make do.'

'Pretty much.' We started walking back up towards Spitalfields together, glad to leave those towering warehouses and the rattle of trains behind. 'You need friends in a place like Whitechapel. It's not the sort of place where it's advisable to keep yourself apart because you never know when you're going to need someone,' I said, echoing almost word for word the advice that Poll herself had given me when I'd first appeared on the streets of

Whitechapel a year earlier, on the run from France and terrified for my life.

I gave the girl walking beside me a sidelong look, taking in her neatly plaited and pinned up red hair, her faded but clean blue dress and her well looked after boots. She was carrying a brown paper bag in her hand, a slight sheen of grease and waft of soft dough suggesting food inside. My stomach growled again and I idly considered robbing her if I got the chance but then, more than a little appalled at myself, resolutely shoved the idea away. 'It's lonely too though.' Lonely, exhausting and frightening.

She nodded as if she understood then changed the subject. 'My Pa says that in the olden days they used to call this Ducking Pond Row because there used to be a ducking stool for bad tempered wives out this way. Eventually the name got changed to Duck's Row and then finally Buck's Row as it is now.' She looked back at the stretch of pavement where Poll had been found and where another small crowd was beginning to gather. 'Hard to imagine a pond here, isn't it?'

'Is your Pa a teacher then?' I asked with a laugh although I felt a little sad inside because my Pa used to talk the same way to me when we went on our walks together around town. He knew about all sorts of things like the Roman soldiers who used to live there and the warrior Queen with a blue painted face who came and burnt the whole town down because they mistreated her and her daughters. He loved history, my Pa.

The girl shook her head and went a little red about the ears. 'No, he's a policeman,' she said in a low voice, shooting me a quick look to see my reaction.

'Oh.' An awkward silence fell broken only by the growling of my stomach, the rumblings and shouts from Whitechapel Road and the distant barking of a thousand dogs.

'Sorry,' she said at last with a smile. 'He's not one of the bad ones though,' she added as an afterthought. 'I know there's some who aren't so nice. He's not like that.'

'I don't think any coppers, and especially not the ones on the take, think they're bad,' I said with a shrug. Her face fell and I felt guilty enough to rush to make amends. 'I'm sure your Pa isn't one of them though.' What was it Emily had said in the kitchen earlier on? 'Thick as mince and mostly on the take as well'? I hid a smile.

We turned on to Hanbury Street, a long grotty road that would take us straight back to Commercial Street. 'So what's your name then, copper's girl?' I asked cheerfully, seeing as we were clearly walking back together.

She smiled. 'Cora. What's yours?'

I briefly considered giving her one of the false names that I occasionally used but then gave a small shrug and decided to tell the truth. 'I'm Emma but everyone calls me Em.' I grinned. 'Emma always reminds me of my Ma when she was in a temper and shouting out of the door for me to come home and get a beating.'

The sun had come up now and people were thronging the streets, plenty of them sitting on their doorsteps or on the pavements sharing mugs of beer and tea with neighbours and keeping a cursory eye on the scruffy little ragamuffin children playing in the middle of the road. People always liked to say back then that the people of the East End didn't care for their children, were little better than animals in fact, but that wasn't true at all. Oh, it's true that hardly anyone could afford proper schooling and decent clothes and food for their offspring but they loved them fiercely nonetheless. If someone had done for a child the way that Poll was killed then there would have been riots on the streets that day and the murderer dragged out from whatever hole he was hiding in to be torn from limb to limb by a mob of angry women.

Cora and I strolled along Hanbury Street in companionable silence, enjoying the feeling of sunshine on our faces and the light breeze in the air. It still stank of course: of dirty bodies, smoke, old dinners and the refuse from the stables and tanners yards that nestled among the houses, but that breeze was just enough to lighten the mood a little and chase away the worst of the stench.

'You remember the last time I saw you?' I said after a while, as carelessly as I could. 'At the mortuary?' I carefully watched her face and saw her go pale and then look for a moment as if she was going to deny all knowledge of that day before finally giving a small nod.

'I remember,' she said in a low voice as if she wished that she didn't. 'We met on the doorstep, didn't we?'

'That's right.' We were walking past a pub, one of the ones that didn't encourage women to drink inside so that a small cluster of blowsy old tarts hung about outside, glowering sourly at the world from over the rouge stained rims of their gin glasses. 'Martha, the woman who got stabbed, had something of mine, you see,' I said, treading carefully. 'An envelope with something inside it. I thought it might still be on her when she was killed but when I went to have a look…' I let my voice trail away and looked at her hopefully, hoping that would be enough to nudge her into telling me if she had the pendant.

Cora stared at me for a moment, her eyes wide with panic, then resolutely shook her head. 'I didn't see it,' she said, looking flustered and a bit pink about the ears.

I sighed, now knowing full well that she was lying. 'It's just that it was very precious to me,' I persisted, thinking that precious was an understatement right now when I didn't have a pot to piss in and needed the money it could have made me to survive a few more weeks on the streets. 'It was a keepsake of another friend who got murdered and I'd dearly like to have it back again. It didn't fall on the floor or something did it?' I was quite proud of that touch, which gave her an easy excuse for owning up to taking it.

She stopped walking then and looked right at me. 'I didn't take anything,' she said, her voice rising a little so that people turned to stare at us. 'I never saw no envelope nor nothing else either and I certainly didn't take it.' She was bright red now, her cheeks almost clashing with her hair and I hastened to calm her before she started to cry and involved anyone else, not that I need have a care about that as no one on Hanbury Street would be interested in gawping at two girls having a fight. They'd seen it all before a hundred times over.

'It's alright,' I said gently, putting my hand on her arm and making myself smile. 'I was just wondering if you'd seen it, that's all.' I started walking again and after a moment she hurried to catch up with me. 'I didn't mean to upset you,' I said, half tempted to drag her into an alleyway and beat her up a bit until she told me the truth.

She blinked away some tears then gave a tentative nod. 'I know,' she said. 'I know that you had to ask.' She couldn't quite meet my eyes, knowing as well as I did that she was lying and probably fully aware that I knew it too. I sighed again. So this was how it was going to be, was it?

We were almost at the top of Hanbury Street now and about to turn on to Commercial Street where presumably she'd go her way and I'd go mine. I smiled at her. 'Well, it was nice meeting you, Cora,' I said, starting to stroll away and thinking that I was clearly never going to see my pendant again and that, more pressingly, I needed to thieve something quick smart so that I'd have enough money for food and somewhere to sleep.

'Wait,' Cora said, surprising me and probably herself as well as she'd gone a bit pink again. 'Do you want something to eat?' She waggled the paper bag at me then opened it to reveal a stack of shiny bagels inside. 'My Pa sent me out for them but he won't mind if we have a couple.'

I laughed. 'Bagels?' I said, doubtfully taking in her red hair and the dusting of freckles across her nose. 'You Jewish then?'

Cora laughed and shook her head. 'No, not Jewish,' she said as we turned and walked up towards Christ Church to find a spot to sit and eat. 'My Pa loves their food though. He's always buying bagels from the bakeries on Brick Lane and Middlesex Street and you should smell our rooms when he's bought some of that pickled fish they have as well.' We went past the Ten Bells and she paused as I exchanged the usual pleasantries with a couple of tarts sitting on the pavement outside. 'It's silly really but I used to think we weren't allowed into their shops but they're nice, the Jews around here. Really friendly.'

We went through the gates of Christ Church then walked up the white stone steps to the entrance, skirting around the homeless people who spent their days sitting there waiting for the shelters to open. 'What would your Pa say if you brought a Jew boy home with you?' I said, putting my hand into the bag and pulling out a bagel before sitting down on a step and taking a tentative bite. It was deliciously chewy and not at all oily as I thought it would be. 'Would he be alright about that?'

Cora sat down beside me and considered this for a moment, thoughtfully chewing on her bagel. 'I don't think he'd mind,' she said at last. 'He's kind my Pa and likes almost everyone. I don't think it'd happen though. I don't think they're allowed to go with us in that way and, well, we all stick to our own, don't we?' She sounded a bit wistful and I glanced at her curiously, wondering what secrets she was hiding.

'It won't always be like that,' I said after a moment, gesturing down crowded, dusty Commercial Street with my bagel. 'There's all sorts here in Whitechapel - Jews, Yanks, Chinese, Poles, Russians, Irish, you name it, all mixed up together. That's why I like it so much.' I took another bite from my bagel and swallowed. 'It feels like you can be whoever you want to be.'

She gave me an amused look and I felt a little crestfallen as I suddenly realised what she saw when she looked at me - a scrawny little runt of a girl with her roots showing through her dyed blonde hair and a lot of big ambitions that were going precisely nowhere. But if I expected her to poke fun at me, I was very wrong for instead she put her arm around my thin shoulders and hugged me close. 'I know just what you mean,' she whispered.

I finished my bagel and she immediately offered me another one. 'My Pa won't mind,' she encouraged me with a shy smile as I plunged my hand into the bag. 'They're good, aren't they?'

I grinned. 'To be honest, pretty much anything would be delicious to me right now,' I said, chewing on the bagel. 'This takes a lot of beating though.'

Her forehead creased with concern. 'Are you often hungry?' she asked.

I shot her a look. 'Pretty much all the time,' I said. 'Don't feel sorry for me though, copper's girl. It's my choice to be here.'

She sighed and turned her face away. 'Why don't you go home?' she said hesitantly. 'If things are so bad here?'

I laughed and shoved the last bit of bagel into my mouth. 'You're the second person to say that to me today,' I said, licking my fingers then wiping my hands on my skirt. 'The simple answer is that I don't think they'd want me there any more, not after the life that I've led.'

'You could just not tell them what you've been doing,' Cora said, hugging her knees and gazing over at Spitalfields Market which lay directly opposite the church.

I shrugged. 'I think they've probably already guessed,' I said with a sigh. 'I haven't been home for two years, not since I was fifteen. If a girl's been gone that long then it's because she's either dead or up to no good.'

'So where are you from then?' she asked, turning her attention back to me.

I laughed and sat back against the hard stone step behind. 'One of the first rules of Whitechapel is that you never ever ask anyone where they came from,' I said reprovingly. 'Surely you know that by now, copper's girl?' She looked so mortified that I instantly relented. 'I'm from a village near Colchester in Essex.'

'So not hard to get back home then?' she said with a smile. 'If you were to decide to leave.'

I sighed and shrugged, pretending to brush a crumb off my skirt so that she wouldn't see my face and the tears that welled up suddenly, hot and shameful, in my eyes. 'Not hard at all,' I said, angrily brushing the tears away. 'If I were to decide to leave.' The market across the way was buzzing with activity and I still had work to do if I was going to be able to pay for a bed for the night. 'Anyway, I'd better push off now,' I said, standing up and looking down at her as she stayed sitting on the step.

Cora nodded a little sadly. 'What was she like?' she said suddenly after a pause, looking up at me and squinting in the sunlight. 'Your friend, the one that got killed. What was she like?'

I stared down at her and considered my words carefully. 'She was poor,' I said at last. 'Poor and trying her best to survive, same as all of us. She thought she'd done the right thing, getting married and having children with some man but then life got in the way just like life always does and then the next thing she knew, she was here in Whitechapel, sucking sailors off for a couple of pence, starving hungry and scared for her life most days.'

Cora looked horrified. 'That's so sad,' she said. 'Pa says...'

'Never mind what your Pa says,' I interrupted her fiercely, burning all over with a sudden anger. 'I could show you a thousand like her in Whitechapel. A hundred thousand.'

'I know.' Cora stood up and put her arm around me again, pulling me tight against her. 'I've seen them too.'

I let her hold me for a moment then gently pushed her away. 'I've got to go,' I said, rubbing my hand across my damp face. I hated crying, it made me feel so weak and pathetic. 'I've got to make a living otherwise I'll end up like poor old Poll.'

Cora sighed. 'Do you need money?' she asked, feeling in her apron pocket. 'All I've got is sixpence but that's enough to buy you somewhere to stay isn't it?'

She put the coin in my hand and I stared at it for a moment before closing my fingers around it. 'Are you sure?' I asked, astounded by her generosity. After all she'd only just met me and for all she knew, I'd just go straight off and spend it on gin or worse. Then again, if she'd gone off with the pendant and sold it herself then this was basically my money anyway so what difference did it make?

She smiled and nodded. 'Course I am.' At least she didn't insult me as some might have done by pointing out that it was only a sixpence and not worth making a fuss about. In my world, even tuppence was worth a fuss. 'Anyway, I have to go too. My Pa will be wondering where his bagels are.' She gave me a shy look. 'Mind how you go, Em.'

'You take care too,' I said as she started back down the steps. 'And if you come across that envelope, make sure you tell me about it.' I hated myself for asking, for mentioning it again, especially after she had been so kind to me, but I had to do it. 'Keep an eye out for it in the station. Maybe someone there's got it?'

Cora went red. 'I'll see what I can do,' she said before darting away down the steps and back on to Commercial Street, where she was soon lost in the crowd.

CHAPTER ELEVEN

I saw Cora just once over the following week, strolling a few yards ahead of me through the crowds on Brushfield Street. She was walking with a girl a few years older than her who had the same bright red hair that gleamed like polished copper in the mellow autumn evening sunshine. I smiled to myself when I saw passing men actually stop and stare at them both in the street, knowing that Cora probably didn't notice them at all and would be mortified if anyone pointed out the attention she was unwittingly getting.

They soon vanished from sight and, still smiling, I turned on to Commercial Street and headed straight to the Britannia on the corner of Dorset Street. I'd had a good day picking pockets at the heaving Middlesex Street market and could easily spare some pennies for a few beers before I headed back to my lodgings on Thrawl Street.

'Alright, Em?' Marie was sitting at a beer slicked table by the door and hailed me cheerfully as soon as I stepped inside and was assailed as usual by the hot beery, fetid aroma of the pub. Her cheeks were a rosy pink thanks to the heat and probably one too many gins. 'How's your day been, my pretty little darlin'?' Definitely one too many gins then.

'Not bad.' I grinned at her then swaggered off to the bar to buy my beer. As was usual for a Friday night, the Britannia was packed that evening and I had to shove my way through to get to the counter where the landlady Mrs Ringer and a couple of harassed looking barmaids were doing their best to serve everyone as quickly as possible. By the time I got back to the table, Marie had been joined by Annie, who was staring sourly into her pint glass and had a faded black eye and Joe who smiled at me as I approached while Marie pulled a face and gave a tiny warning shake of her head, which I took to mean that he still didn't know about her extra source of income so I wasn't to say anything about it.

'You should try and get a job here,' she said cheerfully as I sat down and took my first sip of beer. 'Mrs Ringer's been on about getting a new barmaid again.'

'Why don't you do it?' I asked, remembering too late that Mrs Ringer was very strict about not employing tarts to work behind her bar.

Annie sniggered into her drink. 'Why do you think?' she muttered, rolling her eyes over at poor hoodwinked Joe as Marie glared at me.

'I expect you're too busy,' I said, trying to recover what was rapidly descending into a very awkward situation. 'Looking after Joe and all that.'

Marie smiled and tapped me on the arm to show that I was forgiven. 'That's right,' she said, nestling her head against his shoulder as he looked down at her fondly. 'I've got a man to look after, haven't I? You haven't though, Em.'

Annie gave a nasty laugh and slammed her pint glass down on the table. 'She don't want one neither,' she said, swivelling her small blue eyes over to me. 'Nothing but trouble they are.' We all knew that Annie had been married once upon a time but had been forced to leave her husband and six children when her drinking got out of hand. Her husband had paid her a decent allowance for a couple of years before dying and now she was like the rest of us, piss poor and struggling to survive.

'Oh knock it off you eejit,' Marie said, reaching up to kiss Joe's cheek. 'They're not all bad, just look at my Joe here. Soft as shite so he is.' I loved how her accent became more floridly Irish the more drunk she got.

'What happened to you, Annie?' I asked, pointing to her fading black eye and a particularly livid bruise on her forehead. I wasn't really interested but thought it might be best to change the subject. 'Got in a fight with a lamp post again?'

She heaved a great sigh. 'Got into a fight in here with that stinking bitch Eliza, more like,' she said with a dark scowl that could have curdled milk. 'Caught the thieving cow nicking tuppence from a friend of mine so she smacked me in the face.'

Marie pulled a face. 'She's a nasty one, that Eliza,' she said, throwing her head back as she polished off the dregs of her gin then straight away getting up to buy another, shaking off the restraining hand that Joe gently placed on her wrist. 'Oh, feck off and leave me alone will you? I've had a hard day and need a drink.'

She staggered off to the bar and Joe looked at me almost apologetically. 'I don't like it when she gets like this,' he said miserably. 'It's not her fault though. My Ma was the same. It's just life, innit? It's hard for some.'

'I'll drink to that!' Annie squawked, raising her glass.

In fact we drank to it several times over that night while the sun set across the rooftops and darkness fell on the dingy streets of Whitechapel. Someone sat down at the out of tune piano at the back of the pub and played a few jaunty tunes while some tarts drunkenly sang along, their cheeks flushed and eyes closed as they crooned the well worn melodies then danced together around the tables. A bit later on one of the local prize fighters, a short bully boy with cauliflower ears, an eye that had been punched shut and a nose that had been broken several times over, came in and bought a round for everyone in the pub with his winnings then asked the men back to a fight being held in a warehouse on Buck's Row later that night. I shivered a little when I heard the name, remembering Poll and the sad spot where her body had been found. I hadn't been back since and fully intended never to go there again.

Marie, Joe and I stood up to leave at midnight to carry on drinking at their place while Annie stayed sitting at the beer soaked table, holding her head and complaining that she'd drunk her doss money and would have to go out to earn it all over again. 'I'd lend it you if I had it,' Joe said, putting his hand on her shoulder as Marie gently slapped him and told him to shush and come along with us. 'But I haven't got tuppence to scratch myself with right now.'

Annie gave a grunt of thanks and supped the last of her beer before standing up as well. 'I'll go back anyway,' she said gruffly. 'Maybe I'll find someone to bed down with tonight.' This was always an option for the truly destitute who didn't have enough money to pay for a doss - find someone else who had eight pence for a double and screw them in exchange for a bed for the night. I'd done it myself more than once and pitied whatever poor chump got persuaded into being Annie's bed partner for the night.

The four of us fell out on to Commercial Street just as the clock on Christ Church over the road struck midnight, it's tall white tower looking oddly eerie that night as it stretched up towards the navy blue sky, where a few dark clouds scudded ominously overhead. 'More rain tomorrow,' Joe said with a knowing nod to the sky as Marie linked arms with him and impatiently dragged him off down Dorset Street while Annie and I followed more sedately behind.

'You'll be alright, won't you?' I said to her as we edged carefully around a drunk heaving his dinner out all over the street as a crowd of small ragged children watched and shouted encouragement.

She shrugged, pulling her skirts closer as the vomit splattered all over the pavement behind us. 'Course I will,' she said smugly. 'I always am.'

We reached the archway for Miller's Court and said an awkward goodbye before I followed Marie and Joe's retreating figures past Stephen, who was slumped asleep and snoring in the shop doorway and down the narrow alleyway that led to their room while Annie staggered further up the street to Crossingham's Lodging House, where she was staying.

'Ssh, I've got a bottle of gin,' Marie said as she let me in. 'I've had to hide it under my bed so that no one will nick it. There's some right thieving bastards around here so there is.'

I looked at the table where Joe was taking a swig from the bottle. 'Still no glasses then?' I said with a grin as she shut the door behind me.

Marie shrugged. 'We've got mouths, haven't we?' I found it hard to believe that Joe was apparently so completely lacking in curiosity about where the apparently unemployed Marie was getting the money for treats like bottles of gin but if he was at all suspicious about what she was getting up to while he was looking for work, he gave no sign.

I stayed there for most of the night, always intending to leave after the next swig from the bottle but then always staying for another half hour more. Grumpy and short tempered though she undoubtedly was, Marie could also be great company and she was on top form that night, telling funny stories about her childhood in Ireland, singing songs she'd picked up from rare trips to the local music halls and resolutely putting the world to rights until she finally passed out in the early hours with her head on the table amidst a mess of gin spills and pork scratchings.

Joe yawned as he got up from his chair to carry her to the bed. 'She'll be regretting this in the morning,' he said with a grin. 'She needed cheering up though, Em. She's been right down lately.'

I nodded, getting up from my chair and standing awkwardly by the door as he rolled Marie carefully onto the bed then eased a blanket over her. 'You really love her, don't you?' I said as I watched how gently he touched her.

He smiled and nodded. 'With all my heart,' he said simply. 'She's a good girl really and if I only had the money, I'd marry her in a trice.' He cast an anxious look back at her to check that she was still asleep then lowered his voice. 'I worry sometimes that if I don't then she'll start whoring again, especially now that I'm out of work and we need the money.'

If there was a question hidden in his statement I chose to ignore it. 'I'm sure she wouldn't do that to you, Joe,' I said softly, feeling wretched as the lies spewed from my mouth. 'She knows how it would break your heart.'

He smiled then, the worry clearing from his face. 'I hope so,' he said as I lifted the latch to go. 'I don't think I could bear it if she went back to that life again, especially if it was all my fault.'

I said goodbye and staggered back up the passageway to Dorset Street. The pubs were all shut now but the streets were still busy with whores strolling up and down plying their trade and the usual suspects hanging about the street corners looking for trouble. I pulled my shawl close around my shoulders as I hurried along, trying my best not to catch anyone's eye and tightening my grip on the sliver of cut glass that I kept in my pocket as a rudimentary weapon just in case. I knew those streets well enough after over a year living on them but even so the shadowy courts and alleyways of Dorset Street were enough to strike fear into any heart on a night like that.

'Tuppence for a suck,' a tall dark man in a cloth cap hissed to me from the shadows as I walked past the Britannia, all shut up now with the lamps turned off for the night and with a couple of tramps trying to sleep in the doorway.

'No chance,' I said with a laugh, relieved to still have enough money left for my bed that night. I remembered with a pang that Emily had made me promise not to stay out all night and quickened my step as I crossed the now nearly empty Commercial Street where the usually daytime bustle had been replaced by a few carts making deliveries to the market, some stray tarts still grumpily touting for business outside Christ Church and the usual stream of weary eyed men heading off to work. She'd gone all jittery and nervous since Poll turned up dead and wouldn't stay out much after night fall any more, convinced that there was a killer on the loose.

'Em!' I was just turning towards Thrawl Street when a voice called to me from in front of Christ Church. 'Over here.' I turned, half expecting to see Cora again but instead Annie stepped out of the gloom looking tired and in desperate need of a good wash.

I gave a sigh and strolled over to her, thinking wistfully of my bed at Wilmott's. Lousy and flea ridden though it may be, I still thought of it as mine and had even learned to take some small comfort from the almost companionable snores and sighs of the two other women who shared the room with me. 'Alright, Annie,' I said. 'I was just on my way home.'

'You stopped out late,' she said with a laugh. 'Marie full of gin and talking shit as usual then?'

I grinned. 'You could say that,' I said cordially as we walked up the road a bit towards the corner of Hanbury Street.

'Is that bloke of hers still living in cloud cuckoo land about where she gets her money and why McCarthy hasn't kicked them out yet?' she asked with a mean glint in her small eyes.

I stopped dead. 'Best not talk about that,' I said coldly. 'It's none of our business what Marie gets up to.'

Annie screwed up her face. 'Suit yourself,' she said glumly. 'Although I wouldn't want to be in your shoes nor hers neither when he finds out that she's been telling him fairy tales. He's a blethering idiot if he really believes that the likes of McCarthy lets them stay there out of the goodness of his heart.' She spat on the pavement. 'McCarthy's sort don't have a heart. He's like all men -

out for all he can get and a bit extra besides.'

I turned to go. 'Night, Annie.' I left her on the corner and walked away ignoring her muttered 'Stupid cow' directed at my departing back. Something made me turn back though when I got to the other corner outside the Ten Bells and I saw Annie, all smiles now of course, talking to the man in the cloth cap who had offered me tuppence for a suck. 'Good luck to her and him too, the poor bastard,' I thought to myself with a grin as I headed towards Thrawl Street and bed.

Something nagged at me though as I walked. Something about the man and the way he had loomed over Annie in the darkness, his hand gestures quick and impatient as he talked to her. I'd seen him before but where? No doubt I'd just passed him in the street or maybe he'd stayed at the same lodging house or perhaps he'd stood me a drink in the Britannia once upon a time, plenty of fellows had after all. I gave a shrug and tried to think about other things as I turned my feet towards Thrawl Street but the feeling of unease still lingered and in my mind's eye I saw flashes of wet cobbles, of a pale out-flung hand splattered with blood and a man, a dark man in a cloth cap kneeling over a…

'Bloody hell.'

I heard the Christ Church clock chime half past five as I turned back and raced up Commercial Street to the corner of Hanbury Street, where I had last seen Annie and the dark man together. There was no one there, of course there wasn't, and I couldn't see her further down the street either nor anywhere on Commercial Street.

I stumbled down Hanbury Street then, my heart thudding like crazy in my chest, as I looked from side to side, wondering where she had gone and not knowing what I planned to do should I find her. The dark and desolate road, lit only by a few street lamps that were too distantly placed from one another to help much and in fact made the street seem even darker in contrast, was empty with only a handful of upper storey windows lit up, probably due to market traders getting ready for the day ahead. I strained my ears as hard as I could as I walked stealthily along the pavement, listening out for any sound, however faint and feeble, that would lead me to Annie but all I could hear above my own echoing footsteps was the usual barking of dogs, crying children, the distant tooting of a train whistle and a couple of women having a blazing row in a house further down the road.

I was almost at Brick Lane when I remembered Cathy telling me once that the local whores liked to use the yard behind number twenty nine to do their business, mainly because it was completely enclosed but also because the front door was left permanently unlocked due to the constant coming and going of the lodgers who lived in the house. 'They don't half give you an earful if they catch you back there though,' she'd added ruefully, rubbing at the ghost of a bruise on her cheek bone.

With a feeling of almost unbearable dread, I turned back to number twenty nine, a nondescript and dilapidated three storey house that formed part of a short terrace, and then took a deep wobbly breath before nervously pushing the front door, which stood slightly ajar as if in grotesque invitation, open.

Holding my breath against the dank smell of damp walls and rancid cooking that assailed me and thinking that I was going to faint at any minute from fear, I walked on tiptoe through the small hallway and then down the gloomy narrow corridor that led straight out to the yard at the back of the house. 'Annie?' I whispered as I reached the door. My voice was dry and feeble with terror and the hairs on the back of my neck rose when for one awful moment I thought I could hear someone breathing somewhere in the dismal darkness behind me. 'Oh, Annie, say something if you're there.'

My heart hammering in my ears, I stood on the top of the steps that descended down the yard and peered out into the murky night, straining my eyes as I peered into the far corners of the yard which had a privy and a work shed huddled together at the end. At first I could see nothing and gave a sigh of relief. She must have taken him somewhere else further down the street and was probably already on her way back to Dorset Street with fourpence in her pocket and a smug smile on her face.

I turned to go and in that moment caught sight of something lying in the narrow recess between the steps that I stood on and the wooden fence that separated the yard from the one next door. Almost forgetting to be frightened, I peered down at what appeared to be a woman's boot lying abandoned on the ground, only to realise a split second later that the boot was one of two lying together and that both were attached to a pair of podgy legs that were drawn up from the ground with the knees hanging open as if in parody of intercourse.

The hammering in my head grew ever louder as my eyes followed the legs up to the body then staggered back against the door frame in shock and fright when I saw what he had done to her, hardly able to comprehend what I had just seen: the ripped and bleeding flesh where he had cut her open, the grey and blood smeared pile of what I thought must be her guts lying across her shoulder and the terrible gashes across her throat so deep that for one awful dizzying moment I thought that he had actually taken her head off.

And above it all was Annie's face, her eyes wide open and staring at nothing, her mouth slack and hanging open with the tongue just visible. There was a smear of fresh blood on her chin and there were new bruises on either side of her jaw where he must have grabbed her face as he slashed her throat.

My legs trembled so hard that I could barely stay upright and I was about to give myself over to the darkness and the pounding in my head that threatened to overwhelm me when there was a whisper of something moving behind my back and a voice, a man's voice that I had heard just once before and hoped never to hear again. 'Remember me, Emma?'

Chapter Twelve
Alice, September 1888

It was a beautiful morning, bright and fine and clear and I could feel my spirits lifting with every bump of the road as my father's carriage bowled along busy Shoreditch High Street on its way to Whitechapel. I'd been going to the Whitechapel Women's Mission on Lamb Street for over a fortnight now and had actually started looking forward to my days spent working alongside Miss Lawler. Certainly coming home exhausted but happy and full of purpose every evening was a marked and very pleasing contrast to what I now saw with some shame was a previously very indolent and directionless life.

I looked out of the window as we turned on to Commercial Street, enjoying the familiar sight of children running along the pavements and local women drinking together outside the pubs, cackling over their pint glasses as they exchanged the morning's gossip. Two weeks working in Whitechapel had shown me that there wasn't really any point wasting my energy being shocked by the way people lived there, but that I should instead simply embrace them for the honest truth of what they were and focus on the positives about life in the East End such as the close knit relationships that people forged for themselves in those desolate, ramshackle streets and their seemingly irrepressible sense of humour.

As we passed the Commercial Street police station, I looked up as always at the window with the red geraniums, hoping to catch a glimpse of the redheaded girl who had cheered me up so much the first time I had gone there but as usual there was no sign of her and the window was tightly shut despite the heat of the day. The police station looked busier than usual though with a large crowd, mostly of women, gathered around the great double doors, all shouting and shaking their fists, that peculiarly impotent gesture so beloved of the English.

We pulled up in Lamb Street shortly afterwards and I was ready with a smile and a sixpence for the ragged children outside the Mission house as I got down from the carriage. They were all wearing socks and sturdy boots now thanks to my allowance that month and it no longer broke my heart quite so much to look at them. 'Lovely day, isn't it?' I said to the eldest boy, the one who liked horses, as I handed him sixpence. 'Be sure to keep it hidden and spend it only on food for you and the little ones, Charlie.'

He grinned, showing a few missing teeth. 'Course I will, Miss. Thanks very much, Miss.' He made a funny little bow then secreted the coin deep within his threadbare shirt. 'Have you heard about the murder, Miss? Some tart got her head almost chopped off and puddings cut out on Hanbury Street last night.'

'How horrible!' I wasn't entirely sure that I understood what Charlie had said, especially given his apparent lack of love for the letter 'h' but I'd comprehended enough to know that yet another unfortunate woman had come to a deeply unpleasant end only a few yards away from where we stood. 'Make sure you keep yourself safe, won't you?'

'Ooh, I will, Miss!' he said cheerfully over his shoulder before shepherding the other children away. 'Reckon he's only after the ladies like you though not nippers like us.'

I smiled and hopped happily up the steps, only to be greeted at the door by Mrs Lightfoot, who took me by the hand and drew me quickly and firmly into the house. I noticed that she stuck her head out and looked left and right before closing the front door behind us. 'Everything is in a terrible uproar today,' she said with a sigh as my ears detected the sound of exaggeratedly loud weeping and shouting coming from upstairs. 'There's been another one of these awful murders, this time not too far away on Hanbury Street and it's upset our girls.'

I dropped my bonnet and shawl carelessly on a chair and started to remove my lilac kid leather gloves. 'Charlie told me all about it,' I said. 'He said something about her 'puddings' being cut out.' I grimaced at the recollection.

Mrs Lightfoot went a little pale. 'The things those children hear,' she said with a sad shake of her head. 'He's right though, it seems that the lady had her throat cut and was then disembowelled.' This last said in a shocked whisper as if saying it aloud would bring ruination on us all.

'Out on the street?' I said, aghast.

She shook her head. 'No, well, not exactly. It all happened in the backyard of one of the houses. Apparently it's commonly used by the local working girls as a quiet place to take their clients.' She motioned to the gloves that I still held crushed in my hand. 'You'll ruin those gloves if you don't put them down,' she said gently, taking them from me and placing them carefully on top of my raspberry pink silk bonnet and shawl. 'Try not to dwell on it, my dear. Life must go on.'

I followed her up the creaking wooden stairs to the schoolroom, where Miss Lawler, dressed in her favoured mannish white linen shirt tucked into a lightly bustled skirt of black cotton, was doing her best to maintain order amidst all the noise and upset. Some of the girls were hugging each other and crying while others were sitting on their desks, eyes round with horror as they swapped whatever gruesome titbits they had gleaned about the murders. This was the third woman to have been killed in the last two months and what had at first seemed like a couple of isolated incidents was now very much beginning to look connected. No wonder the women of the area were terrified and, it had to be said, not a little excited.

'Miss Redmayne!' Miss Lawler, strode between the desks to me and took my hands in hers with her usual strong grip. 'You braved the dangerous streets of Whitechapel to visit us then?' she said with a satirical gleam in her dark eyes.

I laughed. 'I'm afraid that I have only just found out what happened here last night,' I said, a trifle ruefully. 'I would still have come anyway though.'

'As I am sure will many others,' Miss Lawler said, taking my arm and leading me from the room. 'Nothing quite like a murder to bring the philanthropic ladies to an area in droves. I expect that we'll be inundated with offers to help by the end of the day.'

She closed the door firmly on all the noise and took me across the landing to the small room where Mr Mercier usually met with the women who needed his help. 'Oh no...' I started to say as she put her hand on the handle then blushed and looked away.

116

'Oh no?' Miss Lawler raised one thin dark eyebrow. 'Still at odds with our Mr Mercier then?'

I grinned, not a little shamefacedly. 'You could say that,' I said. 'I don't think he likes me very much.' If I'd expected to completely confound Mr Mercier by returning to the Mission again after my first visit, I had soon been proved sorely wrong when he'd greeted my triumphant re-appearance with nothing more than a shrug of his broad shoulders. And if I had thought to mollify him by producing a wooden box filled to the brim with several dozen bars of the finest French rose soap to be distributed among the girls of the Mission, I was disappointed there too.

Miss Lawler chuckled. 'Oh, he'll come around in time,' she said with a lop sided smile. 'He moves in rather more radical circles than you and me and it's given him all sorts of peculiar notions.' She gave a shrug.

'He hates me because I am rich, you mean?' I said, feeling my anger rising. 'I can hardly be blamed for that!'

She smiled and put her hand on my arm. 'Of course he doesn't hate you,' she said, looking amused and, for a second, really quite mischievous. 'Quite the reverse, I should think.'

I stared at her in confusion but before I could say anything more, she put her hand back on the handle. 'Anyway, shall we go in? There's someone I want you to meet - one of our girls from several months ago who didn't last very long but whom I try to help whenever I can. I've been trying to persuade her to come back to us but, well, you know how it can be.' She'd told me several times that some of the young women they reached out to were highly resistant to giving up the easy camaraderie of street life even if it meant creating a more secure and prosperous life for themselves. 'I hadn't actually seen her for quite a long time until she turned up on the doorstep this morning, white as a sheet and completely scared out of her wits.'

'The poor girl,' I said, my anger sliding away to replaced with a strangely empty feeling. 'Is it to do with this ghastly murder?'

Miss Lawler nodded. 'Or at least, I think it might well be. They all know each other around here so it may be that she simply knew the victim or perhaps it's something more serious than that.' She smiled and shrugged. 'Or maybe it's all down to something completely different. Who can tell?' She turned the handle. 'I just thought that as you are so good at speaking to the girls here then perhaps she might talk to you about what is troubling her.' She gently pushed the door open and we stepped into the room.

The chintz blinds had been pulled up so that sunlight streamed in, creating bright pools on the floor and highlighting the shimmering motes of dust that floated slowly through the air. Mr Mercier was leaning against the window when we entered and turned with a smile, which became a frown when he saw me standing at Miss Lawler's elbow. 'I don't see what use this will be,' he said, his tone terse and not for the first time I wondered what precisely it was that he saw when he looked at me. Some spoiled rich girl no doubt, frolicking in the slums of Whitechapel in the manner of Marie Antoinette with her sheep. Playing at being poor in the full knowledge that I would get to go home every night to my own comfortable, clean bed and luxuries that were virtually unheard of on these dismal streets.

I lifted my chin defiantly. 'There's no harm in trying,' I said briskly, eyeing him with as much contempt as I could muster. How dare he make me feel small and useless. How dare he judge me because of things that I couldn't help and without making the slightest attempt to get to know me. I'd show him. I turned my attention to the small figure that lay crumpled on the threadbare blue velvet sofa, which at first I took to be a child but then realised was actually a girl not much younger than myself with saffron bleached blonde hair, enormous grey eyes set in a pale thin face and dressed in a gown of flounced pink cotton that had long since seen better days.

'This is Emma,' Miss Lawler said kindly, giving the girl a reassuring smile that she timidly returned. 'Like I said, she came to us early this morning. It's fortunate that I was unable to sleep and already downstairs making myself a cup of cocoa or I might not have heard her knocking on the front door.'

Emma spoke then in a slightly nasal accent that sounded more rustic than the Cockney I was speedily getting used to. 'I'm ever so sorry, Miss,' she said, wringing the thin fabric of her skirt between her fingers. 'I didn't want to wake you.'

Miss Lawler sat beside her on the sofa and took her hands in hers. 'It's quite alright, Emma,' she said with a smile. 'I have told you often enough that the doors here are always open to you should you need help.' She looked quickly at Mr Mercier but he gave a shake of his head. 'I should like to know what it was that brought you to us though.' Her voice became gentle. 'I am sure you have heard by now that there was a murder in Hanbury Street last night. Was it perhaps connected to that? Did you know the woman who was killed?'

Emma drew back then and pulled her hands away. 'I don't want to talk about her,' she said in a low voice, looking utterly terrified. 'Begging your pardon, Miss, as you've always been so kind to me but please don't make me tell you about it.'

Miss Lawler sighed then reluctantly nodded her head. 'Then I shall say no more,' she said. 'For now.' She beckoned me over and Emma shot me a quick curious look. 'Have you met our latest assistant, Miss Redmayne?' she said.

If Emma looked terrified before, she was petrified now and actually recoiled away from me with a look of abject horror and something else that may well have been guilt. 'Redmayne?' she said, her voice hoarse. 'Did you say Redmayne?'

I smiled in what I hoped was a reassuring way. 'Yes, that's right,' I said, not a little alarmed by her reaction to my name and desperately trying to think of what might have caused it. 'Perhaps you have heard of my father?'

'I've never heard of no Redmayne,' she said abruptly before dragging herself off the sofa and hurrying to the door, roughly shouldering away Miss Lawler's attempt to catch her in her arms. 'I have to be off now, Miss,' she said, yanking the door open. 'I can't hang about here drinking tea with you stuck up lot when I need to make some money for my doss.'

I immediately felt in my reticule for a sixpence which I held out to her, almost apologetically. 'Here, have this,' I said.

The girl paused for a moment in the doorway and stared first at the coin in my hand then, more searchingly as if looking for a resemblance to someone, at my face, the skin between her eyebrows creasing into a frown. 'I can't take your money, Miss,' she said at last, almost angrily before whirling around and running as fast as she could down the stairs.

I remained frozen to the spot and only felt able to turn back to the others when we heard the front door slam shut behind the fleeing girl. 'I have no idea what just happened,' I said, feeling a bit frightened and also more than a little mortified to realise that my cheeks were red and hot with embarrassment as they both stared at me.

'Oh dear,' said Miss Lawler with a nervous laugh, not quite meeting my eyes. 'I do hope that isn't the last that we see of her.'

Mr Mercier was more forthright though and immediately strode out of the room and went to the top of the stairs as if deliberating going after Emma, before giving a tiny shrug and coming back again. 'She obviously recognised your name from somewhere,' he said to me, almost accusingly.

'Perhaps she has seen a print of one of Miss Redmayne's father's paintings?' Miss Lawler intervened brightly. 'They're quite popular, aren't they?'

'Yes, alas,' I said with a sigh. Much to my despair, prints of his more mawkish history paintings proliferated on the heavily patterned walls of middle class London so that I was forced to admire them wherever I went. This was a source of much annoyance to me as my own tastes tended more towards the Impressionists or, more recently, the works of Mr Whistler.

Mr Mercier gave an impatient grunt. 'Bad art though they may be, that doesn't explain why Emma ran out of here in apparent terror at the mere mention of Miss Redmayne's name.' He folded his arms and looked at me challengingly. 'Can you not think why that might be?' he said.

I shook my head, swallowing down my irritation that he should describe my father's paintings as 'bad art'. It was one thing for me to not admire his work but quite another for some jumped up and entirely obnoxious little lawyer to do so. 'I have no idea,' I said, my brain finally waking up from the shock and beginning to whirl with possibilities. 'I can only assume that it is a case of mistaken identity.' Or that she had heard my name from someone else. My heart gave a sudden leap of excitement. Could this be the link that I had been waiting for? I'd hardly dared to question any of the girls at the Mission house about Beatrice's whereabouts, thinking it best to build their trust first before I started asking about her.

'That must be it,' Miss Lawler said in her brisk way. 'She was already so rattled that she must have got you mixed up with someone else.' She gave a frown and went to the window, which

120

overlooked the street. 'I do hope that she comes back. The poor child could do so much better for herself than she does.'

'Couldn't they all?' said Mr Mercier wryly, settling himself back down behind his desk.

She sighed and gave a little shrug. 'That is true but I see a potential for something in Emma. I do wish that she would let us help her.' She gave a nod to Mr Mercier and shepherded me from the room. 'I wouldn't take it personally,' she said to me with a concerned look. 'She's obviously had a huge shock this morning and I think that it must have overset her a little. If anyone is to blame it is me for having taken a stranger in to speak to her.' She gave me a quick hug. 'Come, let me make you a cup of tea. You look like you could do with it.'

I managed to make myself smile. 'It is really of no matter,' I said, following her downstairs to the hall. 'I am sure it can't have been anything to do with me.' I thought of the girl's panicked expression, the fear in her eyes, the way she had looked at me when I offered her money and became more convinced than ever that this Emma knew something about my sister's whereabouts and that furthermore, whatever she knew wasn't very good. 'Where does she usually live?' I asked as casually as I could as we crossed the hall to the kitchen stairs. 'Does she live on the streets?'

Miss Lawler shook her head. 'No, she lives in a common lodging house on Thrawl Street, I believe. She told me this morning that she used to share a room with one of the women who was murdered last month, Polly Nichols, I think her name was. Poor child.' She settled me at the large scrubbed wooden table in the centre of the kitchen then busied herself with a large black iron kettle. 'That's why I thought she might have known last night's victim as well. These women all tend to know each other, you see. It keeps them safe, I suppose, if they all know each other's business.' She laid out two mismatched china cups. 'No saucers, I'm afraid,' she said with a laugh. 'They don't last very long here for some reason.'

'Obviously not safe enough,' I said a little dourly, remembering Charlie's gleeful 'some tart got her puddings cut out'.

Miss Lawler gave me a look. 'Obviously,' she agreed before turning away to wrench open a large blue and white striped tin biscuit barrel. 'The girls baked these yesterday and they're very good.' She put some thin ginger biscuits on a chipped jade green plate and put it in front of me. 'It breaks my heart to see bright young women like Emma living the way they do, sleeping rough and never knowing where their next meal is going to come from. It's so unnecessary.' She sighed and sat down opposite me. 'So cruel.'

'Is she a…' I thought of my father's disapproval of what I was trying to say and blushed, unable to go on.

'A prostitute?' Miss Lawler grinned at me then put her head to one side in a curiously bird like gesture. 'Yes, I think she was, once upon a time but not any more. Nowadays she lives by her wits as you and I might call it.'

'You mean that she is a thief?' I said with a smile, taking a biscuit.

Miss Lawler laughed, a great rich sound that echoed in the corners of the kitchen. 'Yes, that is precisely what I mean.' She sighed and got up again as the kettle began to boil on the stove. 'We really must stop speaking in euphemisms when it comes to the women of Whitechapel. There's no shame really in what any of them do to survive.'

I bit into my biscuit, which was delicious just as she had said. 'I'm sure that Mrs Lightfoot wouldn't agree with that,' I said mischievously.

'Not one little bit,' Miss Lawler agreed cheerfully, toasting me with the kettle.

Chapter Thirteen

I spent the rest of the morning helping Miss Lawler with the lessons in the school room, hiding my impatience to set out in pursuit of the mysterious Emma beneath my usual patient smile as I listened to the girls reading aloud from improving books and corrected their handwriting. I had formed my plan while demurely sipping tea in the kitchen and listening to Miss Lawler talk about her plans to buy the adjoining house and expand the Whitechapel Women's Mission into an actual school and if I initially quailed at the thought of taking to the streets of Whitechapel on a doubtless hopeless hunt for a lapsed prostitute and known thief, I hastily suppressed such qualms by reminding myself why it was exactly that I had come there in the first place.

Beatrice. I thought of her now as I watched a trio of girls bend their heads over their books, their tongues sticking out of the corners of their mouths as they laboriously copied out a poem by Christina Rossetti. 'In a far foreign land, upon the wave edged sand, some friends gaze wistfully across the glittering sea. 'If we could clasp our sister,' three say, 'now we have missed her!' 'If we could kiss our daughter!' Two sigh across the water.' Oh Bea.

I waited until they had trooped noisily downstairs for their midday meal before telling Mrs Lightfoot that I wanted to go for a short walk and would be back soon. Luckily she was too busy frowning over a pile of tradesman's bills to pay much attention to me and merely waved me away with a vague smile. If she'd been less busy then my leaving the premises would perhaps have been more fraught with difficulty - she had, after all, promised my Aunt Minerva to look after me and Whitechapel, even if the Mission was an oasis of well bred calm in the midst of chaos, was hardly the sort of area where young ladies were encouraged to walk out alone. However, the deed was done and, terrified that she would realise her error and call me back, I snatched up my bonnet and shawl and hastened out into the bright sunshine.

I closed the green door behind me and stood for a moment at the top of the steps, shielding my eyes with my hand as I gathered my bearings and, almost breathless with mingled excitement and trepidation, decided where to go first. To my left there lay the dark and intimidating warren of streets around Spital Square while on my right there was the noise and bustle of Commercial Street with Christ Church looming white and angular over the rooftops. Wishing with a great deal of regret that I had had the foresight to ask someone where Thrawl Street actually was, I took a deep breath and stepped down onto the pavement then walked quickly away.

I'd hoped that Charlie or one of his small acolytes might be hanging about and able to guide me for the price of a few pence to Emma's lodging house but they'd all vanished, probably in search of food and odd jobs in Spitalfields Market, which seethed with small children running about and getting under the feet of the stallholders, who stood hands on hips, confident and loud in front of their wares. They should all have been in school really and as I risked my neck wending my way between the thick Commercial Street traffic, I wondered how much it would cost to send them to one of the local board schools. If they would even go, which was dubious as like the women Mrs Lawler had described to me, plenty of the children here were equally resistant to giving up their free and easy life on the streets for a more respectable existence. I had a feeling that Charlie might be different though, especially if I enticed him with the prospect of being able to work with his beloved horses one day if he would only learn his letters.

Still lost in thought I looked up to see that I was standing at the top of Hanbury Street, the scene of last night's murder and where even now a large crowd was gathered outside one of the drab nondescript houses that lined the left hand of the street. The body would have been taken away many hours before, especially on such a warm day, but a few unhappy looking young policemen remained outside the battered front door, occasionally shoving back the crowd as it threatened to swamp them and storm inside in search of gory trophies.

'We want to see the body!' someone, a woman, called and there was much laughter. I smiled myself even though the sight of them all straining against the policemen and buzzing with excitement at the merest scent of death made me feel a bit sick.

I turned away and carried on down Commercial Street, attracting a few curious looks but mostly left alone as I went past the Ten Bells on the corner of Church Street and then loitered, suddenly indecisive, for a moment outside Christ Church, which looked depressingly grubby and ill tended and not nearly so impressively majestic close up. I really had no idea which way to go now and again shielded my eyes with my hand as I looked back up Commercial Street towards Lamb Street, wondering if perhaps I should give up and try again some other day when I was better prepared.

'Can I help you, Miss?' I looked round to see a grubby faced woman who could have been aged anywhere between twenty and forty hopping from foot to foot as she tried to get my attention. She had long greasy dark hair that she hadn't even attempted to pin up but instead allowed to trail over her shoulders and down her back and her feet beneath her tattered grey green cotton dress were bare and caked with mud from the streets.

I hesitated then gave a nod, after all what had I to lose? 'I'm looking for Thrawl Street,' I said. 'There's a girl there called Emma that I must speak to at once.'

She grinned, revealing huge gaps in her teeth. 'I know Emma,' she said in a strong Welsh accent, holding out a grimy hand. 'You give me fourpence and I'll take you straight there so I will.' Seeing my hesitation, she leaned in close, so close that I could smell the dank aroma of stale beer, sweat and urine that rose from her dress and added: 'You can trust me. I know it ain't safe round here for the likes of you, but you stay close to me and I'll see you there in one piece.'

I gave a nervous nod. 'Very well then,' I said, thinking that I was making a big mistake but not knowing what else to do. 'I will give you the money once you have taken me to Emma's lodgings.'

She grinned again, that awful toothless leer. 'Fair enough, Miss.' She turned and led me down a street that branched off from Commercial Street, beckoning for me to follow. 'She's dossing down here. I just seen her.' When I didn't immediately go after her, she gave an impatient snort and spat on to the pavement.

'Come on then! What you waiting for?'

I sighed and followed her down the road, which was short and lined with grey miserable looking houses with broken window panes and straggling rags hanging in the place of curtains on most of them. A few grim faced women stood with folded arms on the worn down doorsteps, their grimy faces set in furious glares as they yelled at the dozen or so ragged children playing with a ball and a couple of wildly barking and slathering dogs in the middle of the road. Some of them flicked contemptuous looks over at me as I went past and nudged each other but no one tried to approach me, much to my relief. It reminded me a little of some books I had read long ago about an explorer who had travelled down the Nile and encountered several African tribes in the process. He too had described the way the native people kept their distance, according him just the odd glance but never deigning to actually attempt to communicate with him. He had also written at length about how unspeakably lonely and out of place he had felt, as if he had been transported to a different world where he, who had considered himself so civilised when he first began his journey, had rapidly begun to feel himself the alien in their midst, the one set apart from his fellow man, the outcast.

'It's a bit rough down here,' my companion said with a sly smile, breaking into my thoughts. 'I wouldn't come down here at night, if I were you. There's all sorts out on these streets.'

'Like whoever killed that woman on Hanbury Street,' I said, keen to show my knowledge, however sparse, of local events.

She gave an indifferent shrug. 'Oh, her,' she said dismissively, leading me off the street and down another that was equally as dreary. 'She was a miserable old bitch.'

We silently turned off the street and onto another, just as horrible as the last two, only this one was almost completely deserted but for a couple of men, who sat on their doorsteps with their legs stretched out in front of them, both carving or whittling pieces of wood into pegs, which they slung into tatty baskets beside them when they were finished. We stopped beside the entrance to a dark alleyway. 'She's down there,' the woman said, holding her hand out for the money. 'I did as you asked now pay up.'

I stared at her, not really wanting to go down the alleyway.

'Aren't you going with me?' I said. 'I said I would pay you when you took me to Emma.'

'And so I have,' the woman snarled. 'She's down there.' She jerked her head at the alleyway. 'Off you trot.'

'I think not.' I looked over at the men but their eyes were cast firmly down at their work, almost as if they were deliberately trying not to look at us, which would be typical, I supposed, for these streets. See no evil, hear no evil and no evil shall come to you. 'Why should I believe you?'

She heaved a great sigh, as if I was the one being completely unreasonable. 'Who else are you going to believe? Now look here, you asked me where Emma was to be found and I did as you asked and now you don't want to see her? Is that it?' She pointed down the alleyway. 'Honest to God, Miss, she's staying down there.'

I deliberated for a moment, my gut instinct was that she was lying through her scant remaining teeth while my head was telling me that I really had no choice here but to go down the alleyway because really, what else could I do? I had no idea where I was, there was no one nearby willing to help me and above all there was a chance, however slender, that she was actually telling the truth in which case running away now might mean another step back in my search for Beatrice. I took a deep breath. 'You come too,' I said, rummaging in my reticule for her money. 'I won't pay you otherwise.'

She gave a shrug, making that horrible dank smell rise up again towards me. 'Suit yourself,' she said gracelessly before sauntering into the gloom of the alleyway. 'You coming then, your Majesty?'

What else could I do but raise my skirts slightly above my ankles to prevent them trailing in the filth, both animal and human, that I could see festering on the cobbled floor of the alley, then take a deep breath and follow her in, immediately wishing that I hadn't as soon as the damp and stench of old urine and worse rose up to hit me about the nostrils. 'Good God.' I almost dropped my skirt in my haste to get inside my reticule to find a handkerchief to hold over my nose.

My guide sniggered. 'You'll get used to it,' she said in what I thought was a rather ominous way. 'It doesn't smell so bad after a while.' Probably not when you yourself smell equally as horrible, but of course I did not dare say so.

The alley was mercifully short and it didn't take too long before we reached the small court that lay at the far end. 'Here you are. It's over there.' The woman paused at the end of the alley and pointed across the way to a broken door covered in blistering, peeling grey paint and mildew. 'It's not much but it's home.'

Feeling somewhat relieved, I stepped into the court, which was open to the sky and lit by the few stray rays of sunlight that had managed to straggle down between the tall dark buildings that glowered overhead. In the near distance I could hear a train, dogs barking and, from somewhere near at hand, a woman laughing and singing an old folk song while the air was heavy with the smell of smoke and fried fish that floated down from a slightly ajar window overhead. 'Is it this door here?' I said, turning back slightly just as there came a sudden whoosh of air that made the hairs on the back of my neck rise up and every muscle in my body tense as if about to take flight. I should have known what was coming. Oh heaven help me, I did know.

The blow to the back of my head felled me at once and I crumpled on to the ground, the sunlight dancing like stars in front of my eyes as I tried to lift myself up from the foul and muddy ground. 'Oh no you don't.' I closed my eyes and, my head rolling with sickness and pain, braced myself for the next direct hit which I knew would knock me unconscious and leave me at her mercy.

Instead there came a sound of scuffling from somewhere behind me and with a groan, I rolled over, my heavy skirts caught frustratingly around my legs, in order to see what was happening. The stars were fading now and the sickness retreating so that with a bit of effort I was able to screw up my eyes and make out the surprising sight of Mr Mercier making brisk work of seeing off the woman who had led me to this miserable place. At some point she must have been joined by an accomplice as he was now holding by the throat and shaking a scrawny man in a filthy shirt and red waistcoat, a splash of colour against the smoke blackened walls of the alleyway.

'Are you alright, Miss?' I turned my head towards this new, softer female voice, which turned out to be a grave mistake as the stars immediately returned and everything threatened to turn

128

dark once more.

'Is she conscious?' This was Mr Mercier's voice and I felt rather than heard him come closer until he was kneeling beside me and lightly resting his cool fingers against the pulse in my wrist. 'What a pity that we could not have arrived sooner.'

The stars danced away again and I looked up at the pale, anxious face of a young girl with pretty grey green eyes. 'How's your head?' she asked with a rueful smile that brought the dimples into her cheeks. 'She gave you quite a whack but you should be right as rain soon enough.' Her long red hair fell forward over her shoulders as she leaned down to feel my forehead with the back of her hand.

Red hair. Even in my feeble and befuddled state I knew that I had seen her before and when I closed my eyes I saw her luminous and gleaming against the star spangled gloom, her hair, decorated with amber and crimson geraniums, hanging down around her thin face as she laughed and beckoned to me from within the winding, fetid darkness of an alleyway that seemed to go on forever.

I stared up at her, willing her to understand, to acknowledge the fact that it was she who had brought me here in the first place and that it was all her fault - the locket, the Mission, the alleyway, everything. It was all because of her. 'I know you,' I said with an effort as the stars began to spin more wildly inside my head and Mr Mercier tried to shush me into silence. 'From Whitechapel.' And everything went dark.

Chapter Fourteen

By the time I regained consciousness the girl had vanished and instead the first thing I saw was Mr Mercier who had somehow managed to lift me up off the dirty ground and carry me to the arguably more salubrious surroundings of a nearby public house, where I awoke on a faded red faux velvet covered bench with a pounding headache and a terrible thirst. Someone, presumably Mr Mercier, had balled up a jacket and thrust it roughly beneath my head to act as a pillow, while someone else, presumably not Mr Mercier but more probably the cheerful blonde landlady who upon seeing I had awakened now hovered solicitously over my head, had pulled my skirts down neatly over my ankles to preserve whatever scant modesty remained to me after I had been deposited unceremoniously and completely unconscious onto her premises.

'Well, thank the Lord for that,' she said with a look of satisfaction as I attempted a polite smile then lifted my head to take a curious look around. 'I thought you was a goner for sure no matter what the quack had to say on the matter!' She turned to mischievously nudge a small slight man with a shock of greying hair and spectacles balanced rather perilously on the end of his large nose. 'Saving your presence, Doctor Llewellyn, I'm sure.'

The doctor gave a good humoured chuckle then leaned over to rest his hand lightly against my forehead. 'Now, now, Mrs Ferrar, there was never any danger of that as well you know,' he said over his shoulder in a rich Welsh accent. 'I told you that this young lady would be right as rain in next to no time.' He smiled reassuringly at me as Mrs Ferrar took herself off to deal with some customers who were standing waiting at the polished dark wood bar. 'You took quite a bump on the head, Miss Redmayne but there was no serious damage done.' He lifted my eyelids, first one then the other and looked into my eyes before giving a small nod of satisfaction. 'I was worried that you might be concussed when I was first called here but I believe that you fainted rather than collapsed as a result of injury.'

I smiled at him, liking his brisk but friendly manner enormously. 'Well, that's a relief,' I said, shocked by how dry and rusty my voice sounded. I lifted my hand gingerly to the back of my head and winced when my fingers connected with a huge bump. 'It feels as big as another head,' I said with a laugh. 'Oh dear.'

The doctor grinned. 'Oh, it's the merest trifle,' he said, straightening and looking around for his doctor's bag. 'Head bumps always feel much more enormous than they actually are when you can feel but not see them.' He turned to Mr Mercier and the two men shook hands. 'You've had more than your fair share of blows to the head, Henry so I know that I can rely on you to make sure the patient gets home in one piece.'

Mr Mercier grinned. 'You know me too well,' he said with a laugh, looking more friendly and natural than I had ever seen him, which gave me a small pang of something strange and rather unwelcome. Regret? Wistfulness? Surely not.

Doctor Llewellyn looked for a moment as if he might actually be about to ruffle Mr Mercier's tawny hair but instead he merely gave his hand another brisk shake, patted me on the shoulder and sauntered off, jamming his hat on to his head as he went.

'I liked him,' I said with a smile, struggling to sit upright and wishing that someone would bring me a drink. 'His bedside manner is much more friendly than that of my own doctor.'

Mr Mercier looked at me and to my disappointment I could see the shutters come down, wiping away his easy, good natured smile and draining the cheerfulness out of his eyes. 'I hope that you don't mind me sending for Doctor Llewellyn rather than one of the fancy Harley Street doctors that you are no doubt used to, Miss Redmayne,' he said flatly, his voice dripping with cold formality.

I sighed, clearly he wasn't going to make this easy for me. 'Not at all, Mr Mercier. I hope that you will allow me to recompense you for any charges he may have brought.' I looked about in some panic for my reticule and eventually located it underneath my skirts.

Mr Mercier shrugged. 'The doctor and I are old friends so he made no charge.'

'Nevertheless…' I began but he cut me off with an impatient gesture of his hand.

'I don't want your money, Miss Redmayne,' he said in a low voice that vibrated with something that sounded suspiciously like anger. 'I don't even want your gratitude.'

I met his eyes, determined not to be cowed by him. 'So what do you want, Mr Mercier?' I said, ruthlessly ignoring the dull ache of my head and scrambling to sit up even straighter even though actually I just wanted to lie down and sleep.

'What do I want?' He glared at me. 'I don't want anything from you.'

To my horror, I felt tears prick the corners of my eyes and knew that I had to get out of the hot, over crowded pub as quickly as possible before he realised that he had made me cry and my pathetic, shameful weakness was exposed once and for all. 'I'm sure that I don't know what I could have possibly done to make you so angry with me,' I muttered as I slid down from the bench then held on to the table edge for support as a wave of dizziness threatened to overcome me and send me back into the darkness again. 'Clearly you have decided to dislike me no matter what I do.' I couldn't look at him, I was too angry and I brushed his hands angrily away as he reached out to steady me. 'Good day to you, Mr Mercier.'

I turned and staggered from the pub, ignoring Mrs Ferrar's squawks of concern from behind the bar and the annoyed mutterings of the customers that I brushed past in my haste to get away. 'Miss Redmayne!' I heard Mr Mercier call out to me but the sound of his voice only made me walk faster until I was almost running by the time I had shoved the doors open and made it out onto the street, where I was immediately blinded by the bright sunlight. 'Miss Redmayne.' Unhampered by a headache and apparently unaffected by the contrast between the gloom of the public house and the brightness of daylight, he made it outside almost at the same time as I did and now stood before me with a worried frown between his storm grey eyes.

I deliberately looked away from him and drew myself up to

my full height, which was still a few inches shorter than his shoulder but made me feel better nonetheless. 'I have no need of your assistance, Mr Mercier,' I said with all the hauteur that I could summon and wishing that my aunt could hear me now. How she would have applauded to hear me finally put him firmly in his place. 'Clearly my presence here in Whitechapel is displeasing to you and I would hate to prolong the unpleasantness for any longer than I have to.' I should have rested more for even as I spoke, I could feel myself sagging back against the wall, almost fainting again.

He took hold of my forearms then and held me straight and when I looked up at him again I saw that his generous lips were twisted into a reluctant smile. 'You look like you could really do with a drink,' he said.

My reputation, if I had any remaining to me after that afternoon's events, would barely survive if word ever got out that I had accompanied a man into a public house but I found that I didn't care one jot and there was barely any hesitation before I gave a rueful nod of my head and followed him back inside.

Mr Mercier grinned down at me. 'I don't think there's much chance of any of your high society friends spotting you in here with me,' he said, almost as if he had read my mind or, more likely, seen the momentary worry about my tattered reputation flash into my eyes. 'And there's even less chance that any of the denizens of the Princess Alice will find their way to Mayfair to tell the tale.'

I was confused for a moment, thinking that he meant to mock me again, but then belatedly remembered that I had been unconscious when he brought me there and looked up at the pub sign that swung overhead, which had a crude portrait of the Queen's daughter Alice overlaid with a flamboyant 'Princess Alice' rendered in now flaking but surely once resplendent green and gold paint.

Mrs Ferrar gave a sigh of relief when she saw me somewhat sheepishly come back inside behind Mr Mercier. 'You look like you need some more rest, Miss,' she said, vigorously polishing some glasses with a none too clean cloth. 'Let our kind Mr Mercier here take care of you for a bit before you start gallivanting about again.'

He turned to me with an apologetic smile. 'I've lived in Spitalfields all my life and my family have been here since they fled to the area from France in the seventeenth century,' he said with a shrug. 'Everyone here knows me - which can be both a blessing and a curse.' He settled me back down onto the bench, even meticulously covering my ankles with my skirts until I slapped his hands away. 'I'm afraid I don't know what there is for a young lady to drink in here,' he said, a little abashed.

I smiled at him. 'I'll have a brandy if such a thing is to be had,' I said, trying not to think about the dirty cloth that Mrs Ferrar was using to polish the glasses. 'Failing that, I will have whatever you think best.' It was galling of course to defer to his judgement in such a way, but the events in the alleyway had rattled me completely and left me feeling even more than ever like a stranger in their midst. I felt adrift and badly in need of a guide and if Mr Mercier was the only one to hand then so be it.

He nodded and went off to the bar, returning a few moments later with a pair of large brandies, one of which he placed in front of me. 'I'm sure it's not as fine as the sort of thing you have been used to...'

'Oh shush,' I said, taking a large sip of brandy, which turned out to be not nearly so bad as he was implying. I took another sip to make sure then fixed him with what I hoped was a steely look worthy of Aunt Minerva herself. 'You really have the most ridiculous chip on your shoulder, Mr Mercier.'

He paused and looked at me for a moment over the top of his glass before putting it back on the table. 'Of course I have,' he said. 'Wouldn't you have one too if you were forced every day to see the injustice that this city is rife with?'

'You are not poor, Mr Mercier,' I pointed out.

He laughed then, not pleasantly. 'Does one have to be poor to notice or care about the suffering that the lower classes endure in this allegedly great metropolis of ours?' He picked up his glass again and took a large swig. 'Come now, Miss Redmayne, and here I was thinking you had deigned to come amongst us in the guise of a philanthropic lady.'

'You don't know me at all,' I said quietly, watching my brandy swill around the glass to avoid meeting his eyes. 'You don't know why I came here.'

He looked at me with a frown. 'You're right,' he said after a short pause. 'I don't. I could hazard a guess though.'

I gave a shrug and took another sip of my brandy. My headache had gone and I was beginning to feel oddly exhilarated by our conversation. 'You'd be wrong,' I said, looking at him.

'Would I?' He leaned back in his chair, looking so thoroughly pleased with himself that I had to fight a sudden urge to lean across and box his ears. 'So you're not really interested in helping the poor of the area?'

'Well yes but…'

'So there's more to it?' He drained his glass then slammed it down on the table. 'Then I'm standing by my original assessment that you are just another bored little rich princess trying to catch the eye of some benevolent peer or trying her desperate best to outrage her parents.'

'Princess Alice,' I said with a rueful little shake of my head. 'Oh now you really are talking nonsense.'

Mr Mercier raised one dark eyebrow. 'Am I?' He leaned forward, resting his elbows carelessly in a slick of spilled brandy. 'Surprise me.'

I looked at him and caught my breath as I considered telling him everything, thinking that obnoxious as he undoubtedly was, he would at least prove a worthy ally if I was to navigate the back alleys of Whitechapel in search of my sister. On the other hand though, this was a secret that I had kept close to my heart for over a month now and I was somewhat loath to give it up so easily and especially to someone who had demonstrated several times that they disliked me. If I was going to confide in anyone then surely it should be Lucasta or Patrick or, God help us all, Minnie rather than this arrogant jumped up prig of a man.

'Miss Redmayne…' Something in my face must have touched him for he took hold of my hands and when I hazarded a glance at his face I saw that there was nothing but concern in his eyes. 'I did not mean to…'

I let out my breath in a deep sigh, interrupting him. 'I have a sister,' I said. It was time to let it go. 'Or I had a sister. I don't yet know which it is.' I gave a nervous little laugh and finished my brandy, immediately wishing that I had already had another lined up.

He frowned and his grip on my hands tightened. 'A sister?' he said before putting his handsome head to one side and considering this for a moment as I looked everywhere but at him, willing the tears that had welled up in my eyes at the mere mention of Beatrice to abate and leave me in peace. 'And you think that she might be here? In Whitechapel?' He was sharp, I'd allow him that.

I nodded. 'I have not seen her for six years,' I said in voice so low that he had to strain to hear properly. 'She simply vanished one night and I don't know where she went.' I remember my hysterical tears the next morning and my parents and aunt telling me that she had gone and not to talk about it any more for it was too distressing. I wondered now if perhaps I should have ignored them and asked more questions, no matter how upsetting it was for everyone else. Surely someone knew something and wasn't telling? I felt sick with shame for having remained silent for so long. 'I have no idea what became of her.'

'Until now?' he prompted me when I fell silent. 'You think that she might have come here?'

'I don't know what to think, Mr Mercier,' I said almost pleadingly. 'All I know is that her locket, a trinket that I myself had given to her just before she left, was pushed through our front door almost four weeks ago inside an envelope written in her hand and upon which another hand had written 'From Whitechapel'.' I was crying now and he looked around in panic, signalling to Mrs Ferrar that she should bring more brandy, which she immediately did, pressing my shoulder kindly with her plump hand before she went away again.

'Here,' Mr Mercier handed me my glass and then, as an afterthought, produced a red cotton handkerchief from the depths of one of his coat pockets. 'It's clean,' he said with a smile as I reluctantly took it. He watched in silence as I took a sip of the brandy then carefully dried my eyes. 'I'm sorry,' he said eventually once I was composed once more.

I looked up at him in surprise. 'What for?' I asked. I still had his handkerchief crumpled up in my fist and I offered it back to him now only for him to impatiently wave it away.

'I'm sorry that I misjudged you,' he said simply. 'I was wrong and I am sorry for it.' He sighed. 'You must be able to appreciate how it must have looked to me though? We get them all the time down here in Whitechapel - spoiled little rich girls looking to shock their parents or attract some man by hanging about the poor and playing lady bountiful until they either get bored or get their own way and off they go again.' He takes an angry sip of his brandy. 'I had no reason to believe that you were going to be any different and, damn me, but the people of this area deserve better than the half hearted patronising cosseting of yet another stuck up little brat who'll move on and forget them once she's got what she wanted out of the exercise.'

'Is this how you speak to Miss Lawler?' I asked faintly. I'd gleaned from the gossip over my father's dinner table that Miss Lawler was in possession of a fortune that would make most peers sick with envy. 'You don't treat her the same way as me.'

'That's because she isn't the same as you,' he said wearily, running his fingers through his long hair. 'She's not here to make a dash or to cause a genteel little scandal. She's here to help, to work. No one who has ever met her could ever doubt that.'

I nodded, agreeing with him. 'She is remarkable,' I said before giving a small wry smile. 'You are correct in some respects, Mr Mercier,' I said hesitantly. 'I did come to Whitechapel with entirely my own selfish agenda but that has all changed now and mainly because of Miss Lawler and the sincere admiration that I have for her work. Who could see her and not be inspired?'

He toasted the air with his glass of brandy and took a deep swig. 'Who indeed?' he said, relaxing back into his chair and grinning at me. He looked suddenly very young and I remembered for the first time that he was really not all that much older than me, maybe twenty two at the most.

'Are you in love with her, Mr Mercier?' I asked suddenly.

He looked shocked. 'Me? With Miss Lawler?' He laughed. 'No, there is nothing like that between us.'

'She's very pretty,' I persisted, feeling suddenly very brave and also like I'd had maybe one too many brandies. 'And rich,' I added wickedly.

Mr Mercier grinned. 'Too rich for me,' he said, finishing his brandy.

'She could buy you your own practice,' I said, warming to the idea now and beginning to wave my arms about in my excitement, 'and you could help her with the Mission. I think it would be perfect.'

'I think you've had too much to drink,' he said wryly, moving my glass just out of reach and then, to the surprise, I think, of both of us, suddenly reaching across to tuck a stray straggling curl that had fallen across my face in my enthusiasm behind my ear.

I sighed and closed my eyes for a moment, surprised by how much I enjoyed the touch of his hand against my skin. He jerked his hand away as if scalded and a heavy silence, pregnant with uncertainty and awkwardness, fell between us. 'I know that you think me stupid and frivolous,' I said sadly at last, when I could no longer bear the suspense.

He smiled. 'I know that you are the sort of girl who thinks that an expensive bar of the finest Parisian rose scented soap is a suitable gift to make to women who can't even afford to eat on most days.'

I shrugged, tired now of his relentless disapproval. 'I did that to annoy you,' I said wearily.

'It worked.' He held my gaze for a moment as again that silence fell between us then gave an impatient little shrug and got to his feet. 'I should take you back now. They'll be wondering where we are.' He extended his hand to me.

'Perhaps they'll think we've eloped,' I said, although the words felt like ashes in my mouth. 'Or murdered each other.' I put my hand in his and let him pull me gently to my feet. 'You won't tell anyone will you?' I asked, suddenly anxious.

'My lips are sealed,' he said so grimly that I did not dare press the matter any further. He was a man of his word though, I had discerned that much and with that I had to be content.

With a final nod and smile at Mrs Ferrar, we went out again on to busy Commercial Street, where as usual the pavement was crowded with people and carts and carriages rumbled relentlessly down the mud and dust covered road. He planted his hat on to his head then without looking at me offered me his arm. 'Stay close,' he said. 'I don't want to lose you again.'

I put my hand on his arm and let him lead me back up the road towards Christ Church. 'How did you know where to find me?' I asked when he paused for a moment to point out Thrawl Street, which was not so very far away, I now realised with a pang

138

of embarrassed annoyance from the point where I had stopped and fallen into the wrong hands.

'I followed you,' he muttered.

I stopped dead, causing the labourers walking behind us to complain loudly then shove roughly past us. 'You followed me?' I said, shocked.

Mr Mercier nodded, unable to meet my eyes. 'Oh, I had no designs on your person, Miss Redmayne so you can stop staring at me as if I am some sort of Bluebeard who preys on defenceless maidens. I just happened to see you leave the Mission and thought that perhaps I should keep an eye on you to ensure that you didn't come to any harm.' He looked at me then and gave a rueful sidelong smile that made him look boyish again. 'I had a feeling that you might not know where you were going. Of course, it was not my intention to interfere if my suspicions didn't prove to be accurate.'

'And yet, I still managed to be whacked over the head,' I said, trying to make myself angry, 'so you can't have been keeping all that much of an eye on me.'

He sighed and urged me to keep walking. 'I'm afraid that I lost sight of you when one of my former clients apprehended me in the street.' He gently touched his chin and I saw for the first time that there was a new bruise beneath the stubble.

'He hit you!' I said with more delight than I ought perhaps to have felt.

Mr Mercier grinned. 'Alas, yes, he did. It was one of my less successful cases.'

I laughed. 'This is why you need a rich wife, Mr Mercier. She could pay for you to have bodyguards.'

'Perhaps.' We walked together past Christ Church, which looked much more dignified now in the mellow light of the late afternoon sun. I was shocked to see that it was almost six. 'How long was I unconscious for?' I demanded.

He shrugged. 'Quite a while. It was very tiresome.' We were almost back at Hanbury Street and it was at that moment, reminded quite suddenly by a flash of red hair in the midst of the crowd that still hung about the house where a woman had been murdered that morning, that I remembered the girl. 'I know you,' I'd said to her.

139

'Who was that girl?' I asked trying to hide the urgency in my voice. 'The one who was with you.'

Mr Mercier looked down at me, not smiling now. 'Her name is Cora. Her father is a police sergeant in the Whitechapel station. She's a sweet girl.' He took hold of my arm and propelled me carefully but relentlessly between the traffic until we were standing on the other side of Commercial Street. 'Why?'

'I thought that I recognised her,' I said vaguely, looking up at him from beneath my eyelashes and jealously wondering if I had detected a trace of softness in his voice when he referred to this Cora as a 'sweet girl'. No, not jealous. Never jealous. I gave myself a shake.

'I know.' He led me down Lamb Street to the Mission house. 'You said so at the time.'

We were at the door now but neither of us made any move to go inside. 'Did she run away as well?' I asked lightly. 'Like the other girl, Emma?' I'd almost forgotten about her in the midst of all the fuss.

'Ah, Emma.' He gave me a curious look. 'You were looking for her, weren't you?'

I considered lying but then gave a nod. 'I thought that perhaps she might know where my sister is.' I looked down at my boots, once so shiny and now covered in dust and mud which would no doubt earn me several reproachful looks from Minnie when I got home. 'After all, someone must know.'

He considered this for a moment. 'The person who put the locket through your door knows something,' he said. 'Perhaps start with them?'

I nodded grimly. 'Perhaps I will.'

Chapter Fifteen

I stayed away from the Mission for several days, unwilling to return until both my head and wounded pride had been healed. If anyone, especially keen eyed Miss Lawler, thought there was anything unusual about our absence that afternoon or, more to the point, my distinctly dishevelled state when we returned then they were obviously, much to my relief, too polite to comment on it.

Minnie was less restrained though and disapproval radiated from her as with pinched lips and downcast eyes, she silently helped me out of my mud stained dress then gingerly put my boots aside to be cleaned. 'I won't ask what you've been up to for I'm sure I don't want to know,' she said reprovingly as she examined the dirt encrusted into the once pristine white hem of my petticoat.

'Oh, Minnie,' I said, irritable now that the warming comfort of the brandy had worn off. 'I was attacked and beaten around the head in an alleyway, if you must know.'

She had the grace to look a little contrite then but I could still hear her muttering when she went off to the bathroom to run my jasmine scented bath. Too tired and aching to be annoyed, I wrapped my pink Chinese silk robe around myself and unlocked the drawer beside my bed where I kept my most precious things. On the very top there lay the photograph of Beatrice and me along with the amber pendant and envelope that it had arrived in. 'From Whitechapel,' I whispered, lightly touching the scrawled writing.

Emma and Cora. I was now more certain than ever that they held the key to my sister's whereabouts and was thoroughly resolved to smoke them both out and discover the truth. There was something though about Emma's frightened expression and precipitous flight from the Mission and the look of mingled consternation, fear and guilt that crept across Cora's face when I said that I knew her that gave me pause for surely they would not have reacted as they had done if all was well. Could it be that..? No, I would not and could not think about it. Beatrice was alive but for some reason determined not to be found and that's all there was to it.

I looked again at the envelope, at the dark rusty stains around the edges that could be blood. But of course it wasn't blood but something else. Rouge perhaps? Or dye. I remembered Cora's astonishing red hair, the shade sported by Venetian prostitutes in the sixteenth century and made so popular by Titian and then later on Rossetti. Did she dye her hair? Surely not. Emma did though but it was a brassy sunflower yellow that she favoured rather than the colour of fallen autumn leaves. Beatrice's colouring had been like that of a Boucher nymph, all huge rolling blue eyes, pink cheeks, pearly white teeth and tumbling corn coloured tresses. Had she dyed her pretty hair red and splattered dye on to the envelope?

'Your bath is ready, Miss,' Minnie called from the bathroom and with a sigh I closed the drawer.

I kept to myself for the next week, immersing myself in my books, art and music until I was forced back into company again by one of my father's dinner parties, which thankfully Aunt Minerva had already agreed to preside over so there was no need for me to pin a false smile to my face and play hostess, although it fell to me to oversee the actual arrangements.

'Seems like you do all the hard work and Lady Coudland gets all the credit,' Minnie grumbled as she laced me into a new Parisian evening gown of pale apricot silk trimmed with lace at the bosom and elbows and with sequinned sunbursts spangled all over the narrow bodice and down the elaborately swagged bustled skirt.

I laughed. 'Oh, I don't mind at all. I'd much rather arrange flowers, order extra ice and decide where everyone is to sit than have to pretend to be pleased to see people that I actually have absolutely nothing to say to.' Not that I had actually arranged any flowers of course - as usual Papa had insisted upon ordering huge arrangements of hot house white and pale pink lilies and peonies in from his favourite Mayfair florists and all I had had to do was tell the maids were to put them.

'Well, it should be a splendid evening anyway,' Minnie said as she got down on her knees to arrange the folds of my skirt to her satisfaction. 'And you've got lovely weather for it too so you'll be able to go out on the terrace later on.' She was right - there had been glorious sunshine all day which had now settled into a soft orange and pink autumnal glow over the rooftops. 'Maybe Lord Woollam would enjoy that too.'

I glared at her. 'That's enough, Minnie,' I said crossly, sitting down heavily in front of my dressing table. I always hated reprimanding her when she had overstepped the mark, hated the way that things would become awkward between us as we slipped back into the roles of mistress and servant again rather than the friends that I hoped we were. 'I'm sorry. I think I have a headache.'

'That's quite alright, Miss. I didn't mean to speak out of turn,' Minnie said stiffly, starting to do my hair. 'You haven't been out much lately. It's probably doing you no good to be cooped up here for days on end.' She gave me a curious look in the mirror and I knew that she was wondering what exactly had happened to me the last time I went to Whitechapel.

If only she knew that even I had no idea what had happened that afternoon or how it had changed me. I could hardly bear to recall the moment that I was attacked, just thinking about the darkness and dancing stars was enough to send me dizzy and sick again and as for the hours I had spent afterwards with Mr Mercier, they were not to be thought of at all.

I thought of him now though as Minnie teased my hair up into a chignon and decorated it with small diamond and topaz starbursts that almost matched the ones on my dress and smiled a little to myself as I imagined his intense disapproval should he ever see me all dressed up for one of my father's parties. It was probably for the best that he never would, even if the thought made me feel oddly sad. Arrogant and impossibly rude though he might well be, there was a tiny part of me that wanted to take him out of Whitechapel and see him in my own world, introduce him to Papa and my friends (although perhaps not Patrick) and let him get to know the real me.

'I don't think you need any rouge this evening, Miss,' Minnie said with a knowing look that brought me back to earth with a bump. 'You're blushing already.'

My cheeks were still shamefully warm half an hour later as I mingled with our guests and made the usual perfunctory small talk while waiting for dinner to be announced. Despite Papa's usual protests that that evening's dinner party was to be an informal affair for just our closest friends, he had, again as usual, been unable to resist inviting enough people, the usual array of artists, politicians and wealthy patrons, to fill our dining table to its fullest capacity. I gave an inward sigh, remembering how it had been when my gentle, quiet Mama was alive and able to restrain his more extravagant impulses. There had been parties then too but not nearly so frequently or on the same scale as nowadays.

'Wonderful flowers as usual, Alice,' Lady Brennan murmured to me in passing. Exquisitely dressed as always, she was wearing a jade silk gown that emphasised the marble paleness of her skin and rich dark gleam of her eyes and hair, which she wore pinned with artful carelessness on top of her small head.

'My aunt deserves all the credit,' I said modestly, mindful that I was not the hostess that evening.

Lady Brennan laughed, making the emerald and diamond earrings she was wearing glitter wickedly in the flattering candlelight that my father insisted upon employing instead of gaslight on these evenings. 'Oh come now, I detect your exquisite touch everywhere. I don't know how your father will manage without you.' This last bit was said with an arch look and nod across the room to where Patrick was standing beside the fireplace with my father and Lord Brennan.

I smiled. 'It is lucky then that he won't be forced to do so for a long time to come,' I said, wondering what people were saying about me. How awkward if talk of an engagement had already leaked out. I saw Lucasta making her way through the crowd towards us and turned to her mother with an apologetic smile. 'I do hope you will excuse us but I haven't seen Lucasta for far too long and am dying to catch up with her.'

Lady Brennan gave a false little society smile and stepped aside as her daughter came up and took my arm. 'Of course. It's always such a delight to see you two girls together.' She didn't look delighted though and not for the first time I found myself

144

wondering if she actually liked me at all.

'It's not you,' Lucasta muttered as she dragged me off to the terrace. 'She's like that with everyone at the moment. I think it's the change coming upon her, like the Lady of Shallot's curse only in reverse.'

'The change?' I was confused, the loss of my mother and sister had left me at something of a disadvantage when it came to such womanly matters although I was sure that Aunt Minerva would be only too happy to oblige should I ever feel in need of any intimate advice. I shuddered at the thought of it.

Lucasta nudged me. 'You know,' she said. 'When a woman's flowers stop and she can't have babies any more. They get really upset about it for some reason.' She shrugged. 'I have no idea why - it sounds like a blessed relief to me.' She firmly closed the glass doors behind us and led me over to the parapet overlooking the garden.

'Don't you want to have children?' I asked my friend curiously as she fished her silver and enamel cigarette case out of her reticule and flicked it open with a sophisticated air that I longed to emulate.

Lucasta shrugged. 'I suppose that I will have to have at least one, one day but I can't say that I am thrilled by the prospect.' She lit a cigarette and took a deep, blissful drag. 'Isabella was the same, I think. Why do you think there's only me to carry on the family name?'

'Maybe there were other attempts?' I said gently. I knew that my own Mama had had several sad little miscarriages in between Beatrice and myself, which explained the long gap between us.

Lucasta shrugged again and blew out a perfect smoke ring. 'Maybe,' she said with a complete lack of interest before cocking her blonde ringleted head towards me. 'So how is Whitechapel?'

I sighed, wondering how much I could tell her. 'It's very different to how I expected,' I said carefully, thinking of Henry Mercier and his slow smile.

Cigarette in hand, Lucasta peered at me through the gloom. 'Why are you smirking?' she demanded with a frown. 'Have you met a man? Oh my God, you have, haven't you?'

'Of course not,' I said with a nervous laugh as I felt my cheeks go hot and red again. 'How utterly bizarre you are being. Quite ridiculous, in fact.'

Lucasta impatiently waved my protests aside. 'Who is he?' she said. 'Gracious, is he some piece of Cockney rough? Or have you managed to winkle out a gentleman for yourself? Come on, spill the beans.'

I sighed. 'There isn't anyone,' I said firmly. 'I haven't met any young men and certainly none that you would care to hear about. It isn't exactly a hotbed of handsome young millionaires, you know.'

'Pshaw.' Lucasta blew out her cheeks in annoyance and took another drag from her cigarette. 'Have you told Patrick about it?' she asked, pretending to examine her nails but really watching me closely from beneath her long eyelashes.

'Of course I haven't,' I blustered, appalled by the very idea. 'And besides, there is nothing to tell.'

'Oh, give it a rest,' she said with a grin. 'As usual, you forget that I've known you all your life, Alice Redmayne and can tell straight away when you are lying.'

I stuck my tongue out at her. 'Now you just sound like Aunt Minerva,' I said. 'I'm sure she said exactly the same thing to me not so long ago.'

'Perhaps you should try telling less lies then,' she retorted with a cheeky look before dropping her cigarette on to the ground and grinding it to dust beneath her heel. 'Anyway, I have news of my own.'

'Oh?' I raised an eyebrow, relieved to have Lucasta's attention stray elsewhere even if I wasn't foolish enough to think that she had finished with my own diverting little situation quite yet. 'What have you been up to? More kissing unsuitable young men after drinking too much absinthe?'

'We didn't just kiss.' My friend grinned. 'Anyway, it's not that - it's this.' She lifted up her saffron yellow silk skirts and innumerable lace and ribbon edged petticoats to reveal a pale blue swallow tattooed into the pale skin of her inner thigh. 'What do you think?'

I stared at the tattoo then, suddenly embarrassed because of where it was, quickly looked away. 'Gracious, Lucasta, how on earth are you going to explain that away on your wedding night?'

'Oh pooh.' She laughed. 'I have no intention of marrying the

146

sort of feeble milksop who would be shocked by this, no matter what my parents have planned for me.' She dropped her skirts and brushed them down with a smug look. 'They are all the rage among the court ladies, you know. It's whispered that even Lady Randolph Churchill has a tattoo of a snake on her wrist.' The dark haired and frankly gorgeous Lady Randolph Churchill, formerly the American heiress Jennie Jerome, had been Lucasta's most adored idol ever since she'd smiled and waved to her across the way at the opera.

I sighed. 'I suppose you think that I should get one too,' I said, resigning myself to the inevitable.

Lucasta laughed. 'Oh gracious no, it's far too dashing for you, my dear!' She stuck her tongue at me. 'Although if you're going to run off with your East End paramour...'

I glared at her. 'I'm not running off with anyone,' I said.

She put her arm around me. 'Oh come now, you know that if you did then people would excuse it as all being down to your Italian blood.'

I laughed then. 'I am not actually Italian, as well you know,' I said. 'I just happened to be born there.' It was true. Papa had dragged a pregnant Mama and Beatrice out to Rome with him while he made sketches for what he intended to be a grand series of paintings about the infamous Borgia family with Beatrice posing as Lucrezia Borgia, looking lush and beautiful with her long fair hair studded with rubies and hanging unbound to her knees. He promised Mama several times that they would be returning to London in time for my birth but in the end she had given up, hired a local midwife and settled in for my birth, which occurred in a lavish Renaissance palazzo overlooking the Tiber.

'Same difference,' Lucasta said with a smirk. 'Maybe you should go there on honeymoon. I can picture it now - you, your Cockney dreamboat, the blood red waters of the Tiber at night, the majestic beauty of the Vatican and... '

'I'm not getting married, Lucasta,' I interrupted her patiently. 'No matter what half of London seems to think.'

We were called in to dinner shortly after that and went in together, arm in arm and ignoring Aunt Minerva's hissed reminders that we were supposed to be escorted in by two of the eligible young gentlemen present, who now stood awkward and

147

partnerless in their white gloves at the back of the drawing room until my aunt suggested they stroll in together.

I'd arranged the seating plan so that I was in between my father and Sir John Steer, one of his elderly artist friends that I had known all my life and who always amused me with his tales of his travels abroad. However, when I reached my chair he was nowhere to be seen and Patrick was sitting there instead of him, with a look of perfect innocence on his handsome face that told me immediately that he was not the culprit responsible for swapping the place cards.

'Have a lovely time,' Lucasta whispered to me with a laugh as she released my arm and skipped away to her own seat on the other side of the table. 'Oh, don't look so cross, darling. I only did what you really ought to have done for yourself.'

'I can't believe you didn't place me next to you,' Patrick said with a comically reproachful look as I awkwardly sat down beside him. 'Do you really prefer Sir John to me?'

I couldn't help but laugh. 'Oh absolutely,' I said in a whisper. 'He's quite the Casanova when you get to know him a little.'

'Really?' Patrick looked down the table to where the doddery, pink cheeked Sir John was nervously taking his seat next to Aunt Minerva. 'Well, he certainly looks the sort. Will your aunt be safe from his devilish charms, I wonder?' We looked at each other and grinned, all awkwardness vanishing between us.

'So why didn't you want to sit next to me?' he asked after a moment's silence as the footmen hired for the evening served the soup course, a thin vegetable consommé and poured wine into our fine red crystal goblets, an artistic affectation of my father's which always made me uneasily feel like I was drinking blood.

I felt my cheeks go warm at the directness of Patrick's question. 'I didn't want people to talk,' I mumbled, not quite meeting his eyes.

'But don't they always talk?' he said in some surprise, putting down his soup spoon with a clatter. 'Or do you mean in a more specific way?'

I looked at him then and saw that his face was filled with nothing but concern. 'I think you know what I mean,' I said in a low voice.

Patrick sighed and nodded. 'Yes, alas, I do.' He took hold of my hand beneath the cover of the table. 'Well, I can think of at least one thing we can do to make them stop talking,' he said gently.

Now I really was blushing. 'There's two things actually or, well, technically three. We could both marry other people.' I gently but firmly removed my hand from his grasp.

He looked dumbfounded. 'Marry someone else?' he repeated as if he hadn't quite understood what I was suggesting. 'Alice? Is there someone else?' He lowered his voice to a barely audible hiss. 'Someone that you want to marry?'

I pushed my soup bowl away untouched. 'Of course not, Patrick,' I said with a nervous laugh. 'You're as bad as Lucasta. I can't so much as look at a man without her hearing wedding bells.'

We both laughed then looked across the table to where our friend was simultaneously charming the socks off a pair of middle aged artist friends of my father, both of whom were very handsome in a rather louche Bohemian way and had quite shockingly rakish reputations, which made me wonder if perhaps Patrick's place card was not the only one she had tampered with.

The soup bowls were efficiently whisked away to be replaced by a fish course of sole fillets in a rich creamy wine sauce and I picked at this without enthusiasm as I listened with half an ear to the conversation between Lady Brennan and the gentleman next to her that was going on beside me. A conversation which, I realised with a jolt, had strayed on to the topic of the recent spate of murders in Whitechapel.

'Of course, what can one expect from the savages that live in such an area?' Lady Brennan said with a sniff of disapproval. 'They're little better than animals.'

'Come now, my dear, surely that is being a little unfair to animals?' her husband interjected from across the table, which had the effect of making the conversation more general as everyone turned their heads to see what they were talking about. 'If animals behaved like the creatures in the slums of Whitechapel, we'd be doing them a service in having them put down.' He looked smugly around the table as if expecting applause.

I'd known Lord Brennan all my life and had never really had much of an opinion about him, other than the occasional wish that he would have a little more care for his daughter Lucasta's feelings. Now though, I absolutely disliked the man and wished that I had the courage to say so.

'That's a little harsh, don't you think?' Patrick said smoothly and I looked at him in gratitude. 'The people of Whitechapel are as deserving of respect as any of us. More so in fact when one considers the difficult conditions that they are forced to exist under.' His hand again reached for mine beneath the table and this time I didn't pull away.

'They don't have to live that way though,' Lord Brennan said with a fatuous smile. 'Why can they not make themselves useful to society and live like all the rest of us instead of choosing to live like beasts?' He heaved a great dramatic sigh and looked around the table, which had gone completely silent now as everyone listened to him. 'Oh, I'm sure that most of them bemoan their fate and curse the cruel ill luck that brought them so low but what do they do to try and change matters, that's what I want to know.'

Patrick gave a low, mirthless laugh. 'Oh come now, my Lord, surely you aren't suggesting that a street child from Whitechapel has the same advantages as, say, someone of your own standing?' He shook his head as if in disbelief. 'I'm sure that if every child in Whitechapel had several hundred thousand pounds in the bank, a title and an education at Eton and Oxford then we, and they, would have nothing to worry about.'Lord Brennan shrugged. 'They'd spend the fortune on gin then pawn the title to buy more,' he said briskly, rubbing the ends of his fingers together as if literally brushing the dirt of Whitechapel from them. 'Such loathsome creatures will never change. We'd be better off sending them all off to the colonies.' There were some nods of agreement around the table but I was heartened to notice most of our guests were staring fixedly down at their plates with expressions of dismay. I looked down the table to Aunt Minerva and noticed that Sir John had placed his hand gently on her arm as if restraining her from launching into an attack. I found myself wishing that she'd just shake him off and say what was on her mind. She never had much time for the Brennans. 'At least then we'd never have to see any of them again or hear about their miserable lives or these tawdry murders.'

'Out of sight, out of mind,' Patrick muttered. 'How

convenient.' He sighed and took a sip of his wine before smiling again. 'Of course, you forget, my Lord, that Miss Redmayne has been working in Whitechapel for the last few weeks and probably knows more about the area than either of us.' He turned to me and smiled, giving my hand a reassuring squeeze beneath the table. 'Is that not so, Miss Redmayne?'

Every eye around the table turned to me and I felt my cheeks redden and go hot under the weight of their scrutiny. 'That - that is true,' I faltered, first staring down at my plate then, after taking a deep breath to steady myself, looking up and straight into Lord Brennan's cold dark eyes. 'You are wrong about the people who live there, my Lord,' I said softly. 'They are not perfect, it is true, but who is? I certainly don't think they are any worse than us - after all, they have the same weaknesses and strengths, the same virtues and vices as anyone around this table. If their vices overwhelm them then it is our fault as much as theirs for it is we, with our gifts of both wealth and ability who seem hell bent on keeping them in their place.' I thought about bright little Charlie and his poor little barefoot friends; of Emma with her pale hungry face and terrified eyes; of Miss Lawler, so earnest and desperate to assist in any way she could and I felt my heart swell with pride. 'Lord Brennan, they are not beasts or animals, they are people just like you and I and as such deserve our respect.' I slid my eyes around to Patrick and saw him give a small, almost imperceptible nod. 'In fact I would go so far as to say that if our society as a whole is judged by how it treats the poor, sick and needy then I'm afraid that I find us very wanting indeed, no matter how civilised we may think we are.'

An uneasy silence fell across the table, broken only by the gentle clattering of plates as the footmen discreetly removed one service and brought in the next, as I stopped speaking and looked away from Lord Brennan's astonished gaze. 'Well done,' Patrick whispered to me, giving my hand one final squeeze before releasing it.

Lady Brennan gave a high pitched nervous laugh that suggested that she'd already had too much to drink. The huge egg shaped rubies around her throat gleamed wickedly in the mellow candlelight and I remembered Lucasta telling me that they had once belonged to an Indian Maharajah who was murdered, torn to pieces in fact, by his harem of wives because of his great cruelty towards them. 'My dear, you are far too soft hearted,' she said, leaning forward in an almost conspiratorial manner as if it was just we two at the table.

'That ought not to be considered a failing,' I replied with a smile that I knew did not quite reach my eyes. 'Perhaps we should all be a little more soft hearted when it comes to those less fortunate than ourselves.'

'I rather doubt that,' Lord Brennan interposed, clearly unwilling to let the subject go. 'I must say, and I hope you will allow this liberty from someone who has known you all your life, that I am more than a little alarmed by the effect your work in Whitechapel is having upon you, Miss Redmayne. You are becoming quite the little radical. Next you will be wearing absurd smocks and trousers like the so called ladies of the Rational Dress Society and standing for Parliament.' There was a polite laugh along the table, which he acknowledged with a smug little smile and bow of his head before turning towards my father who had been sitting in silence at the head of the table the whole while, observing in his usual gentle way but saying nothing. 'I am surprised at you, Edwin, for allowing such a thing.'

My father heaved a great sigh then and carefully put his glass of wine back on the table. 'Gracious, Richard,' he said with a smile and a wink across at me, 'what on earth gives you the impression that I have any control over anything that happens within my own household?'

Chapter Sixteen

After dinner we went to the drawing room where an up and coming young opera singer with the improbable name of Mademoiselle Anastasia Nightingale was waiting to entertain us with some arias. She sang beautifully and I could feel my residual anger about Lord and Lady Brennan's snide behaviour flow from me like water as I listened. 'She really is superb,' Patrick whispered to me. He'd accompanied me out of the dining room and then elected to sit beside me too, much to my aunt's obvious and rather mortifying delight.

'I wish that I could sing so beautifully,' I said, unfurling my fan and waving it slowly in front of my face. It was an unseasonably cold evening and the combination of a lit fire, candlelight and press of several bodies crowded together into the drawing room had made it intolerably hot. 'Would I have to change my name to something more musical though? Perhaps Alice Sparrow would suit me?' I smiled at him and he grinned back.

'I think your name is quite musical enough,' he said gently as the last aria ended and we all politely applauded. 'Or at least it is to me.'

I smiled but said nothing.

'You really were quite astonishing earlier on,' he continued in an undertone as we all got up and some of the guests, including him, prepared to leave. 'I had no idea that you were quite so passionate about the plight of the people of the East End.'

I gave a tiny shrug. 'I must confess that I had no idea either,' I confided as I led him out to the hallway. 'It's true though. I am proud of the work that we do there and only wish that I could do more.'

He nodded, suddenly serious. 'You should be proud,' he said, feeling in his pocket for a card which he pressed into my hand. 'If you ever have any need of me, if there is ever anything that I can do to assist then you will let me know, won't you?' He put his finger to my chin then and tilted my face upwards so that I was looking into his eyes. 'Promise me, Alice?'

It was the first time since childhood that he had used my first name, having abandoned the practice as soon as I started putting my hair up and lowered my hemlines, and I gave a little smile to acknowledge this and approve it. 'I promise,' I said in a low voice. 'Must you go now?' One of the footmen was already advancing towards us with Patrick's hat, black evening cloak, gloves and walking stick in his hands and I suddenly found myself desperate to keep him there with me just for a little while longer.

'I'm afraid that I must,' he said regretfully. 'Like a total idiot, I arranged a business meeting for first thing tomorrow morning and must have all my wits about me for the task. You have no idea how much my lawyer and estate manager love to confound me.' He laughed and put his hat on then took the walking stick as the footman arranged the cape carefully about his shoulders. 'I will be back to see you soon though, no doubt.'

I smiled and slipped the card into the tiny watered silk reticule I wore hanging from my wrist. 'I do hope so,' I said just as there was a knock on the door which made us spring apart almost guiltily. 'Gracious, who could that be? I don't think there was anyone missing from dinner?' I looked around for my aunt but she was still in the drawing room, holding court with my father, who was showing off some of his latest sketches.

One of the footmen went to open the door and I was astonished to see Mr Mercier standing on our doorstep, looking very unsure of himself and dressed in a rather shabby oversized black overcoat with his bowler hat tucked under his arm. There was a short, painful pause, during which he looked like he desperately wanted to leave, before I swallowed down my ridiculous feeling of disappointment and went towards him with my hand out stretched. 'Mr Mercier,' I said as smoothly as I could, smiling at him. 'What a pleasure to see you.'

He stared at me silently, ignoring my hand and my smile faltered as I realised how he must see me - the price of my lovely apricot silk dress could feed a family in Whitechapel for six months, my diamond earrings could keep a girl off the streets for two years. I pulled back my hand and looked away as a stab of shame shot through me.

'I'm sorry to intrude,' he said at last very formally, clearing his throat before he spoke. 'I didn't know that you would be entertaining tonight. I assumed that —'

I felt my cheeks go warm as I looked at him again and met his eyes, which were just as cold and hard as I'd feared they would be. 'No, no, there is no need to apologise. You weren't to know.' I felt Patrick come up behind me and turned to him in relief and some embarrassment. 'Lord Woollam, this is Mr Mercier from the Whitechapel Women's Mission.'

The two men looked each other in silence before Patrick held out his hand with enviable and very practiced aplomb. 'I am very pleased to meet you, Mr Mercier,' he said cheerfully. 'I'm most exceedingly interested in the work that our dear Miss Redmayne is doing in the East End.'

Mr Mercier nodded but said nothing and there was another pause as Patrick clearly cast about for something else to say. 'I've been thinking that perhaps I ought to make some sort of donation,' he said at last as I looked at him in surprise. 'To see Miss Redmayne so inflamed with enthusiasm about the Mission has made me realise that I don't do enough to help.'

Mr Mercier gave a nod. 'That would be very kind of you, my Lord,' he said but I could tell by his expression that he didn't believe a word of it, that he thought my friend was just another bored rich aristocrat trying to make himself look good by making promises that he had no intention of keeping.

I watched them both together, taking in the contrast between Patrick's fair good looks and Mr Mercier's dark stockiness as they warily looked at each other. I could tell that Mr Mercier was longing to be as rude and dismissive towards Patrick as he used to be to me, but the fear of angering a potential sponsor for the Mission had completely taken the wind out of his sails. As for Patrick, he was his usual urbane, friendly self but his eyes as they rested upon Mr Mercier and flickered every now and again towards me were hard and calculating.

'Why did you come here?' I asked eventually when the silence went on for a smidgen too long. Of course the question sounded much more polite, less accusatory when I rolled it over in my mind a second before asking but it was too late to do anything about it now.

Mr Mercier pulled his gaze away from Patrick and looked instead at me. 'I wanted to bring you something,' he said with a shrug, matching my rudeness with plenty of his own. 'I didn't know if you were coming back to the Mission but thought you might have need of it at some point.' I raised my eyebrows in some confusion and he felt inside his coat pockets, eventually bringing out a battered envelope which he looked at thoughtfully for a moment before almost reluctantly handing over to me. 'It's the address that you wanted. I probably ought to have just sent it,' he added a little ruefully, feeling the back of his neck with his hand in a gesture that I knew meant that he was feeling awkward and like he really ought not to have come. 'I just thought that —'

'Well, it's certainly very kind of you to bring it all this way,' Patrick interrupted smoothly. 'After all, Whitechapel is no small distance away.' I looked at him quickly, thinking that perhaps he meant to mock Mr Mercier but there was nothing but sincere appreciation in his expression.

'Some things are better delivered by hand,' I interposed a little crossly, wanting to reassure Mr Mercier, who was now eyeing the door as if considering escape, and thinking of the other envelope, the red stained one in my drawer upstairs. 'At least now you know that it is safe with me.'

He smiled then although the rest of his expression was unreadable. 'Is it?' He turned back then to Patrick and gave a slight bow. 'It was nice to meet you,' he said.

'Likewise,' Patrick agreed affably. 'I will contact the Mission tomorrow about making a donation.'

'And who is this then?' Her timing perfect as always, Lucasta appeared in the doorway and I gave an inward groan of apprehension, dreading whatever was inevitably going to happen next. If my face gave away my trepidation, she gave no sign of noticing but instead grinned and tripped carelessly over to us, her bright blue eyes fixed curiously on Mr Mercier. 'Is this one of your's, Alice?'

I could have cheerfully slapped her but instead I just smiled and shook my head. 'No, absolutely not one of mine. Mr Mercier is his own man and belongs to no one.'

Lucasta laughed and opened her white ostrich feather fan which, like her tattoo, I had been assured was all the rage amongst the Princess of Wales' ladies in waiting. 'What a pity,' she purred, looking Mr Mercier over quite shamelessly.

I hazarded a look at him, half expecting him to be all a-blush and flattered by her attentions but instead he was pale with anger, with his full lips drawn together into a forbidding line. 'I really should go,' he said to no one in particular before turning and rushing from the house.

'Oh dear, I think you scared him off,' Patrick said with a wry smile at my friend, who gave an unconcerned shrug.

'Clearly he should learn a bit more about our ways then,' she said tartly, closing her fan and turning to me with an impish look. 'I thought you said there aren't any handsome young men in Whitechapel?'

I glared at her then, before I really quite knew what I was doing, lifted my heavy silk skirts above my ankles and ran out of the door and down the stone steps after Mr Mercier. Unable to see him straight away in the gloom and heavy clammy fog that swirled around the streets of north London that night, I guessed that he must have gone towards Canonbury station at the end of the street and turned right before hurtling clumsily down the road, hampered by my high heeled boots and heavy, swagged skirts.

'Mr Mercier!' I called into the smoky darkness. 'Please wait!' A dark shape that could have been a man loomed out of the fog just ahead of me and my heart leaped with hope as I called again: 'Please don't go!'

He turned and looked at me then, his face shadowed. 'Wait.' I panted slightly as I came up to him and rested my hand against my side where my tight corsetry was digging into my flesh. Perhaps I should have joined the Rational Dress Society after all. 'I just wanted say…'

'Yes?' He sounded impatient and keen to be on his way.

'It's very kind of you to come all this way.' I waved the envelope at him, still gasping for my breath and shivering in the damp night air.

He frowned and shrugged. 'It's really nothing.'

'It's not,' I said, pushing the envelope down the front of my bodice. 'It's really not. You didn't have to come all this way but you did anyway, just to help me.' I held my hand out towards him. 'I really appreciate it.' He didn't take my hand and I slowly withdrew it, distressed by the barrier that had sprung up between us again just when I had thought that it was gone forever. 'Thank you.'

He half turned as if to go but then turned back to me and this time there was a light in his dark grey eyes as he looked at me. 'Are you ever going to come back to the Mission?' he asked.

I nodded. 'Yes.' I hadn't been certain, had indeed been rather dreading my return to Whitechapel in fact but now I knew that I had to go back. I had to see my quest to the very end, no matter where it led me.

'Good.' Mr Mercier nodded and looked down at his shoes, which desperately needed cleaning, causing me to feel a brief, entirely unworthy and hastily repressed stab of embarrassment that my friends, particularly the always exquisitely turned out Patrick should have seen him thus with his dirty shoes and scruffy overcoat. 'You have been very much missed.'

I felt ridiculously pleased. 'Have I?' I asked, smiling now, the shoes and shabby coat forgotten. 'By everyone?'

He smiled and shrugged. 'Perhaps.' We heard a train whistle in the distance, an unearthly eerie sound, wailing like a banshee through the thick grey swirling smog. 'Miss Redmayne...' He hesitated.

'Mr Mercier?' I prompted when he still didn't speak.

He sighed and shook his head almost regretfully. 'It's nothing. I did not mean to speak out of turn and I certainly didn't mean to ruin your party.'

I laughed. 'You didn't ruin anything,' I said. 'It was just one of Papa's get togethers. He likes to entertain.' I smiled and shrugged. 'I am not quite so fond of it. I would prefer a quiet life.'

'I don't think a quiet life would suit you,' he said in a low voice and again I realised how I must look to him, all dressed up in my peach silk gown with diamonds at my ears and throat and even dotted about in my hair. I knew what it must have cost him to come to me here in Highbury and I also knew that I had somehow disappointed him dreadfully, that what he had found here confirmed all of his worst thoughts about me.

'I know what you must think of me,' I said, faltering over the words in my desperate haste to make amends, to make him understand that this was not all there was to me and that the barriers that he had clearly erected between us were just figments of his imagination. 'I know you think me rich and spoiled and ridiculous and perhaps I am all of those things but that is not all that I am, Mr Mercier.'

He gave a brief curt nod. 'I know that,' he said before giving a sudden smile. 'I also know that you can hold your brandy and have worryingly little care for your personal safety.'

I smiled too. 'I told you that I am ridiculous,' I said a trifle ruefully. I folded my arms around me as the fog swirled and thickened around us. Just beyond my line of sight I could see dark moving shapes of other pedestrians and every now and again a carriage would pass by, the usual brisk clip clopping of the horse's hooves muffled and made dull by the smog. 'I just wish I knew…'

He stepped closer to me. 'Knew what?' he said softly, so softly in fact that I had to lean forward to hear him.

I hesitated for a moment. 'I wish I knew what you want me to be,' I said at last, rather miserably. 'It seems like everything about me is wrong.'

He frowned then. 'I don't want you to be anything,' he said slowly and carefully as if to impress every word upon me. 'You are as you are, Miss Redmayne.' He nodded in the direction of my house, which was mostly obscured by the swirling fog, bar the soft amber lights that glowed at the windows. 'Are you engaged to Lord Woollam?' he asked.

I paused then shook my head. 'No, although everyone wants us to be,' I said. 'We've known each other all our lives, you see.'

He nodded but didn't smile. 'You make a handsome couple,' he said flatly.

'Do we?' I laughed. 'I'm not so sure. We fight like cats in a bag and I'm fairly sure that if we did marry then one of us would end up horribly murdered by the other before the end of our honeymoon.' A horse and carriage clip clopped slowly past in the fog and I suddenly felt the chill in the air with a renewed vigour and heartily wished that I'd had the presence of mind to snatch up a wrap before running out of the house. 'I should really go back now.' I gave him a quizzical look and extended my hand again while yet again he ignored it. Good grief. I sighed loudly to let him know how tiresome I thought he was being then turned away with a shrug. 'Thank you for coming all this way,' I called over my shoulder as I started to slowly fight my way through the fog back to the house. 'I really do appreciate it.'

I heard his footsteps behind me and before I could do anything to prevent him, he had put his arms around me and turned me around to face him. 'I like you just as you are,' he said quickly and urgently before, oh lord, he pulled me to one side so that we were hidden behind a wall then lowered his head to mine and kissed me as I clung to him in the most unladylike manner.

'Mr Mercier,' I whispered against his lips as he pulled away for a moment. I opened my eyes and stared up at him in wonderment as his arms tightened around me and pulled me close again, first trailing his warm mouth down the side of my neck then making for my lips again. 'Henry.' I opened my mouth and kissed him back, feeling intoxicated at first but then gradually nothing at all. Perhaps my expectations were simply too high after all those weeks of frantic daydreaming and wishing or perhaps we just didn't fit together as well as I had so tremulously hoped, but there was something wrong and after a while, although I let him carry on kissing me, I began to wonder just how long I could politely leave it before I moved away.

'Alice…' In the end it was he who broke away first and released me. 'We shouldn't do this. You're on the verge of getting engaged to someone else and I, well…'

I stared at him, still feeling the weight of his tongue upon my own, the roughness of his stubble against my chin. 'I'm not on the verge of getting engaged to anyone' I interrupted with annoyance.

He gave a short laugh. 'Of course you are,' he said. 'I saw the way that you and Lord Woollam looked at each other. I don't know you well enough to know precisely why you've convinced yourself that you aren't right for each other but my guess is that you're spoilt, Miss Redmayne, and you're having your little bit of fun with someone who can't hurt you before it's time to settle down and play wife.'

I glared at him. 'That's not true,' I said furiously. 'I'm not spoilt and I'm certainly not having any fun.'

'Not at my expense anyway,' he snapped.

'So why did you kiss me just now?' I demanded. 'Or did I entrap you into it like some sort of siren.' I gestured at the fog that surrounded us. 'The current weather conditions are certainly very apt for such activities, aren't they?'

He sighed and ran his fingers through his hair. 'I kissed you because I wanted to,' he said. 'And because I thought you wanted it too.'

I stared at him then, I think to the amazement of both of us, I started to laugh. 'I did want it,' I conceded with a rueful smile as he stared at me in astonishment, 'and I'm glad that it happened.' I looked at his face, which was just as comely as ever but not really as handsome as I had remembered it during my time away from Whitechapel. 'I'll admit that I was just a little bit infatuated with you, Mr Mercier but to be honest, I don't think that we are very well suited either.' I lifted a hand to stop him speaking. 'No, this isn't about money or where we live or our respective backgrounds or anything as tiresome as all that, it's simply that I think we are just too different in our attitudes and aspirations.' I smiled. 'If Patrick and I wouldn't survive beyond the honeymoon, I doubt we would make it past the announcement of our engagement being posted in the newspapers.'

'Or our first kiss,' Mr Mercier said softly and with, I like to flatter myself, the slightest touch of regret.

I sighed. 'Exactly.' Again I offered him my hand, only this time he took it and we shook hands as formally as strangers. 'I wish you all the best, Mr Mercier,' I said as cordially as I could.

'And may I be the first to offer my congratulations, Miss Redmayne?' he said, clearly struggling to hide his annoyance.

I smiled and shook my head. 'I meant what I said,' I said with a laugh. 'Cats in a bag.'

I watched him walk away until he had vanished into the fog and the muffled sound of his footsteps died slowly away. I could have run after him again, of course I could, but to what end? It was clear to me now, and in fact had probably always been clear to me deep down, that my wistful daydreams about making him a part of my life had indeed been nothing more than ridiculous fantasies, childlike in their simplicity and just as pathetically unrealistic. In fact, although his words had stung more than I could bear, he was quite right in his cruel estimation of my

161

motivation - I was indeed a spoilt little rich girl indulging in a preposterous fancy for someone who could never really hurt me, safe in the knowledge that the man that I knew deep down, however much I fought it, was really right for me would wait until I was ready for him. Poor Patrick.

'I have been such an idiot,' I said to myself as I turned to go back to the house. 'What was I thinking?' It wasn't so much my sheer foolishness that stung though, it was the look on Henry Mercier's face when he looked at me in all my finery, it was the sheer and palpable disdain that he had for everything about me. I could see now that the main obstacle in the way of Henry being a part of my life was not so much the differences between us but rather Henry himself and at that moment, my stupid girlish and ridiculous longing to make him a part of my world was replaced by a sort of shamed wish that he should never return to it.

Patrick and Lucasta had already gone by the time I got back home, shivering with cold and no doubt looking suspiciously disheveled although the staff were far too well trained to so much as bat an eyelash at either that or at my pulling the now very crumpled envelope out from inside my tight bodice. My fingers shook with impatience and nerves as I ripped it open and let it drop to the floor then quickly scanned the small scrap of paper inside.

'Emma has moved on from Thrawl Street to Crossingham's lodging house at 35 Dorset Street. I thought you might like to know although, and I am well aware that my advice is falling upon deaf ears, I would absolutely NOT advise that you attempt to go there alone. H. Mercier.'

I crumpled the paper in my fist then marched purposefully across the hall to my father's study, a gloomy book lined room that I rarely had occasion to enter and mostly associated with my mother's final illness when I had been sent downstairs from her sick room several times in order to fetch a favourite book from the well stocked shelves. I don't think I had set foot inside since then and my heart was in my mouth as I gently pushed open the door and stole inside.

The study smelt strongly of leather bound books, cigar smoke and the sweet incense that my father loved to burn in beautiful blue and white porcelain burners when he was relaxing with a book. I smiled as I went over to the desk, thinking how the mingled scent of incense and cigars would always bring him to mind, just as the smell of lavender and rose face cream would forever remind me of my mother.

Her portrait, serene, pale and limpid eyed in primrose yellow silk and muslin, hung over the fireplace in the study and I glanced up at it with a smile as I quickly sifted through the pile of pamphlets and books that littered the desk, hunting for my father's battered pocket atlas of London. I'd learned my lesson now and was determined never again to approach the dark and warren like streets of Whitechapel without proper preparation.

'Where on earth it it?' I wondered aloud as I scattered letters, receipts and leaflets all over the desk in my search before giving up and turning my attention to the drawers. The top one was locked, unsurprisingly enough, but the one below slid open and proved to be stuffed full of even more seemingly random pieces of paper: letters from admirers, invoices for painting commissions, bills from father's tailor, all shoved in together with no thought for order. I smiled wryly as I remembered my poor Mama's despair over father's untidy and disorganised ways and how he had blithely kissed it away, always reminding her that she only had herself to blame for choosing to marry a Bohemian artist rather than the peer that her parents had lined up for her hand.

I pulled out a sheaf of papers, some of which were yellowed with age and looked to be several years old and idly looked through them, thinking that perhaps it might be time for him to hire a proper secretary to keep his affairs in order and that it was wonder he ever got paid when he seemed to have such scant regard for bills and invoices when a letter somewhere in the middle captured my attention.

It was the return address at the very top that first caught my attention: Panacea House, Rayleigh, Essex. I may not have known very much about the world but I had heard of Panacea House, a well known, very exclusive and reputedly shockingly expensive 'rest home' for women suffering for nervous complaints or to put it another way - a lunatic asylum for inconvenient aristocratic ladies. It was one of those places that upper crust families like Lucasta's or my own, I suppose, sent girls and women who didn't quite fit in or were deemed liable to cause a scandal with their errant or erratic behaviour. It was either that or marriage to whoever would have them.

I let the other papers fall back into the drawer as I quickly read through the letter, which was dated from October 1882 and then, my eyes wide with shock and disbelief, read it through yet again, forcing myself to slow down and carefully take in each and every word. I could hardly believe what I was seeing, could hardly believe that I had been so soundly deceived in such a way and not just me but everyone else as well. Or had they? Was I the last to know?

'This changes everything,' I said to myself as I shakily tucked the letter and Henry's note into my reticule and dashed from the room.

Chapter Seventeen
Cora, 1888

The inquest was already well under way in the Working Lad's Institute on Whitechapel Road when I sneaked in through the heavy double doors and slid into one of the few remaining seats left at the back of the room, which was packed full of people, mostly women, all craning their necks to get a better view of the coroner as he spoke so that my view was obscured by a sea of dark bonnets and nodding heads.

'Hot in here, isn't it,' someone said close by and I turned to see Emma grinning at me from a seat just behind. I smiled back, noticing how much thinner and paler she looked and how despite the broad grin there was something wary about the way that her eyes, which were under shadowed by dark smudges of exhaustion, didn't quite meet mine.

'Boiling,' I agreed, pointlessly fanning myself with my hand as I looked around. It was autumn's last warm blast of the year and we were all sweltering in the small room which reeked of oniony sweat, bad breath and, oddly, old fish. A few women were patting lavender oil behind their ears in an attempt to freshen themselves up but they need not have bothered as the sweet spicy scent was no match for the rank smell that surrounded us all.

'What did I miss?' I whispered to Emma, ignoring the cross looks and pointed sssh's of the people around us.

She gave a delicate shrug. 'Nothing much,' she said with a hint of her usual chirpiness. 'Just the usual he said and she said. The doctor who examined poor old Annie is up next which should be more interesting.'

I shuddered. I'd already heard what was done to the woman found in Hanbury Street - even though Pa tried to keep us from finding out about it, it was impossible not to hear the rumour and

165

gossip that churned around the police station during the days after the murder. 'He almost took her head clean off,' Ned told me in a whisper when I was hanging about with him in the yard, enjoying the sunshine in between my chores while he puffed almost angrily on a cigarette while glancing uneasily over his shoulder in case one of the Sergeants came out and caught him. 'He cut it all around and yanked on it but it didn't come away, see.'

I must have gone pale or looked queasy or something because Emma leaned across and awkwardly patted my arm. She was wearing grimy black fine knitted mittens with a tear across the top and her fingernails were broken and thick with grime. 'Are you sure you should be here?' she asked in concern. 'It's not a pleasant business. I can tell you what happened later on if you'd rather go.'

I shook my head. 'I want to hear it for myself,' I said before turning back to the front where a small dapper looking man with a neatly clipped grey beard and small glasses was taking the stand. To my relief it wasn't Dr Killeen but one of his colleagues, Dr Phillips, a kind, gently spoken man whom I knew by sight from his occasional forays into the station. He coughed nervously before he began to speak and removed his glasses, played with them a bit then replaced them several times before addressing the room. 'I think that it might be advisable if any children, women or people of a nervous or gentle disposition leave the room before I begin,' he said with a frown that took in the gaggle of women who sat agog and eager for gory details on the front few rows, their children perched, bored and yawning on their laps. 'The evidence that I am about to present is of a rather, shall we say, distressing nature.'

He paused and looked pointedly at the women, clearly waiting for them to get up and leave, but instead they merely stared back at him, folded their arms and settled themselves more comfortably in their chairs, making it clear that they were not to budged. 'Ah.' Clearly knowing when to concede defeat, the doctor rustled the papers in front of him one last time then addressed the room again, first describing the scene when he had first seen the body of Annie Chapman in the yard off Hanbury Street then, with another pained look at the women on the front rows, continuing on to her many injuries.

I sank back against my chair as I listened, wondering not for the first time, why on earth I had come here to hear all of this. I suppose the truth was that since seeing the body of Martha Tabram laid out on the mortuary slab and then the sad and desolate site where poor Poll Nichols had met her end, I'd felt some sort of strange connection to these murdered women, had wanted to find out more about them.

'The throat had been severed as before described. The incisions into the skin indicated that they had been made from the left side of the neck. There were two distinct, clean cuts on the left side of the spine.' He paused and removed his glasses again and rubbed the skin between his eyes as if weary. 'They were parallel from each other and separated by about half an inch. The muscular structures appeared as though an attempt had been made to separate the bones of the neck.'

There was a ripple of horror through the room as we all winced, taking in the import of those words. Ned was right, he really had tried to pull her head right off. This was no man, it was a monster. A monster, furthermore, who walked among us still for I knew from my father's anxious expression and earnest pleas to we girls not to go out at night that he and his colleagues were no closer to catching whoever was responsible for these dreadful murders.

Dr Phillips paused until the hubbub of appalled muttering had died down then continued at a slower pace, carefully referring to his notes as he went. 'There were various other mutilations of the body, but I am of the opinion that they occurred subsequent to the death of the woman, and to the large escape of blood from the division of the neck.' He looked across to the coroner, who had gone ashen as he listened. 'I'm sorry,' he said, spreading his hands out apologetically. 'From these injuries, I am satisfied as to the cause of death and I feel that perhaps I ought not to go into further details of the mutilations, which could only be painful to the feelings of the jury and the public.' The women gave a great collective groan of annoyance - why else did he suppose that they had come there - and he cast them a reproachful look.

The coroner nodded his assent to this, also looking with annoyance at the women, who shushed then and whispered angrily to each other. I looked back at Emma, expecting to see her grinning away at the macabre pantomime being performed before us, but was surprised to see her staring in rapt and unsmiling attention at Dr Phillips as he started talking again, even leaning forward on her chair with her hands clasped tightly around her knees.

'It must have been a very sharp knife,' he said turning to nod at a portly dark haired man in a check suit who stood to the side: Inspector Abberline, a seasoned detective with many years prior experience of Whitechapel and the East End, who had been sent from Scotland Yard to solve this case as quickly and efficiently as possible. Pa said that he was a good sort with a quick brain but I knew from Ned that the other policemen were being rather less complimentary about him, disliking his quiet manner and resolute insistence on following police procedure to the letter. 'A knife with a thin, narrow blade.' I thought of the stab wounds on Martha Tabram, the blood that had oozed out on to her dress, her flabby face and the foul stench of death that had surrounded her as his voice droned on in the background. 'There was no evidence about the body of the woman of a struggle having taken place. I am positive that the deceased entered the yard alive as I made a practical search of the passage and the approach to the house and saw no trace of blood.' Another pause. 'I am of the opinion that the person who cut the deceased's throat took hold of her by the chin, and then commenced the incision from left to right.'

I heard Emma give a small sigh behind me and turned again, this time meeting her eyes. 'I've heard enough,' she said and got up to leave. I hesitated just for a moment before I stood up too and hurried after her, stumbling over feet and ankles in my haste not to lose her. I turned just once at the door and saw with a blush that Dr Phillips had paused again and that everyone had turned to watch us leave, including Inspector Abberline who was looking at me with interest and, more worryingly, recognition.

'Emma, wait!' She was already half way along the street, hurrying along with one hand holding her shawl about her shoulders and the other clamped to the front of her black bonnet to stop it falling off as she charged head first through the crowds, clearly determined not to be caught up with. 'Emma!' She obviously wasn't going to stop and wait for me so I had no option but to run after her, bunching my skirts up so that I didn't trip over them.

'Emma?' I was panting by the time I caught up with her. 'What's wrong?' I put a hand on her arm to stop her and was a bit surprised when she didn't just shake it off and go on her way but instead came to a halt and turned slowly and clearly unwillingly towards me.

'Nothing.' She muttered, not quite meeting my eyes. 'Nothing's wrong. Why would it be?'

'Why did you run out of the inquest then?' I said. We were standing in the middle of the pavement on Whitechapel Road, which was jam packed with the usual wandering throng of traders, housewives in their aprons with baskets slung over their arms and small children darting in and out of the traffic. On the corner of Osborn Street there stood a trio of sad faced flower sellers, hoarsely shouting about their wares above the din of the traffic while further along a knife grinder was cheerfully sharpening knives for a queue of women. I thought of Dr Phillips' evidence about the murder weapon at the inquest and quickly looked away. 'What's wrong?'

Emma turned on me angrily, almost snarling. 'There's nothing wrong so just bloody leave it, why don't you.' This time she did yank her arm away from my hand then gathered her grubby yellow shawl tighter about her shoulders as if trying to protect herself. 'Just leave me alone.'

I was confused, this wasn't the Emma that had waved me cheerily off from the steps of Christ Church all those weeks ago. This pale, trembling, wild eyed girl was someone else, was a total stranger in fact and I wondered what on earth had happened to her since the last time we'd met. 'What's going on?' I whispered, pulling her to the side out of the way of the jostling crowds, some of whom stared at us curiously as they milled around us. 'Are you in trouble?'

She laughed nastily. 'You could say that,' she said, twisting up her grubby face to stop herself crying. 'In a manner of speaking.'

I put my arm around her painfully thin shoulders and hugged her close. 'Maybe I could help you?' I wasn't sure how exactly but it felt good to make the offer.

Emma gave a wavering smile. 'There's no one on God's earth who can help me now,' she said wearily before giving a rueful little shrug. 'And there's no one that I trust enough to help anyway.'

Did I imagine the resentful look she gave me as she said this? 'You can trust me,' I said falteringly, wondering what was going on and hoping that it wasn't anything serious.

'Can I?' She shook off my arm and backed away, frowning. No, I hadn't imagined that look of mingled resentment and anger that glinted in her eyes. 'We both know that that isn't true.'

I stared at her. 'I don't know what you mean.' I did though, of course I did. She'd asked me before about the envelope, the one that I'd taken from amongst Martha Tabram's pile of shabby belongings at the mortuary, and I'd lied about it. Would I still lie about it now though?

'You're lying,' Emma whispered, reaching out to grasp my wrist with her thin fingers. 'What did you do with it?' Her eyes bored into my mine and although I desperately wanted to look away, I couldn't. She gave me a little shake. 'What. Did. You. Do. With. It?'

I tore my gaze away then. 'I gave it back to her,' I mumbled.

She released me then and took a step back. 'You did what?' she said, confused. 'Gave it back to whom?'

I shook my head, not really wanting to tell her about my pathetic trip to Highbury but knowing that I must nonetheless. 'The girl on the envelope,' I muttered. 'Alice Redmayne. I gave it back to her.'

Emma stared at me for a moment, her eyes and mouth wide open with shock before, to my immense surprise, she released my arm and fell back against a doorway wheezing with laughter. 'You gave it back to her? That stuck up bint from Highbury? No wonder she's been hanging about in Whitechapel like a lost lamb,' she said, wiping tears from her eyes. 'Well, that's a turn up for the books and no mistake.'

Relieved that she didn't seem to be angry any more, I plunged on with my explanation, feeling my cheeks go a little warm with embarrassment as I went. 'I wish that I'd never taken it. They all think I'm weak as milk so I wanted to prove that I wasn't by seeing the dead Tabram woman and then taking something that belonged to her to prove what I'd seen.' I paused as Emma's laughter came to a hiccuping end and she began to intently listen.

'I didn't know that it was yours, I swear that I didn't and I didn't mean to exactly steal it either. I'm not a thief,' I boldly asserted even though the evidence clearly disproved this. 'Of course, once I'd shown it to my sister I didn't know what to do with it. She thought I should put it back where I found it but I wanted to see this Alice Redmayne for myself, I don't know why…'

'So you went up to Highbury and gave it back to her,' Emma finished for me with a tiny smile and a look that was almost admiring. 'Well, I can hardly blame you for that. I was curious too but didn't think to actually go up there and see for myself. Perhaps I should have done and saved us all a lot of trouble.'

I nodded. 'I didn't get to see her though,' I said ruefully. 'I got scared, wrote that it had come from Whitechapel and posted it through the door of her big house then ran off before she could catch up with me.'

Emma laughed again then and, just for a moment, I saw a flash of the merry, confident girl that I had left behind on the steps of Christ Church. 'She's here in Whitechapel now,' she said musingly. 'I was wondering why she'd come here and now I think I know.' She put her arm through mine and we walked together up Osborn Street, apparently reconciled although I still felt wary and worried about saying the wrong thing and angering her again.

'I've seen her too,' I said as we went up Wentworth Street. 'She got knocked over the head in one of the alleyways off the Old Montague. I went to help her with Mr Mercier.'

My voice, always my betrayer, must have softened when I said his name for Emma drew back and gave me a sharp measuring look. 'Mashed on him, are you?' she said slyly. 'Well, he is a handsome one, isn't he? He's not my type, mind but I can see why you girls might go all silly over him.'

I pursed my lips together and shook my head. 'I don't know what you mean,' I said, realising with despair that I was probably blushing furiously. 'He wouldn't notice the likes of me anyway.'

Emma sighed and put her head to one side, observing me thoughtfully. 'Oh, I don't know about that,' she said with a smile. 'You're a bit of a looker. Or would be if you maybe curled your hair a little and wore brighter colours.'

I stared at her. 'Do you really think so?' I said, reaching up to self consciously pat my red hair. Pa said it was beautiful but the other children at school had called me 'Carrots' and tugged on my plaits until I cried. They'd never have dared to treat Cat like that but I was quieter and considered fair game.

Emma grinned. 'Of course. Haven't you noticed the way men stare at you when you walk past?'

Now I really was blushing. 'Not Mr Mercier though,' I mumbled. 'I don't think he really notices me.' I sighed. 'I think he's soft on Miss Redmayne. Now she's a real beauty, isn't she?'

Emma laughed then and gave me a quick hug. 'And to think that it's your fault that she's here at all,' she said. 'After all if it wasn't for you taking her that bloody envelope, she probably wouldn't have come here, would she?'

I turned and looked at her. 'But why is she here?' I said. 'Is she looking for me or is it something else?' I remembered the heavy feel of the pendant in my hand, the elaborately curling engraving on the back. 'Beatrice,' I whispered. 'Is that who she's after?'

Emma turned away from me and a sort of darkness passed across her face. 'Maybe.'

I stopped then and planted myself in front of her, resisting the urge to wag my finger scoldingly in her face as my sister would have done to me. 'What is going on, Emma? Who is Beatrice and what's all this got to do with the murdered women?'

She looked at me as if she was going to deny all knowledge but then gave a curt nod. 'Fine, I'll tell you but you mustn't breathe a word to anyone and especially not that Pa of yours.' She held up her hand as I began to protest. 'I know he's a good sort and not like the flashy coppers on the make you get around here but you can't trust any of them, not really.'

'You can trust my Pa,' I said stoutly.

She shrugged, obviously unconvinced. 'Let's go for a drink. You look like you could do with one and I'm parched.' The Princess Alice pub, its once colourful sign sun faded and peeling, was at the end of the road and she took my hand and dragged me along to it, ignoring my feeble protests. 'Oh come on, it's not like your beloved Pa will ever find out that I've set your innocent little feet on the road to ruination or anything.'

CHAPTER EIGHTEEN

I let her lead me in through the doors to the grimy public bar with its rickety, beer stained old tables and dirty sawdust strewn floor where she boldly plonked herself next to the bar and ordered two bottles of beer from an elderly barman, who peered at us disapprovingly from beneath his huge tufty white eyebrows, assessing our potential for troublemaking, before giving a small shrug and turning away to get our drinks.

'I can't have beer,' I said, mindful of a promise I'd once made to my Pa that I wouldn't take to drink. He was always saying that he'd seen too many girls and women come to ruination through the demon drink to lose my sister and me to it as well.

Emma made an impatient sound. 'Oh, don't be such a baby. One bottle of piss weak ale isn't going to wreck your life.' She paid the barman and handed me my bottle. 'Gin though is quite a different matter,' she said with a wink before chinking her bottle against mine. 'Chin, chin.'

I stared dubiously down at the brown glass bottle in my hand then gave a small shrug and raised it to my lips. I was already a thief and a liar, I might as well add drunkard to my sins as well.

'What do you think?' Emma said, nudging me with her elbow.

I rolled the warm beer around my mouth and tried not to grimace at the metallic tang which reminded me of the time I fell over in the street and accidentally bit my tongue, filling my mouth with blood. 'It's not bad.' It wasn't exactly pleasant either but I wasn't about to say so, sharply aware as I was that she could probably barely afford to pay for it.

'Liar,' she said gaily before taking another swig of her own drink and wiping her mouth with the back of her hand.

We sat in silence for a while, sipping our beer and half heartedly listening to the buzz and drone of conversation around us. Like most of the pubs on Commercial Street, the Princess Alice had a mixed clientele of tarts, market men and everything in between. It was popular with the women of the area as it was one of the few pubs that didn't make them stand outside with their drinks and there were quite a few of them in there now, clustered like flies around the sticky tables and emitting gusts of laughter and gossip.

'So what's this all about then?' I asked eventually as the silence stretched on between us.

Emma gave a heavy sigh and rolled her eyes. 'I was hoping you'd forgotten about all that,' she muttered against the head of her bottle.

I grinned. 'Not a chance,' I said.

She carefully put her bottle down on the bar and turned to me. 'You promise that you won't go blabbing this all over the Chapel?' she said grimly. The Chapel was how some of the local tarts liked to refer to Whitechapel, which had the effect of making it sound much nicer and rather less Godless than it actually was. 'Only if word gets out then I'm done for.'

I gulped. 'Surely it can't be that bad?' I said.

She shook her head. 'It can and it is,' she said before abruptly leaving the bar and making her way to a recently vacated table in the far corner. 'I don't want anyone listening in,' she said over her shoulder as I grabbed my bottle of beer and scrambled to follow, pushing my way gently through the crowd, which was buzzing with the latest gruesome titbits from Annie Chapman's inquest, which had just ended. It didn't take long for news, especially bad news, to spread through Whitechapel - by nightfall there wouldn't be a garret or cellar in the whole area that didn't know what was done to poor old Annie, God bless her.

I settled myself on a low wooden stool next to Emma and turned to her expectantly as she arranged her shawl around her shoulders and fluffed up her fair hair a little. 'Alright, it's like this,' she said at last after taking a long swig of her beer. 'Beatrice or Bea as she was then was a girl I knew in a knocking shop in Calais. I say 'was' because...' her voice trailed away and she looked away. To my surprise I saw that she was almost crying.

'She died,' I said softly.

Emma shook her head. 'She was murdered,' she said furiously, the raw rage back and bubbling over inside her as she looked into the past and saw things that I hoped never to even imagine. 'Butchered.'

'Like the others?' My throat felt suddenly parched so that my voice came out as a nervous little squeak.

She gave a brisk nod. 'Just like the others.' She picked up her bottle and passed it nervously from hand to hand then pressed it against her cheek. 'She was alright was Bea. A bit long in the tooth maybe to still be working as a tart and the other girls thought she was a bit of a fancy piece as well, probably on the run from some rich man or other after cleaning him out, although I never thought she was looking down on us all or nothing.' She took a drink and pulled a face as if she'd only just realised how bitter the taste was. 'She had lovely things though and was nicely spoken, not in a lah dee dah snotty sort of way but in a nice way.' She looked at me. 'Just like that Alice your Mr Mercier is so mashed on.'

'He's not my Mr Mercier,' I broke in.

Emma shrugged impatiently. 'Oh leave it out. Do I look like I was born yesterday?' She put her bottle down on the table and carried on, rubbing her hand across her eyes as if suddenly weary. 'Anyway, that was Bea. A nice girl who deserved better than she got.' She sighed. 'A bit like all of us, I suppose.'

'How was she related to Miss Redmayne though?' I asked, feeling a bit confused and still not sure how all of this related to the current spate of murders in Whitechapel.

Emma pursed her lips and put her head to one side as she considered this. 'No idea,' she said at last. 'Maybe she was her governess or old nanny or something? I don't think it's very likely that a flash toff like Miss Alice would be related to the sort of girl who winds up ripped to pieces outside a French knocking shop.'

I nodded in agreement, remembering the Redmayne's big house in Highbury, their haughty butler, the atmosphere of wealth and luxury. 'I think you must be right,' I said. Even after she'd been knocked down in an alleyway, with dirt on her dress, blood trickling down her smooth high forehead and her long hair falling down around her ears, Alice Redmayne had looked like quality and was plainly completely out of place in the stews of Whitechapel. 'She came here anyway though,' I said. 'She must be trying to find her.'

175

Emma nodded. 'Oh she's looking for her alright,' she said thoughtfully. 'I've heard these upper crust girls can get quite attached to their old nannies and whatnot so that's not entirely surprising.'

'But to come all the way to somewhere like Whitechapel?' I said, doubt creeping in. 'And for someone who might very well be dead.'

'Who is dead,' Emma corrected me and we both fell silent as we contemplated the fact of Miss Redmayne's imminent disappointment. 'Poor cow. She has no idea.'

I drained my bottle almost without thinking. 'She needs to be told,' I said with a firmness that I did not entirely feel. 'One of us should tell her what happened.'

Emma shrugged. 'Maybe,' she agreed but I could tell that she was unwilling. Who wouldn't be? It's no easy task to tell someone that one of their nearest and dearest had been killed in cold blood. My Pa had done it hundreds of times, this was Whitechapel after all, and told me once that it never got any better, that it was just as hard and painful every single time to see them crumple and hear them cry.

'I'll get us both another drink,' I said, barely waiting for Emma's silent nodded assent before I went off to the bar, my head reeling with what I had been told so far and slightly worried about what further revelations were surely imminent. Despite my initial misgivings, I was beginning to feel quite at home in the Princess Alice and wouldn't have objected to settling there for the rest of the day in fact although I suspected that Cat might have something to say about that as she was expecting me back by evening.

I returned to the table with two more bottles of beer, one of which I placed in front of Emma before I sat back down on my stool. She looked morose but managed to greet me with a wavering smile. 'I suppose you're wondering what all of this has got to do with me and you?' she said. 'Isn't it obvious though?'

I shook my head. 'Not really,' I said although looking at her pale unsmiling face and the way her hand trembled as she picked up her bottle was making me feel a bit sick at heart as if something big and terrible was about to happen. 'Do you think it's the same killer?'

She pressed her lips together and nodded. 'Yes,' she said, toying nervously with her drink. 'It's the same man alright. I saw him out of our window in Calais.'

I stared at her, aghast. 'You saw him?' I said a little too shrilly, which made a few people near our table turn and stare at us curiously. I blushed and lowered my voice to a whisper. 'You actually saw him?'

Emma nodded dismally. 'Not well enough to be able to recognise his face but...' She hesitated then took a swig of beer. 'He got a better view of me. Stupid cow that I was, standing there in plain view, gawping from the window like some sort of ruddy half wit.' She wiped away some tears and looked away, setting her face into an expression of stony indifference.

My heart stopped. 'He saw you?' No wonder she looked terrified, no wonder she'd lost some of her spark. 'Is that why he's here? To find you?'

She shrugged. 'No idea,' she said in a small, broken voice. 'My friend and I thought we'd be safe here in Whitechapel. She'd been here before, you see, and knew that it's the sort of the place where a girl can hide herself away and avoid any trouble.' She gave a grim little smile. 'Or so we thought at first.'

'Until the murders started again,' I said, reaching across the table to take her hand in mine.

'Until the murders started again,' she agreed, squeezing my fingers. 'I saw him on the night that Annie Chapman died,' she went on. 'I went to the yard on Hanbury Street trying to find her, to stop her going with him but it was too late and he came up behind me just after I found what was left of her.' Her grip on my fingers tightened even more. My Pa had come back from Hanbury Street shattered and silent after spending the morning keeping guard over the Chapman woman's butchered body so God only knew how Emma had felt when she saw it in the dead of night with the killer himself breathing down the back of her neck. 'He knew my name,' she said so quietly that I had to lean forward to be able to hear her. 'I thought I was going to die right then and there but he just said my name and then he left me alone in the darkness.' She looked at me then, her eyes wide with horror and fear. 'I swear to God, Cora, I thought I was a goner.'

'So why is he killing all these other women instead?' I said

177

dully, wishing with all my heart that I'd never set eyes on that blasted envelope, had never set foot in the bloody mortuary because then none of this would be anything to do with me. It would all be happening to someone else, be someone else's problem, not mine.

Emma shrugged. 'How would I know?' she said, starting to sound panicked. 'He's got to be a raving lunatic to do the things that he does, tearing women to pieces in the street then walking away without a care in the world. Who knows what's going through his head?' She tapped the side of her skull then picked up her drink again. 'I thought maybe that he's trying to scare me or that it's a sort of message perhaps, just letting me know that he's here and knows who and where I am.'

'What about your friend?' I said, still feeling a bit sick and fighting the urge to look over my shoulder to see if he was there watching us now. 'Did he get a look at her as well?'

'Marie? I don't know.' She sighed, frowning. 'Besides, she's got her own worries right now with her bloke and landlord and all the usual bloody boring rest of it.' She leaned back on her stool and fixed me with a challenging look. 'I suppose you won't want to be seen with me now?' she said, not, I was pleased to note, without some regret.

I shook my head. 'Don't think that,' I replied, forcing myself to smile, keeping my eyes on hers. 'We're friends aren't we? Of course I still want to see you.'

'You sure about that? You heard what he said that bugger done to Annie,' she said fiercely, leaning forward and gripping both of my hands in hers so that I couldn't pull away. 'That's what he's going to do to me and to you as well if you hang about me long enough.'

I swallowed hard, determined not to reveal how terrified I was. 'Seems to me that if he's been watching you and seeing who you're hanging about with then it's too late for me to be worried about that, isn't it?' I even managed a laugh although it was a pretty mirthless one. 'Seems to me that we'd be best off sticking together.'

There didn't seem to be much to say after that so we sat in silence, lost in our own thoughts as we finished our beers then, still quiet and thoughtful, went our separate ways.

Chapter Nineteen

It was winter when we first moved into the police station. Ma had been dead and under the ground for three months by that point and I remember missing her desperately as we dumped our makeshift bundles of clothes and bedding on to the floor and stared around us at the plain whitewashed walls, the dusty shelves and the grease streaked windows that overlooked Commercial Street. Aunt May, brisk and efficient as always, clicked her tongue against her teeth as she looked around then quickly set to work, first directing us to put our things into our rooms then calling us back to help her clean and tidy up. 'This will make you all a cosy home once it's all spick and span,' she said to me, hugging me close as I began to cry again. 'You'll be happy here, Cora, just wait and see.'

I hadn't believed her at the time - it was still, after all and when all was said and done, a police station and not precisely the pretty cottage with roses around the door that I had always dreamed of. Even as we scrubbed the table and windows then swept the floors, we could hear the policemen downstairs marching about in their heavy boots and calling to each other, their voices gruff and manly, their laughter harsh and a little frightening.

'I don't really like the idea of you girls living close to so many men,' Aunt May said in a quiet voice, looking dubiously first at Cat and then, more lingeringly, myself. 'Although I am sure that your father knows what he's about in bringing you here.' Again there was that dubious look. 'You will be careful, won't you, my dears? You'll do as your Pa tells you and stay away from the other policemen?'

I hung back and said nothing, mainly because at that time I didn't really understand what she meant or what I was supposed to be careful about but Cat, who knew better as always, grinned and gave our aunt a quick, fierce hug. 'Of course, Aunt May,' she said. 'And I'll keep an eye on our Cora too so don't worry about her either.'

I thought about all of this now as I walked up Commercial Street to the police station. As Aunt May had predicted, it had indeed become a happy home to us all to the extent that now, after all these years, I couldn't really imagine living anywhere else and it even felt a little peculiar to me that other people lived in places that didn't have dozens of policemen shouting, marching and laughing underfoot. It would probably have been too noisy a home for many folk but I took a strange comfort from the sounds that drifted up from the police station below, particularly late at night when I lay sleepless in the bed that I shared with my sister and listened with my eyes sleepily half closed to the singing, shouts, slammed doors and murmurs that came from down below.

The sun had gone in and there was a drizzle of light rain that had come on with the usual suddenness of that time of year, so that I was slightly damp by the time that I had reached the blue painted main doors of the police station. Usually I would walk further along the street then skirt sideways into the back yard but on this day I lifted my chin and marched boldly in through the front door.

'Alright, Cora?' one of the mutton chopped Sergeants called from behind the desk as I strode in, his lined face showing no great surprise to see me. It was the job of the older Sergeants like my Pa to man the main desk and deal with any enquiries that came in while it was the lot of the younger men to walk the beats around the district. 'Your Pa is around here somewhere if you want to see him?'

I smiled and shook my head, pulling up my apron to dry my hair and then my face. 'Not if he's busy,' I said. Everyone seemed to be busy in the station that day, from the officers bustling about, their brows creased with worry as they whispered together about the recent spate of murders and that morning's inquest to the usual huddle of drably dressed, sickly looking men and women slumped miserably on the bottom of the cells.

The Sergeant sighed. 'We're up against it and no mistake,' he said miserably. 'I've never known anything like it.' I knew that he

180

meant - Whitechapel was as lawless and brutal a place as they come but murder, and particularly when committed with such savagery, was still very much out of the ordinary here, not because of any hallowed respect for the sanctity of life or anything like that, but because it was considered pointless in a place where no one had anything worth stealing and no one blinked an eyelash if a couple wanted to part ways so there was no need to kill an unwanted spouse if you wanted to shack up with someone else. Such murder as we saw here was of the petty and sad variety - mothers killing their unwanted children, men beating each other about the head in a bar room brawl, drunken beggars turning on each other in their gin fuelled madness. Certainly not anything like the horrors that we had seen in the last few months.

'You'll catch whoever is doing it,' I said consolingly, even though I didn't really quite believe it. 'He'll make a mistake soon enough. He has to, really. It's only down to sheer luck that he hasn't been caught so far, isn't it? I mean someone as mad as he clearly is can't be all that cunning, can they?'

I looked to him for reassurance but he just sighed again, more heavily this time. 'I hope so.' His face brightened then as another, more cheerful, thought struck him. 'Mind you, there's plenty of folk saying that he's gone up north to Gateshead. There's a girl been murdered up there too, throat cut from ear to ear and left out on the street for all to see. Maybe he isn't even here any more so we're all worrying about nothing.' He sounded hopeful, which I suppose was tough cheese for the girls of Gateshead.

The glass panelled door behind him opened and I instinctively drew back as Inspector Abberline appeared, a deep frown between his fine dark eyebrows. 'Sergeant,' he nodded politely to the officer behind the desk before turning to me. 'It's Sergeant Lee's girl, isn't it?' he said with a gentle smile. 'Cora?'

I bobbed a small uncertain curtsey. 'That's right, sir,' I said so quietly that he had to lean forward to be able to hear me. 'I live upstairs.'

Abberline nodded. 'You were at the inquest today,' he said.

I nodded shamefacedly, expecting to be reprimanded but instead he surprised me by smiling and beckoning me forward. 'Come with me,' he said, lifting up the hinged section of the desk counter so that I could pass through to the other side. 'I would like to talk to you if I may, Cora Lee.'

Shivering with nerves, I followed him through the door to the inner sanctum of the station, a confusing warren of whitewashed corridors, cells and briefing rooms, all of which swarmed with uniformed police officers who nodded deferentially to Abberline and peered curiously at me as I wandered, pale, terrified and convinced that I was about to be arrested, in his wake.

Eventually we arrived at his office, a makeshift affair next to door to that of Detective Inspector Reid, that had clearly been hastily cleared up for his use just before his arrival a few weeks beforehand. He held the door open for me as I entered then closed it firmly behind us before gesturing that I should sit down on the falling apart leather chair that had been pulled close to the shabby, paper and book littered desk. 'Please be seated, Miss Lee,' he said gently. 'There is no need to be afraid of me. I wished only to make your acquaintance.'

I gave a little nod then quickly sat down, carefully folding my hands together in my lap and, with some effort for I was still very frightened, turning my gaze on to him as he perched, somewhat uneasily on the edge of the desk, pushing some papers out of the way as he did so. 'This office is a mess,' he said with a nervous laugh gesturing around him at the piles of books on the floor, the unmade cot bed in the corner, the dog eared notes, sketches and photographs carelessly pinned to the board behind him. I took one look at these then had to look quickly away - a gesture that he noted with an almost imperceptible nod. 'There's supposed to be a woman who comes in to tidy but she has yet to materialise. I'm beginning to suspect that she might be a figment of my imagination.'

I found my voice then. 'That would be Mrs Walsh,' I said quietly. 'She is married to one of the Sergeants and is supposed to come in and clean. She acts as matron to the lady prisoners too if they require it and takes charge of any children that come in.'

'A most necessary woman then,' Abberline said with a smile. 'I should be pleased to make her acquaintance.' Again he looked sadly around his office.

'She's ill at present,' I said. 'It's just a cough my sister Cat says but Mrs Walsh, well, she worries and says that it is either influenza or consumption or worse.'

Abberline laughed then. 'Oh, she's like that, is she?' he said with a rueful smile. 'I have an aunt who likes to always imagine herself more ill than she actually is. I expect that she will outlive us all one day. Their type always do despite all their pills and potions and fretting.'

I smiled politely but my eyes returned again to the three grainy photographs pinned to the wall just behind his head. 'What did you want to see me about?' I said, this time unable to drag my gaze away. There was Martha Tabram again, her face flabby and pale in death and her mouth hanging half open just as it had done when I had seen her in the mortuary. Next to her was the thin, careworn face of Poll Nichols, her eyes slightly open and pale hair drawn away from her forehead. Emma had told me that in life, Poll had been a lively little birdlike woman, fond of cracking jokes, a little vain about her relatively youthful looks and always happy to join in a singalong around the piano, get a round in if she had the money or offer a comfortable shoulder to cry on. Like Martha, she was a thief but such an inept and rather pathetic one that no one ever really got angry with her about it.

Annie Chapman, however had been a whole different kettle of fish according to Emma and I looked at her face with interest, shuddering a little as I noticed the piece of white card that had been placed over her neck to hide the terrible wounds that had been inflicted upon her throat. There was no way to disguise the awkward way that her head lolled to side though or the bruised puffiness of her cheeks and eyes. 'She'd been through the wars had Annie,' Emma had said to me earlier. 'Had a hard life and didn't care who knew it. You should have seen her. Proper hatchet faced she was with an expression like a bulldog chewing on a nest of wasps.' Clearly, she didn't look much better in death than she had alive.

'I see that you are interested in the photographs,' Abberline said quietly. 'But of course, you have seen Martha Tabram before, haven't you?'

I gasped and looked quickly away. 'I don't know what you mean,' I said, my hands trembling and fluttering in my lap. 'I've never seen any of those women before in my life.'

He smiled and shook his head. 'Dr Killeen says that he caught you looking at her body in the mortuary,' he said, still in that

183

gentle voice.

I shook my head but really there was no point denying it. 'You won't tell my father?' I whispered, feeling my cheeks go hot and red with shame as I imagined Pa's reaction should he ever hear about what I had done. It was bad enough that Cat should know, even though I knew that she would never tell.

Abberline hesitated for a moment then shook his head. 'No,' he said slowly. 'I won't tell him.'

I nodded. 'Thank you.' I looked up at him then and met his kind hazel eyes. Most of my father's fellow sergeants thought that Abberline was too soft, too yielding and preferred the more brusque and forthright manner of the head of H Division's CID, Inspector Reid, a no nonsense sort of man with bristling dark whiskers who was rumoured to be a committed atheist and whose unlikely hobbies included visiting stone circles and going up in hot air balloons then putting on a parachute and jumping out of them. No one knew yet what Abberline's hobbies were but I hazarded a guess that they would be rather less exciting than those of Inspector Reid. 'I don't know why I did it,' I said.

He smiled. 'I expect you wanted to see for yourself,' he said with a small shrug. 'I would have done much the same thing at your age. It's only natural to be curious about death, especially when it is so violent and on your own doorstep as it were.'

I gave a small, flickering smile. 'Dr Killeen made me feel very unladylike,' I murmured. 'I don't think he thinks that girls are supposed to be interested in such things.'

Abberline laughed. 'You should try telling my wife that,' he said with a wry smile. 'She and all her friends are desperate to hear all the latest gory details of these murders, especially now that it is all over the newspapers and I suspect that it is mostly ladies who read that infernal rag The Illustrated Police News as well.' He sighed. 'And you saw the front rows of the inquest, rammed full of local women all lapping up every horrible detail. Poor old Dr Phillips was no match for them, I fear.' He reached across the desk and picked up a plain tin cigarette case. 'You didn't stay to hear all of it though, did you?' He took out a cigarette and lit it with a match which he then shook and flicked into an overflowing bin by the side of the desk.

'No.' I shook my head, feeling suddenly uneasy again. 'I didn't like to hear about what was done to her.'

He sighed and took a drag on his cigarette. 'And your friend?' he said, screwing up his eyes as some smoke blew towards him. 'The girl with fair hair? I've seen her around Whitechapel before. Isn't her name Emma or something like that? Emily perhaps?'

I shook my head, suddenly on my guard. 'She isn't my friend,' I said stiffly.

'Isn't she?' He sighed and exhaled a plume of blue grey smoke. 'Ah well.'

I stood up then, pushing my chair back so that it squeaked on the tiled brown floor. 'I really should get back,' I said. 'My sister will be wondering where I am and as for my Pa…' Someone was bound to have told him by now that Abberline had asked me into his office and he'd be wondering why and probably thinking that I'd been caught in some wrong doing.

Abberline smiled and nodded. 'Yes, you should go,' he said vaguely, turning away to hunt for something among his mess of papers and books. 'I have probably kept you here long enough.'

I nodded then scarpered as quickly as I could before he changed his mind and called me back again. The back rooms of the station, which smelt as always of male sweat, boiled tea, sour milk, tobacco smoke and pease pudding were quiet now as I made my way back to the front lobby - there were just a few younger officers lounging about and whispering together furtively in one of the briefing rooms while in the distance there was the low rumble of Inspector Reid bellowing orders at some poor cowering sap.

'It's when the girls like that start to get murdered that we've got to worry,' I heard one of the young policemen say as he jerked his pointed chin, which was covered with the merest dusting of stubble, in my direction. 'Let's face it, no one really cares what happens to the sloppy old tarts, do they?'

I almost stopped and told him that he was wrong, that people did care, that I cared what happened to them but to my shame I didn't. Instead, I just felt my ears go very hot and red and carried on walking, feeling glad that my Pa didn't feel the same way as him for after all, as he'd said to Cat and I after the Chapman woman was found dead in that backyard not too far away, 'They're all someone's daughters and some of them are wives,

185

sisters and mothers too. It's a cruel world, so it is, that has brought them to this.'

'Are you alright, Cora?' I would have recognised Mr Mercier's voice anywhere and instantly turned to look at him, feeling half shy, half tremulous with excitement as always. If I was a dog, I'd be wagging my tail at him, I thought, rather disgusted with myself. Why can't I be more like that Miss Redmayne he's so keen on? She never looks pleased to see him, quite the reverse in fact.

'I'm fine and dandy, Mr Mercier,' I said, trying to look as uninterested as Miss Redmayne always did but without her beauty and poise to assist me, I no doubt ended up looking completely idiotic instead. 'I was just looking for my Pa.'

He sighed and took a step forward from where he had been leaning against a doorframe. 'I thought I saw you at this morning's inquest,' he said. 'I must confess that I was surprised to see you there.'

My heart stopped but I managed a careless shrug. 'I didn't see you there, Mr Mercier,' I said, knowing that I sounded incredibly defensive but unable to stop myself. 'I was just curious, that's all. My Pa talks about the murders all the time so I wanted to hear about it for myself.'

He looked at me for a long moment, his eyes considering but not unkind then nodded. 'I suppose it is only natural to be interested,' he said at last. 'After all, women are being killed in the most brutal manner imaginable in your own area so of course you want to know everything you can about it.' He moved closer to me with a look of concern, while I stared helplessly up at him, putting all the love that I felt into my eyes and wishing that he'd look the same way at me. 'You aren't scared though, are you?'

I shook my head. 'No, sir,' I said. 'My Pa doesn't like me to go out at night anyway and besides... well...' I stumbled over my words but my meaning was clear and he gave another nod.

'The killer isn't murdering girls like you, is he?' he said. 'But what if he did?' We walked together along the corridor that led back to the front lobby of the station. 'Do you think that would change things, Cora?'

I looked up at him. 'I don't know what you mean, sir,' I said although I thought that perhaps I did. What had the young policeman said just now? 'It's when the girls like that start to get murdered that we've got to worry.'

Mr Mercier gave a lopsided grin. 'Oh, I was just wondering aloud, Cora,' he said, holding the swing door into the lobby open for me to pass through. 'I was just wondering if perhaps people would pay more attention, take greater action if a,' and here he paused for a moment as he clearly tried to think of the right and kindest words, 'different sort of female was being targeted.'

I nodded. 'You mean, would people care more if he was killing young girls like myself?' I said. 'My Pa thinks so. He says it's not fair that people think it's alright to treat the street women badly and behave as if they deserve the bad things that happen to them. He says that they deserve to be cared about just as much as everyone else. He says that if we'd cared more about them before they felt so hopeless that they went on the streets to survive then things like this wouldn't happen.' I stopped and like a child put my hand over my mouth, not having meant to say so much.

Mr Mercier looked at me in silence for a moment then smiled. 'Your Pa sounds like a man after my own heart,' he said. 'I wish that there were more men like him in H Division.'

'I'm very proud of him,' I said quietly, my cheeks blooming crimson. We were standing in the lobby now and I could see the policemen behind the desk watching us curiously.

'And so you should be,' Mr Mercier said before giving me one last sad smile and strolling over to the desk.

'Where've you been?' Cat demanded crossly when I finally emerged a few moments later, red faced and panting, at the top of our stairs. 'I was expecting you home hours ago. I want to hear all about the inquest.'

I sighed. 'I'm here now, aren't I?' I pushed past her into the kitchen and threw myself down on to one of the chairs. Cat had been working on a wedding gown and the table was covered in cloth to protect the fine silk and lace from the usual stains and debris of every day life. A series of distant thumps, bumps and gleeful shouts told me that our brothers were in but fully occupied in their room.

She pulled a face and sat down opposite me. 'You said you'd help with this dress,' she said resentfully, almost reverently picking up the trail of lovely lace that she was painstakingly attaching to a swag of silk at the front of the skirt. 'It has to be perfect you see and your stitches are smaller than mine.'

I felt immediately contrite. 'I'm sorry, Cat,' I said. 'The inquest went on for longer than I expected and then Inspector Abberline wanted to talk to me about something.' A rather self important tone sneaked into my voice as I said this. We didn't know very much about Abberline but we'd spent a lot of time speculating about him. I felt quite pleased that I'd been the first to actually speak to him - in his own office no less.

Cat dropped the lace into her lap with surprise. 'What did he want to talk to you about?' she demanded, her eyes round. 'Have you been up to no good again?'

I shook my head. 'Of course not!' I said with much indignation. 'Although he knew all about that,' I said ruefully, pulling the wicker work basket towards me and selecting a needle and bobbin of cream thread. 'Well, about most of it anyway.' He didn't know about the missing envelope or if he did then he was keeping it back for some other occasion.

Cat looked startled. 'Is he going to tell Pa?' she asked in a fearful whisper. 'Did he give you a telling off?'

I shook my head. 'No,' I said, still feeling confused about what had just passed between Abberline and myself. It had seemed like such a nothing filled sort of conversation but I'd been aware of deeper currents underneath, of things that were being deliberately left unsaid and other things that were being asked of me even though I was not quite aware of them. 'I think he really wanted to know about a friend of mine,' I mused.

'You don't have any friends,' Cat scoffed, picking up her lace and bending over her work again.

That's what she thought.

CHAPTER TWENTY

The next few weeks passed quickly. There were no more murders, much to the relief of everyone in Whitechapel and the obvious annoyance and disappointment of the journalists that still swarmed around the area, desperate to sniff out any story that might keep the sensation alive in the minds of the newspaper reading public. It was front page news, you see and according to my Pa, everyone in London, in the whole country even, was talking about the horrible murders in Whitechapel, taking the case apart piece by piece and pretending to feel concern about the conditions that people lived in there.

'I hate all these do-gooders about the place,' my Pa said angrily over dinner one evening. 'They pretend to give a damn about the people of Whitechapel when really all they care about is making themselves feel better at our expense.'

I thought of Miss Redmayne then, who was still working at the Whitechapel Women's Mission most days then going back to her big house in Highbury in the evenings. I knew for a fact that she wasn't really here to help but even so there was always a glow about her, a look of satisfied contentment that suggested that she had found some sort of peace in her work among the fallen women and girls of Spitalfields.

I kept my distance from her though, mainly because I didn't want her to recognise me again and ask awkward questions but also because I didn't want to see her hanging about Mr Mercier. Just the thought of them together, of him smiling down into her eyes, made me hurt where I thought my heart must surely be.

I saw Emma even less often - generally in the distance as I went about my chores on Commercial Street but once I caught sight of her walking beneath our kitchen window in the station and I threw it up and hailed her. She'd looked up, startled then grinned and waved to me before calling something up that I couldn't quite hear over the rumbling of carts and carriages and shouts from the nearby market.

It was to be a few more days before I managed to speak to her properly though. I was just on my way down Brushfield Street, where my sister had sent me to pick up some fresh bread, eggs and milk for our pantry when she came running up behind me, her cheeks pink and eyes shining with exertion. 'There you are,' she said, coming to a halt in front of me. 'I've been looking everywhere for you.'

I smiled despite myself. 'Have you?' I said, feeling pleased that she gone to the trouble of looking for me. 'I'd have thought I'd be easy enough to find.'

Emma shrugged and put her arm through mine so that we proceeded together down the street. 'Not if you don't want to go near the police station, my girl,' she said with a wink. She looked plumper, cleaner and healthier than she had done the last time I saw her and even seemed to be wearing a new dress, a simple affair in pale blue sprigged cotton with only a few buttons missing from the front. 'I've got a job,' she said, grinning with pride. 'I'm working as a barmaid in the Britannia on the corner of Dorset Street which doesn't pay too badly and it's live in as well so I'm not sleeping in doss houses no more but am sharing a room with two other girls up above the pub.'

'So you're safe then?' I asked, not liking the idea of her unprotected and vulnerable to attack in the cheap rooms that sprang like mushrooms in the dank, damp abandoned houses of the district.

She nodded, still smiling. 'Yes, I'm safe,' she said. 'No more lodging houses and there's a barred door between me and Whitechapel every night.'

I smiled too. 'Oh, I'm right glad for you,' I said, meaning every word. 'You'll be able to save up now and everything.'

She laughed. 'Save? Oh, I don't know about that, Cora.' She smoothed down the front of her dress. 'What do you think? I got it on Middlesex Street for a song on account of all the missing buttons.'

'It's lovely,' I said before adding shyly: 'I can find you some buttons if you like? We always have spare ones lying about from our jobs. I'm sure I can find you some pretty ones that won't look too out of place.'

She stopped and gave me a quick fierce hug. 'That's kind of you,' she said. 'I'd like that. I've never been too handy with my needle and thread so it wouldn't occur to me to sew new buttons on. You should see my darning.' Something, a memory perhaps, made her eyes darken then and she moved her head slightly as if to shake it away out of her head.

'What did you want to see me for?' I asked after she'd pulled away. I hadn't had many friends in my life so the idea that someone might want to simply pass the time with me for no particular reason was a novel one. Emma, on the other hand, was obviously the sort of person who made friends with ease so I was under no illusion that this meant anything much to her. 'Has something else happened?' I whispered.

She tucked one hand back under my arm and waved the other airily before her. 'Oh no, nothing like that,' she said, her smile slipping a little so that I instantly regretted saying anything. 'I was just wondering, now that I have some money see, if you'd like to come out on my night off.'

'Come out?' I stared at her, a little bewildered. 'And do what?'

Emma laughed. 'Oh, you know, the usual,' she said. 'We could go to a music hall maybe. I've got a friend who comes into the pub and who reckons he can get us in to the Pavilion music hall on Whitechapel Road for free so then we'd only have to pay for our drinks once inside.' We'd reached the shop I was heading for and now stood on the pavement in front of it. 'What do you think?'

'A music hall?' Pa and Cat wouldn't like it but I couldn't prevent a throb of excitement entering my voice as I repeated those magical words. 'A real music hall?'

She grinned. 'Of course it's a real one, you dummy,' she said. 'How about it? I'm off for most of tonight so could come and get you at about nine if you can get away?'

'I'm usually in bed by then,' I said doubtfully. 'And Pa is working on the front desk tonight.'

'All the better,' Emma said brightly. 'Just wait for that sister of yours to nod off then sneak out. I'll wait for you outside your yard.' She made it all sound eminently possible and normal but I must have allowed a little of my doubts to show on my face for she leaned forward and hugged me again. 'Oh, Cora,' she said, 'how old are you now? Almost seventeen? You should be having some fun, my dear.'

'I do have fun,' I said staunchly if a little doubtfully.

'Do you?' Emma asked with a cheeky look and then she was gone.

I had my doubts, of course I did, but there was never any real chance that I wouldn't go out to meet her. The lure of the music hall, a glittering treat that I had longed for as long as I could remember but which had always remained apparently impossible, and the prospect of seeing Emma again were both enough to ensure that I was wide awake and clambering clumsily back into my clothes at just before nine after having waited impatiently for over half an hour for my sister's usual stream of night time chatter about the day we'd had, her plans for the boys and some small worries about Pa and the longevity of the side of bacon in the pantry to slow almost to a standstill then be gradually be replaced by the heavy breathing of deepest sleep.

'You came then?' Emma whispered to me out of the darkness after I'd carefully sneaked down the stairs then crossed the yard, hesitating just for a moment before opening the door out to the street. I whirled around and saw her leaning against the wall by the privies. She was wearing a different dress, this time of dull black silk, stained, worn through and shiny in places but still impressive enough to make me look down at my pink flowered cotton frock with slight dismay. 'I thought I might as well wait in here,' she said with a small shrug, patting the silly little black velvet hat she wore pinned on top of her blonde curls into place. 'It's better than loitering about outside on the street.' She caught me looking at her dress and smiled. 'I borrowed it from Molly, one of the Irish girls at the Britannia. She's ever so nice like that. I expect she'll want something in return though.'

I grinned at her. 'One day I'll take you upstairs to meet everyone,' I said, not really interested in Molly from the Britannia. 'I think you'd like my sister.'

'But would she like me?' Emma replied with an arch look as she pulled open the street door and stepped out on to the street. 'After all, I'm leading you astray aren't I?'

I laughed and linked arms with her. 'Oh, I wouldn't say that,' I said. 'Besides, I'm fairly sure that my sister already thinks I'm something of a lost cause.'

Emma slid me a wry sidelong look. 'Because of your propensity for looking at dead bodies and stealing from mortuaries?' she said with, I hoped, no hint of any ill feeling. 'I can't imagine why she should think that.'

'Quite so,' I said. 'This can't possibly be as bad as that.'

We were walking down Commercial Street together and, being unused to being out at such a late hour, I looked around myself with gleeful interest at the life and noise that still teemed in the streets from an elderly man sitting on the step of the Ten Bells and throwing bread crumbs angrily to a group of pigeons to a cluster of thin cheeked giggling match girls in battered old bonnets admiring their reflections in a shop window to two grim faced middle aged women arguing and almost coming to blows over a red nosed scrawny man who stood somewhat shamefacedly to the side to a sad huddle of half starved looking young men standing outside the pub and counting out their pennies to see what they could afford to drink if they all pooled in together. 'I love it here,' Emma said suddenly, much to my surprise. 'I feel at home in Whitechapel. I feel like I know it even better than my own village.'

'My Pa says that some people are more suited to city life than living in the countryside,' I said. 'He grew up in Suffolk and says that he'd never want to go back to that quiet sort of life where everyone knows everyone else's business and nothing much happens.' I remembered his wistful face that afternoon in Southend. 'He misses the sea though,' I added softly.

Emma snorted. 'There's always the Thames,' she said. 'Although I suspect it's got more rats than the sea and I wouldn't fancy the chances of anyone who tried swimming in it.' She pulled me across the road to the Princess Alice. 'Let's have a couple of drinks before we go on our way,' she said with a wink.

'Let me buy them,' I said, feeling my cheeks go pink. 'It's just that I know you were counting on selling that pendant for money and I feel bad about giving it away especially to the likes of Miss Redmayne, who doesn't want for anything.'

She stared at me. 'I don't mind about all that,' she said. 'I mean, I did at first but I don't now.' She smiled. 'Oh, I was mad as hell when I first guessed what had happened but I know that you

193

were just acting for the best and it's not like I needed the money really is it?' She pulled me into the pub, which was hot, noisy, stinking of armpits, spilled beer and gin and packed to the rafters with the usual gaggle of drunken flirtatious dollymops, slumming soldiers, sour faced old tarts, market men and locals. 'Honestly, Cora, I wouldn't let it trouble you.'

'Well I do,' I said doggedly as we fought our way through the throng to the bar at the back of the room. 'I wish I'd never done it.'

She didn't hear me though over the din of the piano in the corner being amateurishly played by a drunken soldier, whose fellows clustered about him singing a popular song and the shouts and laughter of the punters at the bar, all yelling and waving their money in the faces of the poor harassed barmaids. Emma had confidently pummelled her way through the crowd to the bar and was cheerfully joining in the general pushing and shoving that was going on there so I turned away and looked around the room, looking with interest at the various different groups at each of the low tables and thinking how shocked my Pa would be if he knew where I was now.

He'd made both Cat and I promise not to go out after dark, had been quite adamant in fact so I felt a little sick with shame to be going against his wishes although obviously not shamed enough to turn around and march straight back home again. 'The murdered women have all been of a certain class,' he'd told us a little awkwardly. 'They weren't decent young girls like you but older women who'd had hard lives and who worked on the streets.' Bless my Pa - Cat and I were both Whitechapel born and bred; we knew tarts when we saw them and there was no need to be coy when talking about them around us. 'I can't promise though that things might not change one day,' he went on, pulling off his boots with a sigh. 'He's clearly insane after all and might very well get bored with such easy targets and then where will we all be?'

Where indeed. It wasn't like Pa to speculate about the motivation that lay behind the murders or other crimes that went on in Whitechapel. His job was to catch whoever was behind it and ensure that justice was done and that, to the letter, was what he generally did and nothing more or less. This worry and speculation was entirely new but not, perhaps, completely

194

surprising - after all, as Abberline had said, all of London was at it so why shouldn't be the poor devils paid to police the streets of the East End have their fun also?

When we had finished our drinks, Emma took me down to the Pavilion music hall on Whitechapel Road, a huge and to my innocent eyes opulent building with a passing resemblance to a Roman temple or, more blasphemously, Christ Church on Commercial Street with huge columns on either side of the entrance and a stately triumphal arch two storeys up that towered over the neighbouring buildings. It turned out that Emma knew one of the boys on the ticket stall outside, a surly looking lad with straw coloured hair, a crust of raspberry coloured acne and a painful looking stye on one eye and after some muttered conversation between them he waved us inside with a cheerful nod and a wink. 'You enjoy yourself now ladies!' he called.

'Here we are then,' Emma said cheerfully as she led me by the hand through to the stalls, which were crammed full of people, all craning their heads to watch the stage where a small, rather chubby looking young woman with fair hair was belting out popular songs one after the other while flouncing up and down the stage in a fuchsia pink dress. Most of the audience, especially the women, was enthusiastically singing along, their eyes rapturously closed as they swayed together in time with the music. It was everything that I had hoped it would be and more.

'Do you want a drink?' Emma shouted to me above the din, miming the motion of raising a glass to her lips and grinning.

I nodded and then, suddenly afraid that I might lose her in the midst of the crowds that pressed in around us, followed her as she turned to go to the bar that had been set up at the back of the hall and where a huge throng had gathered to wave their money in the air and loudly clamour for service. 'Gin?' Emma mouthed to me over her shoulder before disappearing into the crowd then emerging again clutching two full glasses a few moments later.

'The barman here is another old friend of mine,' she explained as she handed over my glass. 'These beauties were on the house.'

'Beauties?' I took a wary sip of the gin then started coughing as the fiery liquid seared my mouth and throat. 'Are you sure about that, Em?'

She grinned. 'Oh, you'll get used to it in time. They don't call it mother's ruin for nothing, you know.'

'I've never quite understood that name,' I said, chancing another sip then wincing as it burned its way down to my stomach.

Emma laughed and raised her glass to me. 'You will, my dear.' She took a generous swig, clearly well used to the drink's throat burning qualities. 'You will.'

We pushed through to the front of the stalls and spent the next few hours staring enraptured at a series of acts that ranged from a few plump lady singers, a sweet couple called, rather improbably, Lucian and Delilah, who duetted several love songs ('I bet they hate each other in real life,' Emma whispered to me during their act. 'Just look at the way she's glaring at him when he isn't looking and if her name is really Delilah then I'm the bloody Queen'), Mademoiselle Zara who claimed to have spirit messages for various members of the audience, a magician who seemed to saw one young woman in half and then make another disappear entirely and then, most thrillingly of all, a team of acrobats from Italy who bounded, twirled and leaped across the stage in their spangled brightly coloured costumes until I felt quite dizzy watching them.

'Oh, it's marvellous,' I exclaimed to Emma, clutching her arm when it was all over and it was time to go. I couldn't stop grinning at the people around us. 'Thank you for bringing me here.'

She smiled. 'Still fancy a career on the stage, do you?' she asked, throwing her arm around my shoulders. 'I can just imagine you up there singing your heart out.' She'd had several gins by this point and was beginning to slur her words, stagger against me and make expansive arm gestures when she spoke.

'Can you?' I felt myself blush. 'Ever since I was a little girl, I've wanted to go on the stage and sing. Everyone says that I have a nice voice but I don't think I'm as pretty as those girls up there.' I'd had one too many gins too but while it made Emma more voluble than ever, it made me feel despondent and a little tearful. 'They're ever so beautiful, aren't they?'

'Nonsense,' Emma cried, pinching my cheek until it hurt. 'You're prettier than all of those fat frumps put together. Don't they have mirrors in that police station of yours?' She linked her arm through mine and together we staggered through the crowd, which was slowly drifting out of the stalls and on to the street. 'Fancy another drink? I know a place on Houndsditch that stays open all night long and is always packed to the rafters with nice looking young soldiers. You'll love it.'

I was just shaking my head in despair when a young man in a shabby tweed suit appeared out of the throng and planted himself in front of us. 'Alright Em?' he said. He was very tall with short clipped dark hair, sad pale blue eyes and a quick shy smile that made his long face light up and dimples appear in his cheeks. 'Long time, no see.'

She paused, frowned then rubbed her eyes, a childlike gesture as if she didn't quite believe what she was seeing. 'Albert?' She smiled then with genuine pleasure. 'Albert Sinclair! It's been far too long.'

'You can say that again.' He pulled her into a fierce bone breaking hug. 'What've you been up to then? I haven't seen you for years! Last I heard you were working as a model in Paris.'

She shook her head. 'I left France months ago,' she said smoothly, shooting me a look that warned me to hold my tongue about what she had really been up to in France. 'I'm here in Whitechapel now, working in the Britannia on Commercial Street. It's not much but it keeps me going. How about you?'

'Same as always,' he said cheerfully. 'Working for my Pa's firm back home in Coggeshall. He's about ready to retire now so I'll be taking over soon. It's hard work but, well, the prospects are good and it'll all belong to me one day.' he shrugged as if he didn't care but it was clear from his expression that he was pleased as punch with how his life was turning out.

'How do you two know each other then?' I asked, curious despite myself and wondering how such an apparently ill matched couple had got acquainted. For a couple they had once clearly been judging by the awkward way they were looking at each other and that hug that had gone on for just a fraction too long before Emma gently prised herself out of it.

There was a pause before both Emma and Albert started talking together at the same time then laughed and had a squabble, which Albert won, about who should carry on. 'We knew each other back home in Essex,' he said with a shy grin. 'Only Emma here was a cut above me in those days and had all the boys running about after her. I never stood a chance really.'

'That's not true,' my friend said flatly as if she had suddenly sobered up. 'I was never a cut above you, Albert. You could have had me for the asking if you'd only had a mind to it.'

An awkward silence fell as they stared at each other, the smile draining from Albert's face as he looked at my friend. 'Don't say that, Em,' he said at last, just as a small dark haired girl appeared beside him and put one tiny lace mittened hand on his arm in a gesture that clearly denoted a claim of ownership. He looked down at her with a frown as if trying to remember who she was then smiled apologetically. 'Oh, I forgot, this is Sarah.'

'Sarah?' The two girls stared at each other and I felt Emma's arm tighten around my waist. 'Are you..?' She looked at Albert and he nodded then looked away as if embarrassed. 'Oh, that's nice.' She started to laugh just a little too shrilly and I looked at her in concern. 'No, it is. Really nice and so lovely to see you both.' She was too drunk to hide her dismay and I realised that it was up to me to rescue her from this.

'I think we should be going now,' I said, tightening my hold on her arm as Albert gave me a brisk and rather relieved nod. 'Let's be off now, Em,' I whispered to her as she sagged against me, suddenly drunk and helpless again. 'Let's go and get that drink, shall we?'

She nodded, not laughing any more. 'Bye then,' she called to Albert and Sarah over her shoulder as I led her away. 'See you again some time.' She let me take her out of the stalls then stopped suddenly and leaned against the smoke and mildew stained wall. 'I didn't do very well back there, did I?' she said with a rueful smile as she wiped away a stray tear. 'I hate how these things always take me by surprise. It's always the way, isn't it? You think you're over the bugger and then suddenly he pops up large as life and it just hits you, right here.' She thumped her chest hard enough to hurt then looked away as more tears trickled down her flushed cheeks.

I didn't have much of a clue what it was like, never having had a lover, but I nodded sympathetically, remembering the pang I felt whenever I saw Mr Mercier looking after Miss Redmayne with that sickly doe eyed expression. 'You didn't do too badly,' I said soothingly as I rubbed her back and shoulders, feeling close to tears myself. 'I don't think they know how upset you are.'

'Upset?' She angrily scrubbed at her eyes and pushed herself away from the wall. 'I'm not upset. Bloody man. She's welcome to him.' She hurried out of the music hall and for a while I lost her in the crowd before finding her again sitting on the edge of the pavement, her arms folded across her chest as she sulkily gazed across Whitechapel Road. The pubs were closing up for the night now and the road was packed with people, mostly drunk, milling about and getting in the way of the horses and carts that still plodded up and down the road.

'Are you sure that you aren't bothered?' I asked as I bunched up my skirts and gingerly sat down next to her making sure to avoid a huge steaming plop of horse excrement on the road.

Emma grinned. 'Alright then, yes, I'm not too happy but what can I do?'

I sighed and put my head on her shoulder. 'What happened?' I asked quietly.

She gave a short laugh. 'What do you think always happens?' she said with a shrug. 'We saw each other, he liked the look of me and I lost my heart to the big useless lump.' She pulled a crudely rolled cigarette, cadged earlier on from a man at the bar, from where she had tucked it behind her ear then took an almost empty box of matches out of her bosom before striking one on the pavement beside her.

'That's not all is it?' I said, prodding her on.

She shook her head and took a drag on the cigarette before coughing into her hand. 'No, that's not all,' she said miserably. 'I thought I was too good for where we came from.' She gave a hoarse mirthless laugh and frowningly examined the burning end of the cigarette, which glowed in the darkness. 'I thought I was too bloody good to be stuck there for the rest of my life, seeing the same faces every day and everyone knowing everyone else's business. He wanted to marry me but I turned him down and ran away.'

'You wanted to marry him though,' I said as she took another shaky drag on the cigarette.

She blew out a grey coil of smoke. 'Course I wanted to,' she said. 'I couldn't though. I just couldn't bring myself to do it so I told him that I didn't love him, that I didn't even like him in that

199

way and that was that.' She took one last drag on the cigarette then threw it angrily away. 'You should have seen his face when I said it,' she said. 'I'll never forget how he looked, the poor bastard.' She got up from the pavement and gave a careless shrug. 'Anyway, it's all ancient history now, especially as he's with this Sarah now and all that.' She held out her hand and pulled me to my feet.

'Do you think they're married?' I mused. 'Or just stepping out together?'

She shook her head. 'Who knows,' she said furiously. 'And who cares? I don't. They're welcome to each other.'

I opened my mouth to reply then shut it with a snap. What was the use after all? She'd clearly made up her mind and that was that. We went past the entrance to the Pavilion, heading in silent agreement up towards Houndsditch and that final drink of the night. 'Alright there girls?' Another young man, this one short with sandy hair and looking much less pleasant than Albert Sinclair, stepped out of the dusk, grinning and leering at us both from beneath his tattered bowler hat. 'Fancy a night on the town?'

Emma pulled herself upright. 'No, thank you,' she said with enormous hauteur, pulling me past him.

'Now then, Miss, no need to take on like that,' he said, adroitly stepping in front of her and snatching at my arm. 'No need to look down your nose at me when I'm just being friendly.' He tugged me closer to him as I gave a yelp of pain and fear. 'See.' He put his arm around my waist and pressed a very damp slobbering kiss on my cheek as I recoiled away from him.

Emma whirled around, her eyes narrowing. 'Let go of my friend,' she whispered from between clenched teeth and then when he just laughed and tugged me closer: 'I said, let go of my friend.'

'Make me,' he snarled, pulling me even closer into his sweaty embrace then clumsily kissing me as I tried to push him away, almost sobbing with panic about what he was going to do next, which in the event turned out to be rolling about on the pavement, clutching his face in agony as blood spurted from his nose and Emma nursed her bruised knuckles while a small crowd gathered to point and laugh at his much deserved comeuppance.

'You were warned,' my friend said coldly before taking hold of

200

my hand and stepping over him as he lay, groaning and cursing on the blood splattered ground. 'Come on, Cora, I think we both need a drink after that.'

Chapter Twenty One

We hadn't gone far down Whitechapel Road, skirting around the buskers and gaggles of drunk men and women that hovered about the edges of the filthy pavements, when we heard the first distant blast of a policeman's whistle coming from the direction of Commercial Road. There was nothing unusual about that sound in the middle of Whitechapel of course but there was something about that mournful wail echoing over the dark rooftops that made us both stop dead and stare at each other.

'Has he done it again?' I said.

Emma shrugged as if she didn't care but her face was grim. 'Who knows?' she said. 'I'm not hanging about here to find out though.'

'Do you think it's one of your friends?' I persisted as she hurried along the street and I tried to keep up with her.

'I hope not,' she said. 'I really bloody hope not.'

We weren't the only ones disturbed by the sound of the policeman's whistle and as we almost ran along Whitechapel Road, I could see people turning their heads from side to side as they wondered where it had come from and what had happened, their faces pale and panic stricken. 'It can't be another murder,' I heard one woman say to another. 'He's gone up north, ain't he? There's been nothing doing here for almost a month since poor Annie got ripped up.'

'Just keep going,' Emma urged me, taking my hand and pulling me along the street. 'It's bound to be nothing but let's get out of here just in case.'

By the time we reached the end of Whitechapel Road, the news that another woman been found killed in a yard off Berner Street had travelled ahead of us. 'Just had her throat cut this one,' the spotty adolescent tart who told us at her pitch outside St Botolph's church at Aldgate said with a peculiar touch of regret. 'There was no ripping up this time. The bobbies reckon he got interrupted before he could finish the job.'

I felt Emma shudder beside me. 'Poor bitch,' she said. 'It doesn't matter what he did or didn't do, the fact is that there's some poor woman lying there dead and the ruddy coppers aren't any closer to catching whoever is responsible.' She tugged me away from the girl who was already staring past us with a hopeful smile at a likely looking group of drunk and very noisy City men staggering across from Minories.

'I expect we'll find out who it is soon,' I said as we hurried up towards Houndsditch.

'I don't want to know,' Emma said gruffly.

'What about that friend of yours from France?' I said as we continued up the street. The area wasn't particularly well lit and there was something creepy and distinctly forbidding about the gloomy old City streets which were practically deserted at that time of night. There was still no way that I would rather be anywhere else though - this was the first time that I'd ever gone out so late at night and I was determined to make the most of it as who knew when it would happen again?

Emma turned on me. 'What about her?' she said.

I faltered and fell back from the expression on her face. 'Aren't you worried about her? She was there too, wasn't she? She saw him as well and he saw her.'

Emma shrugged. 'Marie can look after herself,' she said but she couldn't hide the look of worry that flashed across her face. 'Maybe I should go and see her later on,' she grumbled. 'Just to make sure that she's still in one piece.'

'Where does she live?' I asked, gasping as I tried to keep up with her swift pace.

'Never you mind,' Emma replied sharply before swiftly relenting. 'Sorry, old habits and all that. She's got a place on Miller's Court that she shares with her bloke. He's a nice sort, probably a bit too nice for Marie in fact, if you know what I mean.'

I didn't know but nodded anyway. 'You said that she's got her own worries.'

Emma nodded, unsmiling. 'Oh nothing like this but little

things, you know how it is. She owes rent to her landlord and he's started asking for it in kind only her boyfriend, well, he doesn't...' she broke off and grinned as a bedraggled looking woman with messy auburn hair that straggled from beneath a wonky black bonnet came staggering towards us down the street. 'Cathy! Where the bloody hell have you been?' she exclaimed. 'I haven't seen you for ages.'

Cathy grinned back at her. 'Down in Kent picking hops, old cock,' she said cheerfully. 'You should try it sometime, Em, you make a bit of cash and get ever so brown. Just look at my arms!' she held out her hands in front of her so that we could admire her tan. 'Not very ladylike but who cares about that?' She was clearly the worse for wear and reeked of gin, most of which seemed to have gone down the front of her brown linsey bodice and threadbare black short jacket which was trimmed with bedraggled dark fur at the collar and cuffs.

'Ooh, lovely hair your friend has got,' she said with a grin, reaching over to touch my hair which was starting to straggle in annoying ringlets around my neck. 'What a nice shade of red. I bet you have all the boys after you, don't you, sweetheart.'

'So what have you been up to tonight?' Em said, smiling. 'I didn't see you in the Princess Alice earlier, which makes a change.'

'I got chucked in the old nick, didn't I?' Cathy said with a grin that showed off the gaps between her remaining teeth. 'The coppers picked me up on Bishopsgate earlier on and put me in the cells until I'd sobered up enough to be let go.' She laughed. 'Apparently I was doing an impression of a fire engine, bells and everything. Can you believe that? I'm damned if I can remember any of it though. Drunk as a lord I was.'

Emma burst out laughing. 'Bloody hell, Chick, how much did you have to drink?'

'More enough, Em, my old mate. More than enough,' Cathy said with a wink, straightening the length of gaudy red gauze that she had tied around her neck as a rather jaunty makeshift scarf. 'Only I spent all my pennies and now I don't have enough for a bed for the night.' She laughed. 'Always the bleeding way, isn't it? I'll have to go and earn it all again now although I don't know how, I'm sure, as it's the middle of the bloody night and I can barely stand up as it is.'

'You'd best get inside if you can,' Em said, pulling her shawl closer around her shoulders. 'There's been another murder just off Commercial Street.'

'Poor cow.' Cathy pulled a face. 'Still that means the rest of us are safe tonight, doesn't it? He's not likely to have another go, is he?' She laughed. 'I dunno about you, but I reckon all this murdering must really take it out of him. I can hardly walk up the street these days without thinking I'm going to die from exhaustion so Gawd knows how he feels after he's done all this slashing and strangling.'

Em sighed but she could stop herself smiling. 'Even so…'

'Besides, I know who he is,' Cathy continued, tapping the side of her large nose. 'I seen him.'

Emma stared at her. 'No, you never,' she said flatly.

Cathy looked indignant. 'Yes, I bloody well did,' she said. 'I seen him on the night Poll was killed, talking to her on the High Street.'

'Keep your voice down,' Emma said, looking around nervously. 'Why didn't you go to the police.'

Cathy shrugged. 'Why do you think?' she said vaguely. 'Anyway, I'd best be off or I'll never make enough to get some kip tonight. My head hurts something awful now. Bloody police.' She gave my hair one last lingering and rather wistful pat, waved rather vaguely to us both then staggered off up gloomy Duke Street, tunelessly humming to herself and straightening her black straw bonnet as she went.

'Will she be alright?' I asked as we stood for a moment together, watching her go, giggling a little to herself as she tripped over a kerb.

Emma sighed. 'Course she will,' she said, turning away. 'Cathy always lands on her feet. She was one of the first friends that I made here when I came back from France.' We carried on walking up the street. I was feeling almost completely sober now and was beginning to think wistfully of home and my own warm bed. Emma gave me a sidelong look. 'Still fancy that drink or should I be getting you back home?' she said with a smile.

I sighed. 'You won't think me very boring if I want to go back?' I said shyly.

Emma grinned and nudged me with her elbow. 'Course not,'

she said. 'We should do this again though. It was fun.'

I grinned back at her. 'It was.' And in it's own way it was, it really was. Behind us we heard a woman's high pitched gurgling laugh and I gave Em a look. 'Sounds like Cathy's found a customer,' I said. 'Didn't take her long.'

'No, it didn't.' Emma turned and looked uneasily over her shoulder to where we had last seen Cathy, drunk and singing softly to herself as she took off down the street. 'Maybe we should just…' She broke off and turned back the way we had come.

As usual I hurried to keep up with her. 'You don't think there's anything wrong do you?' I said as I hopped along at her side. 'You said yourself that she knows how to look after herself.'

'I know what I said,' Emma said grimly. 'It just seems odd, that's all. Something doesn't feel right.' She gestured around the dark, quiet street. 'This place is virtually deserted and yet she found someone right away?' We'd reached the top of Duke Street and she pushed me back with her arm so that we both stayed out of sight. 'I just want to be certain, that's all,' she whispered to me with a smile that didn't quite reach her eyes, 'and then we can both go home and sleep it all off.'

'The man you saw with Annie,' I said, feeling my heart begin to pound painfully in my chest at the very thought of him, 'you don't really think that he is…'

Emma shook her head, still with that same uneasy look about her eyes. 'I don't know what to think any more,' she said. 'I just want to make sure she's alright, that's all.' She took my hand and squeezed it hard. 'But as long as we stick together he can't touch us, can he? That's what's going to keep us safe. It's just one man with a knife and there's two of us, remember that.'

'Cathy was on her own,' I said quietly. 'We should have made her come along with us.'

Emma shrugged. 'Maybe we should but remember that she needed to make money to pay for a bed for the night,' she said with a sigh. 'Me and you can stay together because we don't need to make money on the streets but what are the tarts supposed to do? They can hardly go about in pairs, can they?' She gave me a sly look that I didn't quite understand but guessed alluded to things that she considered me too young and innocent to comprehend. 'Well, not most of the time anyway.'

'I wouldn't know,' I said, more haughtily than I had perhaps intended.

Emma gave me a lop sided smile. 'No, you wouldn't, would you.' She sighed then after peeping around the corner pulled me down the dark street, which was overlooked on both sides by tall old houses with wooden shuttered windows. 'Just follow me and keep your voice down,' she whispered urgently as we crept along, keeping close to the wall. 'If she's entertaining an actual client then she won't thank us for interrupting.'

I decided not to answer that but instead stayed close to Emma as she sidled quietly down Duke Street until we came to the entrance to Church Passage, a narrow and very gloomy alleyway that led down to Mitre Square. 'You don't think she's down there, do you?' I whispered to Emma, praying that she wouldn't insist that we went down the passage, which looked very dark and daunting in the gloom and reeked of urine and other filth.

'I don't know.' Emma took a step forward then hesitated, clearly as unwilling as me to go down the fetid and very unpleasant alley. 'Let's try one of the other ways into the square. There's another passage from the market on St James Place and, failing that, we can go in through the Mitre Street entrance.'

I stared at her, impressed by her apparently unending knowledge of the local streets and alleyways. 'How do you know all this?' I asked, trying to keep my astonishment out of my voice.

Emma grinned at me and tapped her head. 'It's all in here,' she said. 'I dunno, I just like to walk about, that's all and I tend to remember stuff as well. It used to drive my sisters and brother mad when I was at home.' She'd never mentioned her siblings before and I was about to open my mouth to ask about them when she gave a quick shake of her head and put one finger, which smelt of gin and tobacco, to my lips. 'Later,' she said.

We carried on up Duke Street then took a left turn on to St James Place, a small square with a few empty stalls left standing around the edges and heaps of refuse littering the cobbles where it had been swept away then forgotten after a day's trading. 'It stinks, doesn't it?' Emma said, holding her nose in a theatrical manner. 'Still, you should come down here in the summer. There's flies everywhere then. And worse.' She led the way across the square, weaving in between the stalls and occasionally kicking away a festering cabbage until we reached the arched entrance to another passageway, this one shorter and less forbidding than the other.

'After you,' she said with a grin as we both hesitated at the edge, drawing whatever courage we had remaining to us from the flickering greenish light cast by the gas street lamp beside us. 'No?' She shrugged and took a step into the gloom. 'Fair enough.'

I took a deep breath then followed her, staying as close as I could as the darkness closed in around us. In the distance I could see the pathetically meagre gleam of another street lamp standing close to the other end of the passage but it did little to relieve the fearful, dank murkiness that surrounded us as we tiptoed towards Mitre Square. Knowing that it was unwise to speak, I let my mind race with thoughts - some wild and panicky, others more rational but none the less tainted with purest fear. Mostly I just wondered what on earth we were doing as after all Cathy was no doubt already long gone and safely on her way back to Whitechapel with fourpence jingling in her pocket and a jaunty song on her lips. It seemed senseless really to be creeping about in dark alleyways when there was a murderer who knew at least one of us by sight on the loose somewhere nearby and one woman already slaughtered that night.

Emma had reached the end of the passage and turned to me to put her finger to her lips in warning. Her face looked pale and sickly in the dim green light cast by the nearby street lamp and her eyes were wide with apprehension. 'Wait,' she whispered before stepped out on to the square, keeping close to the wall until she reached the railings close to the passage entrance.

I hesitated for just a moment before following her, my heart pounding with fright as I hid behind her in the shadow of the railing and peered across the murk to the other far corner of the square which had no street lamp and was cast into darkness. 'He's there,' she whispered, her breath warm against my cheek. 'Can't you see him?'

I followed the direction of her gaze, past the green glow of the street lamp in front of us to the dark corner across the way which was overlooked by a pair of wooden gates that led presumably to a yard and a large redbrick warehouse with 'HORNER & CO' written boldly on the wall in white paint. The entire square, possibly once elegant in times now long gone forever was overlooked on all sides by hulking smoke blackened warehouses with a few boarded up and empty houses scattered in between. It was a miserable spot - no doubt bustling with life and activity during the day but desolate and abandoned at night.

It took a few moments for my eyes to adjust to the darkness beyond the street lamp's glow which really only served to light up the immediately surrounding area and plunge everything any further away than that in even deeper gloom and at first I couldn't hear anything that suggested that we were not alone in the square. 'Where..?' I began but Emma shook her head angrily.

'Listen,' she hissed and so I did until the distant sounds of the sleeping city: the melancholy wail of a train whistle, a couple drunkenly squabbling on the next street, dogs barking, a baby crying all faded away to be replaced by the dank and heavy nothingness of Mitre Square. 'Just listen.'

I closed my eyes then and suddenly it came to me - first Emma's ragged breathing beside me then the dip of a breeze as it brushed past my face and then finally the faintest scrape of metal across brick and a soft sound half way between a gasp and a moan. My eyes snapped open, a cloud moved across the moon and I saw him then just as Emma did and as she had done all those months ago in Calais: the black shape of a man, outlined like a silhouette against the velvety darkness as he leaned over the splayed out body of a woman, her hand flung out helplessly against the cobbles, her skirts pulled up almost to her waist and a silvery grey coil of intestines thrown across her shoulder. If it was Cathy then very little remained to identify her now for he had sliced off her nose, slashed at her face and was even now cutting at one of her ears as if trying to remove it.

My first instinct was to cry out in fear and disgust but Emma as always was too quick for me and before I'd even realised what I had seen, her hand was fastened firmly across my mouth and she was holding me tight against her body as her eyes pleaded with me to keep quiet. 'Hush now, Cora,' she whispered. 'Hush now.' I struggled against her but that only made her hold me tighter as if she didn't trust me not to run across the square or scream the place down, alerting him to our presence.

It was at that moment that we heard a dull tread of feet to our left which let us know that someone was making their way steadily and without concern down Church Passage. It alerted the square's other inhabitant as well for a second later we heard a muffled exclamation as he straightened up and looked down almost regretfully at the body spreadeagled on the ground. There was no time to hide and as the footsteps came closer, Emma and I in one accord moved back and pressed ourselves though a small gap in the railings, then turned our faces away from the lamp's miserable glow.

The man crossed the square towards us, not exactly unhurried but not running either and I felt my blood turn to ice within my veins as his footsteps came closer then paused for a second as he stopped for a moment by the lamp to look back over his shoulder at his work. He then carried on at a quicker pace up the passageway that we had just come down, passing so close to us that I could almost feel the whisk of his coat as he went past, the heat of the blood being pumped around his body, the crackling of his energy. I could almost smell him and I was sure that he could smell us too but even though I expected him to stop, to hesitate then come towards us, he did not.

Emma leaned against me with a sigh as we listened to his footsteps hurrying up the narrow cobbled alleyway to freedom and I knew that she felt as sick and faint with trepidation as I did. I quickly took hold of her hand to reassure her but before I could say anything the mysterious interruptor had arrived in Mitre Square, mere seconds after the killer had vanished out of it. He paused for a moment beneath the lamp at the end of Church Passage and I saw with much relief that it was a City policeman, looking tired and bored after a long night on the beat as he wearily opened the shutter on his hand held lamp to cast a light around the square.

'Let's go,' Emma whispered to me as he slowly circled the light towards the far corner where Cathy's body lay sprawled on the cobbles. 'We can't be found here, Cora. There'd be too many questions.'

I nodded agreement and moved stealthily but as quickly as I dared, the cold sweat of purest fear trickling slowly between my shoulder blades, towards the entrance to the passageway with Emma following close behind, panting and stumbling as she went.

We'd just made it to the relative safety of the alley's darkness before all hell broke out in the square as the unfortunate bobby's lamplight fell on the body and he gave a spluttering cry of fear then rushed in a horrified panic towards it, blowing his whistle in short shrill blasts as he went.

'Run! Now!' Emma whispered to me, giving me a little shove in the small of my back that sent me hurtling up the passageway as fast as my legs could carry me. 'Don't look back, Cora. Don't ever look back.'

'But what if,' I gasped, bunching my skirts above my knees so that they wouldn't hamper my flight, 'what if he's up there waiting for us?' He'd gone up the same passage only a few moments before us after all so it was entirely plausible that he was still there, lurking in the darkness, waiting for us to appear. Waiting with his knife.

'Never mind that,' she said as we burst out of the passage together and found ourselves back in St James' Place, which was mercifully empty but slowly coming to life as the policeman's shouts and whistle blows woke up the few residents, making them turn up their gas lamps and stumble, yawning and tousle haired out of bed and to their windows to see what was happening. 'We can't stay here,' Emma whispered, grabbing my hand and tugging me back the way we had come to Duke Street.

We didn't stop running until we were back on Houndsgate, where Emma let go of my hand and doubled over, clutching her arms around her stomach and panting with exertion. I leaned against a wall and silently watched her, ignoring the painful lurch of my own stomach and the terrible trembling of my legs. 'Well?' I said at last, feeling suddenly utterly exhausted and longing more than ever for the safety of my own bed, for the comforting presence of my sister Cat. 'What happens now?' My tone was almost pleading as I expected her to reassure me, to have a plan, to put things right. After all, if anyone could solve this, it was Emma. 'What are we going to do?'

She met my eyes and shook her head despairingly, reading my thoughts and knowing that she was going to have to let me down. 'I haven't got a bloody clue what we are going to do,' she said.

Chapter Twenty Two
Alice, November 1888

The elegant Brennan house on Eaton House was already full to the rafters by the time we arrived, fashionably late as always, for Lucasta's birthday ball. The weather had taken a distinctly chilly turn over the last couple of days and I shivered as I handed my fur edged stole over to one of the maids waiting in the marble floored hallway, which was lined with beautiful Greek statues brought back by Lord Brennan from his many extended visits to the continent.

'My dear Edwin,' our host greeted us himself, arms so outstretched that I caught a glimpse of dark hair on his forearms as his wrists shot past his cuffs. 'And the lovely Miss Alice as well.' He gave me an approving look. 'Looking beautiful as ever. That shade of teal green really suits you, my dear and I suppose we should all be grateful that you haven't come dressed in trousers or whatever heinously unflattering mode the ladies of the Rational Dress Society are favouring at the moment.'

I smiled and turned away with replying. I'd known Lord Brennan all my life but had never felt quite at ease with him, mainly because of the tense atmosphere that followed he and his wife wherever they went but also because in my mind he would always be 'Lucasta's Father', a distant, often moody, unapproachable man who took very little interest in our childish games and ostentatiously winced whenever we laughed or sang too loudly.

'There you are.' It was Lucasta, glowing and lovely in pale pink silk that shimmered with mother of pearl sequins and fine gold embroidered lace. 'Late as usual, I see.' She tried to pout but then grinned and laughed, catching at my hand and almost dragging me into the ballroom away from our fathers who remained in the hall to discuss Lord Brennan's latest acquisition of several warehouses in Wapping, which he was planning to lease out to various businesses. 'Have you arranged to dance with anyone?' she called over her shoulder.

I shook my head. 'Of course not,' I said as we pushed our way through a gaggle of girls standing with their cross looking mamas at the side of the room. They were tapping their feet and swaying from side to side beneath their tightly laced sugared almond coloured gowns as they wistfully watching the more fortunate girls being swept around the dance floor in a waltz by their partners.

Lucasta stopped for a moment and looked at me with one eyebrow arched. 'Not even Patrick?' she said in surprise.

I nodded firmly. 'Especially not Patrick,' I replied brightly. 'I haven't seen him for weeks.'

'Oh.' Lucasta sighed then took my hand again and took me out through the french windows that led out onto a small terrace overlooking her mother's precious rose garden. 'Have you fallen out with him?' She closed the door behind us and pulled her blue enamel cigarette case out from her reticule.

'Of course not,' I said crossly, folding my arms across my body in a vain attempt to keep warm.

Lucasta shrugged then offered me the open cigarette case, which I waved away. 'He's here tonight,' she said, putting a cigarette into her mouth then lighting it with a match which she then carelessly flung on to her mother's best white roses below the balustrade. Lady Brennan had only two enthusiasms in life as far as I could tell: her ridiculously spoiled pekinese and her rose garden. 'I do wish you would decide if you want to marry him or not.' She blew a plume of grey scented smoke into the air.

'What makes you think that he wants to marry me?' I said, not quite meeting her eyes. 'Besides, perhaps we wouldn't suit.'

'Oh, don't talk such nonsense, darling.' Lucasta laughed and took another drag on her cigarette. 'Seriously, Alice, if you don't want him please do feel free to pass him my way.'

I laughed and held out my hand for her cigarette. 'I'll see what I can do,' I said, taking a small drag then posing in what I hoped was a sophisticated manner with the cigarette held airily between my fingers.

'Failing that, I wouldn't say no to that dish you met in Whitechapel,' Lucasta said with a wink.

I hesitated for a moment before forcing myself to smile. 'Mr Mercier?' I handed back the cigarette. 'You're welcome to him.'

'Am I indeed?' Lucasta sighed and took another drag on the cigarette. 'Did you hear what happened over there?' she said, abruptly changing the subject.

I looked at her. 'The murders? Of course I heard. All of London is talking about it.' It had been the hot topic in the capital and probably the entire country for the past four weeks with everyone exclaiming over both the killer's audacity and the gruesome manner he mutilated his victims. He'd murdered two women in the space of under an hour almost a month before - the first had been discovered with her throat cut but no other mutilations in a miserable little yard near Whitechapel High Street while the other had been discovered in a square within the precincts of the City, ripped apart with her nose sliced off and her cheeks cut to ribbons. It turned my blood to ice just to think about it but my Papa's dinner guests a few nights ago could speak of nothing else as they spooned raspberry and rose syllabub into their mouths. I'd had to leave the room in the end as the juxtaposition of dripping red food and avid talk of facial mutilation was making me queasy.

'Oh, yes, of course, I suppose that you are on the spot as it were, aren't you?' Lucasta said airily. 'I expect you get to hear all about it from the girls at the Mission.'

'Not really,' I said, turning away. 'I haven't been there for a few weeks. Papa is working on a new painting and is keeping me so busy posing for him that I barely have time for anything else.'

'Oh God, what tragic heroine it this time?' Lucasta said, her eyes wide. 'Boudicca? Iphigenia? Ophelia?'

I shook my head, laughing. 'No, Anne Boleyn preparing for execution. Apparently my sad but brave expression is quite exceptional.' I smiled to myself, thinking of the long hours spent posing as the doomed queen, draped in crimson velvet and with swags of pearls around my neck, in my father's studio at the bottom of the garden.

'How utterly ghastly.' Lucasta flicked her cigarette into the rose bushes and turned to give me a quick hug. 'You won't go back there, will you?' she whispered. 'Papa says that this violence can only escalate and soon the killer won't stop at street girls but attack other classes of women too. I would hate for you to be in any danger.'

I sighed. 'I'm not in danger,' I said. 'Please don't fret, Lucasta. It's not like you.'

She gave a rueful smile. 'It's not, is it? Ah well.' We both turned as the door opened behind us, only to relax when Patrick appeared in the doorway, smiling in his usual charming way but looking ever slightly as if he expected to be told to go away again.

'I don't mean to intrude,' he said, looking at Lucasta and then, almost unwillingly and for the briefest of moments, me. 'Your father said that you might be out here.' He sniffed the air, which was clearly scented by Lucasta's Turkish cigarettes but said nothing.

'You aren't intruding,' my friend said lightly. 'We were just talking about the murders in Whitechapel.'

'Jack the Ripper,' Patrick said with relish. 'Isn't that what the press are calling him.'

'What a splendid name,' Lucasta said with a delighted shudder. 'I wonder who dreams these things up?'

'He himself if the papers are to believed,' Patrick said with a shrug. 'Apparently he signed a letter off with it.'

'Oh, how wonderful and was the letter written in blood?' Lucasta's eyes shone. 'Oh please do say that it was. I can't imagine anything more delicious.'

Patrick grinned. 'Naturally,' he said, still not looking at me. 'I believe there is a law somewhere that states that murderers aren't allowed to write in anything else.'

I hid a smile behind my hand. 'We should return to the ballroom,' I said, rubbing my bare upper arms. 'It's freezing out here.'

'Oh lord, I see my mother heading this way,' Lucasta said with annoyance as she peered through the glass door. 'I'd better play the dutiful daughter for a while.' She gave us both a cheeky smile over her shoulder then pulled the door open and vanished.

Patrick sighed. 'We should return as well,' he said, still not looking at me and sounding colder than I had ever heard him. 'I would hate to give rise to gossip.'

'Of course,' I said in a low voice as he offered me his arm. Once upon a time we would have joked about how being found alone together would be playing into my father's hands but the words turned to ashes on my tongue and I couldn't say them. Instead, I clutched at his arm, forcing him to turn and look at me. 'Patrick,' I said, my voice sharper than I had intended but at least I managed to make him look. 'Please.'

He shook his head. 'What is it, Alice?' He didn't smile. 'Have I offended you in some way?'

'No of course not,' I said, smiling at him and wondering what had happened between us. 'You could never do that.' I hadn't seen or heard from him since the night of Papa's party several weeks before and his absence had made my heart ache in a way that I hadn't thought possible and which made my brief infatuation with Henry Mercier seem even more pathetically childish. I'd desperately wanted to write, to ask him how he was and why he hadn't visited but the silence had felt so deep, so profound and so final that I hadn't dared breach the chasm that had suddenly yawned between us. 'I haven't seen you for such a long time,' I said lamely.

He sighed. 'I was called away to the family estates in Scotland,' he said. 'I expected to be back before now but you know how these things can be…'

I didn't know, of course but I nodded as if I did. 'I wish that you had written.'

He smiled then, but it wasn't altogether pleasant. 'Do you?' He shrugged and brought out his own battered silver cigarette case which was monogrammed with what I knew to be his family crest. 'I'm afraid that it didn't occur to me.' He flipped open the case and selected a thin cigarette which he then lit with a practised flourish.

I took a deep breath. 'Have I done something wrong, Patrick?' I asked. 'This isn't like you.'

'Isn't it?' He gave me a sidelong look as he leaned against the balustrade. 'Perhaps I should have been more like this in the past.' He examined the glowing end of his cigarette, a frown between his eyes. 'We all make mistakes though.'

'You don't,' I said, feeling a strange sensation of panic rising within me. 'You never make mistakes.'

'Don't I?' he said maddeningly before looking directly at me then turning away again. 'I wish that…' He broke off and took another drag from his cigarette.

'You wish what?' I moved to stand beside him and put my hand on his arm. 'What is it, Patrick? Why have things gone so wrong between us?'

He laughed, a sharp, brutal sound. 'Why do you think, Alice?' He shook my hand from his arm. 'I saw you, you know. You and Mr Mercier.' He frowned down at his cigarette again and I realised with a pang of shock that he was drunk. 'He's not right for you.'

'Oh, don't be such an awful snob, Patrick,' I snapped.

He shrugged and tossed his cigarette over the parapet. Lady Brennan's precious roses would be decimated at this rate. 'You know damn well that I don't mean it that way,' he said angrily. 'Don't try to put words into my mouth, Alice. I would feel exactly the same way no matter who he was.' He looked at me almost pleadingly and his voice softened. 'I don't think he's good enough for you.'

I stared at him then gave a small shrug. 'I'm not sure what that means,' I said sadly. 'There is nothing special about me.'

'No?' Patrick took my hand in his own firm, warm grip and I felt a throb of relief that things seemed to be returning to normal. 'Now you are the wrong one, Alice.'

I stared at him, my dearest friend whom I had known for most of my life, who had covered up my scrapes, taught me French verbs when I had struggled with them, kissed me better when I fell and hurt my knee, spent hours listening to me cry about Beatrice after she had vanished. There had never been a time when Patrick had not given me his full and undivided attention, when I had not basked in the warmth of his complete and unadulterated admiration and care. Not until now. I shivered, feeling left out in the cold more ways than one. 'I don't love him,' I said in a low voice. 'I thought that I might come to do so but then it just never seemed to happen.'

He stared at me. 'So there is no grand romance?' he asked, his fingers tightening around mine.

I shook my head. 'None whatsoever and there never was.' I gave a small rueful smile as I remembered how badly I had wanted Henry Mercier to kiss me and then how my infatuation for him had dwindled away after it had happened, after I had realised so clearly and with such painful clarity that his feelings for me would never really change and that mine for him were nowhere near as strong as I had built them up to be.

'Poor fellow,' Patrick said grimly. 'I saw the way he looked at you.'

I felt my cheeks go red with a potent mingling of shame and embarrassment. 'I was infatuated at first,' I whispered. 'How could I not be? He was so very different to anyone I had ever met before and so utterly indifferent to me.' He still kept hold of my hand and I was grateful for it as the warm clutch of his fingers gave me courage to carry on. 'In fact he seemed to actively dislike me so much that it rather piqued my interest.'

Patrick smiled. 'You women are all the same,' he said, not unkindly. 'Always running after the men you can't have and ignoring the ones who would do anything for you.'

'Perhaps we don't want to have things done for us,' I pointed out crossly. 'I don't need rescuing, Patrick.'

'I know,' he said with a smile, 'but please allow me the luxury of pretending that you do every now and again.'

'Mr Mercier wasn't like that,' I said, feeling suddenly very weary. 'He never wanted to do anything for me. In fact on the one occasion when he had to help me out, he seemed inordinately angry about the fact.' I looked at Patrick from underneath my eyelashes, afraid that I might say the wrong thing and lose him forever. 'We only kissed once but after that it seemed as if all the things that I had found so fascinating, so invigorating even, became utterly exhausting. He never could have loved me, you see and I began to find his endless disapproval of who I am dispiriting.' I gave Patrick's hand a reassuring squeeze - having been totally unable to meet his eyes after my confession about kissing Mr Mercier, which I suppose told me everything I needed to know about my true feelings for the man who stood so silently by my side. 'We would have ended up hating each other.'

'You have no regrets then?' Patrick asked. The music from the ballroom swelled behind us and I heard a woman neigh with laughter close at hand.

I paused, hesitating for a moment to make sure that my answer was absolutely truthful. 'No, none.' I shrugged lightly. 'We are friends, I think, but nothing more than that.'

'And how does he feel about that?' Patrick moved closer to me now and I leaned against him.

I shook my head. 'I don't know,' I said truthfully. 'We haven't really spoken about it and to be honest I've hardly seen him since it happened.' I smiled up at him. 'I've actually been avoiding him as I feel so awkward about the whole thing but I suspect it meant as little to him as it did to me.' It was the truth but it still stung my pride to admit it out loud.

Patrick sighed and pulled me close. 'I think that my problem is that I don't think anyone is good enough for you,' he said quietly against my hair.

I smiled up at him. 'Even you, Patrick?' I asked.

He smiled back but it didn't quite reach his eyes. 'Especially me, my dear.'

I sighed and shook my head, allowing him to pull me further into his embrace and wishing that I could stay there, safe within the circle of his arms for all eternity. 'I have missed you so much, Patrick,' I said. 'I have badly needed to speak to someone over these last few weeks but didn't know where to find you.'

'You should have written to me,' he said, pushing me away a little so that he could look down into my face. 'I would have replied at once,' He smiled a little, 'however furious with you I happened to be at the time.'

I smiled back at him and rubbed my aching temples with my fingers. 'I didn't want to trouble you,' I said, ruefully thinking of all the times I had sat down at my little desk and prepared to write to him but then in the end had not. 'I didn't want to trouble anyone.'

He frowned. 'Is everything alright, Alice? I don't think that I have ever heard you sound quite so forlorn before.'

I shook my head. 'I don't know.' I thought of the letter that I had found on my father's desk and which now lived in my locked drawer along with Beatrice's pendant, photograph and the envelope. Henry Mercier's note was there too - armed with a map and full directions, I had gone to the address he gave me but the girl Emma had already vanished and I had no hope of finding her again. 'I found something out about my sister and don't quite know what to make of it.'

Patrick nodded. 'I see.' He pulled his cigarette case out again and flicked it open, this time offering it to me.

'Shouldn't you be getting back to the ball and doing your duty by all those desperate looking debutantes and their pushy mamas?' I said as I helped myself to a cigarette then waited for him to light it.

'My place is here,' he said briefly, shaking the match out and throwing it over the balustrade. 'As they all very well know.' He took a drag from his cigarette and blew a series of perfect smoke rings up into the air, the great show off. 'So what did you find?'

There was something about his voice, a sort of studied insouciance, that made me look sharply at him. 'You know all about Panacea House, don't you?' I said, my voice catching.

He hesitated for a moment then nodded. 'Not all about it, no,' he looked at me apologetically, 'but enough.'

I gave a great sigh and broke away from his arms. 'How long? How? Did Papa tell you?' I leaned over the balustrade and stared out into the murky gloom of the garden. He came up behind me but made no move to touch me again.

'Your Papa told me some of it,' he said. 'He thought that I ought to know.' There was no need to ask why my father had thought Patrick should know but still I felt a surge of anger against them both that they should have discussed the matter behind my back while apparently happy to leave me in ignorance of it all. My father and aunt, I could just about forgive for I knew that they acted as they did purely out of a desire to protect me from the truth, that they had believed it better for me to know nothing at all than to be distressed. They had been stupid, yes but not intentionally cruel - or so I was determined to believe. 'Have you been there?' he asked.

I shook my head, suddenly tearful. 'I know that I should,' I said. 'I know that it is wrong of me not to have gone there already but I couldn't bring myself to and I don't know what to say once I am there.' I looked at him then. 'What does one say, after all?'

He put his hands on my shoulders and drew me gently towards him. 'I don't know,' he said. 'I don't know.'

Chapter Twenty Three

Torrential rain lashed relentlessly against the carriage windows as we lumbered through the countryside towards Rayleigh in Essex. I stared miserably through the glass at the grey, depressing countryside and only occasionally stole a few shy glances across at Patrick who sat opposite me, apparently lost in thought.

'What an awful day,' I said at last before giving a tiny shrug. 'Although, to be fair, it certainly suits my mood.'

He smiled and reached across the gap between us to take my hand. 'I am with you,' he said. 'There is nothing to be afraid of.'

I gave him a wan smile. 'Are you sure about that? It seems to me that I have much to be afraid of.'

He shook his handsome head. 'I know that it must seem that way, Alice, but it really won't be as bad as you fear and once this is over with…'

'Yes, what then?' My tone was harsher than I had intended and I felt my cheeks redden with embarrassment as I turned my face away to stare again out of the window. My eye was caught by a group of small children running, whooping and laughing down the street in the village we were passing through with newspapers held aloft above their heads in a vain attempt to hold off the rain. I felt a sudden longing to be outside with them, gathering my heavy grey silk skirts above my knees and running through the puddles as my hair fell down about my ears. 'What will happen, Patrick?'

He sighed. 'Once this is all over then I should hope you will feel able to continue with your life.' He released my hand and sat back in his seat, turning his head to follow my gaze out through the rain dappled window. 'I know how much Beatrice's disappearance devastated you and I was hoping that knowing what has become of her will mean that you are able to carry on with your life as before.'

I reached up and trailed one finger down the mist of condensation that had gathered on the inside of the window, watching in fascination as it turned to water and dripped away. 'I don't know if that's possible,' I whispered. 'Although I suppose that in the end it will all depend on what we find at Panacea House.'

My father thought that I was on my way to the refuge in Whitechapel and I dreaded to think what he would say should he learn the truth - that we had picked up Patrick at Canonbury Station and then headed straight out of London towards Essex. It would, perhaps, have been a better idea and more anonymous to go by train but there was always that danger that someone who knew us both would see us together so we decided to take a carriage instead. It could have been worse though - the coachman had known me all my life and, like most of the staff at our house, colluded only too happily with my plans knowing that they would be well rewarded for their silence and there was no chance of being turned out by my soft hearted father should the deception be discovered. My aunt, of course, was a different matter but I rather thought she would be completely mollified by the fact that Patrick was with me and so didn't worry too much about her reaction should she find out.

'Am I doing the right thing, Patrick?' I said. I'd been happy in my own way before the envelope with Beatrice's locket had landed on the chill marble floor of our hallway or, at least, I had supposed that I was. Now though, I wasn't sure as a restlessness, a sense of something missing that had throbbed below the surface threatened to overwhelm me.

Patrick looked at me and shook his head. 'I don't know, Alice,' he said. 'Only you can know the answer to that.'

I felt in my reticule and brought out the letter that I had found on my father's desk then handed it to him. I had read it so often now that the words were seared across my memory.

'My dear sir,
I am writing to let you know that your daughter, Miss Beatrice Redmayne is settling in well at Panacea House and no longer requires

222

any significant methods of sedation. She is sleeping and eating well and has even been playing the piano in the evening, which brings everyone much pleasure.

I do not advise visits or any form of communication at the present time as it may lead to a relapse of her nervous condition but I am sure that all of this may be resumed in the future when she is more herself again.

I will, of course, let you know immediately if there is any change in her condition.

Yours etc.
Mrs Smith-Welsh.'

Patrick said nothing as his eyes scanned the letter then handed it back to me. 'I can't believe that she has been there all this time and that no one thought to tell me,' I said. 'I hope that she does not think that we have all forgotten about her.'

'I am sure that she does not think that,' Patrick said in a low voice, taking my hand again and gazing at me most earnestly. 'I have heard that these places can be damnably strict and you can see from the letter that they discouraged any communication until she was better.'

'But surely she must be better by now?' I said, pushing the letter back into my reticule. 'This was written six years ago. You remember how she was, don't you?' I stared at him. 'She was perfectly normal, perfectly sane and yet this letter makes it sound like she was some sort of madwoman or some wild creature that must be cut off from the world.' I felt tears welling in my eyes and angrily dashed them away with the back of my hand. 'There is something very wrong here, Patrick, and I am determined to get to the bottom of it.'

He smiled. 'I have no doubt at all that you will,' he said. 'This doesn't explain the locket and envelope though.' I had told him everything while making the arrangements to travel out to Panacea House together and would always be grateful for the careful way he had listened to every single word, for his absolute and wholehearted belief in everything that I had said no matter how preposterous it had seemed once uttered out loud.

I shrugged. 'I'm sure that there is a perfectly straightforward explanation,' I murmured, gazing moodily out of the rain and mud splattered window. 'Perhaps this girl Emma was a fellow inmate of Panacea House and stole them from her?'

Patrick nodded. 'That does seem like the most likely scenario,' he said quietly.

We arrived at Rayleigh shortly afterwards and as if by magic, the rain cleared up so that I was able to push the window down and relieve some of the stuffiness in the carriage as we rolled up a pleasant and well tended street lined with shops and pretty pale stone houses. 'I suspect that Panacea House is on the outskirts,' I said, smiling up at the rainbow that was just beginning to shimmer into life above the rooftops. 'How fresh everything smells after a really good rain shower.' I took a deep breath then settled back into my seat. 'Have you ever been to Italy, Patrick? The air there smells extraordinary when the rain has stopped.'

'I went to Venice and Naples when I was younger,' he said, stretching his long legs out in front of him and wincing when they wouldn't go as far as he would like in the cramped conditions of the carriage. 'I would like to go back one day. Perhaps we should go together after...'

'Let's not talk about that now,' I said quickly, cutting him off.

'But we will talk about it?' He ran his fingers nervously through his thick hair, which he was wearing a little longer these days. The gold signet ring on his finger caught the light and dazzled me.

I sighed and shrugged. 'Yes, one day but not today.' I looked at him pleadingly. 'Please, Patrick, let's not do this now.' I gave a shaky laugh. 'I know that I have compromised my reputation by travelling so far alone with you but I do hope that you haven't been colluding with my father and aunt to use this as a means of forcing me into matrimony.'

He grinned and shook his head. 'No, but I'm willing to wager that they will be most disappointed not to have thought of such a ruse themselves.' He leaned forward and caught both of my hands in his. 'Very well, Alice, I won't speak of it now but after we have returned to London, I will be making an appointment to speak to your father at the very earliest convenience.'

I hesitated for a moment then nodded. 'As you wish,' I said in a low voice. 'I know when I am beaten.'

Panacea House did indeed lie on the outskirts of Rayleigh and we passed out into open countryside with rolling fields, clumps of trees and a few scattered cottages before finally turning in through a rather forbidding looking stone gatehouse topped with crenellation and a large lozenge decorated with a coat of arms. 'This is much grander than I had expected,' I remarked to Patrick as we rolled up a long winding driveway that passed through dense woodland before coming to an abrupt end in front of a large pale stone house built in an austere Georgian style with columns holding up a pediment at the front and a pair of small wings attached to the sides.

'Whoever owns this place must be raking it in,' Patrick said appreciatively as our carriage came to a halt in front of the house and the coachman jumped down to pull open my door.

'Well, according to Lucasta, this is the most fashionable place to send wayward young ladies,' I said tartly as I descended on to the gravel then drew the short veil that edged my hat down over my eyes.

Patrick jumped down behind me and then after a moment's hesitation offered me his arm. 'Shall we?' he said.

I looked up at him, suddenly frightened and nodded. 'Don't desert me,' I whispered from lips that felt suddenly dry and bloodless.

He squeezed my hand. 'I will remain by your side until the very end,' he said with a meaningful look that made the blood rush into my cheeks and gave me the strength to walk the few yards to the front door, which already stood open with a pert faced little maid standing beside it.

'Welcome to Panacea House,' she said in a distinctly Essex accent as we approached. Her eyes flickered over us both and I saw a frown appear between her dark eyes as she clearly wondered if we were merely visitors or if Patrick was bringing me in to be committed and I started to feel vaguely panicked in case someone appeared from the shadowy hall between her with a straight jacket. What was the procedure in these places anyway? I looked around curiously, taking in the avenue of lime trees that led to a pleasant garden at the side of the house and the pretty pink and green curtains that hung at the window nearest to us. It didn't look like the formidable institution that I had been imagining but more like a rather charming private home.

'I am Lord Woollam and this is Miss Redmayne. We have come to see Mrs Smith-Welsh,' Patrick said, clearing his throat nervously. 'We have some questions about a young lady who has been residing here.'

The maid nodded and led us into the hall, which was large, painted a soft shade of periwinkle blue and lined with portraits. 'I will let her know that you are here,' she said. 'If you will just follow me into the parlour?'

We silently went across the hall to a room at the back of the house, which was papered with pretty Japanese wallpaper painted with peacock feathers, lush exotic flowers and tiny golden fish. Pale green watered silk curtains hung at the windows and I pulled one aside to peer across the lawn at the back of the house, where I could see about a dozen young women walking together - some in pairs with linked arms and bright heads close together and others alone, either reading from a book or just staring into the distance. I had vaguely expected the young ladies of Panacea House to wear some sort of uniform but instead these girls were dressed as fashionably as any you might see at a Mayfair garden party or taking the air in Hyde Park.

I looked for Beatrice among them but they were too far away. I thought that perhaps one of the blonde girls, who was wearing pale pink and was sitting alone on a bench at the very far end of the lawn, might be her but it was impossible to tell at such a distance. 'It's really quite pleasant here,' I said to Patrick as I regretfully turned away from the window. 'Much nicer than I expected.'

'I'm so pleased,' a woman's voice said in tones of amusement and with a shock I turned to see that a dark haired middle aged lady dressed in pale grey silk that I took to be Mrs Smith-Welsh had entered the room and was now surveying us with frank curiosity. 'Did Rosie bring you tea?' she asked, moving towards me with a smile. 'She's very new and really rather hopeless but what can you do?' She went to a blue silk bell pull that hung beside the highly decorated white plaster fireplace and gave it a sharp tug. 'As you can imagine, we have quite a high turn over of staff here at Panacea House.'

I couldn't imagine and looked doubtfully at the window, through which I could still see the pale dresses of the young ladies walking in the garden. Mrs Smith-Welsh followed my gaze with her own and gave a small, tight smile. 'I do wish that all of our young ladies were as well behaved,' she said enigmatically.

A very flustered Rosie appeared a few moments later, tucking her hair back under her neat white linen cap then wiping her hands down her apron. My aunt Minerva would have been appalled but I rather warmed to her. 'You rang, Mrs Smith-Welsh?' she said breathlessly as if she had been running.

'Tea, Rosie,' Mrs Smith-Welsh said with a thin lipped smile. 'And cake, I think?' She turned to Patrick with an apologetic shrug as the maid scampered off again. 'I expect that I really ought to offer you something stronger but as you can no doubt appreciate, we consider it unwise to have strong spirits on the premises lest it excites the young ladies.'

Patrick nodded. 'Of course,' he said. 'Tea will do perfectly well.'

Our hostess motioned that we be seated then, after we had perched on one of the very uncomfortable jade silk covered sofas arranged either side of the fireplace, turned to me with an arch of her eyebrow. 'And what can I do for you, Miss Redmayne?' she said smoothly. 'I do, of course, recognise your name but...' she made an expressive little gesture with her small plump hands that indicated that she had no idea what I was doing there.

I took a deep breath and decided that it was best to be bold than waste time beating around the bush and probably getting nowhere. 'I have come to see my sister, Beatrice Redmayne,' I said, reaching into my reticule for the letter that she herself had sent six years before. 'I believe that she is a resident here.'

'Is that so?' Mrs Smith-Welsh put out her hand for the letter and scanned it quickly before handing it back. 'I remember writing this,' she said. 'That poor girl.'

'So she was here then?' I said, clutching at Patrick's hand.

Mrs Smith-Welsh nodded briskly. 'She was indeed,' she said carefully, 'but no longer.' She looked from me to Patrick and then back again. 'I am so sorry, my dear, but she left Panacea House just over a year ago.'

I stared at her in amazement. 'She left?' I gasped. 'But where has she gone?' I looked around at Patrick but his expression was just as confused.

Mrs Smith-Welsh opened her mouth to reply but then closed it again with a snap as the door was pushed open without ceremony and Rosie entered, flushed and panting under the weight of a large silver tray laden with a pretty pink floral tea service and cakes arranged on a china plate. She flicked me a curious look from beneath her sandy lashes as she placed the tray on the table in front of the fireplace and started to arrange the tea things.

'How many young ladies do you have living here?' Patrick said, breaking the uneasy silence that fallen in the room. 'It is a much larger establishment than I had anticipated.'

Mrs Smith-Welsh gave him a polite smile. 'We have around thirty young ladies living here at any time.' She watched warily as Rosie poured the tea. 'Some of them are here permanently but others are here for a rest.' She looked at me. 'Society life can be so very exhausting, can't it? Some of our young ladies come here for a few weeks or perhaps a month to recuperate before returning to their usual life.'

Rosie finished pouring the tea and straightened up. 'Will that be all, ma'am?' she said to her mistress before whisking from the room without waiting for an answer.

'She won't last long,' Mrs Smith-Welsh said with a sigh, handing me my cup of tea. 'They never do.'

I took a polite sip of my tea then put the cup back on the table in what I hoped was a business like manner. 'Why did my sister leave?' I said.

Mrs Smith-Welsh paused in the act of raising a piece of seed cake to her lips and coughed before replying. 'I don't know,' she said candidly. 'I know that she wasn't entirely happy here but I didn't realise that she was unhappy enough to want to leave.'

I digested this. 'But where did she go?'

Mrs Smith-Welsh sighed and put the piece of cake back on to her plate then sat back, wiping her hands on a lace edged napkin. 'I have not the faintest idea,' she said. 'She left no clues as to her current whereabouts so I rather presumed that she had gone home. Naturally, I immediately wrote to your father to make him aware of the situation.' She frowned. 'I expected him to come here and talk to me about it but he obviously did not see fit to do so.'

'It's possible that we were abroad at the time,' I murmured, trying to remember where we were a year ago. There had been a trip to Paris in the spring and then three months in Italy across the autumn. Had Beatrice gone back to Highbury only to find us all gone? I felt cold at the thought of it. What must she have thought of us all, carrying on with our lives as if she did not exist? What must she have thought of me?

'That would certainly explain it,' Mrs Smith-Welsh said, lifting up her cup and taking a sip of tea. 'We were all very worried at the time as it was so unexpected.'

Patrick gave a discreet cough. 'Do your young ladies often just walk out?' he said. 'I was under the impression that the residents of Panacea House were on the whole compelled to remain here until given permission by their families to go home.'

Mrs Smith-Welsh reddened slightly. 'That is quite true, my Lord, but in this case I am afraid there was a lapse in the usual security arrangements and Miss Redmayne was able to leave.' She sighed. 'It happened very late at night when we were all in bed or at least should have been. We found out later that she had managed to befriend one of the maids who let her out of her room and then helped her to find her way to Rayleigh, where we believe that she caught a train to London. The maid was, of course, immediately dismissed.'

I felt like crying. I suppose that most people would describe Panacea House as tranquil but the silence felt like more like a sepulchral hush to me. 'Did she have many visitors?' I asked in a low voice.

Mrs Smith-Welsh shook her head. 'No, I'm afraid not.' She took another sip of tea and watched me over the rim of her cup. 'Your parents and aunt came a few times but then shortly before she vanished, her behaviour deteriorated and I advised them to stop visiting as it was causing distress.' She did not say to whom but I could imagine it all so clearly - my father, red eyed and silent with misery; Aunt Minerva, weeping into her handkerchief and Beatrice..?

'You say that her behaviour deteriorated?' I said, still holding onto Patrick's hand as if my life depended upon it. 'What do you mean by that?'

'Ah yes, well, by that I mean that she became erratic, hysterical and really quite difficult to manage,' she put her cup back on the table and regretfully eyed the seed cake. 'There were several

229

unfortunate outbursts particularly during...' her voice trailed away and she cast a meaningful look at Patrick.

'Oh, yes, I see.' The monthly courses were referred to as visits from Lady Montrose in my family due to a rather awful aunt of my mother's whose regular visits had been a source of much annoyance to her as a young girl.

Mrs Smith-Welsh leaned forward and took my free hand. 'I am so sorry that I couldn't be more helpful, my dear,' she said kindly. 'I think you should know though that she spoke about you all the time.'

A tear snaked down my cheek. 'I wish that I had known,' I whispered. 'I have thought her lost for all these years.'

'And now she is lost in truth,' Mrs Smith-Welsh reminded me gently. 'Do you have any idea where she might have gone?'

I hesitated then shook my head. 'I thought that I had an idea but now I am not so sure.' I looked at her and then down at my hands. 'You see, until now I had believed that she had simply vanished and that no one knew where she was. I was warned at the time not to ever mention it as it was too distressing for my mother but I have always believed or rather assumed that my family exhausted the usual official channels while trying to find her and then, having drawn a blank, decided to carry on with their lives as best they could.' I clasped my hands together and looked back up at her again. 'I have only known the truth for a few weeks and was relieved to think that I had been mistaken and that she has been safe and alive all along.' I looked at Patrick and he took both of my hands in his. 'It is very hard to think that I have lost her again.'

Mrs Smith-Welsh sighed. 'I am so sorry, my dear, to be the bearer of sad tidings.' She lifted her eyes to the ceiling and gave a little shrug. 'I often think that families are so silly about such things. If only someone had told you the truth at the outset then none of this would have happened, would it?'

I wasn't so sure about that - after all, Beatrice was genuinely missing and I was now absolutely certain that someone in Whitechapel knew what had happened to her. I stood up abruptly, almost upsetting the tea things and looked down at Mrs Smith-Welsh with a frigid smile. 'If it is not too much trouble, I wonder if perhaps I might see where my sister lived while she was here?'

I could see that it was on the tip of the other woman's tongue to refuse me but then she gave an unwilling nod. 'I'm not sure how that will help but I will gladly oblige you, Miss Redmayne,' she said, looking not at all glad, in fact quite the reverse. She looked to Patrick, who had also risen to his feet. 'I think that perhaps you should remain here, Lord Woollam. I do not mean to be discourteous but some of our young ladies can be somewhat excitable in the presence of gentlemen.'

Under better circumstances, Patrick and I would have had a good laugh over the idea of his presence causing young ladies to become excitable but as it was he just gave a grim little nod and saw us on our way before resuming his place by the fire, stretching his long legs out in front of him and helping himself to a hefty slice of seed cake, scattering crumbs all over himself and the floor as he did so.

Chapter Twenty Four

Y ou say that you have thirty young ladies here,' I said as I
followed Mrs Smith-Welsh across the hall and then up the
sweeping white wooden staircase that led to the upper
floors of the house. 'Are they all free to walk about as they please?'
As we climbed the stairs, I could hear distant sounds of laughter,
singing and someone playing a piano rather incompetently with
many dropped notes but much enthusiasm.

Mrs Smith-Welsh sighed. 'Not all, no,' she admitted, absent
mindedly patting a bunch of keys that swung at her waist. 'Many
of our young ladies are temporary boarders who have been sent
here by their families to get some rest but most of the others are,
well...' her voice trailed away as she led me down a long bright
corridor that was lit from above by a series of large skylights that
allowed in the mellow autumnal sunlight. 'There is no obvious
difference in their treatment but we have specialist staff on hand
to deal with them if there is any need for restraint or therapy.'

'You said that a maid let my sister out of her room,' I said,
hurrying alongside her. Mrs Smith-Welsh was an uncommonly
fast walker. 'Do you lock all of the girls in at night?'

She turned and looked at me in surprise. 'Oh yes, Miss
Redmayne,' she said. 'Of course we do! Although we like to give
the impression that this is a nice cosy country house, the fact
remains that our young ladies are still patients and have been sent
here for their own good. Their families pay handsomely to have
them here and trust us to ensure that they are properly cared for,
which is a responsibility that we take very seriously.' She sniffed.
'Certainly our security arrangements failed when it came to your
sister but we were not to blame for that and have taken measures
to ensure that such a thing will never happen again.'

She stopped at a door at the very end of the corridor and after pressing her head to the wood for a second, gave a sigh and knocked. 'As your sister wasn't considered to be a danger to herself or others, she was lodged here in the main house. The more, shall we say, erratic of our ladies are lodged together in one of the side wings of the house, where they are cared for and treated by more specialised staff.'

'You mean doctors?' I said, feeling sick at heart and also rather afraid although I couldn't quite explain why. Perhaps it was all down to the odd atmosphere in the house but I found myself wondering if our visit was a ruse to get me here without any fuss so that I too could be incarcerated until I agreed to marry Patrick. I imagined myself beating my hands against a barred window as he vanished from sight in the carriage then gave myself a little shake. What nonsense.

Mrs Smith-Welsh nodded. 'We have four doctors on site permanently and a consultant in London who comes to help with the more complicated cases.' She stepped back as the door was suddenly opened and a young woman, perhaps just a couple of years older than myself, appeared and looked at us both curiously.

'Yes?' she said rather abruptly with a Scottish accent, her eyes running over me before returning to Mrs Smith-Welsh with a hostility that I entirely appreciated for I was rather feeling it myself. 'I was reading.'

'I hope you don't mind, Miss Fairchild, but I was wondering if perhaps I could just quickly show Miss Redmayne here your room?' She was effusive with her politeness and I discerned at once that she was a little afraid of Miss Fairchild, a rather rawboned creature with bright blue eyes and flaming red hair that she wore pulled back in a severe chignon that did nothing to soften her features. 'Her sister stayed here you see and she has expressed a wish to see it for herself.' She gave a fluttering laugh that I guessed was supposed to indicate how foolish my request was and how sorry she was to have to give in to it.

Miss Fairchild however had given a small start at the mention of my name and turned to me with rather more warmth. 'So you're Beatrice's sister then?' she said, looking me over again. 'You don't look much like her, do you?'

I smiled and shook my head. 'No, not in the slightest. My nursemaid always used to joke that I was a changeling baby that had been left in the night by fairies as nothing else could account for how different I was to the rest of my family.'

Miss Fairchild looked me up and down then silently stood aside so that we could enter her room, which was large and cheerfully decorated and overlooked the garden at the back of the house. She had been telling the truth about being interrupted reading as there were several books, mostly forbidding looking tomes about science and nature, scattered all over the colourful patchwork quilt that covered the bed. The rest of the room was messy but not lamentably so, with books covering virtually every available flat surface and very little trinkets of the usual sort to be seen other than a photograph of a harsh faced elderly man, presumably her father, that stood on the dressing table alongside a pot of face cream, a glass bottle of lavender water and a rather elderly silver backed brush with a few fiery strands still caught between the bristles.

'What a lovely room,' I exclaimed sincerely, feeling the sadness that had gripped me since we first arrived at Panacea House begin to lighten a little. I crossed to the window and looked down over the garden where the other girls were still walking together. In the distance I could see trees and soaring above them what I believed to be the spire of Rayleigh Church. 'You have such a nice view.'

Miss Fairchild gave a graceless shrug. 'It's all very well if you like that sort of thing,' she said grumpily. 'I'd much rather be at home in Scotland.' She shot an accusatory look at Mrs Smith-Welsh who fluttered her hands nervously.

'All in good time, Miss Fairchild,' she said soothingly. 'Your mother has written to say that you may return for Christmas if you are willing to compromise a little.'

'I'll be here forever then,' Miss Fairchild said truculently.

'Let us hope not,' the other woman replied crisply. 'When will you girls learn that it is easier by far to use honey to trap flies? You won't gain anything to your advantage with a sour disposition and these childish acts of rebellion.' She sounded really quite aggrieved and I looked at her with interest, breaking off my perusal of the pretty matching wallpaper and curtains, both of which were decorated with huge blooming pink and blue roses. 'Honestly, my dear, could you not unbend just a little?'

Miss Fairchild gave a harsh laugh and turned away to pick up one of her books. 'I am afraid that unbending is not something that I have ever felt able to do,' she said gently. 'It is not in my nature to bend like a reed, to dance for the amusement of others, to pin a smile on my face and do as I am told. Yes, of course my life would be easier if I could only bring myself to do so but perhaps I don't want an easy life?'

'Nonsense,' Mrs Smith-Welsh said briskly. 'Utter nonsense.' She turned to me, having clearly washed her hands of Miss Fairchild, who had retreated back to her bed and calmly opened the book she held in her hand as if we had already gone. 'Have you seen everything that you wanted to see, Miss Redmayne?'

I nodded, feeling a little embarrassed and suddenly desperate to leave. 'Yes, I think so.' I looked apologetically at Miss Fairchild and found that she was looking directly at me with a small smile hovering about her thin lips. 'I am so sorry for intruding,' I said. 'I do hope that I haven't inconvenienced you.'

She gave a grim little nod. 'Not in the slightest, Miss Redmayne,' she said. 'In fact it is interesting to finally meet you as Beatrice spoke so often about you.' I was just thinking that 'interesting' was an odd choice of word to use when she hurried on as if fearful of being stopped. 'We were friends, you see or at least as friendly as one gets to be in a place like this. I liked her a great deal anyway and was sorry when she left.'

'Do you know where she was going?' I asked impulsively, ignoring Mrs Smith-Welsh's look of annoyance.

The girl hesitated and bit her lip then shook her head. 'No, not really,' she said. 'She spoke often about going back to London but that's a common refrain here, I'm afraid. We all have somewhere that we would much rather be.'

'I can well imagine,' I said with a smile before holding out my hand to her which after a moment she took. 'I do hope that your stay here will be a short one,' I said, rather liking her despite her prickly ways and wishing that we could be alone together so that I could ask her more questions about my sister.

'Oh, I rather doubt that, don't you?' she said breezily and I remembered that if she had known my sister then she had been at Panacea House for at least a year if not longer already.

Mrs Smith-Welsh gave an impatient little cough and after one last regretful squeeze of the other girl's hand, I allowed her to hustle me out of the room and close the door behind us. She paused for a second outside and touched the keys at her waist as if considering locking Miss Fairchild into her room but then gave a haughty toss of her head and instead motioned that I should follow her back down the corridor.

'I am so sorry about that,' she said as I hastened to keep up with her brisk pace. 'Miss Fairchild is a rather frustrating case, I'm afraid. Her mother is widowed and the family estate and title turned out to be entailed upon a distant male cousin.' She sighed heavily. 'It is often thus, I believe. However, in this case, the cousin, quite unaccountably I feel, has something of a tendresse for Miss Fairchild and is more than willing to marry her to ensure that she and her mother can continue to live in the style to which they are accustomed...'

'And she is unwilling to do so?' I broke in, feeling my admiration for her grow.

'She is more than unwilling!' Mrs Smith-Welsh exclaimed angrily. 'She is perversely and stupidly resistant and apparently entirely impervious to any form of reason. Her poor mother is quite beside herself and as for the cousin? Well, I can't see him waiting for the silly girl for much longer, can you? Not when there is a large fortune and property to recommend him to other young ladies of a more grateful and obedient nature. It's a wonder that he has remained unmarried for this long!'

'How unfortunate,' I murmured as we crossed a hall and went down another passage, this one lined with prints depicting tragic and inspiring scenes from the lives of various Queens of England. Papa would have adored it, which made me smile to myself as I followed Mrs Smith-Welsh to the stairs and listened to her rant on about Miss Fairchild.

'It's worse than unfortunate,' she said with shrill annoyance, sounding more like my aunt Minerva with every passing second. 'It's absolutely criminal. There really should be a law that compels young women to do as they are told. I am informed that arranged marriages are still quite common on the continent - perhaps if we followed suit things would be much better for everyone.'

'Oh, I'm not sure I agree with that,' I mumbled as I followed her down the stairs to the hall. 'Surely arranged marriages lead to a lot of unhappiness on both sides.'

Mrs Smith-Welsh paused and turned back to me. 'Not in the slightest,' she said. 'Love is such a very inconvenient emotion, don't you find? And, more to the point, such a precarious basis for something as grave as marriage. How much better would it be to form a life long commitment based on logic rather than the sort of romantic flummery to be found in the pages of the very worst type of novels?' She looked me over, her eyes lingering for a moment on the bare ring finger on my left hand. 'I am sure that your family have someone in mind for you, Miss Redmayne. That handsome young peer waiting downstairs, perhaps? Would you really put your own feeble and half formed wants and desires over your father's wish to securely settle you in a position that is worthy of your rank and lineage?'

I stared at her. 'I don't know what you are talking about.' I knew exactly what she meant of course. My duplicity was written, plain for all to see, all over my face. 'Naturally I would always do as my family wishes but I know that what they really want is for me to be happy.'

'Do they?' She shrugged and turned away. 'If I had a penny for every time I've heard a young woman say that within these walls and always quite wrongly.'

I followed her silently back to the sitting room where we found Patrick lounging on the sofa, his cheeks slightly red as if he had been asleep. I cast him suspicious look and motioned that we were leaving. 'I have done all that I can here,' I said. 'I think that we should return to London now.'

He smiled and stood up. 'I'm so sorry, Mrs Smith-Welsh but I seem to have finished off all of your excellent seed cake,' he said with a rueful look as he said goodbye to our hostess. 'You really must send my compliments to your cook.'

As we crossed the hall, the peace of the house was shattered by a series of terrible screams from the upper regions of the house, which were quickly echoed by shouts and cries from other parts of the building. 'Have your young ladies become excited?' Patrick asked, entirely straight faced and with apparent concern.

'It would appear so,' Mrs Smith-Welsh said grimly as a door to the side opened to allow three women in nursing uniforms and a tall white haired man in a brown checked suit who was brandishing a large black doctor's bag to hasten past us across the hall and then up the stairs. 'They should be able to deal with whatever is happening up above.'

I shivered as the nurses sprinted up the stairs, their heavy black boots clip clopping on the wooden steps. 'Does this sort of thing happen all the time?' I said faintly.

Mrs Smith-Welsh gave me what can only be a pitying look and nodded her head. 'Every single day,' she said. 'Which is why we can't keep maids for longer than a few months at a time. They get exhausted with it after a while and who can blame them? Why would honest country girls who have to work for their daily bread sympathise with the sort of pampered, spoiled, ungrateful little madams who end up in a place like this?'

'It's not a lack of gratitude though,' I said to Patrick when we were back in our carriage again and making our way back down the road to Rayleigh. 'It's a sense of outrage that we are supposed to be grateful for all these things that we never asked for in the first place.'

He smiled. 'Oh, I think I know exactly what you mean. Every time some chippy young fellow like that Mr Mercier of yours calls me 'my Lord' with an ironic gleam in his eyes, I just want to beat him about the head while screaming that I didn't ask for any of this and if he wants my bloody title and all the trouble that goes with it then he's welcome to it.'

I gave a wan smile. 'I suppose that is sort of what I meant,' I said. 'Although really, Patrick, I don't think it is something that any man can really properly understand as after all even in your most pampered youth, you were never as protected or kept in so much ignorance as we women.' I sighed and stared out at the gloomy countryside. It was getting late and a heavy fog was beginning to descend upon the treetops and waft across the road ahead of us. 'To be frank, I don't entirely see what we have to be grateful for but Mrs Smith-Welsh would no doubt disagree.'

'I expect she would,' Patrick said. 'What a very unpleasant woman. Anyway,' he reached across the gap between us and took my hands in his, 'what did you find out? Anything juicy?'

I shook my head. 'Not really,' I said. 'What about you? Although I don't expect you discovered anything of significance while shovelling seed cake into your face.'

'Ah, that's where you are wrong,' Patrick said mysteriously.

'It's amazing what you can discover while eating cake.'

I sighed. 'Really Patrick, I can't imagine why anyone would think that we are at all well suited.' I thought with a pang of poor Mr Mercier. What a wretch I was to him.

He laughed. 'Don't you? Oh dear, I see that I shall have to work harder to gain your approval.' He was thoughtful for a moment. 'Is that what the problem is? Do you feel like perhaps this is all just a little too neatly arranged? That it's not romantic enough?' He looked thoughtful. 'I think that I could perhaps fall to my knees at your feet and maybe even squeeze out a few tears in an excess of emotion? Would that do?'

'Perhaps.' Unable to meet his eyes, I carried on staring out at the countryside. 'Or perhaps I am just inherently suspicious of anything that my aunt Minerva approves of.'

'I can't win then, can I?' he said with a sigh.

Chapter Twenty Five

We hardly spoke to each other on the way back to London as we were both wrapped up in our own thoughts. Mine revolved around the girls at Panacea House and what Beatrice's life must have been like there. Patrick's, of course, were a mystery to me but judging by the firm clench of his jaw, I guessed that they weren't cheerful.

It was only when our carriage pulled up at Canonbury Station that he looked at me and reached across to take my hands in his. 'What are you going to do now?' he asked.

'I have to go back to Whitechapel,' I said with a feeling of heavy resignation. 'Those girls must know where my sister is and I am now more determined than ever to know the truth.'

He sighed and withdrew his hands. 'Promise me that you'll take care of yourself, Alice,' he said. 'I don't want to have to go down there to avenge your death.' He gave me a flickering smile then, before I could move back or stop him, leaned across and kissed me on the lips before pulling slightly away and resting his forehead against mine. 'Stay safe, my love.'

'I will,' I whispered, wishing that he would kiss me again but knowing that it would be a bad idea. 'You haven't seen the last of me, Patrick.'

He gave me one last regretful look over his shoulder as he closed the carriage door behind him and then I was alone again. I sat there for a moment watching him as he walked towards the station entrance then tapped on the vehicle roof to let the coachman know that he should move on.

It was starting to rain heavily again by the time I got back to the house on Grosvenor Avenue and I held my hat to my head as I rushed inside, flashing a grateful smile at Swift as I went past him. 'Is my father at home?' I asked as I crossed to the table and pulled off my hat and damp kid leather gloves.

'He is in his study, Miss Redmayne,' Swift said. 'I shall order that some tea be brought to you there.'

I smiled at him. 'You are very good to me, Swift,' I said, patting my wet cheeks and for one second letting my fingers linger on my lips, which still felt the pressure of Patrick's mouth against mine.

'Not at all, Miss Redmayne,' the butler said sombrely but I saw a flash of pleasure in his dark eyes as he turned away.

I hesitated for a moment then straightened my shoulders and crossed the hall to my father's study. It was now or never. I needed to know the truth. I stood for a moment and listened outside the door, just as Mrs Smith-Welsh had done with Miss Fairchild, before lifting my hand to knock.

'My dear child,' my father looked up with a pleased smile as I entered. 'Did you get caught in the rain? What a bore.' He pushed back his chair and stood up then came to my side of the desk and led me towards his fire, which was blazing away merrily in the grate. He never could abide the cold and would insist on having fires lit from the end of August onwards. I dread to think how ruinously expensive this was but it seemed a small price to pay for the cessation of his endless complaints about being cold. 'Is Swift bringing tea? Good, good.'

I smiled politely but could wait no longer. 'Papa, I need to ask you something,' I blurted out. 'It's about Beatrice and Panacea House.'

He stared at me for a moment then sat down heavily on one of the comfortable crimson leather chairs that stood either side of the fireplace. 'How do you know about that?' he said dully, staring down at the floor and not looking at me.

'I found a letter,' I said. 'What happened, Papa?'

He shook his head and for a terrible moment I thought he was going to refuse to tell me but then he seemed to brace himself and began to talk. 'Do you remember Beatrice at all, Alice?' he said, looking up at me then and I saw that his eyes were filled with tears. 'You were very young of course but...'

'Of course I remember her,' I interrupted him brusquely, fighting against my own tears. 'I was eleven years old, not a tiny child or a baby. I remember everything about her.' I sat down on the chair opposite him and pulled Mrs Smith-Welsh's letter out of my reticule. 'Why did you send her away?'

He looked away. 'You think that you remember her but you don't know what she was like,' he said. 'Not really. There were tantrums and terrible... scenes. Your mother found it all so distressing. It was exhausting just to be in the same house.' He sighed. 'Perhaps we did the wrong thing but it seemed like the correct thing to do and then, of course when...' he broke off and looked at me for a moment in silence before giving a shrug and carrying on: 'We couldn't carry on as we were. It would have killed your mother and destroyed our family. We were afraid for you as well.'

'Why afraid for me? Beatrice loved me and I loved her,' I said. 'She would never have done me any harm.'

He stood up and went to the drinks tray that had been laid out as usual on top of a cabinet behind his desk. 'Perhaps not physical harm in the sense that you mean but in other ways,' he said as he shakily poured himself a brandy. I stared longingly at the bottle, thinking I could do with some myself but could hardly dare to ask him to pour me a glass. 'Her behaviour was becoming increasingly erratic and we feared that there might be some sort of incident that would reflect badly on you. It hardly seemed fair to expose you to that so we did what we thought best.' He gave a rueful smile as he settled back into his chair. 'We had already made plans to take her to Panacea House for a rest but then there was an incident that necessitated our moving more swiftly to have her removed from the house.' He took a sip of brandy and closed his eyes, apparently at an end.

I stared at him, hardly able to breathe. 'What sort of incident?' I said in a low voice. It seemed so odd, so completely bizarre to be having this conversation in such a perfectly ordinary way in the well known surroundings of my father's study while all the while I was conscious of the cook and maids downstairs busying themselves making our tea and slicing cake as if everything was just as it always was, as if nothing had changed.

He sighed and opened his eyes. 'She threatened your mother with a knife,' he said baldly. 'I don't know what happened. I wasn't there.' He took another sip of brandy, a larger one this time. 'I should have been. I should have known not to leave them alone together as it had been building up for weeks.'

242

'She threatened Mama with a knife?' I could hardly believe it. 'But why?'

My father shook his head. 'I haven't the faintest idea,' he said. 'Like I said, she was erratic and prone to hysteric fits and becoming increasingly so. Who knows what was in her mind at the time? I don't suppose she knew herself.' He drained his glass with one gulp and placed it on a small table at his side. 'Anyway, after that, you can see why we could no longer have her in the house. I telegraphed Panacea House straight away and within a few hours the arrangements were made and she was on her way.' He looked down at his hands. 'It was no easy task to get her there,' he said with a small wince. 'She fought like a tigress but it was only when I promised her that if she could only be good and do her best to get well again that she agreed to go quietly.'

'How could you?' I whispered, tears now spilling down my cheeks. 'How could you send her away from us all?'

He looked up at me. 'But what else could we do?' he said sharply. 'She was a danger to herself and others. She almost killed your mother and might very well have killed you too. She was fortunate indeed that we sent her to Panacea House instead of contacting the police.'

I couldn't disagree with this and so remained silent for a moment taking it all in, my thoughts running this way and that and always returning to the same thing: that my family had lied to me about everything for six years. 'Does everyone know?'

He gave a weary nod of assent. 'I know that you are angry with me,' he said in a quiet voice, 'and you have every right to be but please believe that I acted only for the best.'

There was a knock on the door, which opened a second later to admit Swift and one of the parlour maids bearing a laden tea tray. My stomach rumbled terribly as I watched them carefully laying out plates covered with sandwiches and cake and I remembered with a jolt that I had had nothing to eat since breakfast - at which point I could barely restrain myself from snatching several sandwiches from the plate and shoving them into my mouth like some kind of savage.

My father and I remained completely silent as the butler and maid laid out our tea things, wincing as if in pain at every chink of silver against china or clatter of tea spoons. Our silence continued after they had gone as I performed my usual task of pouring out the tea and adding milk and a sugar to my father's cup.

'Please don't be angry with me, Alice,' he whispered as he took the cup from my outstretched hand.

I hesitated. 'I'm not angry with you,' I said at last, finding to my surprise that I wasn't. After all, I'd known my father all my life and no matter how painful this was, I still couldn't bring myself to believe that he had acted out of malice. Carelessness certainly and perhaps stupidity, but never malice. What was it that Napoléon once said? Never ascribe to malice that which is adequately explained by incompetence. That was my poor dead foolish Papa all over.

He smiled weakly. 'Well, that's something at least,' he said sadly. 'I always intended that she should come home one day but then her behaviour deteriorated so much that it just never seemed to happen. I hear that she is doing well now though so perhaps in time…'

I stared at him. 'But Papa, surely you know that she isn't there any more,' I said, spluttering over my tea as he looked at me in confusion. 'I was at Panacea House today. I went there to see her and find out what had happened but she wasn't there.' I put my tea down on the table so clumsily that it spilled all over the polished wood. Usually this would earn me a reprimand but for once my father didn't notice. 'She left just over a year ago. Apparently that awful Mrs Smith-Welsh wrote to let you know but I think that it must have happened while we were in Italy.' Again I felt that crushing sense of entirely irrational guilt that we should have been enjoying ourselves in the sunshine while my sister was apparently some kind of fugitive.

'Over a year ago?' My father was aghast. 'But how can this be? Why was I not informed?' He ran his fingers through his greying hair. 'And this woman claims to have written to let me know?' He stood up and went to his desk, which as usual overflowed with scraps of paper, sketchbooks, pamphlets and peculiar odds and ends. He pulled open a drawer and plunged his hands into a mess of papers and old letters, all tangled up with paint brushes, blunt pencils, a yellowing French newspaper and several receipts from art shops. 'But that is impossible,' he muttered to himself as he searched. 'Absolutely impossible.'

I rose and went to stand beside him, wondering what on earth he was hunting for so desperately. 'What is it, Papa? How is it impossible?'

He gave a small cry and pounced on a letter that had been pushed to the side of the drawer. 'Read this,' he said, pushing it into my hands then standing back, slightly flushed, as I cautiously opened the envelope and extracted the letter within, which I saw at once was written on the headed notepaper favoured by Panacea House.

'Dear Sir,

As promised, I am writing to let you know how your daughter is getting on. Although we had hopes that she would be able to receive visitors again very soon, I am afraid that there has been another marked deterioration in her behaviour and that any contact with family members must continue to be discouraged.

I am so sorry to tell you this as I know that quite some time has passed since you were last able to see your daughter but please be assured that we have given the matter much consideration and can see no other option.

Otherwise, she is doing well and continues to eat and sleep as well as can be expected. As we advised, we are discouraging her from the reading of sentimental novels of the sort that are liable to inflame such impressionable young women and instead recommending that she devotes herself to a proper study of far more improving religious and historical tracts…'

I crumpled the letter in my fist and stared at him. 'What does this mean?' I said in a whisper. 'This letter was apparently written just two months ago, which if Mrs Smith-Welsh is to believed is impossible.'

My father reached out and took the letter from me, straightening it between his long fingers. Artist's fingers. I looked down at my own and noticed for the first time how short and stubby my own were in comparison. Perhaps I was a changeling after all? 'But Mrs Smith-Welsh signed this letter herself,' he said patiently, showing me the bottom of the letter where that lady's unmistakable signature, bold and florid in purple ink stood out starkly against the pale creaminess of the expensive paper. 'So she must be lying.'

'But why is she lying to us?' I said, feeling suddenly so weak legged that I had to sink down into one of the chairs. 'I didn't see Beatrice when I was there and I even asked to see her room.' They had had no warning of our visit, no time to prepare, which made me think that everything I had been told that day was the truth - which meant that this letter must be a lie. Or was it? 'I don't know what to think any more,' I said wearily. 'But I think I know where to go to find out.'

CHAPTER TWENTY SIX

After a mostly sleepless night, I was up early and ringing for an extremely disapproving Minnie to come and help me into one of the plain dresses that I usually wore for my visits to Whitechapel. 'I thought you'd finished with all of that, Miss,' she said with a sniff as she finished putting up my hair in an intricate coiled plait, pinning it into place with carved jade headed pins. 'And it's hardly safe there at the moment is it?'

I sighed and picked up my pearl earrings, which I remembered Beatrice wearing before she vanished. They'd been left behind in her room and had been lying forgotten in my jewellery box ever since. Until now. 'There haven't been any murders for almost a month now and I expect there are no more to come,' I said, fastening the earrings then stepping back to take in the full effect in my dressing table mirror.

'You don't know that, Miss,' Minnie persisted with a scowl. 'Seems to me that no one knows what's going to happen next.'

'Well, maybe you are right but I certainly don't feel like I am endangering myself by going there,' I replied reprovingly. 'If it bothers you so much, perhaps you should accompany me to ensure my safety? After all, this Ripper fellow is hardly likely to attack both of us, is he? He actually seems like rather a cowardly sort of chap when all is said and done.'

Minnie looked satisfyingly aghast at this proposal. 'You wouldn't make me do that, Miss,' she spluttered, backing away with hot patches of colour high on her cheekbones. 'You can't. It's not what I'm paid for.'

'Then hold your tongue,' I said sharply, pulling on my gloves and giving myself one last glance over my shoulder to ensure that my outfit of a plain cobalt blue dress with matching fitted jacket was as it should be. 'I will be back in the early evening as usual.'

I didn't feel entirely confident though as I sat in the carriage on my way to Whitechapel and I found myself continually checking my reflection in the window or nervously patting down my skirts and rearranging my cuffs. I hadn't been back to the Mission for a fortnight now and felt anxious about the sort of reception I would get, even though I had written to let Miss Lawler know why I was absent and received a very cordial reply in the return post.

I suppose that I was worried that they might all think that I was just the sort of spoiled and cherry picking philanthropic hobbyist that Mr Mercier was always complaining about, that I had no real interest in the people of the East End or concern for their plight. Even though I had my own personal reasons for wanting to be in Spitalfields, I would have hated for anyone to think that about me and especially not Miss Lawler, whom I now thought of as something close to a friend.

I need not have worried of course. Charlie and his little ragged crew were there outside the main entrance on Lamb Street as usual and grinned and looked very pleased with the coins that I gave them and there was a huge hug waiting for me from Miss Lawler when I stepped inside. My welcome from Mrs Lightfoot was rather more restrained but still relatively cordial by her rather dour standards.

I dared not look about for Mr Mercier as we went up to one of the classrooms where I was to help some of the girls with their writing practice that morning but Miss Lawler managed to preempt that by telling me quite naturally that he was at the police station helping one of their past residents who had been caught stealing from a grocers on Brick Lane. 'He will be sorry to have missed you, I am sure,' she added with an understanding light in her dark eyes. 'He speaks of you often.'

I smiled and dipped my head in some embarrassment. 'That's very kind of him,' I mumbled.

Miss Lawler put her head to one side. 'Yes, he is kind,' she said, almost musingly. 'Even though his manner would perhaps suggest otherwise.' She looked at me. 'I had rather thought that perhaps...' her voice trailed away and she raised one eyebrow enquiringly.

I shook my head. 'No,' I said more brusquely than I had perhaps intended. 'Absolutely not.'

She sighed and gave a tiny shrug. 'Ah well.'

I followed her into the classroom, which was bright with the sunlight which streamed through the skylights and tall windows that lined one of the walls and took a deep breath of the once familiar scent of freshly laundered clothes, chalk dust and female sweat. The usual soft murmur of chatter came to an abrupt end as I stepped inside and I felt my cheeks redden then pale with embarrassment as every pair of eyes turned curiously towards me. 'Long time, no see,' one of the girls, Cassie, a diminutive redhead with a cheeky smile, called out with a wink. 'We thought we'd seen the last of you, Miss.'

I smiled and dipped my head. 'Oh no, you'll have to try harder to get rid of me.' I turned to Miss Lawler and took her hand. 'I mean it,' I whispered. 'I mean to do real good here once this is all over.'

She frowned. 'When what is all over?' she said but I merely shook my head and moved across the room to where a small group of girls were sitting together reading, their gleaming heads, each wrapped with a neatly coiled plait, bent over their red cloth bound books. 'Still carrying on with The Pilgrim's Progress then?' I said brightly as I approached them and they looked up with the smiles of welcome that I had not even realised that I missed but now made my heart give a small sad pang of mingled happiness and sorrow. 'Let's see how you are doing.'

It was several hours before I was able to slip away and after making my excuses to Miss Lawler, I tiptoed out of the room and down the stairs to the hall, which as usual was completely deserted. Mrs Lightfoot had been making pot pourri in the cavernous kitchen downstairs and a huge fresh blue and white bowl of it stood on the table in the centre of the room, filling the air with the soft, spicy scent of roses, geraniums and carnations.

'Miss Redmayne,' Mr Mercier's voice made me jump guiltily before I recovered myself and slowly turned to face him. 'How nice to see you here again.'

'Is it?' I said, feeling distinctly awkward.

He took a step towards me and I lowered my eyes beneath the weight of his gaze, the confused anguish of his expression. 'I thought you were never coming back,' he whispered reaching out to take my hand, which I quickly withdrew before making a big drama out of putting my blue kid leather gloves back on. 'What did I do?'

I looked at him then and shook my head. 'You didn't do anything,' I said in a low voice. 'It was all my doing and I am sorry for it. I should never have behaved as I did, with such shocking impropriety and such thoughtlessness.'

'Impropriety?' He gave a harsh little laugh. 'Now there's something that I would never thought to hear you trouble yourself about.'

I looked away. 'I can't blame you for being angry with me,' I said as calmly as I could. 'Don't presume to know me though. All that you have ever seen of me is a side that I didn't think I even possessed and, furthermore, attributes that belong entirely to your own imagination. You don't really know me at all, Mr Mercier.'

He stared at me then for a long moment then gave one small, cold, clipped nod of agreement. 'No,' he said quietly. 'Perhaps I don't after all.'

I inclined my head in farewell then passed as calmly as I could past him and out of the house, pausing only to bestow a coin on a ragged little urchin that had taken up a station on the worn front steps before closing the door behind me and turning left up Lamb Street.

It was late afternoon and the sun was hanging low over the rooftops as I turned left again up Commercial Street and walked away from the market towards the police station. The street was busy as always, packed with men, women and children of all races and ages, either milling together in small groups or walking as purposefully as I did towards their destinations.

As I walked, I wondered what the Brennans and their friends would make of the scene that unfolded around me as I made my way down the road past the shops, warehouses and tall forbidding houses, all with pitted, smoke blackened walls. Children hurtled everywhere underfoot, howling, screaming and laughing as they went and thumbing their noses rudely at the adults who threatened them with a clip around the ear. Miserable faced women stood outside the pubs, all dressed in plain dark dresses, their eyes fixed on their pints of beer as they swapped the latest salacious snippet of street gossip. Some of them had babies crying or sleeping in their arms and occasionally would glance

250

down at the blanket wrapped little bundles with a look of exhausted resignation.

Men, grimy, surly and smoking pipes, their caps worn low on their brows stood on the street corners or sat forlorn and forgotten on the front steps, reading tattered newspapers or greedily devouring pies wrapped in greasy brown paper. Cats and dogs ran free, snapping and snarling at the children, stealing scraps of pies and slinking into the dank, menacing looking alleyways.

I smiled to myself as I drew closer to the police station, almost enjoying the cacophony of sounds, the barking, shouting, train whistles, crying and rumbling, that surrounded me and wondering how I could ever have thought it discordant and exhausting. Even the smell of the air was like champagne to me that day although really it stank as always of smoke, dung, rotten vegetables, meat pies and poverty. It was filthy, yes, and mostly unpleasant but at that moment, I don't think I had ever felt more alive, more a part of the beating inner heart of the city that I had called home for all of my life.

'Can I help you, Miss?' The policeman behind the desk was young and fresh faced, which had the absurd effect of making me feel incredibly old even though he must have been a few years my senior. 'Have you come to report a crime?' His expression plainly showed that he thought I looked out of place in Whitechapel and had, in his opinion, probably come either to report being robbed or to make some sort of trouble.

I smiled at him. 'My name is Miss Alice Redmayne and I've come to see a young girl who lives here at the station,' I said in a low voice, well aware of the lack of privacy in the lobby where groups of rough looking men and women loitered while waiting to be summoned for questioning. 'I believe that her name is Cora?'

He looked surprised and gave a nervous look back over his shoulder. 'I believe that I know who you mean, Miss Redmayne' he said cautiously, running his fingers nervously through his clipped short hair. 'Although I can't imagine what you'd want with her.'

'It is a personal matter,' I said, 'pertaining to a piece of work she did for me a few months ago.' Mr Mercier had told me a long time before that Cora worked as a seamstress so I trusted that this would be a believable ruse.

251

He hesitated for a moment then gave a nod as if I had passed some arcane test. 'I see,' he said, with the smidgeon of a smile. 'She lives upstairs as you no doubt already know and if she already knows you then I'm sure she won't mind it if you go up to her.' He lifted the top of the desk and came out to stand beside me. 'If you go through that door there then follow the passage to the end, there is a set of stairs. The Lee family live at the very top.' He smiled again, more warmly this time. 'First door on the left.'

I thanked him and after a moment's hesitation made my way to the door that he indicated, pausing in the doorway to look just once back over my shoulder at the crowded, busy lobby where my place at the front desk had already been taken up by a blowsy, drunk looking young woman in a rusty looking black silk dress, the skirt hanging baggy and awkward at the back due to a lack of bustle cage. She was leaning across the counter and collaring the young policeman with a mittened hand, tightening her grip as he tried to struggle away. 'Now you listen here, you young bastard,' she cooed in a distinct but slurred Irish accent as the door closed behind me. 'I'm afearing for my life, so I am and what are you going to do about it?'

I made my way slowly down the passage, which had damp peeling walls then, after a second's hesitation, went up the staircase, which someone had long ago painted a cheerful apple green, all worn away now by thousands of footsteps. As I slowly ascended, I listened to the sounds that floated into the stairwells from behind closed doors - children's laughter, a badly played violin, someone singing a popular music hall song. There was no noise from behind the Lee family's door though, although I stood for a moment and listened, trying to guess what awaited me beyond the white painted wood before I made the decision to knock and have it all over and done with.

There was a flurry of noise from within, a cough, the whisper of skirts and the sound of a chair being pushed back so that it rattled against wooden floorboards. 'Who is it?' a girlish voice called out and then when I did not dare reply, the door was opened a crack and I caught my first sight of her, small, pale and redheaded with wide hazel eyes. 'Oh,' she said as she looked at me and her eyes widened even more with recognition and what I knew to be fear.

'Can I come in?' I said cordially, putting out a hand to prevent her from closing the door in my face. 'I think that we have much to talk about, don't you?'

She hesitated, her cheeks pink then gave a nod and opened the door enough for me to be able to enter the room before putting her head out to make sure that no one had seen then closing it carefully behind us. 'My brothers and sister are all out,' she said, going over to the stove where a kettle was whistling and steaming. 'Would you like some tea? I have cake too, freshly made this morning.'

'That would be most welcome,' I said, standing awkwardly beside the scrubbed table and looking about myself with interest, taking in the cheerful red curtains at the window, the tangle of small boy boots against the wall, the cold pie on the table waiting to be put into the oven and the pile of books and newspapers that lay on one of the chairs beside the stove. 'What a very comfortable home you have,' I said appreciatively, sitting down.

Cora smiled. 'We do our best,' she said, busying herself making tea then slicing pieces of moist cake. 'I suppose that it must seem very strange to you that we should live somewhere like this and not a proper house.'

I shook my head. 'No, it's not strange at all,' I said. 'I think it is wonderful.' I glanced down at my hands then smiled up at her as she handed me my tea in a lightly cracked flower patterned cup. 'It would be very dull indeed if we all lived in the exact same way.' I took a sip of the tea, which was strong and sweet as people here seemed to like it.

'I suppose that it would,' Cora said quietly, putting the plate with cake slices on the table then pulling a chair over so that she could sit opposite me. 'I've seen your house, of course,' she said awkwardly, cradling her cup between her hands and staring down into the brown depths of her tea. 'I hope that you don't mind.'

I shook my head, feeling a little startled. 'No, of course I don't mind,' I said, taking another restorative sip of the tea. 'I am glad that you came. I only wish that you had stayed long enough to let me speak to you.'

She sighed and went pink at the ears. 'I was afraid,' she said with the ghost of a smile. 'I saw the way your butler treated your last visitor and didn't fancy receiving the same treatment or worse.'

I frowned, trying to remember that morning so many weeks before. 'Oh, Mrs Snaith!' I cried. 'Oh yes, she is a very tiresome woman but Swift would never have treated you in the same way. He really is incredibly kind despite his ferocious looks.'

'Will you have some fruit cake, Miss Redmayne?' Cora said, pushing the plate towards me with her fingertips, which I noticed were chewed and ragged. She gave a nod of satisfaction as I took a piece then picked up a child's white linen dress that lay on the table and began to sew. 'I've almost finished this piece of work,' she said apologetically. 'It's due to be delivered tomorrow morning.'

I watched her for a moment, admiring the way her thin fingers deftly plied the needle. 'You sew beautifully,' I said, a little wistfully. 'I've always been so sadly ham fisted with a needle. My aunt used to despair of me when I was being taught embroidery as a child. She said that her pet spaniels could do better.'

The other girl laughed. 'Are they unusually clever animals then, Miss Redmayne?' she asked. Her accent was Cockney, as might be expected, but had its own soft cadence that was very appealing.

I laughed too. 'Not particularly,' I said, 'and please, call me Alice. That is what my friends do.'

She looked at me over her sewing. 'Are we to be friends then?' she asked softly.

I nodded. 'Yes, I believe that we are,' I said before taking a bite from my own slice of cake. 'This is delicious. Is there no end to your talents? I know that Mr Mercier always speaks very highly about you.' I could feel my cheeks go pink as I said his name but this was as nothing to the closed and stony expression that spread across the other girl's face at the mention of him.

'Does he?' she said, bending her head lower over her work. 'That's very kind of him, I'm sure.'

I inclined my head to the side, even managed a smile. 'He's a kind man,' I murmured.

She looked up at me then. 'I thought you were sweet on him,' she said at last, pausing her needle.

I felt oddly flustered beneath her gaze. 'Oh no, not that,' I said at first, putting the cake back on its plate and reaching for my teacup. 'Never that.' She leaned back in her chair, still looking at me in that steady way as I prattled nervously on. 'I admit that I cared for him at first but it was doomed from the very start.'

She laughed then. 'It sounds just like a play,' she said.

'A very bad play,' I agreed, laughing too. 'He is terribly handsome isn't he but it would never have worked out between us, I'm afraid.'

She sighed and dropped her work on to her knees. 'Did you kiss him?' she asked in a whisper.

I looked at her for a moment, gauging what would be the right answer or at least the one least likely to cause upset. 'I did,' I admitted at last. 'Just once.'

'Oh.' She looked down at the dress spread across her lap and fiddled a little with the collar, which was prettily embroidered with bluebells. 'Was it nice?'

'Yes,' I said boldly, my cheeks hot with embarrassment. 'It was very nice indeed but could only ever happen once. We were not at all suited really.'

She frowned. 'I suppose he is rather beneath you,' she said flatly, picking up her needle again. 'Socially, I mean.'

I shook my head as she resumed her sewing. 'No, it wasn't down to anything like that. I am not concerned with such things and am fairly certain that my father wouldn't mind either so long as I was in love with the person.' I took a comforting sip of my tea. 'The truth of the matter is that I realised that someone else would suit me better.' I smiled, thinking of Patrick. 'Has always suited me better in fact, only I was far too blind and wilful to see it.'

A silence fell between us as I thought of Patrick and she quietly got on with her sewing, keeping her secrets to herself but no doubt bracing herself for what must inevitably be said. 'You know why I am here of course,' I said gently. 'I know that it was you who put the envelope through my door.' She gave me one frightened quick look from those huge eyes but carried on sewing as if I had not spoken. 'I am not angry, Cora. I just want to know the truth. I just want to know how the envelope came into your possession.'

She looked at me then, her eyes round with fear. 'I can't…' she whispered. 'I can't tell anyone what happened and especially not you. Oh, please, Miss Alice, please don't make me.'

I leaned across the table and put my hand on her arm. 'I must,' I gently said. 'I'm sorry but I must.'

Her gaze faltered and dropped away. 'Please don't be angry with me,' she said frantically. 'I couldn't bear that. Not on top of everything else.' She looked at me again and I was astounded by the sheer panic in her expression. What on earth had been happening? What had I stumbled into? 'You don't know what it's been like.'

'Then tell me,' I said as calmly as I could manage. 'Tell me everything and I will shoulder it with you.'

What followed was a garbled tale, tearfully and falteringly told of her visit to the Whitechapel mortuary to look at the face of a murdered woman. 'You can't imagine what she looked like,' she whispered with a shudder of sheer revulsion. 'It was terrible and I wished that I hadn't gone.'

I stared at her as she spoke, hardly able to comprehend what I was hearing, that my sister's pendant had fallen into the possession of a woman of the streets, a woman furthermore who had been murdered in the most savage and public manner. 'How could such a thing be possible?' I murmured, thinking that this tale made Beatrice seem even further away than ever. 'How did she get the locket?'

Cora looked away. 'Well, as to that...' She fell silent and twisted her hands in her lap. The dress had already been laid aside and I could tell that she wished that she had some way to occupy her hands as she spoke. 'There is another girl, Emma, who knows more about that than I do.'

'Emma...' I murmured, remembering the thin girl with dyed brassy blonde hair who had rushed out of the sitting room at the Mission. 'I thought that she must have something to do with it.' I sighed. 'I went to find her at her lodgings more than once but she was always one step ahead of me, it seems.'

Cora nodded. 'She lives above the Britannia on Commercial Street now,' she said. 'She's safe there.'

I stared at her. 'Safe?' I felt the cold hands of fear clutch at my heart. 'What is there to be safe from?' I thought of the Tabram woman who had had possession of my sister's locket for such a short time and of the other women slaughtered on these streets. 'Tell me.' She shook her head, trembling now with fear. 'This is about more than the necklace, isn't it?'

She nodded. 'You need to speak to Emma,' she said miserably. 'She knows all about it. It isn't for me to tell you so please don't make me.'

I still didn't know quite what to think when I left the police station shortly afterwards and made my way slowly back towards Lamb Street. Summer was well and truly over now and dusk was steadily falling as I pushed my way through the crowds on Commercial Street, where the shops were beginning to close for the night and the pub lights were coming on, glowing cosily in the encroaching darkness.

For a moment I was tempted to step inside one and order a drink to steady myself but I wasn't quite brave enough. Not yet anyway. Instead I carried on to Lamb Street, mulling everything that I had been told over and wondering what further revelations were yet to come. So deep was I in my morose thoughts that it took me quite by surprise when a woman stepped lightly out in front of me, forcing me to come to an abrupt halt in the middle of the pavement.

'So, you're Miss Redmayne then.' I recognised her at once as the blowsy looking Irish woman from the police station although close up, I now saw that she was actually rather pretty and not all that much older than myself, with curling auburn hair and fine grey eyes.

'I am,' I said, stopping and looking at her, determined not to be intimidated as she swayed closer, enveloping me in her heady and not exactly pleasant scent of spilt gin, damp petticoats and meat pie. 'What do you want with me?'

She gave a careless shrug but her eyes were sharp, picking over every smallest detail of my appearance, pricing and weighing me up to see how much I would be worth to her. 'Well, that depends, doesn't it?' she said with a wink and a flounce. 'Emma told me that you'd come to Whitechapel. She said you'd find us one day.'

I paused. 'Emma?' I tried not to sound too eager but there was no point, of course as she'd already seen the gleam of interest in my eyes.

She grinned. 'That's the girl,' she said chirpily. 'Fair Emma we used to call her in France on account of her hair. I was called

Ginger Marie on account of mine.'

'Oh, you were both in France?' I said politely, wondering what she wanted with me and nervously looking towards the Mission house with the vague hope that someone might come out and rescue me.

Marie nodded. 'That we were, my Lady,' she said blithely. 'Emma and me and Beatrice.'

I stared at her. 'Beatrice?' She had my full attention now. 'Beatrice was in France? But why?'

She grinned again. 'Now, wouldn't you like to know.' She made as if to turn away but I quickly reached out and gripped her arm. 'Ooh, got you now, have I?'

'Just tell me,' I hissed.

She laughed in my face. 'It'll cost you,' she said, pulling her arm out of my grasp then rubbing her thumb and forefinger together. 'Oh yes, I think you'd pay a very pretty penny indeed to hear what I have to tell.'

I drew back and tried to hide my eagerness. 'How much do you want?' I asked cautiously.

Marie gave me a sly look from beneath her eyelashes, sizing me up again. 'Ten pounds would do me,' she said.

I took a deep breath. It wasn't a lot of money really, not to me anyway, but it was a high price to pay if she turned out to be a liar. 'Very well then,' I said. 'Ten pounds.' A couple walking down the street with their arms around each other jostled me as they went past and I almost fell against the other woman.

'Steady now,' she said with a laugh as I put my hand against a damp, smoke blackened wall to steady myself. 'You've got to be careful around here.'

I allowed myself a small smile. 'So I can see.' I looked at her. 'What do you have to tell me then?'

Marie smiled and shook her head. 'Money first, my fine lady,' she whispered, patting my cheek with her hand. 'Come back tonight with ten pounds and I'll tell you everything you want to know and more besides.'

I sighed, resigning myself to the inevitable. 'Where will I find you?' I remembered the stinking alleyway where I had been lured and then hit from behind and gave a tiny shudder. 'Perhaps we could meet in one of the public houses?'

She gave a harsh laugh. 'No, I don't think so, Miss Redmayne,' she said. 'Come to my room, number thirteen Miller's Court later on.' I must have looked confused for she leaned forward and whispered in my ear. 'It's just off Dorset Street. If you get lost just ask for Marie Kelly and someone will point you in the right direction. Everyone knows who I am down there.'

CHAPTER TWENTY SEVEN

L uckily it was just Papa and Aunt Minerva at dinner that evening so there was no need to make anything other than the most perfunctory conversation and there was barely a murmur of protest when I declared myself exhausted immediately after the last course and made my way back upstairs to my room.

'I am worried about that girl,' I heard Aunt Minerva say to Papa as the door closed behind me. 'Of course I am very happy that she isn't gadding about the place as the young people these days are so wont to do but even so, Edwin, I wish that she was having a trifle more fun. It's not pleasant to see her looking so dejected all the time.'

I stood for a moment on the other side of the door and listened as my father murmured some indistinct reply then shook my head and crossed the candlelit hall to the stairs. As requested, Minnie was waiting for me in my room, with my plain grey walking dress laid out ready on the bed.

'Are you sure about this, Miss?' she whispered as I closed the door behind me and immediately began to briskly pull pearl and diamond studded pins out of my hair. 'Whitechapel is a dangerous place at night. I know that you've been safe enough during the day but surely you can see how different this will be?' She moved forward to help me out of my heavy olive green silk dress.

'I will be quite alright,' I said, stepping out of my skirt. 'I know exactly where I am going and do not intend to linger there for any longer than I need to.' I watched myself in the mirror as Minnie dressed me, rather liking the determined tilt of my head, the bright shine of my eyes that only I knew and my maid guessed masked the most profound fear that I had ever felt. 'Besides, I will be well protected,' I said.

'Oh, Miss?' Minnie asked, hardly looking up from her task of fastening my tightly fitted bodice. 'And how might that be?'

I smiled and leaned forward to open one of my dressing table drawers, making her tsk with annoyance as I interrupted her work. 'I took this from my father's study,' I said triumphantly, brandishing a small hand gun in the air. 'He bought it to protect himself against goodness knows what while doing a lecture tour in America and it's been lying forgotten in a drawer ever since.'

Minnie eyed the weapon with frank disapproval. 'Until now,' she said sourly. 'Do you know how to use it, Miss?'

'Of course I do,' I said, putting the gun down on my dressing table. 'Patrick showed me how to load and fire it one summer many years ago and, besides, how hard can it be to point it then pull the trigger?' I smiled back at her over my shoulder.

'Lord, Miss, do you really think you could shoot someone?' she asked, brushing out my hair then pinning it back up again into a simpler style than the one I had sported during dinner. 'I don't think I would have the nerve to dare to do such a thing.'

'At this moment in time, I think that I would dare to do anything,' I said grimly.

It didn't take us long to make me ready and after one last glance at myself in the mirror, I hastily snatched up the gun and fifty pounds that I had extricated from my quarterly pin money, stuffed both into the grey watered silk reticule that swung from my wrist and almost ran from the room.

'Good luck, Miss Alice,' Minnie said as I went and I stopped for a moment in the doorway and looked back at her. 'I hope you don't need that gun of yours,' she added with a wry smile.

'I hope so too,' I said with a shrug. 'God bless you, Minnie.'

I made my way quickly and quietly down the back staircase that the servants used then crossed the terracotta tiled floor of the second hall and let myself out of the back door, which opened out onto the side of the house. After this it was simply a matter of quickly making my way down Grosvenor Road and on to the main thoroughfare where I intended to halt a passing hansom cab.

This proved easier said than done as the first few cabs that appeared were tooled straight past me by drivers who clearly had no wish to pick up a single female, no matter how respectable looking she may be. The fourth driver to pass, however, had no such qualms and stopped straight away beside me as soon as I put out my hand then jumped down from his cab to cheerfully help me up inside then settle his rough tartan blanket over my knees before closing the hinged wooden front of the cab in front of me. 'It's a chilly night and no mistake,' he said, grinning as he patted his horse. 'Now where would you be going, Miss?'

I took a deep breath. 'To Whitechapel, if you please,' I said. 'The top of Dorset Street.'

He stared at me then. 'Are you sure, Miss?' he said, a frown between his eyes as he looked me over, clearly wondering if he had been wrong to think me a respectable fare. 'Dorset Street is no place for a young lady such as yourself, if you'll understand my meaning.'

I sighed and assumed my most haughty manner, which was based in no small part on that of my Aunt Minerva, God bless her. 'I am well aware of that,' I said in clipped tones that allowed no argument. 'It's a terrible bother really as, you see, my maid has run away there and I simply cannot do without her so I have decided to bring her back again.'

He stared me, uncertain as to whether he should believe me or not. 'Your maid, Miss?'

I nodded, looking him right in the eye and curling my fingers around my pistol to give me extra courage. 'Quite so,' I said. 'It's quite irregular, I know but I simply cannot do without her.' I smiled weakly. 'Of course I will pay you handsomely for your time and effort.' I opened my reticule a little so that he could see the roll of notes and gleam of coins within.

That decided it of course. 'Then I shall take you there, Miss,' he huffed, returning to his seat at the back of the cab, 'although I won't say that I am very glad to do so.'

He continued muttering for quite some time but I didn't care as I smiled to myself and settled back against my seat for the ride, rather enjoying this unprecedented solo excursion into the city at night. Usually when I went out this late, it was in the company of either my father or aunt as they escorted me to a ball, party or evening at the opera or theatre. I always felt quite safe, cushioned even from the outside world, inside our comfortable carriage, with windows that barely allowed the noise of the city streets to intrude.

The hansom cab was open at the front, leaving me exposed to the chill, dank air and despite the feeling of increasing trepidation that was growing within my stomach, I still looked about myself with interest as we bowled through a light mist of rain along those dark, foggy streets, which still hummed with life and activity. Many of the shops were still open and of course the public houses spilled their usual comforting amber glow and sounds of good times on to the damp pavements. From the safety of my cab, I stared at the women who clustered around the doors, their pint glasses in hand and eyes darting around them as they spoke, taking in the scene with as much avid curiosity as I.

We were almost there. In the distance I could see the great white spire of Christ church, looming pale and daunting over the dark roofs of Whitechapel. My cab lumbered past the police station and I peered up at Cora's window, hoping to catch a glimpse of her but of course seeing nothing. Instead I saw several policemen streaming out of the station's front doors, all ready and keen to do that evening's beats.

My cab pulled to a halt at the top of Dorset Street, outside the Britannia where I now knew Emma, the other key to the puzzle of Beatrice's disappearance, lived and worked. I got down from the cab and felt in my purse for my coins. 'How much do I owe you?' I asked the driver with a smile.

He told me the amount then frowned down at me. 'Are you quite certain that the girl you seek is here, Miss?' he asked in a low voice. 'I have to say that it doesn't sit right with me at all to be leaving you all alone in such a place.'

I handed him his fare with a little extra. 'That is very kind of you,' I replied with a firm smile that made it clear that no further argument would be tolerated. 'I shall be perfectly alright here though.' I stepped back as he touched his hat to me then trotted off then turned to look through the Britannia's brightly lit up windows, which were embellished with frosted glass vines and bottles. Inside I could see the usual swell of drably dressed people, both men and women, all drinking together in small groups. I looked in vain for Emma's distinctive head of frazzled yellow hair though and after a moment had to concede defeat and move on down Dorset Street.

'How much, Miss?' a man sidled close to me and grinned a

263

terrible toothless smile. 'You're a sight for sore eyes and no mistake.' He stank of smoke and rotten fish and had his cloth cap pulled down low over his forehead.

I took a deep breath and pulled the gun from the depths of my reticule. 'Too expensive for you,' I whispered, pointing the gun at him with what I hoped was an unwavering hand.

He looked from the gun to my face and then back again before backing away, shaking his head. 'Sorry to bother you, Miss, I'm sure,' he muttered, touching his cap then melting away into the night.

I put the gun back into my bag, straightened my shoulders then continued down the street, where despite the lateness of the hour small children were still playing in the gutter while their mothers watched from afar, all clustered together around the open doors of the Blue Coat Boy public house. I felt their eyes on me as I strolled briskly down Dorset Street but did not dare to even so much as glance in their direction, always aware how out of place I was. It reminded me oddly of the time I went swimming in the sea in Italy and felt a moment of wild panic when I realised that my feet no longer touched the bottom and all manner of creatures, unknown and unseen, were swimming beneath me.

It did not take me long to find Miller's Court, a narrow, miserable looking alleyway sandwiched between a down at heel lodging house and a dirty looking grocer's shop. An old soldier, dressed in the ragged remnants of his uniform sat on the ground next to the alley's entrance, his cap lying open on the ground in front of him. I paused for a moment to throw him a penny and was rewarded with a drunken lopsided grin.

'Thankee kindly, pretty miss,' he slurred, one eye screwed up shut as he peered up at me from beneath his lank hair. 'You be watching your step now. These are dark times.' He watched me as I stepped slowly and carefully into the darkness of the alleyway leading to Miller's Court. 'Be careful, young lady.'

It took me a moment to get my bearings once I'd reached the other end as there was more than one door on the court as well as a staircase that led to the upper storeys of the building to the right of the alleyway. I hesitated for a moment, covering my nose against the fetid stink of the privies at the far end of the yard then knocked on the closest door, feeling the thin wood rattle beneath my hand.

A woman was singing on the other side of the door but broke off abruptly when I knocked, after which I heard some coughing and the sound of bed springs squeaking. 'Who is it?' a voice called.

'It's Miss Redmayne,' I whispered. 'I'm looking for Marie Kelly.'

There was the sound of stifled laughter before the door was wrenched roughly open. 'So you came then?' she said in that lilting soft Irish voice, her eyes bright with amusement.

I smiled and inclined my head to the side. 'You doubted that I would?' I said as she held the door open to allow me to step inside. As I pulled my gloves off, I looked around her mean little room, observing the dirty floor, piles of old clothes around the soot blackened fireplace, the unmade bed pushed against the peeling wall, the half eaten fish and chips in newspaper on the litter covered table. 'Do you live here alone?' I asked.

She gave me a sharp look. 'I do now,' she said wearily. 'I had a fellow but he upped and left, didn't he, just like they always do in the end.' She gestured to the fish and chips, congealing in their fat on the table. 'He was here just now actually. I reckon he's still sweet on me, the daft sod.'

'Perhaps he is,' I said, looking about for somewhere to sit as she threw herself down on the bed. 'Men can be so odd like that.'

'Can't they just.' She sniffed then reached under the bed to pull out a bottle of beer. 'Fancy a drink, my Lady?'

I shook my head then moved some clothes off the chair and sat down. 'Let's not waste time,' I said, putting my reticule on my lap then folding my hands around it. 'You know why I am here.'

She sighed. 'I do indeed. You want to know all about Beatrice and what happened to her in France.' She opened the bottle of beer and took a generous swig before wiping her mouth with the back of her hand.

I felt suddenly cold. 'Did something happen to her in France?' I said feebly.

Marie winked. 'Didn't it just,' she said with relish. 'Friend of yours was she?'

I took a deep breath then shook my head, realising just in time that it would do me no good to admit to the true relationship between Beatrice and myself. 'Never mind who she was,' I said. 'I just want to know what happened to her.' I opened my reticule and pulled out ten pounds which I laid carefully on the stained tabletop. 'Here is the money you asked for.'

She glanced at the bank note then offered me the bottle again and gave a tiny shrug when I shook my head. 'Well, she died, didn't she?' she said with a shake of her head. 'Murdered, so she was.'

I stared at her, unable to believe what I was hearing. 'Murdered?' I gasped. 'Beatrice?' I pulled the reticule closer to my body, hugging it for comfort as I would do a child and willing myself not to cry in front of the other girl's cold eyes. The tears could come later when I was alone.

She gave a nod. 'That's right, my Lady,' she said, almost triumphantly. 'Cut to pieces she was, in the courtyard of a whorehouse in Calais. I saw it happen with my own eyes.' She took another swig of beer. 'Emma and I saw it all from our window, so we did.'

'So that's where this all began,' I whispered weakly. 'With you and Emma and Beatrice.' I looked down at my hands and saw that they were trembling. 'You say that this happened in a... brothel. Does that mean that my... that Beatrice was a... was a...'

She raised an eyebrow and grinned at me. 'A whore? Yes, she was, my Lady.' She gave a harsh laugh. 'I know it must all seem very unpleasant for a fine young lady of your sort, all protected and pampered as you have been, but what else can less fortunate girls like me and Emma and Bea do for ourselves if we've got nowhere else to go and no nice rich Papa to save us?'

'She has a family,' I said angrily.

'She had a family,' Marie corrected me coldly, her eyes boring into mine. 'Seems to me that they can't have cared very much about her if she ended up working on her back.'

I looked around the horrible little room again, which was gloomy and ill lit by only a handful of candles, which Marie had stuck into empty gin and beer bottles along the mantelpiece and window sill. 'Is that how things are for you?' I asked dully. 'No family to care?'

She laughed. 'Oh, I've got plenty of family, so I have, but they're all over the sea, aren't they? I don't think they'd be none too happy if they ever got to hear what it is I do to keep bread in my belly but what else can I do?' She took another swig from her bottle then shook her long red hair back over her shoulders. 'You don't seem very shocked considering what a fine young lady you clearly are.'

I looked around the room again, this time noting the damp laddered stockings that hung over the back of the other chair, the chipped washbowl on the floor and the sharp aroma of vinegary chips, fish and sweat that hung over everything. 'I'm not shocked,' I said, 'not any more.'

Marie finished off her beer and put the bottle carefully on the table. 'I'm sorry about Bea,' she said awkwardly. 'She was a nice girl who didn't deserve to die like that.'

'No.' I thought of the stained envelope that Cora had taken from Martha Tabram's corpse, of the other women that had been found dead and mutilated in recent months. 'Was it like the others?' I asked hesitantly. 'The other murders.'

She looked away from me. 'Yes,' she said in a quiet voice. 'It was just like the others.'

I didn't need or want to hear anything more and stood up abruptly, almost knocking my chair back and over in the process. 'I have to go,' I said, angrily brushing away the tears that threatened to overwhelm me. 'You've been most helpful, Miss Kelly.'

She leaned back on her hands and observed me for a moment. 'Have I?' she said. 'Emma told me that you got hold of the envelope that stupid Tabram bitch stole from her.'

I looked down at her. 'That's right,' I said carefully, feeling in my reticule for a handkerchief. 'I have it safely hidden away at home.'

She laughed and shook her head at me. 'Has it never occurred to you, Miss Redmayne, to wonder why your envelope is empty?' She felt under her pillow and produced a stained piece of folded over paper.

'It wasn't empty...' I began to say weakly before trailing off as I stared at the letter in her hand. 'Have you had that all this time?'

'Aha, wouldn't you like to know.' Marie waved the paper vaguely between her fingers as if fanning herself. 'It'll cost you,' she said, predictably enough.

I sighed, my mind and heart still reeling from the revelation about Beatrice. 'I rather thought it might,' I said, opening my reticule and producing another five pounds, which I placed on the table next to other notes. 'Will this be enough?'

She hesitated for a moment then gave a nod. 'I reckon that'll do me just fine,' she said before handing over the letter. 'It's all written in French so I couldn't read it.'

I smiled then. Well done Beatrice. 'Not for want of trying, I expect,' I said wryly as I unfolded the paper and saw how stained and smudged it was.

She shrugged. 'You can't blame a girl for trying. I've always been a curious one. Nosy, my mam calls it. She always said that one day I'd have my nose snapped right off if I wasn't careful.' She watched as my eyes scanned down the page. 'So you can read it then?' she asked almost enviously. 'I tried my best to pick up some French while I was over there but it never quite stuck in my head for some reason.'

'We had lessons,' I said distractedly as I read the letter again, more slowly this time so that not one single word was wasted or lost.

'Mon chérie,

You must be quite the young lady by now, my dear and how I wish that I could see you again with your hair up and the pretty dresses that you must wear. It's been too long since I last set eyes on you. Far too long. I think of you every day though, no matter what. I think of you smiling on your birthday, sleeping in my arms as a baby, taking your first brave steps holding on to my hands and I think of you playing in the garden as a little girl, chasing your hoop through the fallen leaves and shouting for me to watch you as you run.

I didn't mean to leave as I did. I thought that I acted for the best but as usual it was all wrong. I can't tell you where I am now or what I am doing. It would shame us both, I think and I can't bear to have you think of me the way that I think of myself.

I've started to cough blood, Alice. The doctor here says that it is a small thing now but will become a great thing in time. In fact, he doesn't know how much time I have which is why I am writing to you now because I don't know when I will be able to again.

I wonder what you have been thinking about me all these years. I wonder if you think of me at all. In some ways I hope that you do not, that you only barely remember me and have no curiosity about where I went. I think that it would be kinder and safer that way, for you if not for me.

I didn't mean for our lives to unfold the way that they have done. When I went to Mama and told her about the great mistake that I had made, no one could be kinder or more gentle. I was so ashamed but what else could I do? I was just a girl, little more than a child at the time. I couldn't defend myself against him, you see. He was too powerful, too strong. I tried to fight him but it was impossible and afterwards I felt only the shame of what he had done.

Mama and I made our plans carefully and when you were born, on a hot lazy day in Italy, then placed into my arms, I knew that, despite everything, I had done the right thing. Have you guessed yet what I am trying so clumsily to tell you? Have you understood that you are my own? That there is a bond between us that is more powerful than you realise?

Enough now, I think. It is enough for me that you know.
Please don't be angry with me.

Your loving Beatrice.'

'How could I ever be angry with her?' I said as I looked at Marie, hardly able to see her through the shimmering blur of tears in my eyes.

She shrugged. 'I don't know, to be sure,' she said carefully. 'I didn't really get to know her very well. She was quiet and kept to herself mostly.' She looked oddly guilty for a moment and I wondered why. 'She was nice to all us other girls though. Not everyone is in that sort of place. They don't really need to be, I suppose but Beatrice always had a kind word for everyone.'

I nodded and brushed away my tears. 'That sounds just like her,' I whispered, feeling utterly bereft Oh Beatrice, Beatrice. How could this have happened to you? 'She was always a kind girl.' A thought occurred to me then. 'Where did she end up? Afterwards, I mean?' I couldn't quite bring myself to say it yet, that small, stark, violent word. 'I assume that the police took her away and then the body was buried somewhere close at hand?'

269

She gave me a quick cautious look then shrugged her shoulders. 'You'd be right to assume that, my Lady,' she said warily, 'but that isn't quite what happened.'

I stared at her, bracing myself for whatever new and horrible revelation was inevitably coming my way. 'No?'

'No.' She pushed her long red hair back out of her eyes then reached beneath the bed for another bottle of beer. 'Can't afford to pay my rent but I can always afford a few bottles to drink,' she said with a miserable grin. 'It's a right rare old mess that I'm in, so it is.'

I automatically put my hand in my purse and pulled out another five pound note, which she took without thanks and stuffed down the front of her frayed and stained bodice. 'The police never came,' she said after a moment's pause. 'Miss Lisette, who ran the place we were at wouldn't let them be called for and instead got her men, the bully boys who looked after the place, to take Bea away.' She took a swig of her beer, clearly unable to look me in the eyes.

I felt cold and sick but made myself go on to the bitter end, just as I had promised to. 'Where did they take her, Marie?' I asked quietly, twisting my hands together on my lap and digging my nails into my palms to stop myself screaming out with the pain of it all.

She put down the bottle and turned away to the fireplace, still unable to meet my gaze. 'To the sea,' she said in a voice so low that I had lean forward to properly hear her. 'They took her to the sea.'

There wasn't much more to be said after this so I tucked the letter into my glove and took my leave, shaking hands with Marie and wishing her well as I went. I remembered her saying at the police station that she was frightened for her life but when I asked her about this, she almost angrily denied it in a way that made it impossible for me to press the matter further even though the woman was clearly scared out of her wits about something. 'You take care of yourself, my Lady,' she said softly as she closed the door behind me.

I stood alone for a moment in the darkness of the yard and pressed the palms of my hands over my eyes, which were still wet with unshed tears. There was a pain, a terrible empty, lonely ache of sorrow and loss, within my ribcage while my heart felt like it had turned to ashes. This then was the end of my journey, this then was the answer that I had sought for so long, this then was the secret that Whitechapel had been withholding from me.

I looked up at the tall dark buildings that loomed overhead. Night had completely fallen now, wrapping the streets in a dank and comfortless blanket. I could see thin strips of orange light from candles and gas lamps and the occasional shadow as people moved around their rooms. Marie had started singing again - I recognised the song as 'A Violet I Plucked From My Mother's Grave', a miserable ditty but one that was popular with romantic young ladies of a somewhat morbid turn of mind. It was not to my taste though and I hugged my arms around myself against the sudden chill and started to walk back down the alleyway to Dorset Street.

'Alice, my dear.' The voice, so well known and tinged as always with a faint mockery, took me completely by surprise but as I looked back startled and opened my mouth to reply, to ask what on earth he was doing there, a cloth with a sweet, nauseating smell was held in front of my nose and mouth and I saw nothing but a whirl of stars and the buildings overhead closing in until I was completely surrounded by darkness.

Chapter Twenty Eight

I opened my eyes and gave a groan as another wave of sickness coursed through my body. At first I was confused by the sideways view of dozens of sacks all piled up one on top of the other until I realised that I was lying on the floor with my cheek pressed close to a gritty floor that smelt of must and hops.

'I was wondering when you would wake up,' a suavely calm voice said from the darkness behind me. 'I do hope that I didn't frighten you.' He stepped in front of me and I looked up at him almost in wonderment.

'Lord Brennan,' I said, my voice sounding as dull and thick as if I hadn't spoken for a hundred years. I swallowed to try and relieve the terrible dryness but only succeeded in making myself cough. 'What an unexpected surprise.'

He smiled then and offered me his hand. 'Is it?' He pulled me gently to my feet then, courteous as ever, put an arm around me to help me to a chair which stood alone in the centre of the room. 'Apologies for dumping you on to the floor in such a woefully casual manner but I thought you would be more comfortable there until you had woken up.'

I swallowed again. 'Could I trouble you for a drink?' I whispered as I sat down. I looked around for my reticule and eventually spotted it lying on its side against a pile of sacks.

'Of course, how remiss of me.' He turned away and filled a glass with water from a carafe on a low table. 'I really am so sorry, Alice, about the means that I had to employ just now in Miller's Court but I couldn't think how else to make you come away with me.'

I took the glass from him. 'You could have tried simply asking me?' I said before gratefully taking a swig of water. 'After all, I've known you almost my whole life, haven't I?'

He gave me a quick, rather quizzical look. 'Yes, you have,' he said in an odd voice that I had never heard before. He looked across at the reticule. 'I read Beatrice's letter,' he said.

My eyes followed his across the room. 'Beatrice,' I said wearily, rubbing my temples as another wave of grogginess threatened to overwhelm me. 'She died.'

He gave a nod. 'I am sorry to hear it,' he said gravely. 'I had no hand in it though. It is not what I wanted for her.'

'No?' I looked at him then and it was as if I was seeing him for the first time. 'What did you want for her, Lord Brennan?'

He looked away and gave a delicate little shudder. 'Not that,' he said. 'Not a miserable little death far away from home. She didn't deserve that.'

I felt suddenly furious. 'No one deserves that,' I said. 'No one. Not Beatrice and not those other women either.'

Lord Brennan shrugged. 'Tuppenny whores,' he said dismissively. 'It surprises me that you can mention them in the same breath as Beatrice.'

'Does it?' I glared at him. 'You know what happened to her, don't you. After all, why else would you have brought me here?'

He sighed as if I was disappointing him in some way but his eyes sidled away from my face. 'Yes, I know,' he said brusquely, 'and I would have given a great deal for you not to find out.'

I took another steadying sip of my water. 'But I did,' I said quietly. 'I found it all out. Despite you.'

He looked at me then. 'Not all,' he said. 'Not quite all, anyway, but enough.'

'Enough to change everything,' I whispered, my heart hurting as I imagined telling Papa what had happened to Beatrice. I knew that he would blame himself and I would have given anything to spare him that pain.

Lord Brennan smiled. 'Yes, certainly that.' He took my now empty glass away from me and placed it on a table. 'Yes, I think that we can safely say that things will never be quite the same ever again.' He turned to look at me. 'For you anyway.'

That was the first time that I felt afraid. After all, I'd known him all my life so what harm could he do me? What a fool I was. I looked again at my reticule and wondered how quickly I could move towards it. 'For both of us, surely?' I said almost idly, as I prepared myself to spring for the bag. 'After all, you are my father, aren't you?'

He stared at me and for a long, hopeless moment I thought that he might be about to deny the fact but then he gave a nod. 'Yes.' He sighed and gave a small shrug that could have been unconcern but was more likely relief to be able to admit it at last. 'Yes, you are mine.'

I frowned. 'I'm not yours,' I said. 'Not now, not ever.' I remembered all the times that Lucasta had told me how much her father admired me, all the times that she had told me that he was fond of saying how much he wished she could be more like me. 'Does Lucasta know?'

'Lucasta?' He laughed then. 'Of course not and she never will.' He poured some more water into my glass and handed it to me.

I inclined my head and smiled as I politely sipped at the water. 'I am more than happy to oblige in that respect,' I said. 'I have no great wish for the world to know the truth of my parentage.'

Lord Brennan grinned. 'Tsk tsk, dearest Alice, you really do wound me. What have I ever done to make you feel ashamed of me? I can well understand your unwillingness to own your closer relationship to poor dear dead Beatrice but what have I ever done to earn your disapproval?'

I cast a slow meaningful look around the warehouse, which I now saw was piled full of crates and sacks, all stamped with the insignia of a well known tea company. 'Well, there is the small matter of my abduction for a start,' I said lightly.

He smiled and tapped his strong white teeth with the key that he had produced out of his pocket. 'Ah, yes, your abduction.' He came closer and I instinctively shrank back in my chair. 'You realise of course that I can never allow you to go home now that you know the truth.'

I swallowed deep and hard, determined not to let him see an ounce of fear in my expression. 'I rather thought that might be the case,' I admitted, eyeing up the reticule and thinking that I should make a grab for it the very next time he moved out of the way. 'And what do you have planned for me?'

'I originally thought that a prolonged stay at Panacea House might serve my purpose rather well - especially as it was dear Mrs Smith-Welsh who first alerted me to your interest in your sister's whereabouts. She is in my employ after all - as is everyone who works at Panacea House. I'm sure that I could rely on them to keep you silent.' He gave a heavy sigh. 'However, it really wouldn't do at all. After all, Beatrice managed to escape, didn't she and I expect you could too as you seem like a singularly determined young woman.'

I looked him right in the eyes. 'Did you arrange to have her sent there?' I said.

He nodded, looking really quite infuriatingly pleased with himself. 'Not at first, as you know, but later on when she threatened to cause trouble for me. She'd fallen in love, you see, with a most unsuitable young man and when your father refused to countenance the match, she came to me to ask for money in exchange for her silence about what had passed between us all those years before. As the owner and chief patron of Panacea House, it seemed like the perfect solution to have her sent there.'

I remembered the letter. I was just a girl, little more than a child at the time. I couldn't defend myself against him, you see. He was too powerful, too strong. I tried to fight him but it was impossible and afterwards I felt only the shame of what he had done. 'You violated her,' I said flatly, making sure that he could see the flash of cold hatred in my eyes. 'Your friend's daughter.'

He looked away then, unable to meet my eyes and the accusation that lay within them. 'I believed myself encouraged,' he muttered. 'How was I to know? Young women these days are so bold, so openly flirtatious. It's impossible to know what they are really thinking…' His voice trailed away as I thought with a pang of shame of Henry Mercier and the kiss we had so briefly shared and then my avoidance of him afterwards.

'That's not an excuse,' I said. 'She must have been not much more than a child herself when I was born. I'm amazed that you can sleep at night, Lord Brennan, when you think about all the damage you have done.'

He shrugged. 'I think you'll find that I sleep very well,' he said. 'I have nothing to reproach myself with. I could have had Beatrice killed when she tried so ineptly to blackmail me but instead I persuaded your father to have her sent to Panacea House, where she was intended to live out the rest of her days in some comfort. How was I to know that the stupid girl would run away to her lover and end up in some French whore house, presumably after he had tired of her?' He looked at me. 'I can't really be blamed for that you know, although I can well imagine how much it distresses you to hear the truth about your mother. Certainly, I can't condemn you for wanting to pin the blame on to someone else.'

'I blame you because it is all your fault,' I whispered before pushing myself from the chair and making a grab for the reticule, 'and it is you who distresses me, not Beatrice.' I fumbled inside the bag, feeling desperately for the pistol that I had secreted within its depths as he rushed towards me with his hand upraised. 'Where is it?' It had gone. I felt desperately within the depths of the bag, my fingers coming into contact with my remaining money and some coins but the pistol I had taken from my father's study had vanished and I felt my heart sink with despair as I realised that it must have fallen out when I was taken from Miller's Court and no doubt lay there still, waiting for some criminal denizen of Dorset Street to claim it for their own.

'You stupid bitch.' His blow almost felled me and I felt myself reel against a pile of crates arranged neatly against the wall before he grabbed me by the front of my coat and dumped me back into the chair, the reticule hanging uselessly from my fingers. 'I can see that you are becoming quite deranged, Alice.' His eyes were cold and he was breathing hard after the exertion of half carrying, half dragging me across the floor. 'Perhaps an extended sojourn in the wilds of Scotland would be of some benefit to you after all.' He smiled at my look of surprise. 'You didn't think that Panacea House was the only string to my bow, did you? Oh no, I also own a much more select property, run along far more stringent lines, in the Highlands of Scotland. Whereas Panacea House is a delightful rest home for the wayward daughters of the aristocracy, I suppose you could say that its sister residence, Kildaire Manor is more of an asylum.' He smiled and grasped my jaw, forcing me to look at him. 'The staff there were all handpicked by me for their efficiency and discretion. You could bury someone alive there for decades and no one would ever know.'

'You wouldn't dare,' I said, wrenching my face away from his grasp. 'Someone would come after me.'

He shook his head. 'Would they? I think not. It would be an

276

easy matter to persuade your father that you have run away as your mother did and once you are safely ensconced in solitary confinement with a new name and story and an official diagnosis of complete derangement in the wastelands of Scotland, there would be no point looking for you. He could search all the four corners of the globe and never find you again.'

I stared at him, touching my fingers delicately to the blood that I could feel seeping from the corner of my cracked lip. All of the fight had gone out of me now. It was over. I was done. 'You've thought of everything,' I said quietly.

'Almost everything,' a familiar and oh so loved voice behind me said and I turned to see Patrick standing in the doorway, his handsome face hard and unsmiling as his gaze swept over the scene before him. 'Has he hurt you, Alice?' he asked softly, moving forward to take my face gently between his fingers, his eyes sharp with concern. 'Minnie sent a note to tell me where you had gone. While you were taking a tour of Panacea House, I was going through the papers in Mrs Smith-Welsh's office so when I couldn't find you at Miller's Court, it wasn't too difficult to guess where you had been taken and by whom - after all, my Lord Brennan has been boring half of society with talk of his latest acquisitions in the docks. As to the rest of it - even on Dorset Street, the spectacle of a toff hurling an unconscious young woman into the back of a carriage is unusual enough to occasion some remark. '

I smiled as best I could despite the pain of my split and bleeding lip. 'I am only a little hurt,' I said. 'Oh Patrick, I don't think I have ever been so happy to see anyone in all my life.'

He grinned down at me and gently ran a finger down my cheek. 'Finally,' he said softly and with some satisfaction. 'Perhaps I should have arranged for you to be abducted long before now.' He looked up at Lord Brennan, who remained standing as if transfixed on the other side of the room. 'I heard it all,' he said coldly. 'What sort of a man are you to take that which is not freely given, to destroy lives, to show no care or concern for the victims of your selfish lusts?'

Lord Brennan shrugged. 'Oh come now, Patrick, don't play the innocent and expect me to believe that you wouldn't do the same thing.' He lunged towards me, pulling me to my feet and holding a knife to my throat. Patrick was quicker though and no sooner had the knife flashed silver in the corner of my vision but he'd pulled back his fist and punched Lord Brennan full in the face, knocking him immediately unconscious.

I gave a scream as his blood splattered onto my face then stared down in horror at his body, which lay crumpled at my feet. 'Patrick...' I held out my hand to him and he immediately took it, his fingers warm and comforting as they intertwined with my own. 'My God, Patrick.'

He looked down at Lord Brennan's body, his face so pale that one for one awful moment I thought he was going to faint. 'I couldn't let him hurt you, Alice,' he said quietly, pulling himself together and putting an arm around me, 'and I won't let him hurt anyone else ever again.'

I sighed and leaned against him. 'And how do you propose to do that?' I asked. 'Short of keeping him a captive on one of your estates?'

He smiled. 'That's not such a bad idea,' he said. 'However, I think it's enough for now that he knows that we both know what he has done. When he wakes up, I think that he will be immensely amenable to my proposal that he takes himself off overseas for an extended tour if he doesn't want his vicious little secrets to be exposed to all society.'

I nodded, unable to resist giving Lord Brennan's unconscious body a little prod with my toe although I couldn't quite bring myself to fully kick him. 'That seems reasonable enough.' I sighed. 'I just hope that he doesn't take Lucasta with him. It hardly seems fair that she should suffer just because she has such a monster for a father.' And me too, I might have added but didn't because I still couldn't quite face the truth of the fact that this dreadful, wicked man lying bleeding and inert at our feet was my actual father. 'Is it really all over?' I said in a quiet voice, thinking of Beatrice and feeling as if my heart must surely burst from the sorrow of all that I had learned that night.

He nodded and gently pulled me towards him. 'It's all over for Lord Brennan,' he said, kissing my forehead, my eyelashes, my nose and then finally, and almost shyly, my lips. 'But I think we'll both live to see another day.'

Chapter Twenty Nine
Emma, November, 1888

I'll have a pint, Em and have a gin yourself, lass,' one of the regulars, a cheerful Scottish docker with a shock of grey hair and lazy eye called across the bar. 'Cheer up, it might never happen.'

I smiled at him. 'It already has, Jock, it already has.' I served him his drink and necked a shot of gin when Mrs Ringer had her back turned. It was the first drop of alcohol I'd had for a couple of days and I coughed as it made its fiery way down to my stomach, while thinking that there wasn't enough gin in the world to solve my problems.

'You having tonight off, Em?' one of the other barmaids, a pink cheeked girl called Cassie said, giving me a nudge with her plump elbow. 'It's about time you went outside and had a bit of fun.'

I grinned. 'Maybe I will,' I said. 'There's been no murders for over a month now.' I resisted the temptation to claim any responsibility for this - after all, I'd barely set foot outside the Britannia since Cathy was killed and then only in broad daylight with one of the other girls for company. It may have been something of a stretch to say that I had personally been keeping the women of Whitechapel alive and well by negating Jack's need to send me bloody messages but at least I felt like I was doing something to help myself and by extension others.

Cassie laughed. 'I never had you pegged as such a worry wart, Em,' she said, rolling her huge blue eyes. 'That whole Ripper business shook you up good and proper, didn't it?'

I turned away, feeling the smile falter on my lips. 'A little bit,' I conceded with a shrug. 'Hard not to be a bit shaken up when women are being split open like bags of corn in the street.'

She gave an eloquent shudder. 'It's all over and done with

279

now, Em,' she said, moving forward to serve a customer who was gesturing impatiently with his pipe in a bid to get our attention. 'Mark my words. There'll be no more killing.' She winked at me.

I looked out of the window as I briskly rinsed out and dried a pile of dirty glasses. Dusk had long since fallen and the street lamps had been lit so that they cast their peculiar pale green glow on the damp pavements. As I watched, a young couple, thin cheeked and dressed from head to toe in sombre black walked slowly past the pub windows, their heads ducked down and braced against the cold wind and rain, their arms wrapped tightly around each other. For some reason they made me think of Albert and I was forced to give myself an angry shake to dislodge him from my mind. That was all finished. He was someone else's man now, not mine.

'You off then, Em?' I didn't hear Mrs Ringer coming up behind me until her voice was booming in my ear. I liked the landlady well enough although I feared her plump fists, dark currant like eyes that seemed to see everything that went on either side of the bar and far beyond and annoying habit of creeping up behind us.

'In a bit,' I said placidly, taking my time drying the last of the glasses before putting it back on the shelf. 'You don't mind me having the night off do you?'

Mrs Ringer shook her head. 'It's not like you ask often,' she said. 'Not like the other girls. Just don't make a racket when you get back later.' She leaned in close. 'And no bringing any men back with you. We've had more than enough trouble of that sort around here, thank you very much.'

I smiled. 'I wouldn't dream of it,' I said, folding up the towel and putting it on a ledge. 'I've had more than enough trouble of that sort too.' I took off my apron, picked up my shawl then checked my reflection in the mirror that hung behind the bar. I looked pale and a trifle drawn about the face but not too bad really, especially as I'd just spent some of my carefully hoarded pennies on a brown dye to cover up the blonde, which had been more roots than yellow by the time I tackled it. I thought I looked rather nice now or at least not as down on my luck as I had done before.

'You have a good time now,' Cassie whispered as I gave my hair one last pat into place then crossed to the other side of the bar.

'If you do want to bring someone back, I promise that none of us will tell.' It was no more than I'd done for the others several times after all, even if they'd kept me awake half the night with their gasps and gigglings and I'd had to stuff a pillow over my head to help me sleep.

I took a deep breath of fresh air when I came out of the Britannia, pleased despite myself to be out at night again and thinking that perhaps I needn't have left it so long. He'd gone after all. No one had seen head nor hair of him since that night on Mitre Square and it seemed unlikely that anyone ever would again. It really was over. I pulled my shawl tight about my shoulders, put my head down against the wind and turned left up Commercial Street.

'Alright Em?' Several people hailed me from the gloom as I made my way up the street towards the police station, most of them smiling with genuine pleasure to see me. 'Haven't seen you out and about for a while. How's things, darling?' It'd be a wrench to leave them and start again in a new place where no one knew my face or name but it had to be done. The killings had stopped for now but I knew as well as anyone that it could all start up again at any old time and when that happened, I intended to be as far far away as I could manage.

I pushed open the door that led to the back yard of the station then scurried into the building and up the stairs. I hadn't seen Cora since the night Cathy was murdered and didn't know what sort of greeting I would get but I hoped she'd understand why I stayed away. She'd told me once that the Lee family lived on the top floor and so I panted my way up there, my boots rattling so loudly against the painted wooden stairs that they probably had more than enough warning that someone was on their way to them. God only knew what it was like when the policemen in their great heavy boots were on their way up and down to their duties in the station below.

I remembered Cora's father, Sergeant Lee with his great red sideburns and thatch of auburn hair, then and my heart failed me a little as I imagined what would happen if he opened the door to me and not one of his daughters. Cora had told me often enough how kind and polite he was even to the whores of the district but would he feel the same way if one of them tried to befriend his precious daughter?

There wasn't a sound to be heard from behind the door but I didn't allow myself to hesitate for even so much as a second before I raised my hand and softly knocked. It wasn't too late so surely someone would be awake? There was no response and so I knocked again, louder this time and more confidently. 'Cora? Are you there?' I whispered, pressing my face against the wood.

'Who is this?' The door was wrenched open so suddenly that I almost fell into the room and it took a moment for me to recover myself, all under the cold and distinctly unfriendly eye of a tall redheaded girl whom I realised at once must be Cora's elder sister, Cat. 'What do you want?' She looked me over slowly, quirking her pale eyebrows in a way that made it quite clear to me that she knew exactly what sort of girl I was or at least what sort I had once been. 'Who let you in here?'

'The gate was left unlocked,' I said feebly. 'I came to see Cora.'

Cat pursed her lips and for a moment I thought she was going to send me on my way but before she could open her mouth to speak, Cora herself appeared, dressed in neat sun bleached pink cotton and bouncing excitedly behind her sister's shoulder like a puppy. I smiled and relaxed, mentally kicking myself for ever thinking that she might not be pleased to see me. 'Em!' she squeaked. 'I thought you'd run away!'

I grinned and shook my head. 'Not me,' I said. 'Not yet anyway. I'm off though in the morning. I've been saving up and it's time to move on.'

Her face fell. 'Are you joking?' she said in a quiet voice. 'Are you really leaving?'

I shrugged, feeling a bit abashed now especially as her sister was now glaring at me. 'I have to go, Cora,' I said apologetically. 'I've barely set foot outside for over a month now. I can't live like that. You know I can't.'

She hesitated then shook her head. 'No,' she said softly, 'I suppose not.' She looked up at her sister and a faint flush touched her cheeks and ears. 'Emma is a friend of mine,' she said before glancing awkwardly at me. 'We are friends, aren't we?' she asked.

I nodded and would have taken her hand if it wasn't for Cat glaring at me as if she wanted to kick me all the way down the stairs again. 'We'll always be friends, Cora,' I said before taking a deep breath. 'That's why I thought I'd come and see if you wanted to come out for a bit. I don't know if I'll ever be coming back, you see and so it might well be the last time.'

She caught her breath and looked again at her sister, her eyes shining with tears and hope. 'Can I, Cat?' she said. 'Just for a little while? I've finished all of my work and the boys are in bed now so you don't need my help with them any more.'

Her sister hesitated, coldly sweeping her eyes over me again then gave a grudging nod. 'Fine, but don't stay out too late,' she said, her gaze softening as she looked down into Cora's face. 'You don't have much fun, Cora love, do you? I'll tell Pa that you've already gone to bed when he gets in - he won't ever know any different.' Her blue eyes turned to me again and hardened like ice. 'As for you,' she said harshly, 'if so much as a hair on my sister's head is harmed, I'll be looking for you no matter where you've run off to.'

I grinned at her and did a quick salute with my fingers pressed against my forehead. 'I absolutely promise to return her in one piece,' I vowed, 'so help me God.'

'God help you if you don't,' Cat growled before turning away to help Cora find her shawl, bonnet and boots in the chaos of their kitchen as I leaned against the doorframe and watched them. The boys, their younger brothers, may well all be in bed but their home still bore their imprint from the boots piled under the table to the dog eared books littered amidst the dirty plates to the woollen vests that steamed in a neat line before the fire. It was a mess, yes, but it made my heart ache for home and my own younger brothers whom I hadn't seen for two years now. I wondered if they still remembered me then felt ashamed and had to push the thought away, just as I had done with the memory of Albert.

Eventually Cora was ready to go and I gravely offered her my arm as we went down the stairs together with Cat watching us silently from the doorway the whole time. 'I don't think your sister likes me very much,' I whispered when we had finally gone out of sight and heard the click of the door shutting behind us.

Cora smiled. 'She's like that with everyone,' she said. 'She's been very protective of us all since Ma died. I suppose because she's had to become the mother to us all now.'

'It can't be easy,' I said carefully. 'After all, she should by rights have her own husband and children by now.'

Cora nodded pensively. 'I know,' she agreed. 'We all know. One of the other policemen is sweet on her but Cat won't hear about it. She says she's going to stay until Pa doesn't need her any more and who knows how long that'll be when our littlest brother, Alfred isn't even old enough to start school yet.'

I shook my head. 'Well, it's no wonder she's as prickly as she is,' I said. 'I'd be the same in her shoes.'

'It's alright for you,' Cora said gruffly, sounding just like her sister for once. 'You can come and go as you please, can't you? It must be nice to have no ties and no one to answer to.' She sounded wistful and I resisted the urge to take hold of her shoulders and give her a good hard shake.

'Nice?' I said instead. 'Hardly. I'd much rather have a nice family and friends to care that I have gone and to wonder what has become of me. It's not nice to think sometimes that no one cares what happens to you.'

She looked startled. 'I care what happens to you,' she said softly, her grasp on my arm tightening. 'I'll be sorry to see you go, Em and it's not true that you don't have a family to wonder where you are, you know that it isn't.'

We'd reached the bottom of the stairs and I paused with my hand on the door. 'I can't go back,' I said, unable to prevent a craven petulant note from creeping into my voice. 'I can't let them know what happened to me.'

Cora sighed. 'They wouldn't be angry,' she said. 'Not if they really loved you and it sounds to me like they do.'

I shrugged and shoved the door open before pulling her into the yard with me. 'They might not be angry but they'd be disappointed in me, of course they would and that's what I don't think I can bear. My Ma will cry and Pa will look all sad like he's the one that let me down and that's what I can't go back to.' I angrily rubbed at my eyes. 'It's worse than anger. I would know what to do if they shouted and showed me their fists and told me never to come back. I'd know to run and stay away and I'd know that I deserved it. It's the sadness though, that's what I don't like. How can you feel right and decent when you've made your parents cry?'

'I don't know.' She put her hand to the latch and opened the yard door. 'I don't think I could ever feel myself again if my Pa cried over me.' She looked back at me over her shoulder. 'I still think you should go home though.'

I smiled and took her hand in mine. 'Then I think we're going to have to agree to disagree, Cora my love.'

We crossed the road and shambled down to the Ten Bells, which was full to bursting as usual with several drinkers standing outside on the street, nursing their glasses and bottles in their hands and tucking themselves against the wall to hide from the chill wind that blew through the streets that night. 'You off to the parade tomorrow, Em?' someone called as I went inside. The annual Lord Mayor's Parade was due to take place in the City the next morning and as usual most of the East End was looking forward to making a day of it.

'You'll be gone by morning, won't you?' Cora said in a small voice as we pushed our way through the crowd to the bar.

I looked at her. 'Yes, I will,' I said. I had it all planned out - my belongings were all packed up and ready to go, I'd written a note for Mrs Ringer and another for the other girls and after that there was nothing to do but slip out before dawn and make my way to the docks to look for a passage somewhere else. 'You could come too.' The words had blurted out before I could stop them, prompted no doubt by the miserable look on Cora's face and my own pathetic feelings of guilt and remorse.

Her eyes lit up. 'Really?' she said. 'You'd let me go with you?'

I sighed. This wasn't exactly the response I had been hoping for. 'Yes,' I said after a pause, 'of course you can come with me.' After all - why not? It would be safer and more fun with someone else along to share the adventure. 'Wouldn't you rather stay here though?' I asked curiously. We'd made it to the bar and I leaned against it as I tried to catch the barman's eye.

Cora shook her head. 'I sometimes think that I'm going to be stuck here forever,' she said. 'I love Whitechapel or at least, I love it as much as anyone can but I can never forget that there's more to the world than these few dirty streets and all the same faces every day.'

I laughed. 'You should have been a boy,' I said, 'then you could have joined the navy and seen a bit of the world.'

She pulled a face. 'That's what I wish I could do,' she said sadly. 'It's harder for girls though. Just look at Cat - she should be married now with children of her own and instead she has to stay with us. I don't want my life to be like that.'

'You don't think that you should stay as well and help your sister?' I said, elbowing a large man who had encroached on my bar territory out of the way.

Cora flushed. 'I suppose I sound very selfish,' she said miserably. 'I know I am but I can't help it. I want more from my life than this.'

I shrugged. 'Well, I can't exactly blame you for that.'

Chapter Thirty

We stayed in the Ten Bells for several hours, content to sit in our little corner beside the pretty tiled mural of a couple in old fashioned clothes walking together, and drink and talk while rain lashed against the windows and the gas lamps were gradually turned up, bathing everything in a soft amber glow that made even the most threadbare and downtrodden old tarts look softly alluring, especially when you'd had a few drinks.

'I'll miss this,' I said at one point, looking around me with a smile that took in the whores clustered around the bar, the men intently playing cards at the table behind us and the usual noisy, rowdy throng of East Enders enjoying themselves on a cold, rainy night. 'I don't think I've ever felt quite so at home anywhere as I do right here in Whitechapel.'

'Then don't leave,' Cora said. She'd had one too many beers and peered at me tipsily from behind her curtain of red gold hair, which had fallen loose around her face. 'You don't really have to go.'

I felt my face tighten with annoyance. 'I must go,' I said in a low voice, finishing off the rest of my bottle of beer and shoving it crossly away. 'There's nothing here for me now.'

Cora sighed and shrugged. 'You're still thinking about that Albert, aren't you,' she said, waving her own bottle about to punctuate the point. 'You want to get him back. You miss him, don't you?'

'Not a bloody chance.' I glared at her. 'That Sarah is bloody well welcome to him. I've had a belly full of his sort.' I stood up and angrily shoved my chair back. 'I'm getting another drink. You?' She nodded her head and I staggered off to the bar, pulling a few coins out of my pocket as I went and squinting up at the

287

clock set into the wall. It was almost one in the morning and probably about time Cora was back home, safely tucked up in bed under the watchful gaze of her draconian sister. 'Ah well,' I said to myself as I waved the barman over. 'It's not like she gets out much, poor thing.'

'Well well well, fancy seeing you here.' I would have recognised that voice with its fake genteel softness anywhere and immediately stiffened with surprise and dislike when I heard it in such unexpectedly close proximity.

'Lisette.' I turned around then and looked her in the eye. 'It's been a long time.'

'Madame Lisette to you, dear,' she said cordially, taking a drag from her perfumed French cigarette and blowing the violet scented smoke into my face. 'I am sure it is quite a surprise seeing me after all this time.'

I shrugged and turned away briefly to take my bottles of beer off the counter and sling some pennies at the barman who gave me a cross look as he picked them up. 'It's not really a surprise,' I said. 'You over here looking for more poor little geese for your Calais house? Isn't Whitechapel a lot more down at heel than your usual hunting grounds or are you economising?'

She flushed angrily. 'I'm here on a social visit,' she said. 'I do have friends, you know.'

I couldn't stop myself smirking. 'Oh, I know.' I also knew that her career had started on these streets before she was whisked away to a discreetly exclusive knocking shop on Bishopsgate which catered for the more rarefied and occasionally unpleasant tastes of certain City gentlemen.

She looked me up and down, taking in my newly dyed hair, dark blue cotton dress, moth eaten red shawl and battered boots. In contrast she was dressed in a fashionable and immaculate watered purple silk trimmed with deep blue velvet and had a matching hat, complete with towering dyed feathers, perched at a jaunty angle on her brassy ringlets. 'You were missed, you know,' she said grudgingly. 'Several gentlemen asked after you and that Marie as well.'

'Did they now?' I took a swig from my beer, never taking my eyes off her. 'That's nice.' I remembered the 'gentlemen' in Calais - they'd mostly been sailors, townsfolk and the very rare passing toff looking for a bit of rough trade. I don't suppose most of them knew what we looked like above the waist let alone cared enough to miss us.

'There was one gentleman,' Lisette continued as if I hadn't spoken, 'tall and not all that well favoured but he asked most particularly about you and Marie as well after you'd gone. He was most put out when I told him you'd both cleared off to Whitechapel.'

'How did you know we'd come here?' I asked, feeling bored and hoping Cora was alright and not being bothered by anyone. 'We could have gone anywhere.'

'Marie let slip to one of the other girls before you went. She never did have any sense did she?' She paused and adjusted her bodice. 'I saw him earlier on in fact. He said he's still looking for her and I told him where she could be found.' She smiled at my expression. 'I saw her in the Britannia earlier on, you see, falling over drunk and barely able to remember her own name but she told me where she lived alright - said she'd got a nice snug little room on Miller's Court and has no need of my help any more.'

I stared at her. 'You told him that?' I said, taking another swig from my bottle and then another in quick succession. 'You told him where she lives? Bloody hell, Lisette, it seems to me that you're the one without any sense.'

Lisette gave me a haughty look. 'Why shouldn't I have told him?' she asked, drawing herself back from me as if I had stung her. 'What's it to me or to you either if he wants to have his way with her?'

'What is it to me indeed,' I agreed grimly before pushing my way past her and then shoving through the crowd to where Cora sat, pale and nervous looking in the corner. 'Drink up quickly,' I said, thrusting her bottle at her. 'We're leaving.'

She stared up at me, wide eyed. 'What's happened? Why are you looking like that?'

'Just drink up,' I said, nodding at the bottle. 'We've got to go somewhere. One of my friends might be in trouble.' The very worst trouble but of course I couldn't say that.

Cora obediently lifted the bottle to her lips and took a long swig before lowering it and wiping her mouth on the back of her sleeve. 'Is it Marie?' she asked.

I nodded. 'I've always wondered how he knew where to find me and now I know.' I looked back towards the bar but Lisette had vanished - either gone on somewhere else or hidden from view by the crowd. 'Bloody Marie and her big flapping bloody mouth. I knew I couldn't trust her to keep a bloody secret.'

'Oh.' Cora's eyes grew even wider and she took another great swig of beer. 'That's bad.' She clumsily stood up, almost knocking the chair over as she did so. 'We can drink these while walking.'

I took her arm and we shambled out together into the cold misty rain. 'I can feel the winter coming,' Cora said with a shiver as we stood for a moment in the dark looming shadow of Christ Church. 'I can feel it in my bones.'

I smiled at her. 'Albert does that too,' I said softly. 'He gets a prickling at the back of his neck when a storm is coming and his leg aches where he broke it tumbling out of an apple tree as a boy when it's going to rain.'

Cora put her head to one side and looked at me. 'You sure you aren't still sweet on him?' she said with a grin.

'As sure as eggs is eggs,' I said curtly, angrily shoving the thought of him away from me. 'That's all done with now, I told you.' I took her hand and pulled her across the road to the market, which was all closed up and dark now but would soon be humming with some semblance of life again as the market boys started to stream in to unload deliveries and set up their stalls. 'Why didn't the stupid bugger stay in Essex? It was all easier before I saw him again.' I stopped and looked at her. 'I'd managed to forget him, more or less but now he's all I can think about again.'

She put her arms around me and put her head on my shoulder. 'Maybe it means something,' she whispered. 'Maybe it was fate telling you that it's time to go back.'

I shook my head. 'Not to him though,' I said. 'You saw him and that girl he was with. They were married, weren't they, or as good as married.'

She pulled back to look at me then kissed my cheek. 'You don't know that,' she said with a smile. 'Maybe she was his sister?'

I laughed then and pulled her closer. 'He doesn't have a sister,' I whispered, 'but thanks all the same.'

We carried on down the road towards the top of Dorset Street.

The Britannia was still open and I could see Cassie and the other girls yawning behind the bar as they served the last few customers, while Mrs Ringer herself was at the door, bodily throwing a drunk adolescent boy out on to the pavement. 'Touch one of my girls again, and I'll have your bloody hands off,' she screamed at him as he cowered away from her, his cap lying in the dirt at his feet. 'Now clear off and consider yourself lucky that I don't cut your puny little balls off and feed them to my dogs.'

I grinned and took Cora's arm. 'Is she always like that?' she asked, looking a bit scared.

'Yes.' We turned down Dorset Street, bypassing the ragged crowd of tarts on the corner, who were having a half hearted cat fight over some hapless man who had fallen into their clutches. A bit further along, a thin faced bedraggled woman was sitting on a doorstep nursing her baby, who squalled and pummelled her breast with its small fists. I released Cora's arm and felt in my pocket for some coins, which I handed over with an apologetic smile, sorry that I could not give her more. 'Best get inside,' I whispered as she looked up at me in surprise then gave a hesitant, confused smile. 'This is no time to be out with a little one.'

Cora slipped her arm around my waist as we moved away. 'That was kindly done,' she said.

I shrugged, feeling suddenly embarrassed. 'I wish that I could have done more,' I replied. 'I wouldn't have noticed her a few months ago though. I would have just walked past and ignored her and the baby too but now, I don't know, it's like something has changed.'

'I know exactly what you mean,' Cora said in a low voice. 'I think that I have changed too.' We stopped and looked at each other then without smiling. 'It seems like such a long time ago now that I stole that envelope and took it to Miss Alice,' she said hesitantly as I watched her.

'Miss Alice,' I repeated, looking towards Miller's Court and wondering. Marie had stopped off at the Britannia earlier to gloat about luring poor Miss Redmayne to visit her - for all we knew, she might be there still but it seemed more likely that she was long gone back to Highbury, probably never to return.

'Well, well, well,' he stepped out of the shadows as we approached Miller's Court, gingerly skirting around the drunk noisily vomiting on to the pavement. 'Fancy seeing two fine ladies like yourselves in a place like this. Remember me, do you?'

It took me several moments to recognise him in the dim, greenish glow cast by the few street lamps that lined Dorset Street but when I did, I felt my heart sink into my stomach. 'You again,' I said. 'I thought I'd taught you a lesson about bothering me and my friend?' After all, the last time I'd seen him, he'd been sprawled on the mud in front of the music hall after I'd punched him to the ground for refusing to release Cora.

'Well you thought wrong,' he said with a grin that revealed several missing teeth as he pulled out a knife. 'You thought wrong and now it'll be me who's teaching the lessons around here.'

I stopped dead and looked him up and down. 'Really?' I said, pushing Cora behind me. 'Come here and try it.' He stepped forward, snarling and slashing his knife drunkenly and ineptly towards my face. 'Is that the best you've got?' I taunted. 'Did your mother teach you how to fight?'

His face twisted with anger and he jumped forward, raising the hand holding the knife only to find it blocked by my hand as I quickly raised my knee up between his legs. When he dropped, groaning to the ground, I finished him off with a punch to the face which made his nose explode with blood all down the front of my skirt. 'Now, who's learning a lesson?' I shouted, raising my fist to punch him again just as a pair of arms came from behind and raised me up in the air before lifting me away from him. 'Cora?' I looked back over my shoulder but she was nowhere to be seen.

'Now then, missy,' a gruff voice said close to my ear as I was put back down on to the pavement. 'I'm going to ask you to come quietly to the station with me.'

I struggled against him for moment, pushing back with my elbows but then gave up and pulled away. 'Are you going to arrest me, officer?' I asked. 'I was just acting in self defence.' The local policemen were too cowardly to walk down Dorset Street on their own and his fellow was bending over my challenger, who was rolling about and groaning on the ground. 'What do you expect me to do? Stand there and let the likes of him clobber me?' Still worried, I looked around for Cora and with relief saw her standing, still and silent, in a doorway nearby, her shawl pulled close about her face, hiding it from view. She met my eyes and gave a gentle shake of her head. No, her eyes seemed to say. Don't tell.

'You've been drinking,' the policeman said to me with a look of disgust. 'You'd better come along with me.'

I laughed then, unable to stop myself. 'Are you planning on arresting everyone who's had a drink or two tonight?' I said as he took hold of my arm and half pulled me up the street. 'Good luck with that, copper.' I looked back over my shoulder at Cora but she'd already gone, plunging further into Dorset Street, more frightened of her father and sister than whatever lay in wait for her in the dark alleyways of Whitechapel. I feared for her, but what could I do? She'd never forgive me if I drew the eyes of her father's colleagues towards her so all I could do was let her go and hope that no harm would come to her.

Behind us the other policeman was half carrying, half dragging my opponent, grabbing him by the collar and occasionally clobbering him about the head when he put up some feeble resistance. 'Maybe we should put them in a cell together and let them fight it out,' he shouted to the policeman who had me.

'Don't you bloody dare,' I whispered, 'or you'll have a corpse on your hands in the morning and it won't be mine.'

He snorted, pulling me up closer. 'Think we care about that? Think we care about the likes of some gutter rat like him? You'd be doing us a favour, Miss.'

Despite their jokes, we found ourselves in separate cells in Commercial Street police station once they'd taken down our names and given us the usual half hearted talking to about keeping the peace. It wasn't so bad really, I thought, as I settled down on my haunches in the women's cell in the main foyer which I shared that night with the usual motley collection of tarts, vagrants and pick pockets.

'What you doing in here, Em?' one woman, a grubby faced blonde in faded pink silk said, blowing a kiss at the policeman who dumped me without ceremony on the floor then slammed the cell door shut behind him. 'Not like a fast runner like you to end up in the old clink.'

I grinned and shrugged. 'First time for everything,' I said, rubbing at my arm where the policeman's fingers had sunk none too gently into my flesh. 'What you in for, Alex?'

She laughed and raised her skirts above the knees with a sly look. 'What do you think? Only this time I gave him a slap didn't I because he didn't want to pay up, the bastard.'

'Funny how it's always us who take the blame isn't it?' another girl piped up from the other side of the cell.

It wasn't really funny at all though, I thought as I peered through the cell bars, which looked out directly on to the lobby so that the sergeants on duty could keep an eye on us. I knew from bitter experience that there was no point appealing to their better natures and so settled down for the night, making myself as comfortable as I could on the cold tiled floor and trying not to think about what had become of Marie and Cora. 'I've let them down,' I whispered to myself, wishing that I hadn't risen to the bait, had just kept my head down and kept on walking, one foot in front of the other, to Miller's Court. 'I've let everyone down.' I thought of Marie as I had last seen her - flushed with pride at her own cleverness and tapping the side of her nose as she told me about the windfall she was expecting from Miss Redmayne.

'She'll pay a pretty penny for what I've got, so she will,' she'd whispered, leaning in so close that I could smell the gin on her breath. 'And then I'm out of here and straight back home, so I am. I've had enough of London. Time for home, I reckon. Time for fresh air, good food and the hot, sweet arms of a loving man.'

Home. I couldn't bring myself to think of that either but what else was there to do that night but huddle against the wall and think and dream of things that could never be? I pinched myself as Albert's face, earnest and not especially good looking, floated into my mind. There was no profit to me there, no benefit in thinking of things that could only fill me with regret for what I had thrown away. For I had thrown him away, I knew this now, and had no way of getting him back again.

I slumped against the wall, beating my head gently back against it as I let my thoughts drift on. I had failed. I'd failed Polly, Annie, Cathy and even Martha, God rot her. I couldn't take any responsibility for the other woman killed, the Swedish one who had her throat cut the night that Cathy was ripped. She was none of my doing. I knew my man and that was none of his work.

Marie though. I'd let her down so badly. Yes, she was stupid and careless, spinning her silly bloody tales and bragging about things when she should have kept her mouth shut but look where it had got her and no one deserved that. It was all my fault as usual. Mine alone, for it was me who opened the window that night in Calais and shouted down into the yard and it was me who had run down in my nightdress and seen and been seen. It was all my doing. Mine and mine alone. 'I'm so sorry, Marie,' I whispered. 'I'm truly sorry.'

I don't know how long I sat hunched up in the darkness, dwelling on the mistakes of the past and trying not to think about what might be happening in the present. At one point the sergeants behind the desk changed shifts and I watched silently and without interest as two went away and two more, both young and yawning wearily behind their hands with hair that looked like they'd only just tumbled from their beds, took their place.

As the hours passed, the other women stopped chatting, fighting and crying and one by one gave themselves up to sleep, their heads resting either on the cold tiled floor or each other, their mouths falling slack as their snores mingled together. I had no need for sleep and took a sly nip of brandy from a hip flask that rolled out of someone's pocket, determined to stay awake for as long as it took.

One of the young policemen started whistling a merry tune and wandered over to the street door, which he opened before poking his head out to look up at the sky. 'The rain is easing off,' he said, turning to smile at me. 'It'll be a cold morning though.'

'Another country boy,' I said, thinking of my conversation with Cora and wishing with all my heart that she was there with me.

'That I am, Miss,' he said with a grin before strolling to the door beside the counter, which I knew led to the living quarters upstairs.

'Em.' And there she was. Pale and tearful in the same dress that she had been wearing earlier on. 'It's time to go.' She nodded to the young policeman and he stepped forward with his keys clinking between his fingers.

'You sure, Cora?' he said, looking at me doubtfully.

She gave a firm nod. 'Sure as eggs, Ned,' she said and it was only then that I noticed the large cloth bag she carried at her side.

'You're coming too,' I said dully.

She nodded. 'I have to,' she said, stepping aside as Ned

unlocked the cell door. 'There is nothing here for me. Not really.'

'What about your Mr Mercier?' I said, struggling to my feet then slipping out through the open door, hoping to God that none of my cellmates would wake up and notice my departure. There'd be hell to pay if they did. 'He's worth staying for, isn't he?'

She went pink about the ears. 'He's not interested in the likes of me,' she said in a low voice before looking at Ned. 'Don't you go shooting your mouth off about Mr Mercier and me,' she warned him. 'There's nothing going on there.'

He grinned. 'Of course not, Cora.' He gave her a quick kiss on the cheek. 'My lips are sealed.'

She smiled back and handed him a small envelope. 'Give this to Cat, won't you? Just say that I left it on the desk. She'd be mad as hell fire if she knew you'd help me go.'

'I'll keep my mouth shut, never fear,' he said, looking worried and scratching the back of his neck. 'You will be alright, won't you?'

She hesitated for a second then nodded. 'Better than alright.'

Chapter Thirty One

We held hands and ran together down Commercial Street, pausing at the top of Dorset Street to catch our ragged breath. 'It's all the stinking smoke above this bloody city,' I said, half laughing, half wheezing. 'I could run for miles back home.' I looked at Cora as she pushed her hair back from her face. 'I was worried about you earlier on,' I said. 'After that copper carted me off to the cells and I had to leave you all alone.'

She grinned. 'I'm tougher than I look,' she said, 'and I've lived in Whitechapel all my life so I know it like the back of my hand. No need to fear for me, Em. I know what I'm about.' She took my arm and we continued down Dorset Street, now almost deserted except for a few vagrants struggling to sleep on the doorsteps and the heavy tread of a group of drunk men wending their weary way to one of the doss houses at the end.

It was almost dawn and the street would be busy and humming with life again within a couple of hours. Already I could see the sky above us becoming tinged with the purple and here and there I could see gas lamps flickering behind windows. 'I hope we're not too late,' I whispered to Cora as we arrived at the Miller's Court archway.

Her grip tightened on my arm as we went slowly up the dark passageway that led up to the yard and for all her tough talk, I knew she was as frightened as me when we came out the other end and found ourselves standing outside Marie's door. 'Listen,' I said. 'Can you hear anything?'

Cora put her head to one side then shook it slowly. 'Only the pump at the end of the yard dripping and a cat crying upstairs and… and…' She shook her head again and put her bag on the ground as if weary. 'Maybe she's asleep.'

'Maybe.' I pulled gently away from her and put my hand on the doorknob, my heart thudding hard against my ribcage now as I slowly turned it. 'Oh, please just be asleep, Marie,' I whispered as with a creak, the door swung open, sticking a little as it always did.

'Is she there?' I could feel Cora's breath hot against my neck as I slowly tiptoed into the room, which was warm thanks to the fire that blazed in the small hearth with a sharp sickly metallic tang in the air. 'The fire is still going.'

I didn't reply. I couldn't. I was staring at the bed, at the thing on the bed. The thing that used to be my friend Marie but was now little more than a heap of tortured bone, flesh and hair. And blood. So much blood. 'Don't look,' I said to Cora, dragging my gaze away from those wide terrified eyes, the gaping mouth that had been cut away so that her teeth were bared at me in an awful grimace, the bloody wound that used to be her nose. What was it she was always saying? 'My Mam always says that I'll get my nose snapped off one day if I don't stop poking it in other people's business.' I could have wept. 'Jesus Christ, don't look.' It was too late though and I took hold of Cora's shoulders as she gave a terrible, high pitched keening sound.

'Murder. Oh, murder!' she wailed as I slapped her cheeks then pressed my forehead close to hers so that our faces were touching and breath mingled. 'He's killed her, Em. We were too late. Why are we always too late to stop it happening?'

'We were too late this time,' I whispered urgently, grabbing her jaw and forcing her to tear her eyes away from the mess that lay ripped apart and sprawled on the bed. 'Look at me, Cora. Look at me. We won't be too late next time, I promise you.'

She stared at me in horror, her mouth working and her eyes huge, then tore away from my grip and whirled out of the tiny room to the yard, where I heard her loudly retching soon afterwards. 'Goodbye, Marie,' I whispered to the body on the bed. 'I'm sorry that I could not come to you sooner.' I made myself look at what remained of her face for the last time, forcing myself to meet those wide, terrified eyes, to remember how she had been in life, so gay, so lively. That laugh. 'My Mam always says…' 'Until we meet again.'

I slowly turned and left the room, closing the door carefully behind me as I went then, following some odd instinct, putting my hand through the broken window to put down the latch. 'Are you alright now, Cora?' I asked quietly, peering into the gloom of the yard. 'I'm sorry you had to see that.' I could hear her sobbing but could not see her until I took a step into the alley and saw her leaning against the wall, crying and wiping her mouth with the hem of her skirt. 'Cora?'

She looked up at me then and shook her head. 'No,' she said, throwing up her hand to keep me from her. 'Stay away from me.'

I sighed. 'I'm sorry,' I said. 'I don't know what else to say. I'm so sorry.' I took a tentative step towards her and held out my hands. 'Honest. I'd give everything for that not to have happened.' There was no point reminding her that it wouldn't have happened if one of her father's mutton headed colleagues hadn't arrested me when we were a stone's throw away from Miller's Court earlier on as I could see from her expression that she was thinking the same thing.

'What are we going to do, Em?' she whispered, angrily scrubbing at the tears that rolled down her pale cheeks. 'He's coming for us, you know he is.'

She was right of course but I couldn't bring myself to agree. 'We'll think of something, Cora,' I said instead. 'He won't be able to find us after we leave Whitechapel anyway.' I looked at her. 'Unless you've changed your mind about coming with me, that is?'

She hesitated then gave a sad little shake of her head. 'What else can I do?' she said. 'If he's taken your Marie then he might come for Cat next.' She started to cry again. 'I can't let that happen, Em, I just can't.'

I went to her and put a gentle hand on her arm. 'We won't let it happen to anyone else,' I whispered. 'I promise.' I put my arms around her and pulled her close as she sobbed against my shoulder, rocking and shushing her as I would do a child. 'We'll go to Liverpool Street now and see about getting out of here for good. He'll never be able to find us again and if we're not here to menace then he won't have any reason to leave his blasted bloody messages any more, will he?' I felt her nod against me and tightened my embrace. 'Just be brave, Cora. Not long to go now, not long to go until we're free of this place and can put it all behind us.'

She pulled away and looked up at me then, her eyes still wide and frightened. 'I won't ever be able to forget what I just saw,' she whispered. 'Not until the day that I die.'

I nodded. 'Me neither, my love,' I said grimly, thinking again of that raw, bloody face, those wild, staring eyes, the grotesquely grinning teeth. 'Me neither.'

We carried her bag between us and turned our feet towards the nearby docks, our plan being to hitch a ride on the first boat that would carry us away from London, reasoning that if we didn't know where we were going to end up then neither would our man Jack. 'You'll be able to write home though,' I reassured Cora. 'Just as soon as we're all settled and know that we're safe.' She nodded but said nothing and I knew that she was scared of what the future held - after all, so was I and this wasn't even the first time I'd packed up my things and run away in the night. 'It'll all be alright,' I whispered, giving her a quick, fierce hug as we turned down an alley. 'Just wait and see.'

She saw the man who loomed out of the darkness ahead of us before I did and gave a cry of shock and lurched back, dropping her bag as she almost tripped over her own feet in her haste to get away. 'No.' She tugged at my arm but I couldn't move. 'No.'

'So here we all are,' he said, grinning almost cheerfully as he strolled towards us. This was the first time that I'd seen him outside the shadows and I stared at him almost curiously as he came towards me, surprised by how utterly ordinary, how forgettable he looked. I could have walked past him in the street a thousand times or more and not have noticed him. Maybe that's why he did it, why he craved the attention, why he wanted our eyes fixed firmly upon him just as mine were riveted to him at that moment. 'Cosy, ain't it?' There were splashes of blood, Marie's blood, on his grey shirt front and across his face and a slight tinge of pink to his hands as he pulled his knife out from within his shabby black coat. 'I've been waiting for this moment, ladies. Longing for it, in fact.' He stank of old blood and grime, like a slaughter house on a hot day. I could almost hear the flies buzzing as he moved, sense the fear of the animals as they waited to die.

I could hear Cora crying behind me and begging me to run, to come with her, to stay alive but I still couldn't move. I just stayed rooted to the spot as if turned to stone as he walked slowly towards me, his knife glinting wickedly in the dim light. 'You're going to stop,' I said and my voice sounded strange and high pitched and not like my own at all. 'This is going to stop right now.' I turned my head and looked at Cora then. 'Go,' I said to her. 'It's me he wants, not you.'

He laughed then and finally I saw something of the terrible madness that lurked beneath that mundane facade. 'Well, this is unexpected,' he said, coming so close now that I could smell the rotten stink of his breath. 'I have to say that it takes the shine off things a little to have you offer yourself up to me so willingly. I much prefer it when my ladies struggle a little - it makes it so much more fun.'

I made myself shrug even though I was almost fainting with fear inside. 'What other choice do I have?' I said. 'What other choice have you left me?' I could hear Cora's footsteps behind me as I closed my eyes and waited for the blow to fall, for the chill of his knife against my throat. Every sense I had seemed heightened, every feeling was magnified in that moment, as if my body knew that it was breathing its last and was determined to make the most of whatever was left to it - just when I was wishing with all my might that I could faint and not know what was happening. 'Get away from here, Cora,' I called over my shoulder. 'Run and keep running. Don't let him catch you.'

She laughed then, an eerie, high pitched sound that owed more to fear than mirth. 'I'm not going anywhere,' she said and I heard her take a faltering step forward and one single shuddering breath before there was a loud bang somewhere behind my left ear.

The man dropped to the ground, clawing at his chest as blood spilled between his thin fingers and for a split second his eyes rolled up and met my own with an expression of mingled rage and disbelief before he gave a great sigh and died. I stared down at him for a long moment then gave him a cautious prod with my foot before pulling it back and kicking him hard in the face. 'That's for Marie, you bastard,' I hissed before kicking him again and again and again and again and again, harder and harder each time until his face was a mess of blood. 'And this is for Polly, Martha, Annie, Cathy and Beatrice.' I pulled back my foot to kick him again then felt Cora's hand on my arm.

'Stop now,' she whispered, throwing the gun in her hand to the ground and pulling me to her, holding me tightly against her chest as I struggled and cried out. 'It's done, it's finished. He's dead.'

I wept then and wrapped my arms around her, feeling the fear and worry and tension of the last few months slide away, leaving me feeling curiously empty and exhausted. 'Where did you get a bloody gun anyway?' I said at last, gulping and wiping my wet face with the back of my sleeve. 'You didn't steal it from your Pa, did you?'

She grinned and shook her head. 'I found it on the ground in that alley when I was being sick,' she said. 'God knows how it got there but I'm glad that it did.'

I smiled. 'It's like a miracle,' I said. 'Who knew that such a thing could happen on Dorset Street? It's almost as if there is a God after all.' I looked down at the mangled body at our feet. 'What should we do with him?' I asked. 'We're almost at the docks and it's not quite daylight so I reckon we could carry him between us if you're able to stomach it.'

Cora gave a shrug. 'I have the stomach for it,' she said, rolling up her sleeves. 'Let's just get rid of the bastard, shall we?' She knelt over the body and quickly went through his pockets first though. 'There's nothing here,' she said at last, straightening up and pressing her hands against the small of her back. 'No papers, no money, no name, no nothing.'

'Then he most likely won't be missed by anyone then, will he?' I said.

We rolled his body into the dark, fetid water of the Thames that lapped against the wharfs and short piers of Wapping. It was still dark and dawn was still only a faint lilac glimmer in the distance as we stood together for a moment in silent reflection while the man's body sank from sight, aided in its descent by a sack of flour which I'd roughly lashed to his waist.

'So that's it then,' Cora said when there was nothing more of him to be seen.

I nodded. 'That's it,' I agreed with some satisfaction before looking at her. 'You aren't sorry that we didn't leave him to be found by one of your Pa's lot, are you?'

She shook her head. 'No.' She stared down into the murky water. 'Let him rot. I think it's better this way, don't you?'

'I do.'

There was another long silence as we both looked across the water to where the docks across the way were slowly beginning to come to life with men beginning to load and unload boats. 'I suppose we'd best be on our way then,' she said reluctantly. 'There's plenty of boats over there now. We could get on one and be out of here within a few hours.'

I sighed then turned to her. 'Do you still want to go, Cora?' I asked. 'Tell me honestly.'

She looked surprised. 'I thought we were definitely going,' she said. 'You said so.'

'Yes, but that was when things weren't right,' I pointed out with a smile. 'There's nothing to be afraid of now, is there? We can stay in London and get on with our lives without having to always be looking back over our shoulders.' I slid my arm around her slender waist and rested my head on her shoulder. 'You wouldn't have to leave your Pa, Cat and the boys then. You wouldn't have to leave anything.'

I felt her shake her head. 'It can never be the same though, can it?' she said. 'After the things we've done and seen…' She pulled away and ran her hands through her long red hair, which had come all undone and hung untidily about her shoulders. 'I killed a man, Em,' she whispered. 'I can't ever be the same again after that. I feel all undone. I feel different.'

I stared at her then slowly nodded. 'No, you can't ever be the same after that,' I said gently, not really knowing what I could say that would make it all better. 'You're just going to have to make your own peace with what happened though, my love, and learn how best to live with it.' I squeezed her hand, forcing her to look up at me. 'I reckon it'll be easier to do that here, surrounded by the people you love though, than alone with me in a strange place full of strange faces.'

She looked at me for a long moment as if searching for an answer in my face then gave a nod. 'This is my best chance, isn't it?' she said simply. 'My best chance not to hate myself and go mad with the memory of it.'

'It is.' I leaned forward and kissed her cheek. 'We'll get there though, I promise.'

She smiled then. 'You're not going either then?' she asked.

I hesitated then gave a nod. 'No,' I said, picking up her blasted bag and slinging it across my shoulder. 'I'm not going anywhere.'

We walked slowly back to Commercial Street as dawn rose above the city and those well trodden and not altogether beloved streets slowly began to come to life again after a long, dark night. I don't think that I had ever before felt quite so alive and I couldn't stop grinning at everyone who passed us and pausing every now and again to pet one of the mangy stray cats and dogs that hung about the streets on a perpetual hunt for scraps of food and comfort. Every now and again though I would remember what lay waiting to be found in Miller's Court and the smile would fade from my lips as I thought of poor foolish ignorant Marie.

We went to the police station first, slipping silently in through the back yard then saying an awkward goodbye on the doorstep. 'They won't be up yet,' Cora whispered to me, casting an anxious look up at the windows. 'I don't think anyone will have missed me and even if Cat does, she won't say anything so long as I come home again.'

I nodded then kissed her cheek. 'I'll be seeing you soon,' I said, blinking away my sudden rush of tears. 'You know where to find me and, Cora, give that Mr Mercier a chance, won't you? I know you're scared of what might happen but you've faced up to worse things this night.'

She smiled then. 'I'll see you soon,' she whispered before giving me one last nod and vanishing inside, letting the door close behind her.

I turned and wearily made my way back towards the Britannia, which was already open for business, with a steady stream of market porters and grey faced women wandering in and out. I paused for a moment on the pavement outside and looked up at the pub windows and then down Dorset Street, bracing myself for the first cries of distress coming from the direction of Miller's Court. It couldn't be long now before they found her.

'Em.' I turned and there he was, just as I had always known he would be one day.

I stared at him. 'Albert,' I said, thinking how nice it would be to let myself fall into his arms. 'I thought you were with that girl.'

He shook his head. 'Not like that,' he said. 'It was never really going to last and especially not after I'd seen you again.'

304

I sighed, not letting myself believe that this was happening, not yet anyway. 'You should go back to her,' I said wearily. 'I'm no good, Albert. I'm no good at all.' I took a step towards him then paused, not trusting myself should I go further. 'You don't know the half of it.'

He smiled then, lighting up his face so that I remembered why I had loved him so much. 'Let me find out,' he said.

I shook my head. It had been a long night and promised to be an even longer day once Miller's Court gave up its terrible secret. He looked nervously down the street and jangled his hands in his pockets. 'I heard that there was a woman almost had her face cut off on the night that I last saw you,' he said in a low voice. 'I was worried that she might be you.'

I gave a harsh laugh. 'I was worried about that too,' I said before shaking my head again as he looked at me in confusion. How could I ever explain what had happened over the past few months or what had happened that very night? 'Why are you here?' I asked at last, still not moving towards him, not daring to hope.

'To take you home,' he said simply, closing the space between us and taking me in his arms so firmly and sweetly that I gave up being brave and sobbed against his chest. 'I'm here to take you home.'

ACKNOWLEDGEMENTS

I've been a Ripperologist, taking a decidedly feminist slant on the murders in that I focus on the victims and not the culprit, since I was fourteen and got caught up with the utterly bizarre fuss that surrounded the centenary of the Whitechapel Murders in 1988. Although I was born in the Scottish Highlands, my mother's family came from the East End of London and so I'd always felt a special connection to the Whitechapel area and indeed have for a long time considered myself to be a 'cultural Cockney' albeit one in exile.

This book was probably always inevitably going to happen, considering my deep interest in the case, but came into full and proper being after I discovered a few years ago that my great-great-great grandfather was a Sergeant in Whitechapel's H Division in 1888 and was very likely involved in some way with the case - certainly he was based at the Commercial Street station and would have known Abberline and Reid among others. When I found out that he lived with his family in the police quarters behind the station I inevitably found myself wondering what life must have been like for his adolescent daughters to be living at the very heart of the Whitechapel Murders and those rather morbid ponderings eventually took flight and became the basis of this book, whose heroine Cora is based on one of my own ancestral aunts, Clara Lee, who was born in Poplar on the 15th of December 1865 and lived to the grand old age of ninety before dying in April 1956 in Whipps Cross Hospital.

I had great fun writing this book, despite the grimness of the subject matter. It was never my intention to write a whodunnit type thriller but instead focus upon the effects that the murders had upon the women living and working in the Whitechapel area.

Many thanks as always to my husband Dave and our boys for all their love and support while I was writing this book. I couldn't have done it without you, although it may well have taken much less time!

I'd also like to thank my chums in the Whitechapel Society and also on the Casebook and JTR Forums (especially Neil Bell, Neil Storey and Mark Ripper) for all their brilliant chat, theorising and help over the last few years and also the inimitable Cobb brothers and Adam Wood for inviting me to speak on the subject of Mary Jane Kelly at last year's Jack the Ripper Conference. It was an amazing and very special experience that I will never forget. Many many thanks should also go to the Gentle Author of Spitalfields Life (for being utterly lovely and keeping me inspired), my friends (especially the ones who kindly let me borrow their names for this book but most particularly Suzy Nightingale, Rachael Lucas, Zara Drei, Simon Trafford, Aden Bos, Miranda Brennan, Delilah des Anges and Alix Penn!), my blog readers, the people on Twitter who cheerleadered me along, Hendrick's gin, the bar staff in the Ten Bells, all those Ripper Street fans who made a fuss until they brought it back again for series three, Tom Hardy for just existing, Saga Norén for making me feel normal and everyone who has bought and enjoyed (or not!) one of my books. You're all fabulous.